RIVER
OF
ASHES

RIVER
OF
ASHES

ALEXANDREA WEIS · LUCAS ASTOR

River of Ashes
St. Benedict, Book 1

This is a work of fiction. Names, characters, places, and incidents either are the product of the author's imagination or are used fictitiously.
Any resemblance to actual persons, living or dead, or locales is entirely coincidental.

Cover Art by Sam Shearon
MisterSamShearon.com

Cover design by Michael J. Canales
MJCImageWorks.com

Edited by Livia Loren and Liana Gardner

ISBN: 978-1-64548-098-3

VESUVIAN BOOKS

Published by Vesuvian Books
www.VesuvianBooks.com

Printed in the United States
10 9 8 7 6 5 4 3 2 1

To the unheard victims who trusted the "boy next door."

"This is a valley of ashes—a fantastic farm where ashes grow like wheat into ridges and hills and grotesque gardens; where ashes take the forms of houses and chimneys and rising smoke and, finally, with a transcendent effort, of men who move dimly and already crumbling through the powdery air."
– *The Great Gatsby*, F. Scott Fitzgerald

CHAPTER ONE

"The scariest monsters are the ones that lurk within our souls. Edgar Allan Poe," Beau Devereaux muttered as he read the sign on the wall in English lit. "What a load of shit."

He turned to watch the minutes tick by on the clock. The only noise in the stuffy classroom was his teacher's monotonous, raspy voice.

The jarring school bell circled the room, setting him free. Beau headed for the door, not taking time to put his book in his bag. He rounded a corner on his way to the gym and spotted a familiar blonde. Her hair in a messy twist and secured with a claw clip, it reflected her no-nonsense style.

"Leslie." Beau cornered her in the hall. "How's it going?"

Her blue eyes blazed—just what he expected.

"What do you want, Beau?"

He almost laughed. His attention settled on the notch at the base of her neck. It fluttered like a scared little butterfly.

"Can't a guy say hi to a friend?" Beau put his arm on the wall behind her, trapping her between the lockers. "We never talk. Why is that?"

He loved watching her eyes dart about, searching for rescue, but no one would challenge him. No one ever did.

"I'm not your friend." She shoved him back. "Go talk to Dawn."

He curled his hand into a fist. If he couldn't have Leslie, her twin sister was the next best thing. Or so he thought. He'd started dating Dawn to get his mind off Leslie, but it hadn't worked. They looked alike, but Dawn wasn't her sister. She didn't have her sass.

That he still wanted Leslie infuriated him. Beau leaned in, letting his breath tease her cheek. The scent of her skin was like the sweet vanilla smell of fresh spring clover. "One day, I'm going to take you to The Abbey and set things right between us."

"Is there a problem?"

An aggravated, deep voice buzzed in his ear like a gnat. Beau turned around. It was Derek Foster, her trusty watchdog. He spent way too many hours studying with the geek patrol and not enough time partying with the popular crowd.

"No problem, Foster," Beau said. "We were just talking about next week's chemistry test."

A few students gathered near the lockers, watching.

Leslie edged around Beau. "You can't even spell chemistry."

He bristled. That smart tongue of hers begged to be tamed. "That's really hostile. I'm trying here, for your sister's sake."

Derek put a protective arm around her. "C'mon, Leslie. Let's get out of here."

Before Derek pulled her away, Beau wheeled around. Running his fingers through his hair, he stuck out his elbow and landed a perfect shot right to Derek's cheek.

He stumbled back, bouncing off some girls.

"Derek!" Leslie went to his side, pushing Beau out of the way.

Holding in his satisfaction, Beau frowned. "Oh, man. I'm sorry." He put a hand on Derek's shoulder, checking the red spot on his cheek and suppressing a smug grin. "I didn't see you there."

Leslie shot him an icy glare. "You're an ass."

He gave her an innocent expression, reveling in her reaction. "I'm sorry, Leslie. I didn't mean to hit him." Beau spoke loud enough for onlookers to hear. "Stop making me out to be the bad guy. Can you give that attitude of yours a break?"

Derek took Leslie's hand. "I'm fine. It was an accident. Let it go."

Beau offered his best wholesome grin. "You should listen to your boyfriend."

"What's going on here?"

Ms. Greenbriar's screeching voice made all three of them spin around.

The middle-aged principal of St. Benedict High stood with her hands on her hips. "Mr. Devereaux?"

"Nothing, ma'am." Beau gave the principal a big smile. "Just a misunderstanding. I hit Derek with my elbow when I turned. My fault entirely."

Ms. Greenbriar shifted her beady brown eyes to Derek. "Mr. Foster, anything you want to add?"

Derek nursed his cheek. "No, ma'am. It was an accident, just like Beau said."

She tapped her heel on the tile floor, glancing from Derek to Beau. "My office, Mr. Devereaux."

Beau backed away from the lockers as his stomach tightened with anger. "Yes, ma'am."

"What an asshole!" Leslie bolted out of the double glass doors with Derek close behind. A pain shot through her when the sun highlighted the red mark covering his right cheek. *Damn Beau Devereaux.*

For almost a year she'd tolerated his comments and lewd glances, but since she'd started dating Derek, he'd stepped up his game. "I can't believe he punched you like that."

Derek put his arm around her waist as they walked down the stone steps to the parking lot. "It was an accident."

She halted and stared at him, numb with disbelief. "You don't buy his bullshit, do you?"

"No, but what am I going to do about it? Punch him back?" Derek urged her along. "Then I would be the one in Greenbriar's office."

Students on the grassy quad sat on benches, tossed footballs, studied their laptops, and listened to music.

"Does anyone in this town stand up to him?" Leslie shook her head. "He's got everyone believing he's Mr. Perfect and I'm crazy."

Derek slipped the book bag off her shoulder to carry it. "No one thinks you're crazy, least of all me."

The simple gentlemanly gesture melted her heart. Leslie touched Derek's dimpled chin, feeling fortunate. "My hero."

"What did Beau say to you, anyway?"

She shrugged. "The usual."

Hard rock blasted from a nearby car.

Derek glanced at the source of the noise. "I don't get it. How can he date your sister and not like you at all?"

Leslie removed the claw clip and ran a hand through her shoulder-length hair. "Sometimes I think she went out with him to spite me."

"What makes you say that?"

She shrugged and fell in step beside him. "We aren't exactly the closest of sisters. It was always a competition between us when we were younger. I joined the swim team, and then Dawn joined. I wanted to be a Girl Scout, and so did she. I wanted to take riding lessons and guess who went with me. But I gave up competing with her when we got to high school." She gazed at the neatly trimmed grass beneath her feet. "Dawn never stopped. Sometimes I think that's why she became a cheerleader and started going out with Beau—to show me she could."

"I can't see her dating Devereaux to get back at you. He's the richest and most popular guy in town. Isn't he every girl's dream?"

Leslie stopped short, shuddering. "Not mine. There's something off about him."

"He's just used to getting his way. It comes from two hundred years of inbreeding. Don't all those old, rich Southern families marry their cousins? Maybe that's his problem. Too many batshit crazy relatives in his family tree."

A brisk wind stirred as they crossed the blacktop to the car she shared with her sister. The chill wrapped around her, seeping into her bones.

Derek nudged her. "Hey, you okay?"

She came out of her daze, shaking off the bizarre feeling. "Just really sick of Beau."

Derek smiled, and the look in his eyes made her heart skip a beat.

"Want to sneak up to The Abbey? I could show you around. It's pretty cool."

She'd never been to the abandoned St. Francis Seminary College on the banks of the Bogue Falaya River but had heard stories. "Yeah, no." She hit the remote on her keychain and unlocked the doors.

He climbed into the car. "We can skip The Abbey tour and hang out at the river."

She put her book bag in the back seat. "I have no interest in the river. I've told you that."

"No. You told me you used to go there, then stopped."

Leslie wanted to smack him for not dropping it, but didn't. Her life had been empty before she'd met Derek. They shared classes for almost a year before getting the nerve to talk. "Do you remember the first time you spoke to me?"

"How could I forget?" He leaned over the console. "I left class early and found Beau pinning you against a locker. Seems to be a thing with him. Anyway, you threatened to tell everyone his dick was the size of a number two pencil. I was impressed."

She laughed as Beau's horrified expression came back to her. "And you told him to leave me alone and then offered to buy me a soda. Never realized you were so nice."

"Then why did it take you two months to go out with me?"

Leslie started the car. "Because I wanted to see how serious you were."

A bit rough around the edges, with bashful glances and soulful brown eyes, Derek reminded her a little of James Dean with a dark tan—a sign of his Creole lineage. He was from what some would call "the wrong side of the tracks."

The polar opposite of Beau Devereaux.

Leslie didn't care where he came from or what he drove because, to her, Derek Foster was the most perfect guy in the universe. When he finally asked her out, she turned him down. She hadn't wanted to ruin her dreams of him with the disappointment of reality. But she took a chance, and six months later, here they were.

Her stomach fluttered with one glance at him. "If I agree to go to the river, what did you want to do there?"

Derek sat back, eyes on the road and grinning. "I'll come up with something."

CHAPTER TWO

Beau sat on a wooden bench outside Ms. Greenbriar's door in the administrative offices. Arms crossed, he tapped a finger on his elbow while staring out the window. He waited, keeping a lid on his rising anxiety.

Students rushed past the window to the principal's office, but their occasional stares didn't bother him. His mind was on getting to practice. Coach Brewer hated when players were late, and Beau made a point never to show a lack of discipline. Next to his father, Coach Brewer was the only man whose anger he never wanted to incur.

"Beau," *Madbriar* called from her office.

He stood from the bench and put on his best smile. *This will be fun.*

The room was jam-packed with bookcases, a small desk, and an outdated computer.

"Tell me what happened with Leslie Moore and Derek Foster," the principal asserted.

"I was speaking to Leslie when Derek came up. I accidentally hit him with my elbow when I turned around." He cleared his throat and looked at the floor. "I completely understand if you want to punish me for hitting Derek."

Madbriar took a seat behind the desk, her chair squeaking in protest. "Relax, Beau. You're an exemplary student and an upstanding member of this community. No one is questioning your behavior." She sat back and stared at him for a moment. "Ask your dad to give me a call when he can to discuss the new gym addition. I want to see whether Benedict Brewery will donate for the school fundraiser."

Beau folded his hands, keeping the tips of his index fingers together, a thrill of amusement running through him. Everyone always wanted something from him or his family. Being the town's biggest employer made donating to every fundraiser in St. Benedict obligatory. He sometimes wondered how his father put up with all the bloodsuckers.

"Sure. I'll let him know, but he's always happy to help."

She pointed at the office door. "Now, you'd better get to practice."

His tension eased, Beau stood. He wanted to pat himself on the back for an impeccable performance. "Thanks, Ms. Greenbriar."

"And Beau, do yourself a favor."

He gripped the door handle. "Ma'am?"

"Stay away from Leslie Moore." She picked up an open folder. "That girl will be nothing but trouble for you."

He nodded, then hurried from her office, chuckling.

Trouble is my middle name.

The smell of sweat and freshly cut grass greeted Beau as he strutted onto the practice field. He tightened his grip on his helmet. The team was already in the middle of their stretches. He was late.

His belly flopping over the waistband of his gym shorts, Coach Brewer walked between rows of guys, blowing his whistle to keep time with their exercises. One among the team struggled to keep up. Jenson Theriot.

The bungling offensive tackle annoyed the shit out of Beau. He'd missed several blocks, leaving Beau vulnerable in the pocket. The freckle-faced redhead had become a detriment to his team—something Beau couldn't tolerate.

Beau's attention drifted to the metal bleachers and the cheerleading squad working on their routine. Dawn was there wearing a short, white cheerleading uniform. He loved how the bright red St. Benedict dragon, its mouth open and teeth bared, hugged her breasts. The other girls on the squad, whose names eluded him, shouted their silly rhymes for victory and team spirit as Dawn watched them kick, split, and jump.

Dawn turned to the field and, spotting him, waved.

The wind whipped her long blonde ponytail and brushed several strands over her shoulder, making it appear shorter, like Leslie's. Though they were physically identical in every way except for their hair length, Beau wished Dawn was the smart-mouthed bitch he really wanted.

Before he could get away, she came running to greet him. It was the last thing he needed. Coach Brewer would be pissed.

"Hey, honey." Dawn frowned at him. "Everything okay? I heard Madbriar called you into her office."

Her voice wasn't Leslie's. He'd memorized the smoky, sexy sound of her sister. The way she raised her tone ever so slightly when she was about to say something sarcastic. Dawn had none of Leslie's nuances—her voice was utterly lifeless.

Dawn worked hard to portray a wholesome image by avoiding cursing and smoking, which he admired. But her love of cherry-red lipstick and excessive mascara aggravated him. He'd told her more than once not to wear so much, but she didn't listen. She just put on more, thinking he liked it. Beau longed to wipe the color from her mouth.

He gave her a warm smile, hiding his thoughts. "She wanted to talk to me about my father contributing to the gym fundraiser." He looked over at his teammates.

"I heard it was because you were giving Derek and my sister a hard time."

His head snapped back around to her. How dare she contradict him. "No way, baby." He laced his voice with extra charm to sound convincing. "Why would I waste my time on them when I'd rather spend every moment with you."

She squealed.

Putty in his hands, Dawn melted against him, wrapping her arms around his neck.

"I knew it wasn't true," she whispered.

He smelled her skin. It wasn't there—the heady aroma of clover always lingering on Leslie. Another difference between them, but one he was sure only he noticed.

"Beau, get your ass over here," Coach Brewer yelled.

"Gotta go." He unwound her arms. "See you after practice."

"I love you," Dawn managed to get out before he walked away.

He pretended not to hear her while putting on his helmet. Love wasn't what he was after.

A load lifted from Leslie's shoulders the moment the red-brick walls of St. Benedict High were behind her. The months of putting up with Beau had taken their toll, making the school almost feel like a prison. She relaxed her hands on the steering wheel. The cool afternoon breeze ran through her hair as she drove toward Main Street, where rustic storefronts sat between modern buildings. The hodgepodge of styles reminded her of the people in town. An interesting blend of old families who had lived in St. Benedict for several generations, and new families running away from the urban sprawl taking over nearby cities.

Derek touched her knee. "Why don't you like going to the river?"

Leslie glanced at a thick swath of honeysuckle vines on the side of the road, her unease returning.

"All you ever said was you went to the river with Dawn junior year, ran into Beau and his friends, and swore you'd never go back."

"Dawn and I got invited to the river by some seniors. Being asked to party on the river at night was a big deal to me." Leslie's shoulders drooped. "Beau started out talking to me, and I knew he was interested, but Dawn didn't like that. So, when I went to grab something to drink, she stepped in and hit on him. They hooked up and disappeared. I got stuck fighting off his football buddies, who wanted to show me a good time."

Derek scowled. "What did you do?"

Leslie raised her nose in the air. "I started spouting feminist literature, and they ran for the hills."

"That must have been scary."

"It was." Her voice cracked. "When three guys manhandle you, it's terrifying. I didn't have my car, so I walked back to town."

"At night?" His voice rose.

She took in the sunlight skipping across the tops of the buildings. The smell of hamburgers from Mo's Diner filtered through the car. "Staying at the party was dangerous. A virgin hanging around a bunch of drunk and horny football players would only end badly."

Derek moved closer. "I don't want you in that situation again. The only guy I want around you is me."

Leslie noticed a hint of possessiveness in his tone. "But you never try anything with me when you're drunk. Or any other time."

He sat back. "I will when you're ready."

Near the edge of town, tall oak trees covered with Spanish moss replaced the buildings. A gentle breeze ruffled through their leaves. Leslie turned onto Devereaux Road and headed toward the remains of St. Francis Seminary.

Derek put his hand on her knee, then slowly rubbed up her leg. A warm tingle spread between her thighs.

"I want your first time to be special." He bobbed his eyebrows. "But that doesn't mean we can't fool around at The Abbey."

She let her foot off the gas, slowing as the road narrowed, her sense of dread returning. "Are you sure you want to go?"

Derek flashed a boyish grin. "Hell yeah."

The spires of The Abbey appeared as the car cruised along. The ruins of the towering white marble and brick structure rose behind the trees. Leslie slammed on the brakes, not wanting to go any farther.

Derek leaned toward her. "Is something wrong?"

Tearing her gaze away from the macabre structure, she sought refuge in his eyes, and the feeling passed.

"Can we skip the tour of The Abbey? I don't think I'm in the mood."

He lightly kissed her lips. "We can do whatever you want."

CHAPTER THREE

L eslie drove down a tree-lined street of tired old homes with peeling paint, sagging porches, and varying degrees of disrepair. It saddened her to see the residences crying for attention. One of the older neighborhoods in St. Benedict, the atmosphere reflected the work-weary attitude of the people struggling to hold on to their dreams.

She pulled into the cracked driveway of a yellow wooden house. With a rusted tin roof, broken white picket fence, and bent mailbox, the residence mirrored others on the street. Despite its unsettling appearance, the home contained happy memories.

She shut off the engine. "Is your mom still working doubles at the diner?"

Derek shoved open his door. "Yes. Thank goodness."

Leslie got out of the car, astounded by his comment. "What makes you say that?"

He pointed to the bruise on his cheek. "You know how she feels about fighting. I hope she doesn't kill me when she sees my face."

The chug of an approaching engine caught their attention. A blue pickup truck, with a bent front fender and cracked windshield, pulled in beside them.

Leslie blocked the sun with her hand, a sinking feeling settling over her. "I guess you're going to find out real fast."

"Thought I might beat you home." A waiflike brunette with naturally tanned Creole skin stepped out of the truck.

Her beige polyester waitress dress made Carol Foster look older than her forty-two years. It stressed the crow's feet and circles rimming her eyes. But Leslie still saw some of the pretty woman her father once told her about.

Derek helped his mother unload groceries from the truck. "What are you doing home early, Mom?"

"I got the afternoon off." Carol nodded to Leslie. "How have you been, dear?"

Leslie went to Derek's side, nervous. "I'm good, Mrs. Foster."

"I told you to call me Carol, sweetie. No need for all the—" She homed in on her son's cheek. "What happened to your face?"

Derek walked toward the porch steps, ignoring his mother's reaction. "It's nothing."

"Nothing, my butt." Carol grabbed his chin to get a closer look. "Who did this?"

He stepped back. "It was an accident. I ran into Beau's elbow."

Carol's cheeks paled. "Gage Devereaux's son? Why were you fighting with him?"

"I wasn't fighting. He turned around and struck me with his elbow in the hall. No big deal."

The anguish in Derek's voice frustrated Leslie.

"Were you there?" Carol demanded.

Leslie twisted her fingers as her guilt intensified. "He was coming to my rescue."

"Your rescue?" Carol marched toward the porch. "What did Beau do to you?"

Derek waited for Leslie to climb the steps before following with the groceries. "He's been bothering Leslie in the hall a lot lately."

Carol's green eyes widened, and she looked at Leslie. "Why would Beau pick on you?"

"Because he hates me." Thinking of Beau made Leslie queasy. "He has ever since the night he got with my sister. He keeps telling everyone he wants to be friends, but I don't buy it. The way he looks at me, the things he says … He doesn't want to be friends, not by a long shot."

Carol yanked her keys from her handbag. "Sounds like you need to steer clear of him." She unlocked the front door and pressed her shoulder against the warped wood, shoving hard to get the door to budge. "I've been meaning to fix this."

A single mother working twelve hours a day deserved a break, but Leslie didn't know how to help Derek or his mother. Getting ahead in St. Benedict took more than a strong work ethic, it took the good graces of the town patriarch, Gage Devereaux.

Leslie followed Carol inside. The sparsely furnished living room had a small worn sofa, a wobbly oak coffee table, and an old oval rug covering the dull hardwood floors. The only new item was the flat-screen TV mounted on the wall above the dusty mantle.

"I haven't cleaned." Carol ran her hand over her forehead, hiding her worry lines. "But you've seen the place messier than this."

Leslie put on a reassuring smile, her heart aching for the woman. "You should see my room. My mom's always complaining about it."

Carol set her five-gallon purse on a rickety, round table next to the kitchen. "What about your sister? Do you two share your propensity for messy rooms?"

Leslie shook her head as she considered her sister's OCD-like ways. "No. Dawn is the perfect one. Her room is always spotless."

Derek carried the groceries to the kitchen counter. "But her personal life's a mess."

"That's not a kind thing to say." Carol slapped her son's shoulder, frowning at him.

"Why not?" Derek tossed his book bag down. "She's dating Beau Devereaux and thinks he can do no wrong. She's seen him bullying Leslie and blames her for it. What else do you need to know?"

"You don't know that." Her lips set in a firm line, Carol went to the kitchen and flipped on the lights. "Right now, Dawn's wrapped up in having the attention of a guy she thinks is the catch of St. Benedict. Dating the football star and heir to the Devereaux fortune seems like a dream come true. She's probably afraid to ruffle Beau's feathers and risk losing him."

Leslie arched an eyebrow. "You seem to know an awful lot about what Dawn is feeling."

Carol lifted milk from one of the grocery bags. "I was in your sister's shoes once."

More than a little intrigued, Leslie edged closer. "You were?"

Derek put the eggs in the fridge. "Mom dated Gage Devereaux in high school. Didn't I tell you that?"

Leslie gave a wide-mouthed *no you did not* look. She faced Carol. "So, what happened?"

"There isn't much to tell," Carol muttered. "Gage and I dated for a couple of years in high school, and then he went to college in Boston."

"She met my dad after she quit college," Derek interrupted.

"Don't remind me." Carol took a ragged breath. "We weren't even married two years when your father ran off to California."

Derek's father skipping town was a sore spot, so they never talked about him. But Leslie's curiosity about Carol's past with the Devereaux family got the better of her. "Is Beau like his father?"

A slight smile added a touch of warmth to Carol's sad eyes. "I don't know Beau, but Gage was very considerate of other people. Even though he was the richest boy in town, he never acted better than anyone else. I'm going to take a shower." Carol nodded to Leslie. "Good seeing you, sweetie."

Leslie waited until Derek's mother disappeared down the narrow hall. "Did she seem upset to you?" She hooked her pinkie around his. "When I asked about Mr. Devereaux, she changed."

"Nah. She's upset about my face. I'll get an earful after you leave."

Leslie rested her head against his chest, wishing she could stay. "I should go. My mom wants me home for dinner."

She went to the freezer and found a pack of peas. Returning to his side, Leslie gently pressed the bag against his bruised cheek. "Keep this on for a while. I can't have my boyfriend walking around school looking like the other guy won."

Derek chuckled and walked her to the door. It took a stiff yank to open.

After kissing Derek goodbye, Leslie walked to her car, thinking about Carol's connection to Beau's father. There were secrets buried in their small town, especially about the Devereaux family. Hints of their past had circulated among the residents of St. Benedict for as long as she could remember. But Carol's history with Gage had not been one of those tales.

If Dawn continued dating Beau, would she end up like Derek's mother?

The chill she experienced on the road to The Abbey returned. She didn't know why, but the daunting thought of her sister's future made her think of those sinister spires. Unnerved by the sensation, Leslie decided to take the long way home and avoid the area altogether.

CHAPTER FOUR

The beauty of the sunlight filtering through the oaks lining Leslie's street offered a moment of distraction as she drove through her upper-middle-class neighborhood. Nestled in a quiet part of St. Benedict known as The Elms, her house wasn't far from the entrance to the lands owned by the Devereaux Estate.

Leslie pulled up to the three-car garage and cringed when she looked at the clock on the dash.

She grabbed her book bag and headed toward the back door, hoping her mom wouldn't be downstairs.

"You're late again, Leslie Elise," Shelley shouted from the kitchen.

Leslie sighed and shut the door. "Yeah. Sorry."

Her mom rounded the corner in a navy pantsuit, her wavy honey-blonde hair secured at the base of her neck in a barrette.

No doubt about it. Shelley Moore could intimidate the devil himself if she wanted to.

Her mother's blue eyes sparkled with irritation. "You were with that boy again, weren't you?"

Leslie scowled. "His name is Derek, Mom. Not *that boy*. I hate when you call him that."

"And I hate when he makes you late." Shelley pointed a spatula at her daughter, her lips nothing but a thin, angry line.

Leslie followed her mother into the kitchen. She crossed the threshold, her tennis shoes squeaking on the polished brick floor. She hiked her bag onto the counter with a heavy thump. "I was only a few minutes late. It's not a big deal."

"We have rules for a reason." Her mother wielded the spatula again, pointing it at Leslie like a sword. "And you know better. Books on the floor, not the counter."

Leslie deposited her bag next to the breakfast bar. "Where's Dawn?"

"Not home from cheerleading practice yet."

Leslie gritted her teeth. "Is Beau bringing her home?"

"Of course. You know he always brings her home after practice."

Great. The princess gets driven home by her asshole boyfriend, and I get crap for spending ten extra minutes with mine.

Several choice curse words slipped from Leslie's lips.

"What was that, young lady?"

"Nothing. Dad home yet?"

Shelley pointed her spatula at the family room next to the kitchen. "In his office. Go tell him dinner's almost ready."

Leslie hurried toward her father's office. She knocked and pushed the door open. Soft overhead lights stretched across a paper-strewn desk. John Moore's slight frown told her he wasn't happy with what he read. A stack of manila folders lay neatly on the corner of his mahogany desk, each representing a case.

Leslie stood in the doorway and smiled. She couldn't remember when he wasn't working. "Hey, Dad. Whatcha working on?"

John glanced up from the file, his glasses slightly askew. He ran his hand through his hair and leaned back, resting against the leather seat. "I'm finishing up a contract for the brewery."

Lately, he'd been working a lot for Gage Devereaux's company. Benedict Brewery was on the verge of breaking nationally, which meant a lot of late nights.

"How was school? Did you have a good day, Leelee?"

She smiled at the nickname and walked in. She'd always been Leelee to him. "School was good." She slumped her shoulders. "Well, not so good. Beau hit Derek."

John set his glasses on his desk. "Is he okay?"

"Yes. Beau claims it was an accident, but Derek ended up with a bruise on his cheek." Leslie sat on the corner of the desk. "Can you sue Beau on Derek's behalf? For assault, or at least emotional cruelty?"

John folded his hands, a deep line creasing his brow. "You know the law. Derek must file charges or at least seek compensation. Were any charges filed?"

"No. Ms. Greenbriar took Beau to her office, but she won't do anything."

He tapped a finger on his blotter. "I doubt Carol Foster will pursue any legal fight with the Devereaux family."

Leslie perked up, intrigued. "Why? Because she dated Beau's father in high school?"

John narrowed his gaze. "Where did you hear that?"

"Mrs. Foster mentioned it. I got the impression Mr. Devereaux meant something to her."

John picked up his glasses and focused on his paperwork. "They were very close in high school. I remember seeing them holding hands everywhere they went, but everyone knew the Devereauxs never liked Carol."

"Why not?"

John hesitated. "Her father was the brewery foreman at the time, and they were uncomfortable with their son dating the daughter of an employee. I'm sure they discouraged the relationship."

A whole new perspective on the Devereaux family popped into Leslie's head. She'd always thought of them as pretentious, sort of like her mother, but had never considered them cruel. "Foreman, my foot. We both know the reason old man Devereaux didn't want Gage dating Carol, and it had nothing to do with her father's job."

John peered over his glasses at her. "I don't like what you're implying."

Leslie stood and placed her hands on her hips. "Come on, Dad. Carol is Creole. The Devereaux family has never liked anyone who doesn't look like them. I'm sure that hasn't changed."

John smiled. "No, dear. Things are different now."

"Are they? Mom wants me to stay away from Derek because she's a snob and doesn't think he's good enough for me."

"I heard that." Shelley barged into the room. "Just because I don't like your boyfriend, young lady, does not make me a snob."

Leslie faced her mother and squared her shoulders. "Then what justification do you have for the demeaning remarks directed at Derek?"

Shelley glared at John. "You see what your influence has done? Now she's even talking like a lawyer."

He held up his hands. "Don't drag me into the middle of this. It's your argument, not mine."

Shelley folded her arms, smirking exactly like Dawn. "After raising twin girls, I'm better at winning arguments than you'll ever be."

John scanned the paperwork on his desk. "I have no doubt about that."

"Ah, hello!" Leslie waved her hand. "I'm still waiting for my question to be answered."

"Oh, for heaven's sake." Shelley stormed toward the office door. "Get ready for dinner," she announced before leaving.

"Why does she always do that?" Frustrated, Leslie folded her arms. "I ask a question, and she totally ignores me. But Little Miss Perfect can ask about the weather in Cleveland and Mom will give her a three-page report, complete with pie charts and a website."

"Leelee." John's voice softened as he rose from his chair. "Don't you think you're exaggerating?"

"No, I'm not. She hates Derek just because he's not all rich and popular like Beau. But she won't even get to know him. She never lets him come over or bothers to talk to his mom. And whenever I want to go out with him, I have to give her an itinerary, ten personal contacts, and a freakin' urine sample."

John chuckled. "Your mother has her faults, but she isn't that bad."

"Then why does Miss Goody Two-Shoes get to go everywhere with Beau while I face an interrogation just to get pizza with Derek?"

"Because your mother knows Beau. Knows his family. And she trusts him." He held up his hands before she could argue. "People see him as an upstanding kid."

Leslie's hopes of ever getting her mother's approval for Derek sank like a stone in a shallow pond. "What about Derek? What can I do to make her see what a good guy he is?"

"I'm sure she'll come around. You know how resistant she is to change, just like your sister." He patted her shoulder. "Give your mom some time."

Dawn bounded into the room. "Daddy, I can't wait to tell you what happened to me at school today."

"Aaaaand I'm outta here." Leslie headed for the door.

Dawn frowned at her sister. "What's up your butt?"

Leslie spun around and a pang of heartache struck her. They looked so alike yet were so different. She didn't even know Dawn anymore. Beau had driven a wedge between them as wide as the Grand Canyon. Why bother telling her what Beau had done? She wouldn't believe her.

"Nothing's up my butt."

Dawn scrunched her face. "Is this about Beau and Derek getting into it today? Just so you know, my boyfriend told me what happened. You were flirting with him in the hall. Derek got jealous and accidentally walked into Beau's elbow."

Leslie's cheeks burned. "You little toad! Why in the hell would I want a scumbag like Beau when I've got Derek?"

"Girls," John said.

Dawn charged her sister. "You're kidding, right? Beau is so much more than the loser you're dating."

John's voice rose higher. "Girls!"

"Derek's not a loser!" Leslie got in Dawn's face. "He has a better GPA than your Neanderthal."

"What's going on in here?" Shelley burst back into the room.

Dawn pointed at Leslie. "She called my boyfriend a Neander ... something."

Leslie crossed her arms. "Neanderthal, you idiot."

Shelley stepped between the girls. "Enough. There will be no name-calling in this house."

Leslie scoffed. "What about Derek? I can't call Beau names, but she can make fun of my boyfriend? That's not fair."

"She has a point, hon." John eyed Shelley.

"You're not helping," Shelley grumbled. "Leslie, you could learn from your sister's example. Dawn has a future with Beau. What do you have with that *boy*?"

Gutted, Leslie trudged to the door. She stopped and glanced back at her mother. "You're unbelievable."

Would it even matter if her mom knew all the horrid things Beau had said to her? Or the torment she'd suffered for months? No. Her mother would twist it and blame her. So, she would keep her mouth shut.

"Where are you going?" Shelley demanded. "We're about to eat dinner."

"I've lost my appetite." Leslie hurried away, impatient for the sanctuary of her bedroom.

CHAPTER FIVE

Beau strolled down the curved mahogany staircase. He stepped onto the hardwood floor and caressed the newel post shaped like a horse's head at the bottom of the stairs. He admired the taut bit in its mouth and the pain carved into the creature's bulging eyes.

He headed along the hallway, tugging his book bag over his shoulder, the occasional moan of the floorboards echoing around him. He glanced at a massive gold painting of New Orleans, bought by some dead relative a century ago. Family portraits of deceased members of the Devereaux clan littered the white wainscoting-covered walls. He passed the tall cypress door to his father's office, not bothering to check inside. His father was an early riser and probably on his way to the brewery.

At the end of the hall, he turned down a slender corridor to the kitchen and the entrance to the five-car garage. He enjoyed the quiet after his father went to work and before his mother crawled out of bed. It made him feel like everything was all his—for a little while, anyway.

Beau eased around the hammered copper breakfast bar to the refrigerator in the kitchen. When he turned around, Beau froze, afraid to move.

Gage held a coffee mug as he leaned against the black granite countertop. Wearing a long-sleeved shirt and slacks, he came across as more casual than the ruthless capitalist he was. Beau had nothing in common with his father except their height and physical prowess.

He attempted to appear relaxed by shifting his book bag on his shoulder. "Why are you still home?"

Gage inspected Beau and then set his coffee on the counter. "I wanted to speak to you before you left for school."

The condescending tone in his father's voice tightened his chest. It usually signaled a lecture.

"I got a call from Ms. Greenbriar. She said you had a run-in with Carol Foster's boy."

Beau's fingers twitched. Great. The idiot woman had called his father. The last thing he needed was Gage Devereaux up his ass.

"Derek is dating Dawn's sister. I often see him at school." He tempered the irritation in his voice, not wanting to annoy his father. "Leslie and I were talking, and Derek joined us. I accidentally tapped him with my elbow when I turned to leave. I apologized. Everything is fine."

He waited, analyzing his father's every move.

"I've spoken to you before about this." Gage moved closer. "This family is under scrutiny right now. I don't want your actions threatening our business or our name." He gripped Beau's shoulder. "What have I always told you? What is our rule?"

Beau faced his father, standing at attention. "Self-control in all things. Never let anyone see who you really are."

Gage leaned closer. "No matter what anyone says, no matter what they do, you walk away. This includes your girlfriend. Do you understand?"

Beau stiffened at the low, menacing tone in his father's voice. "Yes, sir."

Gage nodded. "Go to school."

Beau stood by the breakfast bar, not moving a muscle as his father headed to the garage. After the door clicked shut, a trickle of sweat ran down his temple. His jaw cramped from clenching. Gage's words spinning in his head, Beau slammed his hand down on the copper bar.

Anger like molten lead ran through him. Beau sucked in deep breaths to calm down—something he remembered from a long-ago therapy session. Then he relaxed his hand on the bar, checking the dent he'd left in the copper. He wiped the smudge away, stepped back, and raised his head.

I am the master of control.

Low clouds heavy with rain hugged the sky above the student parking lot.

Beau drove his silver BMW onto the blacktop and found his usual spot beneath a shady oak.

Students milled around, chatting and laughing. Guys from the team tossed a football over the tops of cars. It was a relaxed atmosphere, just what he needed to dispel the last remnants of his father's warning.

A football dropped a short distance from his door, and a red-faced Jenson Theriot ran after it. He kicked the ball along the blacktop, failing to retrieve it. Some guys laughed nearby.

Beau glared at the redheaded dweeb.

Jenny, your days are numbered.

The awkward teen finally got hold of the ball, and when he raised his head, he spotted Beau sitting in his car.

He offered the junior a smirk. Beau swore the clumsy idiot damn near shit his pants. Jenson took off at a breakneck speed he'd never shown on the football field, heading for the safety of the quad.

Leslie and Dawn pulled into the parking lot, and Beau's grin widened. Leslie was driving, as usual.

Dawn was out of the car as soon as it stopped. He waited until she got to the main entrance before opening his door.

Leslie took her time gathering her things, and he studied her movements. She kept pushing a stray hair behind her ear.

She's nervous. Could I be getting to her?

Beau enjoyed seeing her this way. It made him feel as if he had some mastery over her. He stayed back as Leslie walked toward the side entrance with her head down, clutching the book bag to her chest.

Here was his chance.

He jogged across the green quad as a clap of thunder shook the sky. Leslie stopped at the door, searching through her bag, giving him enough time to reach her.

She had left her hair down, just touching her slim shoulders, and her light blue blouse emphasized the paleness of her skin.

She turned to head back to the parking lot and ran smack into him.

He gripped her arm to keep her from falling, enjoying the opportunity to touch her soft skin. "Whoa, hey there." He kept his voice deep and seductive. "Just the girl I've been waiting for."

Her full, unpainted lips turned downward. Beau pulled her close and Leslie jerked her arm, trying to break free. He dug his fingers into her flesh, loving the fight in her. It made him feel alive.

"What's wrong, darlin'?"

"You're an asshole, Beau. You know that?"

A group of girls rounded the corner, and Beau let her go. He gave them a dazzling smile as they passed by. They giggled and quickly slipped in the side entrance.

Leslie pushed past him, but he placed his hand on the side of the building, blocking her.

He leaned forward, taking in her sweet scent. "Something wrong?"

She arched away from him. "Leave me alone."

"Why? What did I do?" He gazed up and down her body, lingering on her breasts.

Leslie glared at him, her blue eyes on fire. But before she could respond, Dawn ran up and got between them.

"Back off, Leslie."

Her threatening tone surprised Beau. *Where had she been hiding that?* Beau slipped his arm around Dawn's waist. "You need to set your sister straight, baby. If I didn't know better, I'd swear she's mad at me about something."

Leslie pointed her finger at him. "Stay away from me and Derek."

"You need to check your facts, counselor. I don't give a rat's ass about your geek boyfriend." He flashed a brilliant smile, the one he used to get out of trouble.

Dawn curled into his chest, her strong perfume stinging his eyes.

"See? He doesn't give a rat's hiney about Derek. So just drop it."

Beau hated the childish approach Dawn used with her sister, but it proved he had nothing to worry about when it came to her loyalties. That was good. The bigger the divide between them, the closer he could get to Leslie.

Beau took Dawn's book bag from her shoulder. "We on for the river Friday night?"

Leslie rolled her eyes. "All everybody does there is drink and screw."

"You have the wrong idea about what goes on at the river." Beau dug his nails into the strap of Dawn's bag. "We just hang out and have fun. No parents to annoy us, no rules to follow. We can do what we want." He rolled his neck, relieving the tension. "You would enjoy yourself."

"No thanks."

Dawn smirked at her. "Leslie's creeped out by The Abbey. She never wants to go to the river because of it and doesn't even like talking about the place."

With her wide stance and tightly pressed lips, Leslie reminded Beau of an MMA fighter. Dawn had hit a nerve, and he could guess why. He sensed an opportunity. His heart sped up at the prospect of adding to her fears. "Are you talking about the ghost?"

Dawn snickered, grating on his nerves. "What ghost?"

Beau kept his attention focused on Leslie while he spoke, hoping to see her terrified expression. "The lady in white. She wears a white-hooded cloak and haunts The Abbey grounds. Some say she appears when something bad is gonna happen, but others think she's the lost love of a monk who lived at the seminary. You gotta be careful at The Abbey."

Thunder rolled across the sky, and both girls flinched. He couldn't have asked for better timing, but their frightened reactions fascinated him. If only he could recreate the fear in their faces—what a turn-on.

Dawn was the first to break the spell, slapping his arm and giggling. "Beau. Cut it out." She took his hand and pulled him toward the door. "Let's go to class."

He let Dawn lead him away, but not before glancing back at the sister he wanted to possess.

Leslie stared as her sister and Beau walked down the hall holding hands. She hated seeing Dawn manipulated by the sadistic ass.

Lightning streaked overhead as she went inside, spooked by the weather and Beau's eerie story. Leslie had watched his expression as he told the tale about the ghost. He'd almost seemed to enjoy her uneasiness. But why?

Inside, students casually strolled through the gray locker-filled hallway, chatting and checking their phones. Leslie's cell buzzed in her back pocket. She walked as she read the text.

Derek: Running late, love

Warmth chased away the anxiety Beau had caused. Since dating Derek, Beau's choking effect on her had lessened. Having Derek to talk to and share concerns with helped tremendously.

Once past the chemistry lab, the students in the hall thinned. Before she went to her first period class, she sent off a quick text to Derek.

Someone grabbed her from behind, and Leslie dropped her phone. She cocked her arm back to confront Beau with a quick punch to the throat and spun around.

Derek held up his hands, eyeing her tight fist. "Hey, what's wrong?"

Leslie sucked in a deep breath and relaxed. "I thought you were someone else."

He picked up her phone. "Who else would grab you in the middle of the hallway?"

Leslie took her phone, debating what to say. She didn't want to tell Derek how shaken she was. It would only make him go after Beau, and that was the last thing she wanted.

"Nobody. I ran into Beau earlier." She touched the bruise on his cheek, glad it had not turned black and ugly. "It's looking better."

"Never mind about that." Derek took her hand. "What happened with Beau?"

The tension in his voice made up her mind. She couldn't share her fears with him or anyone. She had to keep Derek safe, no matter how much it killed her to remain silent.

"Nothing. His usual crap. I can handle him."

"That guy has some sick obsession with you."

She waved off Derek's concern. "He's dating my sister, so how could he have an obsession with me?"

Derek urged her along the hall. "Who knows. Maybe he hates that you're smart, independent, and the opposite of Dawn. Or he just has a sick fantasy of doing twins."

She tucked her head against his chest. "Isn't that what all guys want?"

"Guess again." He stopped outside her class. "I'm with you, but I'd rather jump off a bridge than spend ten minutes with your sister." He kissed her cheek just as the first bell rang.

Shouting students, lockers banging, and squeaking tennis shoes signaled the last-minute chaos before class.

Derek smiled at her before joining the mad rush for first period and disappeared into the sea of students.

Leslie's heart fluttered as she watched him walk away.

CHAPTER SIX

The final bell rang, and the front doors burst open. A wave of students poured out of the school. Caught up in the tide, Leslie went with the flow until they reached the bottom of the stairs, and the students spread out across the quad. The clouds had vanished, and the afternoon sun filtered down. She stepped to the side, hoping to soak up some warmth while the crowd thinned.

Behind the school was the recently renovated athletic area. New metal stands lined the oval track that encircled the turfed football field. All were generous gifts from Beau's family during his freshman year—along with the announcer's booth and state-of-the-art video equipment.

Leslie adjusted the weight of her books. She enjoyed going to games and watching her sister cheer, but everything changed when Beau cornered her after his first night at the river with Dawn. He confessed he'd slept with the wrong Moore twin.

"Your sister is a cheap imitation of the girl I want."

For months, she kept quiet about his offensive comments. Dawn would never believe it after so much time, anyway, and the rest of the school viewed him as the perfect guy. What could she do?

A loud bang startled her. Guys dressed in red football jerseys and gray warm-ups rushed out of the gym. Hollering and giving each other high fives, the players jogged to the field for afternoon practice. One boy stayed at the back of the pack, carrying his helmet, his red hair reflecting the afternoon sunlight.

"Come on, Jenny," one player yelled at the loner. "Move your ass."

Leslie's fury ignited. She knew what it was like to be an outsider and teased by others.

Coach Brewer, wearing his usual shorts, high tube socks, and St. Benedict Athletic Department knit shirt, trotted toward the field with a player at his side. The coach smiled and patted his shoulder.

Then she noticed the number four on the back of the jersey, Beau's number, and shuddered.

Beau's attention remained on his coach until other players came up to them. They all laughed, knocked Beau's shoulder pads, and slapped each other on the butt.

It was just another example of the Beau other people saw.

Derek walked up and wrapped his arms around her. Smelling his musky scent, Leslie tilted her head, giving him access to his favorite spot on her neck.

He nuzzled the soft hollow. "Let's get out of here."

"Great idea." Leslie threaded her fingers through his.

They crossed the grass to the parking lot and wove through the remaining cars. She hit the remote on her keys and her headlights flashed. The stress of the day evaporated when she got behind the wheel.

Once out of the parking lot, Leslie headed toward Main Street. "Did you get any applications in yet?"

"Yeah. Two." He avoided her eyes. "One from LSU and the other from USL."

She frowned. "None from out of state?"

Derek rubbed the back of his neck. "I'm not sure out of state would be a good fit for me."

"But you talked about going to UT in Austin. It's your dream college."

"The out-of-state tuition is twice what staying here would be. If I'm close by, I can come home on weekends and check on Mom."

A car honked behind them, and Leslie glanced at the green light. She waved an apology and started through the intersection. "Maybe we could go to LSU. They have a great law program. We could even get a place together and save on expenses."

"No way. We're not living together until we're married. I've got my reputation to consider."

"If that's how you feel, Mr. Foster."

He playfully slapped her thigh. "If I could ever get you to The Abbey, I'll make you pay for that."

Anxiety nipped at her. She couldn't keep refusing to go to The Abbey with him. *Just suck it up.*

"All right, all right. Let's go."

His face lit up. "Really?"

Leslie laughed and shook her head. "Yep, really."

She drove past picturesque shop windows displaying everything from clothes to baked goods to art. The quaint, small-town charm was occasionally interrupted by modern, sprawling structures, such as the new drugstore and big chain grocery.

She turned off Main and headed along the single-lane road. The storefronts gave way to homes with colorful gardens and oaks draped with tendrils of Spanish moss. Then the houses grew sparse and disappeared as greenery hugged the side of the road. Leslie slowed to avoid a pothole and heard the rush of the Bogue Falaya River through the open windows.

The trees thinned, revealing the two stone spires of The Abbey. Apprehension snaked through her as she pictured Beau, her sister, and all the unsettling things she associated with the derelict church.

A wall of dense red buckeye bushes swaying in the breeze shrouded the road. Leslie drove through an opening someone carved out long ago. A cleared lot lay hidden beyond the dense hedge, surrounded by thick pines and oaks, with paths leading down a steep embankment to the river's edge.

The lot served those who came in the summer months to visit the river for tubing, swimming, and small watercraft fun. Many parts of the river could barely accommodate a canoe, but the portion at the bend was wide, shallow, and offered a great place for families to gather.

Leslie got out of the car, listening to the sweet refrain of birds in the trees. "No one's here today."

"It's still too early. Everybody from school likes to come after dark." Derek led her to a pine-straw-covered path and to the shore of the rushing river.

Something moved in the dense underbrush. Leslie walked ahead, trying to get a better look. "What's that?"

She crossed several broken branches until she stumbled on something nestled in the foliage. The stench of rotting flesh hit her nose. She gagged and slowed to a stop.

"Wait, be careful." Derek swept aside a few leafy twigs to get a better look.

Flies covered the bloated belly of a white-tailed deer. Deep grooves slashed into what remained of the deer's neck. The poor animal's hindquarters appeared torn away.

Leslie crept closer. "What could do such a thing?"

Derek took her hand and backed out of the brush. "I bet it was the wild dogs."

Leslie let him lead her away from the stench. "What wild dogs?"

He stopped outside of the brush. "They're around here. A couple of weeks ago, Mom said some hunters came in the diner and reported seeing them."

"Where did they come from?" Leslie's voice shook.

Derek guided her to a path curving down a long slope. The roar of the river grew louder.

"There are lots of stories. I heard they were left behind when the monks abandoned the place. Legend has it that when they appear, death is near."

A shudder ran through her.

Derek tugged Leslie's hand. "Come on."

The path widened, and a beach came into view. The outcropping of white sand had a collection of green picnic tables, red barrel trash cans, and fire pits along the river's edge. Around the beach, thick brush covered the shore with limbs from pine trees dipping into the water. The sun sparkled on the gentle waves.

Leslie followed him along the shoreline until they came to a rusted iron gate with a *No Trespassing* sign secured to it. The sign, decorated with crosses and swirls, marked the entrance to The Abbey grounds. Stepping through the open gate, she peered up at the imposing structure.

Two spires of white limestone, shaped like the tip of a sword, cut into the blue sky. A structure of red brick and limestone, the front windows and doors secured with loose scraps of plywood, sat in the middle of a field of high grass. The squat stone building of cloisters behind The Abbey remained intact. The Benedictine monks, who had run the seminary and were responsible for the preparation of future priests, demolished the dormitories, refectory, and library after they abandoned the site. The rest remained because, in the South, it was considered bad luck to tear down churches.

"Some place, huh?" Derek let go of her hand and ventured across the high grass.

A wave of panic shot through Leslie.

The grounds, unkempt after years of neglect, were a hodgepodge of weeds, overgrown trees, and vines.

Why would people come here at night?

"You ever wonder why those monks just up and left?" Leslie was uncomfortable with the eerie quiet. Even the birds had stopped singing. "Everyone says they got a better offer from the seminary in New Orleans, but it seems funny a bunch of people abandoned the place for no reason."

Derek parted a thick pile of tall grass with his shoe. "My mom told me it was falling apart when she was a kid, and the Archdiocese didn't have the money to fix it. So, they packed up the school and sent the monks and all the staff to New Orleans."

"I read that the structure dates back to the 1800s, when the Devereaux family built it as a private church." Leslie eyed the empty belfry atop one of the square-shaped towers. "You'd think they'd want to save it."

Derek nudged her with his elbow. "Maybe the ghost drove them away."

Beau's tale had been in the back of her mind the whole time, but Derek's comment spooked the crap out of her. "By ghost, do you mean the lady in white?"

"Yep." He scanned the land around them. "They say she appears when the moon is full or during storms."

The thought of being alone in such a disturbing place terrified her. "Have you ever seen the ghost?"

Derek searched the thick foliage ahead of them. "Nah. I've never seen anything."

Granite steps appeared as they drew near the entrance.

Leslie kicked herself for letting him talk her into coming to this place. "What about the wild dogs? Have you seen them around The Abbey?"

"Not to worry, love, I'll protect you from ghosts, wild dogs, and Beau Devereaux." He climbed the steps, encouraging her to join him. "But I have to draw the line at your mother. There's no way I'm taking her on in a fight."

On the porch, beneath the cracked and chipped stone arch above the doors, she waited while Derek wrestled with the plywood covering the entrance. Despite the creep factor, the lush green trees surrounding them had a soothing effect. Leslie breathed in the fresh pine scent and mossy aroma of the tall grass. Then a fly zipped past her face.

Thud.

She turned and discovered Derek had pushed a large piece of plywood securing the door out of the way, leaving a nice-sized gap to crawl through. "How did you do that?"

Derek held the plywood to the side for her. "The loose boards have been rigged to open easily."

Leslie dipped her head and looked through the doorway. "You sure it's safe?"

"I wouldn't bring you here if it wasn't, love."

His smile won over her fears.

Once inside, it took a moment for her eyes to adjust. Pinpoints of light shone on a floor covered with clumps of debris. In the roof, thousands of holes, some big and some small, littered the space between the bare beams where parts of plaster had fallen away. Birds' nests of light-colored hay and twigs nestled against blackish beams and shadowy eaves, creating a patchwork design on the ceiling. It reminded Leslie of the quilt her grandmother had made for her as a child.

Derek appeared, shining a beam of light on the floor.

She pointed at the flashlight. "Where did you get that?"

"Me and the guys have been here a few times. We've stashed stuff around the place. We even have sleeping bags and water bottles socked away."

Here she was a nervous wreck while his friends had turned it into their personal campground. Leslie's skin crawled at the idea of spending the night in such a place. "I don't know why you guys come here."

He took her hand, and the beam bounced on the dusty floor. "I don't get why you're so freaked out. It's just an old building. There's nothing sinister about it."

Beau's words about taking her to The Abbey sent a shiver down her spine. Any girl would be at his mercy in such a place. She questioned her sister's choices, knowing she'd been there with Beau.

Derek swung the light across the floor, shining it on dozens of rotted pews, leaves, twigs, crumbled plaster pieces from the ceiling, and skeletons of dead birds. "Lots of animals use this place as shelter. I've seen possums, raccoons, deer, and once, I swear I saw a black leopard running out the back."

Leslie became even more uneasy about being in the building. "You wouldn't happen to have a shotgun in your stash."

"The animals don't bother me, just the people."

Their footfalls echoed through the vast structure as they ventured farther. Leslie kept expecting someone or something to jump out from the shadows. Her only distraction was the intricate carvings atop the arches and the paintings on the walls. Men and angels exchanged timid glances as rays of light from parting clouds shined down.

Paintings of Noah and the flood, Adam and Eve, and other Genesis stories were barely visible on the white plaster covering the arches along the central aisle. In one spot, where the roof remained intact, she could make out the image of Moses holding the Ten Commandments. His eyes stood out the most. It was like they carried the burning wrath of God.

Shivering, Leslie looked ahead to a white archway marking the entrance to the altar. The gleam of the limestone appeared pristine. She got closer to the most sacred part of the old church, and her sense of dread rose. She spun around to face the scattered, rotting pews behind them.

"What is it?" Derek asked, taking her hand.

His voice rattled inside the hollows of the church, adding to her anxiety. They stood under the circular dome where the altar had once been, and then a low growl came from a shadowy corner.

The air left her lungs. Her senses heightened. Seconds ticked by while she listened for other sounds. "Tell me you heard that."

Derek raised his finger to his lips and nodded to a door on his left.

She wanted to run but followed his lead, inching across the debris-laden floor, trying not to snap any twigs or make a noise.

She held her breath as he reached for the rusted doorknob. It turned, and the old, warped door gave way without a creak. Once they were on the other side, Derek gently shut it.

Her heartbeat slowed, and she relaxed her shoulders. "What was that?"

"Wild dog, maybe. I don't know." He put his ear to the door. "I've never heard anything in there before."

"Maybe we should go."

"I'm not going back through the church." Derek glanced around the short hallway, brandishing his flashlight. "We can get out through here." He motioned the beam down a corridor. "There's an opening up ahead."

Leslie clung to him, wishing they were outside. "What is this place?"

"The cells." Derek kept his voice low.

Leslie squeezed his arm and peered into the dim, cavernous corridor ahead, with only patches of light coming through the thick stone walls. "I wish we hadn't come."

"It will be fine, I promise." He patted her hand. "Nothing will hurt you. I won't let it."

They crept along, their feet hitting sticks and fallen pieces of plaster from the crumbling walls. Puddles of water dotted the uneven stone floor along with mounds of dead leaves. The low ceiling had roots coming through it, and the walls were cold and slimy to the touch. Derek shined his flashlight into the first room on the left. It was a depressingly small space composed of four walls and no windows.

It reminded Leslie of a jail cell rather than a place where a person would choose to live.

Scraps of paper littered the ground of the next cell they came across. Another had a rusty metal-framed bed. Several rooms had cracks in their plaster ceilings along with patches of mold. When they stumbled on rat skeletons, Leslie grabbed Derek.

At the end of the passageway, sunlight snuck through a break in the wall. The intrusion was a welcome sight, and Leslie's fear abated. The jagged opening allowed green leaves from the plants outside to reach in, and creeping vines jutted up toward the ceiling. Along the floor, a thick pile of dead leaves hid the lower part of the opening.

"There was a cave-in along the wall here." Derek brushed the leaves aside, revealing a breach able to accommodate one person at a time. "The other cells past this point are too dangerous to explore. We can get out here and avoid going back through The Abbey."

Derek turned off his flashlight and handed it to her. He pushed the leaves back, moved the vines down, and kicked the debris at the bottom away, trying to clear the opening.

While he worked, a glimmering light from inside one of the cells down the corridor distracted her. She flipped on the flashlight and angled it into the tight quarters beyond the cave-in.

The walls in this portion of the structure had deeper cracks. The fissures ran along the entire ceiling and down to the floors. Patches of black mold were everywhere. What struck her as odd was the lack of debris. It appeared freshly swept, with no leaves or rat skeletons littering the ground.

"What are you doing?" Derek said behind her.

Leslie headed to the room where she'd spotted the strange light. "I saw something."

The smell of rot and mold curled her nose. Her skin brushed against the slimy walls, and she cringed. But something compelled her to keep going into the section Derek had deemed too dangerous to explore.

"Leslie, stop."

She ignored him and pressed on, testing the floor with the toe of her shoe as she carefully progressed. Her heartbeat kicked up a notch, but this time a sensation of excitement went with it. She felt like Indiana Jones exploring a lost tomb, waiting for a booby trap to jump out at her.

Leslie's beam of light filtered into the room, and her heart crept higher in her throat. She rounded the edge of the wall and halted.

The cell was small without any windows, but this room appeared lived in. Along the far wall, below a pair of rusted pipes where a sink had once been, was a green cot—army issue. It had a pillow and green blanket neatly stacked on top. At the foot sat a blue ice chest with an assortment of red candles.

Leslie went up to the cot, and her foot tapped something beneath. She bent down and discovered an old CD player.

Footfalls came from behind. She swerved the flashlight to Derek. "Did you do this?"

"Do what?" He shielded his eyes and stepped inside.

She wanted to believe he had no idea any of this was here, but the whole scenario seemed too well-planned.

"What the hell?" Derek approached the cot and lifted the pillow.

She stood back, studying his reaction. "I thought you said this portion was dangerous."

"It is." Derek went to the ice chest and moved the candles to check inside.

She couldn't picture Derek setting this up. That wasn't the guy she knew. "Why would anyone come here for a rendezvous?"

The ice chest closed with a *thunk.* "It's not exactly romantic. If I wanted to have my way with you, I'd bring champagne and take you to a nice hotel."

"But we can't afford a bottle of champagne, let alone a nice hotel." She sighed, inspecting the room.

Derek glanced at Leslie, then directed the beam at an array of mazelike chinks scarring the plaster-covered wall. "It's not going to collapse today, but I wouldn't want to stay here long. Let's go before whoever left this stuff comes back."

He ushered her into the corridor and to the gap in the wall. Pushing the leaves aside, he eased his shoulder through until he disappeared into the sunlight. Then, he stuck his hand back in and wiggled his fingers at her. She grabbed it, smiling, and followed his lead, working her right shoulder into the mass of leaves. They brushed against her face, and she closed her eyes. When she opened them, she was in the midst of an overgrown camellia bush.

Derek urged her forward, and she soon stood in thigh-high weeds. A breeze brushed the tops of the long stalks against her hand. Sunshine hit her face, and she raised her head, soaking up the warm rays, thankful to be outside.

Beside her sat a beautiful triple-tiered fountain with an angel on top, raising her arms to the heavens. A silent witness to the past.

Leslie glanced back at the hidden opening and wondered how anyone had found such a spot. Her fear of The Abbey returned, but this time it wasn't the ghost stories or talk of wild dogs that upset her.

This trip had made Beau's threats even more real. The isolation and helplessness any girl would feel if trapped alone with him would make them an easy target.

How could she get her sister, or anyone else, to see the dangerous predator lurking beneath the brilliant smile and good looks of St. Benedict's golden boy?

CHAPTER SEVEN

The light from the fire pit chased away the shadows from the woods along the outskirts of Devereaux land. Beau warmed his hands as Mitch Clarkson, the towering ebony-skinned player from the football team, recounted their last victory against Martin High. Josh Breeland, the defensive end with arms as big as tree trunks, sat next to him while Jenson Theriot reclined against a stump across from Beau. The redhead's eyes darted between them, appearing unsure.

Mitch popped the top off a beer bottle. "That Boulder kid got past you last week. You didn't see him comin', did ya? Made you miss a block and almost got Beau's ass sacked."

"Almost cost us the game," Beau added.

Jenson put down the beer Mitch swiped from his old man's stash. "Yeah, I know, I blew it. That's why I was surprised you asked me to come out here. I'll make it up to you at the next game. I promise. I'll make every block, Beau. You can count on me."

Beau traced a circle in the dirt with a stick. "I know. You just need a little incentive. That's why we're here."

Jenson peered into the thick covering of pine and oaks surrounding their fire. "You got a sweet place, Beau. I never knew these woods were behind your house. Kind of creepy, though."

Josh cracked open another beer and handed it to Jenson. "The last time we camped out here, I heard a bunch of shit crashin' through the brush. Mitch said it was deer. My guess is a pack of raccoons."

Beau's grip on his water bottle tightened. "It was wild dogs. We get them on the property. My dad thinks they come over from The Abbey grounds. Even shot a couple."

Jenson looked at his two beers. "I shot a buck once. I didn't like it much." He set one of the beers down.

"Then you didn't do it right," Beau insisted. "The fun is tracking down your prey. And make sure it never sees you coming."

"Dude, chug it down," Josh said, picking up Jenson's beer. "Ain't gonna get fun 'round here until you've emptied a six-pack."

"Hell yeah!" Mitch hollered.

Beau grinned at his friends' enthusiasm. He couldn't carry out his plan without them.

Beau stared down at the sleeping giant curled up next to the fire. Jenson drooled as he slept off the beers Josh had practically force-fed him. Beau racked the shotgun in his hand, ready for the festivities to begin. He nudged Jenson's hip with the weapon. "Wakey, wakey, Jenny. We're going hunting."

Jenson stirred, his eyelids slowly fluttering open. Then he bolted upright, wide-eyed.

Beau, Mitch, and Josh stood around him, wearing grotesque dog masks. Beau liked how the shadows cast by the firelight made them look like monsters. He liked the fear in Jenson's eyes even more.

Beau aimed the shotgun at him. "Run, dog."

Jenson scrambled to his feet, pulling at his falling jeans. "What the hell?" He held up his hands. "What's goin' on?"

"Aw, come on, Jenny," Mitch teased, slapping his shoulder. "You're gonna be our prey tonight."

Jenson stood, the vein along his neck pulsating. "Guys, come on, now. Stop foolin'. I don't wanna go runnin' in these woods." He motioned at the trees. "Beau said they got wild dogs—"

The boom of Beau's gun going off pierced the night.

Jenson cowered while Mitch and Josh snickered.

"Run, Jenny, run!" Beau shouted.

Jenson took a step away, not appearing too motivated.

Beau pointed the gun at his head. "I said move." He growled.

Jenson tripped over a log as he hurried to the edge of the firelight. He hesitated before the curtain of darkness that led to the deepest reaches of the Devereaux Estate and glanced back at Beau and his friends. Wiping his eyes, he took in their dog masks, then eased between two tall pines and disappeared.

"Run, Jenny!" Josh called out.

Beau lowered his weapon and turned to his friends. "Chase him down the trail to the point I showed you. By then, he should learn to move his ass faster on the field."

Josh howled, getting into character. He took off into the darkness, carrying Beau's flashlight.

Mitch followed right behind, wielding one of the electric lamps Beau brought from the house.

Beau tucked the rifle under his arm and returned to the campfire. He grabbed a backpack and set out in the opposite direction from the others. He had work to do.

Beau sat by a tree, keeping his lamp off and letting his eyes adjust to the utter blackness around him. He listened to the night, zeroing in on any hint that Jenson was nearby. He breathed in the cool air, feeling powerful. Beau loved the night and relished the mysterious woods around his home. He loved disappearing into them when he was a child, back when he'd sneak out his bedroom window after his parents went to sleep and would roam the dark trails.

Beau learned a lot during his nightly wanderings. He'd set traps, and when he captured something small, like a squirrel or possum, he'd amuse himself. His father caught him climbing back in his bedroom window one night, covered in blood. That was when Gage put in an alarm, bringing his activities to an end.

Thrashing arose to his left. Beau waited by the tree, knowing his prey was near. Nothing moved like a man in the woods, and a frightened one was louder than a bullhorn on a still night.

The bumbling obstacle to Beau's winning season quickly approached. He held his breath, excited by the fluttering in his stomach. He held off his attack until he could see Jenson's thick shape in front of him.

Beau pushed off the ground and tackled the useless fool.

Jenson cried out, and his weight sent him tumbling into a deep hole.

Beau grinned as he heard him groaning from its depths. He removed a ChemLight from the side pocket of his camo pants and cracked it. An eerie greenish light expanded outward, illuminating the old farm well Beau had uncovered earlier that day. "You okay down there, Jenny?"

"Beau?" Jenson sounded petrified. "Is that you? Get me out of here, man."

Beau stepped closer to the edge of the dry well. "Not ready to do that quite yet." He dropped the green light into the hole and saw Jenson cowering against the wall.

"Get me out of here!" Jenson screamed.

"Sorry, Jenny. You, ah, might want to keep an eye out. You're not alone in there."

Jenson snatched up the glow stick and waved it around. Then he froze. The ghostly light illuminated a snake coiled up to the side.

His shriek was music to Beau's ears. "It's hard to say what I put in there with you. It was dark, so I couldn't tell if your little friend is venomous or not."

"Come on," Jenson hollered. "This isn't funny."

"Maybe not to you," Beau grinned. "But I bet you'll move your lard ass and block whatever comes my way from now on."

"I'm sorry, Beau. I'm sorry," Jenson whimpered. "Please get me out of here."

Beau went to his backpack, which rested at the base of a tree. "Now I want you to sit there and think about how you're not gonna screw up again. I can't have you making me look bad." He slipped the pack around his shoulder. "Got that, Jenny?"

"Please, I won't mess up again!"

Jenson's voice reminded Beau of a woman in a horror movie—high-pitched and about to meet her maker.

"No, you won't." Beau chuckled. "Or I might have to come up with a worse punishment."

He flipped on his flashlight and scoured the ground, looking for the trail back to camp. Beau could thank his father for that. Gage was a stickler for making it easy to get around the uncleared portions of the estate.

Tonight, Beau had taken full advantage.

Screams followed him as he moved deeper into the woods. The hours he'd spent planning Jenson's tomblike confines were worth it.

The land around his home was a haven, but he preferred the shores along the river. He might be the heir apparent, but he wasn't in control—Gage was. Only at the river was he king.

Flames danced through the trees. Beau switched off his flashlight and followed the orange glow back to his friends.

Mitch and Josh sat by the fire pit, their dog masks abandoned at their feet. They turned when they heard Beau coming.

"Where's Jenson?" Josh stood and looked behind him.

Beau slipped the pack from around his shoulders and warmed his hands. "Don't know. Lost him in the woods somewhere."

Mitch went to the break in the trees Beau had come through. "But where? We kept him on the path, just like you said, and stopped chasing him at the marker you showed us."

Beau sat down and took a bottle of water from his pack. "You two should go look for him. Make sure he's all right."

"What if he's hurt?" Josh asked.

"He'll be fine. Hopefully, a little wiser and not as clumsy on the field."

Mitch flipped on a flashlight and glanced at Josh. "Let's go."

Beau waited as their crunching through the brush faded. He sat back and looked up at the pinpoints of stars above the treetops. Staring at the sky, he thought about the others he wanted to teach a lesson.

"They'll never see me coming."

CHAPTER EIGHT

B eau sat at the copper breakfast bar, watching a zombie movie on his laptop. He picked at a bowl of homemade mac and cheese— compliments of their cook, Leah. The only light in the room came from above the gourmet stove his mother never touched.

He couldn't remember a time when his mother had cooked or cleaned. He'd even had a nanny until his father insisted Elizabeth take an interest in her son. Family dinners were something he'd seen on TV but never experienced.

A soft overhead light above the kitchen island came on, and the copper pots hanging from the rack above twinkled.

"What are you watching?" Elizabeth trudged in, wearing her favorite yellow robe.

Her drinking robe, as Beau called it.

Noticing the black coffee mug in her hand, he guessed she was out of ice to go with her whiskey.

"A zombie movie." He went back to his mac and cheese, not bothering to turn down the volume.

Her slippers dragging across the floor were like fingernails on a chalkboard.

"I wish you'd pick up your feet," he muttered. For far too long, she'd shuffled around the house like the undead.

Beau watched her out of the corner of his eye. After getting ice, Elizabeth walked back to the counter and stood staring at him.

He tried to ignore her, but her damn gray eyes were like crab claws when they dug in. He paused the movie. "What?"

Her expression was flat. Not a hint of happiness, sadness, remorse, or concern lifted the muscles in her face. He remembered how her smile and beauty used to light up a room.

"Is that all you're eating for dinner?" Elizabeth tapped a finger on the counter close to his bowl.

"What else would you recommend?" He grinned, feeling cocky. "The three-course meal you cooked?"

No reaction. Nothing. The same dull stare she gave him day after day. He didn't know if she was rubbing off on him, but lately, a certain emptiness had affected his ability to give a damn about anything his mother said or did.

"There's steak and baked potatoes in the fridge. Your father grilled tonight before he went out."

Her deadpan delivery irked Beau. "Who's he with tonight?"

A hint of life shone in her eyes. She pulled the lapels of her robe closed. "What are you talking about?"

Beating his mother up over his father's screwing around didn't appeal to him. He had other interests that would be a hell of a lot more satisfying. "Forget it." He stood and took his bowl to the sink.

Elizabeth walked toward him and swept the hair from his brow.

Beau jerked back. "Don't touch me." His tone came out more menacing than he'd intended, but he was glad. It would keep her away. But the eyes frantically searching his face were not the lifeless ones he'd grown accustomed to. Fear dilated her pupils, almost covering the gray.

"What's wrong with you? I don't even know you anymore."

A smugness surged through him. "That's good." He leaned closer, and his mother took a cautious step back, which pleased him. "If you don't know me, no one else ever will."

"What's that supposed to mean, Beau? Don't say that."

The fake motherly concern in her voice pissed him off.

"You know what it means." He went back around the counter to his computer. "Isn't that what you and Dad want? Don't let anyone know who I really am." He picked up the laptop and threw it against the far wall. It exploded into shards, plastic clinking against the floor until silence blanketed the kitchen.

Beau avoided his mother's terror-stricken gaze, furious with himself. He'd lost control. He had one ironclad rule, and he'd broken it.

"Beau, we should talk to your father."

He willed his discipline back into place, fighting the urge for more destruction. "No way." He could not look at her and stepped away to the pantry.

Her shuffling slippers followed him. "You need to talk to someone."

Mindful of his still-seething rage, he gently opened the pantry and got the broom. "Take your ice and go." He went around the counter to what was left of his computer. "I'll clean up my own mess."

Leslie poured soap into the sink, preparing for dish duty. Her mother had demanded she hand-wash every dish as penance for coming home late, and then she'd gone to bed. Leslie enjoyed having the kitchen to herself. She could eat leftovers in peace without the usual Shelley interrogation.

The abandoned abbey bothered her more than ever. The room in the cells gave her a weird feeling. Something wasn't right about the place. She could see why Beau was so fond of The Abbey—it reminded her of him. An empty shell with a lot of secrets.

The door to the garage creaked. Leslie froze, waiting for someone to walk into the kitchen. The light went out, and the heavy pot she had been washing slipped from her hand and clattered to the floor.

"Mom?"

Dead silence.

She grabbed the pot and cautiously stepped toward the door to turn on the light. As she reached for the switch, her fingers touched flesh. Leslie jumped back, heart racing.

The door swung open, and light flooded the room. "Boo!" Dawn giggled.

"Damn it." Leslie relaxed her grip on the pot. "I could have knocked your head off. What the hell are you doing?"

Dawn dumped her book bag on the countertop. "You haven't done the dishes yet? Mom will be so pissed."

"She'll be even more pissed you put your books up there."

Dawn's ponytail, secured with her signature red ribbon, swung over her shoulder as she moved her bag to the floor. She tucked part of her shirt into her jeans as she stood, rubbing her cherry-red lips together smearing her gloss.

Leslie shook her head. It didn't take a genius to figure out what her sister and Beau had been doing. "Why do you have that muck on your lips?"

Dawn smacked her lips together. "Because it turns Beau on. He says he doesn't like it, but I can tell he does. Especially red lipstick. It drives him crazy."

Leslie made a mental note never to wear makeup again. "Where did you go with Beau?"

Dawn twirled her hair around her finger. "We went to the river, but we couldn't stay long. He had some football thing to do with Josh and Mitch."

"The river?" Soap dripped from her hands as she continued washing dishes. "You need to be careful. A pack of wild dogs took down a deer out there. Think about what they could do to a person."

Dawn scrunched her face. She was every inch Shelley Moore's daughter. "I already know about the dogs. Beau told me all about them. He brought his shotgun. We hung out on the beach and made love as the sun set."

Leslie ignored her sister's dreamy expression. "I don't know which image is scarier, you screwing Beau on the beach or him with a shotgun."

"Why don't you like him?" Dawn asked. "He's tried to be nice to you plenty of times, but you just blow him off."

Leslie set a dish aside, struggling with how to respond. "I don't like how he talks to me. Makes me wonder what you see in the guy."

"What I see in him?" Dawn laughed, this time a roaring chuckle, reminding Leslie of her own laugh. "Leelee, are you blind? Beau's rich and crazy good-looking. His family owns the whole damn town. He's captain of the football team, has a banging body, treats me like a queen, and he's great in bed. What else could I want in a guy?"

One of Leslie's soapy hands came out of the sink and rested on her hip. "You slept with Beau that first night at the river. But before he came along, we always talked about waiting until we were sure about a guy."

A glint of apprehension flickered in Dawn's eyes. Leslie had seen that look a million times before. It meant Dawn would try to lie her way out of the situation.

"Beau did want to wait," she muttered. "I was the one who wanted to do it. I wanted him more than any guy I ever met. Maybe I didn't go about it the right way, but it all worked out. I've got my Beau."

Leslie put a plate in the dish drainer. "Every time you talk about him, you go on and on about his family, money, and looks, but never once do I hear you say you love him."

"I do love him."

Leslie raised an eyebrow. "But does he love you?"

Dawn's pert smile slipped, and anger brimmed in her eyes. "Beau was right. All you want to do is break us up."

Leslie set the last of the dishes to the side to dry. "Did he tell you that?"

"He told me I can't trust anything you say about him." Dawn picked up her book bag and marched out of the kitchen.

She was almost through the den when Leslie called after her. "Has Beau picked out his college yet?"

Dawn halted. "Yeah, Tulane."

Leslie walked toward her. "Has he asked you to apply there?"

Dawn played with the strap of her bag. "No matter what you say, you're not going to talk me out of seeing Beau. I trust him. He loves me and wants to make me happy."

"I'm just trying to keep you safe—like I've always done." Leslie softened her voice. "Remember when we were little, and you used to have those bad nightmares about fire, and I said I would always protect you from the flames?"

Dawn glared at her. "We were children, Leelee. I stopped having nightmares a long time ago."

"But I've never stopped trying to protect you."

She tossed the bag over her shoulder. "I don't need your protection. I'm all grown up and can look after myself."

"Just watch your back with him. That's all I ask."

Dawn shook her head and walked away.

Leslie listened as Dawn climbed the steps, wishing she could make her sister understand. She had a bad feeling time would prove her suspicions right, and when Dawn realized the truth, Leslie would be there to pick up the pieces.

CHAPTER NINE

The sky was clear, and the stands were packed as Beau jogged out onto the St. Benedict High football field, surrounded by his teammates. He raised his voice, joining in as the other guys whooped and hollered, getting fired up for the game. The aggressive, tough-hitting, unfettered violence spoke to him.

Red and white banners decorated the bottom of the bleachers with slogans cheering his team to victory. They clashed with the blue and white banners draped across St. Paul's bleachers across the field.

On the sidelines, Beau set his helmet on the bench and glanced at the stands, checking for his parents. His father, an avid football fan, never missed a game or an opportunity to give Beau pointers. His mother was with him. Another command performance insisted on by his father, no doubt.

He scanned the crowd for Leslie and found her parents. Force of habit made him search for her at every game. He imagined she was somewhere with Derek Foster. Fantasies about ripping the geek's head off with his bare hands helped dispel the flow of anger raging through him. Leslie would regret the time she'd wasted on Foster once she understood the depth of his devotion.

Dawn's high kicks distracted him. He enjoyed watching her, especially when she wore her cheerleading uniform. Her thick cherry-red lipstick sent a shudder through him, though. He would wipe it away later.

Another girl on the squad with long, lean legs and a pretty face intrigued him. She looked like the kind of girl who was sweet on the outside, but once you got her alone, turned into a slut. He liked those girls. They always made things interesting.

"Mitch," he called to his buddy a few feet away.

The dark-eyed player removed his football helmet and revealed a head of curly, black hair. "Hey, did ya hear? Jenny quit the team."

Beau didn't bother to tell Mitch he already knew about Jenson's hasty departure—and the reason for it. He pointed to the cheerleaders in front of the stands. "Who's the cute girl next to Dawn?"

Mitch studied the line of girls. "That's Taylor Haskins. She moved here from Los Angeles."

Beau nodded with approval. "California girl. Nice."

"Dude, you better not let Dawn catch you checkin' out another girl. She's gonna rip you a new one."

"I'm just curious. What else do you know about Taylor?"

"Her dad's handling the national campaign for Benedict Beer." Mitch fixed the strap on his helmet. "I thought you knew about that."

"I tune out when Dad talks about business." He kept his eyes on Taylor, examining her curves and her energy. She would never compare to Leslie, but Taylor exuded a snobbish quality, something reminiscent of how his mother, the ice queen, handled herself. The cheerleader would be worth getting to know.

"I envy you, havin' your whole life planned," Mitch said. "I've got no idea what I'm gonna do."

Beau picked up his helmet. "Yeah, well, maybe my old man's plans and mine don't gel."

Mitch punched his shoulder pads. "Yeah, but you got your family's business in the bag, so you can check out other interests. Nothin' wrong with testin' the waters. Could make you appreciate what you've got." With a lighthearted smile, Mitch jogged away.

Beau returned his attention to the cheerleaders as Mitch's words ignited an idea. It was time to test other waters in preparation for the day Leslie would belong to him. Nothing wrong with feeding his fantasies with appetizers to hold him over for the big meal.

He kept his eyes on Taylor as the refs blew the whistle.

I'm gonna like this game.

The aroma of freshly baked chocolate cookies hung in the air of the dimly lit den while one of Leslie's favorite romcoms was paused on the TV. Several lit candles set the mood for date night with Derek.

She did one last check of her favorite jeans and the knit top hugging her curves. Derek liked her fresh-faced, with only a touch of mascara. Dawn's recent obsession with red lipstick had turned her off cosmetics altogether.

She'd spent years working to become the opposite of her twin. It was the only way to guarantee people saw her as an individual and not part of a matched set.

The doorbell chimed, and Leslie's heart skipped a beat. She looked through the window. The porch light streamed across Derek's distinctly handsome features as he waited outside.

She opened the door and ran into his arms. He embraced her, and the world went away. There was no pesky mother in her head, no fights with Dawn, and no Beau.

Derek nuzzled her cheek. "I didn't expect this kind of welcome."

"I missed you."

He leaned back, smiling. "We saw each other earlier."

"Yes, but we weren't alone." She took his hand and led him into the kitchen.

Derek went straight to the chocolate chip cookies cooling on the kitchen counter. He crammed two in his mouth before Leslie could blink.

"I love these things."

Leslie laughed and walked up behind him. "Save some for me."

He playfully grabbed her hand as she reached around him. "No way. If you want a cookie, you'll have to earn it."

Leslie's brow crinkled as he pulled her into his arms. "Earn it? How?"

"A few things come to mind." Derek grinned, staring down at her lips.

"Why, Mr. Foster, what would my parents say?"

"They're not here ..." Derek brushed his lips against hers.

She melted into him, her lips gently caressing his. Their kiss intensified as his tongue softly slipped inside her mouth. He tasted of chocolate and coffee. Leslie trembled against Derek's warm chest as their kiss deepened.

He laced his fingers through her hair and rubbed his thumbs softly on each side of her face as their kiss became more frantic. The combination of his touch and the soft urgency of his tongue against hers made Leslie dizzy. She held him and tilted back to gaze into his eyes.

"Now do I get my cookie?"

Derek sucked in a deep breath and reached for a cookie. "You're killing me. Now come on and show me the movie you picked out."

The crescent moon peeked through a veil of thin clouds while crickets chirped from the azalea bushes. Leslie took a deep breath, appreciating the crisp fall night.

"I had fun." Derek's voice deepened as they descended the porch steps.

Leslie walked Derek to his mom's old truck. "Me, too. Hanging out at my house is better than The Abbey. No wild dogs, either."

Derek chuckled and took his keys from his pocket. "Sure, but there I wouldn't have to duck out before your parents got home."

Her guilt tainted their evening together. "I'm sorry."

Derek turned the key in the lock. "It's okay. I'm used to it."

"I'm sure once my mother gets to know you, she'll love you as much as I do."

Derek slipped his arms around her. "As long as you love me, I've got the whole world." He kissed the tip of her nose. "We still on for dinner tomorrow night?"

"You betcha."

He let her go. "I'll call you in the morning after I pick Mom up from the diner. She's pulling an all-nighter." He nodded to her front door. "Best get inside and hide the evidence I was here before Shelley finds it."

Leslie peered down her quiet street, furious at fate for dealing her and Derek such a lousy hand. She didn't understand why a dick such as Beau Devereaux got to visit whenever he wanted while her boyfriend—the better guy—remained left out in the cold.

"This sucks." Frustrated, Leslie headed back in.

CHAPTER TEN

The screech of a whistle echoed across the field. Beau's adrenaline surged as people in the bleachers roared for the St. Benedict Dragons. Football players crowded around him, hitting his helmet and patting him on the back, celebrating their victory over the St. Paul Panthers.

After shaking hands with the losing team, many players ran to the stands to greet family members and fans.

Before Beau could find his parents, Dawn leaped into his arms.

"You were fantastic."

"Thank you, baby." He kissed her and, put off by her thick lipstick, put her down. "I need to find my parents."

"Oh, they already left," Dawn said. "I saw them walking out with my parents. They must have been in a hurry to leave."

Beau's disappointment tightened his stomach, but he gave Dawn an easygoing smile. "Yeah, Dad mentioned something about a meeting at the brewery."

Dawn gripped his hand. "Come on. I'll walk you back to the locker rooms so we can change and get ready for the party. I can't wait to get to the river."

Beau's gaze drifted to the line of cheerleaders gathering their pompoms and jackets in front of the stands. Taylor was deep in conversation with a cornerback on his team, Wade Farris.

His anger churned. He'd set his sights on her and couldn't have another guy mucking up his plans.

I'm gonna shut that shit down tonight at the river.

A chilly breeze whipped through the open windows of Beau's silver BMW while the steady beat of a banging rock song blasted through his speakers. He got green lights all the way through town, and with his best friends in the car with him, he couldn't wait to get to his favorite place—the river.

Mitch did a drum roll on the front dash. "I hope we get to meet some girls at the party tonight."

"Did you see the ass on that new girl, Taylor?" Josh licked his lips. "I'd like to tap that."

Beau squeezed the steering wheel, imagining Josh's small brain in his hands. What he lacked in smarts, the defensive player made up for in stopping power.

"Breeland." Beau glowered in his rearview mirror at Josh. "Can that shit."

"Dude." Josh's usually gruff voice crept higher. He leaned in, sticking his head between the bucket seats. "What's your deal?"

"She's out of your league," Beau said, sounding cold like his father. "Find another girl."

Josh slapped the seat. "But she's my type. Tight in all the right places."

Beau eased up on the gas. "You don't have a type, dickhead. You've got to get wasted before you can even talk to a girl."

The illuminated white sign of the local grocery came into view.

"And then it's just the ugly ones," Mitch added with a snicker.

"If I have to buy the booze you need to get the balls to talk to girls, then you can listen to what I tell you. Taylor doesn't need your bullshit."

"How come you never drink?" Josh shook his head. "I don't get that. How can you not drink?"

Beau coolly appraised his friend in the rearview mirror, not about to admit the truth. "Because I'm always driving you two boneheads to the river. What do you think my old man would do if I got caught driving drunk?"

Mitch glanced back at Josh. "He's got a point. Somebody's gotta drive."

Beau pulled into the sleek blacktop parking lot and veered to the left, away from where the shoppers left their cars.

He cruised around the side of the long cinderblock building, security lights glaring into his car, and arrived at an empty loading dock.

"You let Freddie know what we need?" Mitch eyed the raised loading dock.

Beau put his car in park right next to a pile of wooden pallets. "Yep. Called him after the game and told him we're going all out tonight."

"I just hope you didn't get more of that cheap rum. I got sick as a dog on that last time," Mitch said.

Beau retrieved his wallet and took out two one-hundred-dollar bills. "Stop whining. You're a lightweight."

A door creaked open, and light covered Beau's car in a fluorescent haze. A stout man with curly hair, wearing a black shirt and white apron, walked outside. The tinkling of the bottles in the box he carried drifted through the air.

"My man, Freddie Bishop." Beau stepped from the BMW. "You got all my order?" He popped the trunk.

Freddie set the box in the trunk. "Yeah." He faced Beau, a little winded. "I'll be glad when you're old enough to buy your own booze, Devereaux. This crap could cost me my job."

Beau handed him the money. "If it does, I'll have my old man get you a job at the brewery. But until then, keep me stocked."

Freddie checked the bills. "Just keep paying me—my girl's pregnant. And make sure you don't leave the bottles on the beach. The barcodes can get traced back here."

Beau shut the trunk. "We'll get rid of the evidence, Freddie. Congrats on the baby."

Freddie pocketed the money. "Give me a little more notice next time."

Back in the car, Beau kept a wary eye on Freddie as he climbed the loading dock steps. After the door closed with a thud, he sat back, his mind buzzing.

Mitch turned to him. "Is there a problem?"

"Nah." His engine hummed to life. "Just glad we got everything we need for the party."

Beau turned onto Main Street and drove to the end of the last row of shops, their darkened windows lit by the antique streetlamps. After he passed the hardware store, he took a left on Devereaux Road.

Beau steered into a cleared lot hidden behind thick shrubs, anxious to join the party. The thump of a deep synthesized bass echoed through the trees. He got out of the car and glanced at the steep embankment leading to the beach.

"Sounds like they started without us." Josh wiggled out from the back seat.

Beau went around to the trunk. "That's just a warm-up. The real party doesn't start until we deliver the goods."

The thick muscles in Mitch's arms bulged as he lugged the box of alcohol down the pine-needle-covered trail. Beau followed, breathing in the night. He cleared the last trees blocking his view of the beach and spotted three roaring bonfires. Logs formed into a teepee sat in freshly dug sandpits. The flames reflected on the murky water, creating eerie shadows next to the narrow waterway.

The instant his feet hit the sand, the heat from the closest bonfire chased away the chill in the night air. A classic tune rocked around him, loud enough to get everyone in the mood, but not so overbearing it drowned out conversation.

His teammates had set the picnic benches close to the bonfires while leaving the round metal tubs, packed with ice, farther away. It kept the ice from melting too quickly and the drinks from getting warm. That was important to him. He wanted his friends to have a good time—and remember he was the guy who made it possible.

Beau swelled with pride. This was his realm, his world, where he could be himself, and there was no one to get in his way.

The river rules, and I rule the river.

Beau patted Mitch's back as his friend checked out two girls sitting on a bench by the fire. "Put the stuff on ice." He reached into the box and retrieved a bottle of vodka. "This is for Dawn."

A roar went up from a handful of revelers on the beach when Beau stepped from the shadows. They raised their beers to him, cheering.

The adoration fed his soul. He'd created this, not his old man. Here, he wasn't Gage's son. He was Beau, and he could do whatever he wanted.

"Hi, honey." Dawn kissed him hard on the lips, smearing her lipstick over his mouth. "You bring something for me?"

ALEXANDREA WEIS AND LUCAS ASTOR

"Would I forget my girl?" He handed her the bottle and took a step back, feeling a little hemmed in. "But go easy. I don't want to bring you home drunk. Your parents won't be happy with me if I do. And you have an image to keep up, remember?"

"I know your rules." She rolled her eyes. "I can get tipsy but never drunk."

The touch of sass in her voice reminded him of Leslie. He wiped the remains of her cherry-red lipstick away and thought of her sister. "We on for our special place?"

Her eyes twinkled in the firelight, but their lack of Leslie's hostility cooled his desire.

"Let's make the rounds first. We need to be social." She grabbed his hand and urged him closer to the nearest bonfire.

He balked at her gesture to wear him like a fashion accessory and let his hand slip from hers. Beau was about to set off across the beach to one of the picnic benches when Taylor sauntered up to them.

"Hey, Dawn, aren't you going to introduce me to the man of the hour?"

Taylor grinned at Beau, not a sheepish smile but inviting, announcing her interest in no uncertain terms. The brazen gleam in her eye, and the way she dipped her noticeable cleavage in his direction, made him hard.

Gutsy move.

He liked Taylor already.

Dawn cuddled against him, tucking her vodka bottle under her arm. She patted his ass—a sure sign she was marking her territory. "Taylor Haskins is our new cheerleader. She was impressed with the game."

"You like football?" He'd never met a girl genuinely interested in the sport before.

"Love it. I think you've got a real talent for pulling it out in a fourth-down situation and converting. You got a knack for reading the defensive line."

Beau couldn't help but laugh out loud. "You sound like a commentator."

Taylor kept her eyes on him, not acknowledging Dawn. "My dad did PR for the NFL before your dad hired him."

Dawn moved in between them and caressed the stubble on his chin. "Didn't you say something about our special place?" She glared at him.

~ 54 ~

Her insistent tone did nothing to distract him from Taylor. "Yeah, baby, in a minute. I'm being social." He kept his attention on Taylor, knowing it would make Dawn jealous. "So, your father's going to put together the national campaign for Benedict Beer?"

"Yep." Taylor nodded. "I hear this is going to be huge for your family's company. Lots of national press. You'll be famous soon."

Ah. That's it. Someone else looking to attach their star to mine. Should have stuck to football.

After giving him a smoldering glance, Dawn turned to Taylor. "We'll be back in a while."

Taylor blushed. "Ah, sure. Catch you later."

Beau watched as she walked away, hips swinging like a bell.

Dawn pressed his chin between her thumb and forefinger, forcing his gaze to her. "Why are you looking at Taylor like that?"

When she sounded like a threatened pit bull, he knew Dawn was pissed. Her jealousy had gotten old. "I'm not looking at her any certain way. Just wondering what she's about."

The rigid muscles in her jaw relaxed. "If you say so."

Beau peeked at Taylor rummaging through a metal tub. She was different. Her bold behavior reminded him of Leslie. She could be a fun diversion.

Dawn rubbed seductively against him. "Want to slip out?"

Beau detected the longing in her blue eyes, and his interest in sex soured. Taking Dawn to his special room in the cells didn't appeal to him anymore. He wanted to try something new.

Beau took the vodka from her. "Sure, baby."

He escorted her along the sandy beach, away from the music and bonfires, to a remote spot surrounded by dense trees casting sinister shadows. He'd used the isolated area as a make-out spot before meeting Dawn. Since then, he'd upped his game and moved his activities to the cells. But the strip of beach, littered with dried twigs and dead leaves, would come in handy for what he had in mind.

When they were far enough to only hear the faint beat of the bass, he kicked a few sticks out of the way and cleared a patch of sand.

"Voila," he said, waving to the spot.

She raised her gaze to the branches overhead, blotting out the moonlight. "Why are we here? What about our room in the cells?"

He had a seat, setting the vodka in the sand. "I picked out this special spot just for us." He snapped up a small rock and tossed it across the gentle waves of the river. "The cells are starting to feel dirty. I want to make you feel like a princess."

Romance wasn't his thing, but he'd learned to embrace it to keep Dawn happy. Until Beau had Leslie, he would have to play her silly games.

Dawn softly squealed as she settled next to him. "Any place you take me is special."

He eased back on the sand, taking her in his arms. "I always want to make it perfect for you." Beau reached for the vodka and cracked the seal. "Here's a toast to us." He handed her the bottle and waited as Dawn took a small sip.

That's not gonna be near enough for what I have planned.

He tipped the bottle to her lips. "This is a toast. You're supposed to take a real drink. Otherwise, it's bad luck."

She twisted her mouth into a funny smile. "Bad luck? I never heard that before."

He nuzzled her ear. "Take another sip, a bigger one for me."

Dawn gave in and he felt his influence over her growing. He was glad she didn't argue. Nothing aggravated him more than when she started with the questions.

After she gulped down a small portion of the bottle, she coughed and covered her mouth.

"That's my girl." Beau took the bottle from her and pretended to take a drink.

She needed to feel comfortable. That was the key—make girls comfortable and they're yours.

He handed her the bottle, frowning a bit to rouse her worry. "You'd better drink some more. You look uptight."

"I'm not uptight." She pushed the bottle back to him. "Why do you think that?"

Beau put his arm around her, his lips against her neck.

"You always say it feels better when you're tipsy." He caressed her thigh. "I want tonight to be good for you."

She eyed the bottle, biting her lower lip as if having a great internal debate. "But what if I get drunk? You always say you don't want—"

He pressed his finger to her lips. "Tonight is about us. No parents and no rules." He set the bottle in front of her. "For me, baby."

She wrinkled her brow. "I don't need to be buzzed to have sex with you."

He clenched his jaw. *Stay in control. Don't let her see who you really are.*

Beau took a breath and regrouped. "But you said you wanted to stop being basic and spice it up." He traced his finger over her lips. "We can't do that unless you're relaxed."

Her forehead smoothed as she picked up the bottle. "What did you have in mind?"

He tilted the bottle toward her mouth. "Something I know you'll love, so drink up."

Dawn took the vodka from him. "Can I ask you something?"

He clenched his fist behind her head, then ran his fingers over the red ribbon securing her ponytail. "Anything."

"Did you ever think about what will happen after graduation? I know you're hoping to go to Tulane, but I was thinking it might be nice if we went to the same college."

Where did that come from?

"You don't have the GPA to get into Tulane."

She set the bottle in the sand. "I know, but have you ever thought about LSU? They have a great football team, and you could get picked up there and eventually go pro like you always talk about."

Beau stared at her in the faint light. How dare she try to change his plans? What made her think she had the right to discuss his future? He quelled the rage rising inside him, not wanting to frighten her. "You never talked about us going to college together before."

"I was just thinking. That's all."

Beau leaned into her, studying her eyes. Dawn never came up with ideas on her own. That's what he liked about her. But who would put such a ludicrous thought in her head?

Then it struck him—Leslie.

"Is this about Leslie and Derek? I've heard they're planning on going to LSU together. Is that what you want?"

"Haven't you ever thought about us after we graduate?" She tugged at the collar of his T-shirt. "Might be hard with me at LSU and you at Tulane. We won't be able to see each other every day."

Beau decided to turn the conversation to his advantage. "I love that, baby." He kissed her. "But you wouldn't want to have me around all the time."

"I would, Beau. Every day. You know I love you."

"Then prove it. Drink a little more for me, so we can do all the things we've been talking about."

She downed more vodka, and he turned his head away, smirking.

Dawn coughed and set the bottle down in the sand. "If I drink much more, I'll be too zonked to enjoy anything."

He pushed the liquor back toward her. "I've seen you toss back way more."

She smacked her lips. "Yeah, but I don't usually chug it like this."

It didn't take long for the vodka to hit her. She had a hard time staying upright and slurred her words.

Beau kissed her neck and waited until she drifted off to sleep against him. Then he gently rested her head on the sand.

Satisfied that she was out, he stood and dusted off his jeans. He looked at Dawn, shaking his head. "You sleep it off. I got somewhere else to be."

Back at the party, Beau mingled. There were a lot of faces he didn't recognize. Students from St. Paul must have heard about the party. He didn't care who showed up on the river, as long as they knew he was the king.

He made his way to the tubs filled with drinks and spotted Taylor with Zoe Harvey. The cute girl with the mahogany skin and great ass was one of Dawn's friends and a real blabbermouth. He'd have to get Taylor away from Zoe. Otherwise, his every movement would get back to Dawn.

He put on a smile and strolled up to them. "Hey, ladies."

Zoe glanced around him. "Where's Dawn?"

"She's not feeling well, so I took her back to my car to rest for a while."

Zoe frowned. "That's odd. She was fine on the ride over here. Maybe I should go and check on her."

Beau clasped her arm, giving it an encouraging squeeze. "Let her sleep, Zoe. I think the vodka just made her a little queasy. She said she didn't eat anything today."

Zoe pulled away, her hazel eyes burning with displeasure. "She skipped lunch today because she was too busy getting all the banners ready for the game."

"I'm sure she'll be fine." Beau turned to Taylor. "There's a guy over there from St. Paul asking about you, Zoe."

Her brassy smirk challenged him. "Sure there is."

Beau pointed to a bonfire on the far side of the beach. He selected a random guy with thick shoulders and buzzed dark hair. "His name's Mike, and he thinks you're cute."

Zoe squinted as she followed his finger. "Mike?"

A muscle worked in his jaw. "Go talk to him if you don't believe me."

Zoe gave him a skeptical glance and walked away.

Beau shifted his focus back to Taylor. "I thought she'd never leave."

Taylor tucked a lock of hair behind her ear. "So, where's Dawn, really?"

For a cheerleader, she wasn't a total ditz, but he doubted she was as sharp as Leslie. "She's up the beach, sulking." Beau moved in closer. "We had a fight."

Curiosity twinkled in her eyes. "About what?"

From the way she rocked her hips to her aggressive flirting, Beau sensed she was ready for more.

"You." He lowered his smoky voice, hoping she would move closer. "She's jealous because I was showing you attention."

She ran the tip of her tongue over her unadorned lips. "But you're her boyfriend, and she's the captain of my cheerleading squad. If she wanted to get even with me—"

"She won't know." He put his mouth next to her ear. "Let's not talk about Dawn. I'm more interested in you."

The aroma of salty sweat mixed with her heavy floral shampoo disappointed him. Why did no other girl smell like Leslie?

He stood back, waiting to soak in her reaction.

There was no blush of embarrassment, no open-mouthed surprise. Desire like flames from the nearby bonfires danced in her eyes.

He had her.

"Is there some place we can talk?" she whispered.

Beau glanced at the people surrounding them. Some sat around the fires chatting, others splashed in the water at the river's edge. A few danced and swayed to the music, while others sat on picnic benches playing drinking games. No one would notice if they slipped away.

"Come with me." He took Taylor's hand and guided her away from the beach, leading her to the rusted iron gate of The Abbey.

CHAPTER ELEVEN

Moonlight danced across the high grass and illuminated the cracked wall in the cells. Beau was glad he'd forgotten a flashlight. Mother Nature set the mood for his encounter with Taylor.

He'd enjoyed flings behind Dawn's back, but none had been with her circle of friends. This could be an exciting challenge.

"What's this place?" Taylor glanced at Beau with a slight crease on her brow.

He imagined how her shimmering hair would feel in his hands. "The remains of the seminary college. Behind The Abbey are the monks' cells. I want to show you my place there."

They reached the fountain with the forgotten angel and Taylor yanked on his hand, stopping him. "Are you kidding me?"

He hadn't expected someone from Los Angeles to be so skittish. West Coasters had a reputation for being mellow.

Beau put his arm around her. "It's cozy and quiet."

Taylor eased away from him. "Sounds creepy."

Instead of getting angry, Beau remained the picture of calm, debating a way to make her trust him. "I know it sounds creepy, but it's not. I've got a cot, candles, and even an ice chest. It's a place to escape, a sanctuary. I only bring special people here." He gauged Taylor's reaction and decided to give her something to win her over completely—honesty.

Well, she would think it was honest.

"I just want to be alone with you without all the noise and interruptions. You ever just want to get away from all the bullshit? The constant pressure to act a certain way. Please your parents, your teachers, your coach—all of it. I get sick of fighting to be the person they want me to be. So, I found this place where I can be me. Does that make sense?"

She slowly nodded. The aggressive tigress retreated, and the quiet girl trying to fit in came to light.

"I understand a lot better than you think." Taylor's smile was tentative but genuine. "I didn't want to move here. I was happy in LA."

Beau inched closer, hoping to get her to open up. "My dad wants me to take over the family business. No matter how much I hate it."

She walked to the fountain. "Yeah, well, your dad has his own company. Whereas mine ..."

Beau moved behind Taylor as she gazed into the black water. He detected a slight sniffle as she kept her face hidden in the angel's shadow. He placed his hand on her shoulder. "What is it?"

She faced him, and the faint light revealed her trembling lips. "I can't say anything. My dad works for yours."

Beau lifted her chin, antsy to discover her secret. Anything could be twisted and used against her, guaranteeing her compliance. "They have nothing to do with us."

Taylor studied his eyes. "My dad couldn't get a job in LA. He's struggled with alcohol. He's sober now and needed a fresh start. But I didn't."

Beau put his arms around her and crushed her to his chest, feeling empowered. "Your secret's safe with me."

She slid her arms around his neck. "What do you see in Dawn Moore? I thought a guy like you would've wanted a challenge." She stood on her tiptoes and bit his lip. "I'll bet you like a woman who knows her mind."

Unlike other girls, Taylor offered a different challenge—a mental one. She gave him a taste of things to come with Leslie.

Done with waiting, he picked up Taylor. Her squeals carried across The Abbey grounds. He hiked her over his shoulder and headed for the crack in the cell walls.

He remembered the first time he discovered the opening. Crammed with cobwebs and dead leaves, the numerous cracks in the walls had given him pause about the integrity of the site, but the dilapidated condition had a plus side—no one would ever venture there. It would be his place, untouched by others.

The first girls he brought there balked at the conditions. But after some cleaning and homey touches, they seemed more intrigued than put off.

At the narrow opening, he put Taylor down. "Stay here and I'll get some light."

She crossed her arms and pouted. "You want me to stay here alone?"

He kissed her, biting her bottom lip. "There's nothing here that can hurt you. The only person to fear is me."

Taylor put on a brave face. "I don't scare easily."

Oh, yeah. He liked her. "I'm counting on it. Just come on."

Beau ducked inside the wall, pulling Taylor behind him. The darkness of the cells took a moment to adjust to, then ribbons of moonlight seeped through cracks, allowing enough light to help him make his way.

He crept along, keeping a firm hold on her hand until a sliver of light reflected off the metal frame of his cot.

He let her go. "Just a sec."

In the room, he made his way to the candles on top of the ice chest. Feeling around, he found the box of matches. The flare took a second to get used to. He lifted a candle and checked the contents of his cell. Everything was where he'd left it.

She waited at the entrance, inspecting the room. "Are you sure it's okay? Someone might walk in on us."

Beau reached underneath his cot, where he kept his CD player and a flashlight. "Everyone stays away because they think it's dangerous."

She touched the cracks along the doorway. "So, how'd you find this place?"

"I got bored when everyone got shitfaced at the river and went exploring. I found the opening in the wall and checked it out. And discovered this." He flipped on the light and pointed it around the room. "Cool, huh?"

Taylor slowly nodded. "It has potential ... I guess."

Tired of waiting, Beau put down the flashlight. "You'll grow to love it. I'm going to give you the night of your life."

He turned her around, curled into her back, and wrapped her in his arms. He kissed her neck as he ran his hands up and down her breasts. Beau liked the feel of her. Taylor had curves and sweet-smelling skin. His touch became more urgent, and he bit her neck.

Taylor sighed, sounding bored. "Is that the best you can do?" She turned around. "I thought you were into playing hard."

Beau pinned her arms behind her. "I always play hard."

She rocked her hips into his. "Then play hard with me."

The request did more than excite him, it freed him. Girls didn't ask for it rough. They wanted sweet and gentle, the way Dawn liked it. But this was an invitation to let the true Beau out.

"Are you sure you want the real me?"

Taylor tilted her head. "The real you?" Her lips lingered temptingly in front of his. "Yes. I want to see what's hiding behind that controlled persona of yours."

He tightened his grip on her wrists, squeezing just enough to hurt. "Then let's have some fun."

She wiggled against him. "Hey, no bruises." She got her hands free and pushed him away. Not hard, but hard enough to make him angry.

Like a rubber band stretched to the breaking point, his self-control snapped. "No, we're gonna do this my way." He picked her up and threw her to the ground.

She hit the floor and looked up at him, fear—dark and primal—in her eyes.

This is my kind of fun.

He climbed on top of her. "Let me explain something. You're in my world now. I own you, your family, your dad's job, all of it. After I'm done, we'll see if you're still in the mood to play hard."

He tore at her blouse, ripping the silky material to shreds.

"Get off me!" Taylor tried to crawl backward to get away.

Beau held her down and struggled to get her bra off.

She punched him in the stomach.

He backhanded her across the face. "Hard enough for ya?"

The sound of her head smacking against the floor sent a satisfying tingle through him.

Taylor groaned as he took off her bra and used it to tie her hands. Then he dragged her across the floor to the wall.

She struggled to fight him as he lifted her onto the cot, but he secured her hands on a curved, sealed pipe jutting from the wall.

Taylor glanced up, battling to free her hands.

He slapped her again. "You had the opportunity to do this the easy way." Beau wrestled her jeans and underwear over her ankles. Her eyes bulged as her expression turned to abject horror. Her terror charged the air in the room.

"Stop it!" She writhed beneath him.

"Scream all you want. No one will hear you." He licked her cheek, tasting the sweat of her fear. "You're mine. I'm going to make sure you never forget tonight."

After he was done, Beau sat back and watched Taylor, relishing his rush. Tears stained her cheeks, a trickle of blood ran down her lower lip, and her body quivered. Her whimpering echoed through the room, adding to his sense of enjoyment. But the high faded when he untied her hands. He'd shown her his true self, and she'd been too weak to take it.

His Leslie wouldn't have acted like such a blubbering mess. She would have glared at him with surly eyes and begged for more.

"If you mention this to anyone, you'll lose more than that fine ass of yours. I'll make sure your father gets fired and his reputation as a drunk is smeared across the country. No one will ever hire him again." He tossed her shirt in her face. "When I want another go, you'll give it to me without the struggle." He grinned. "Well, not completely without. I liked it when you fought back."

Taylor gathered the rest of her clothes. She held the torn shirt to her chest and stood, her hands trembling.

"Go on. Find your way back to the party. And don't let the dogs get you."

She stared at him with bloodshot eyes.

"Oh, did I forget to mention the wild dogs that hunt around The Abbey at night?" He smiled, taunting her. "You'd better run. They'll make a meal of you."

She didn't even put on her clothes before fleeing from the room.

Beau stayed behind, blowing out candles and straightening the cot. The rush of control, the pure pleasure coursing through his veins, was better than the sex and stronger than any drug. He would have to have it again.

Beau put his flashlight back under the cot and quickly checked the corridor outside.

Quiet. Not a sound slipped through the night.

When he stepped through the opening in the wall, the air was crisp but not chilly against his sweaty skin. He felt strong. Powerful. Like a king.

He returned to the isolated scrap of beach where he'd left Dawn sleeping. She was in the same position—on her side with her hand tucked under her chin. He settled in next to her. How could he go from so much fun in the cells to this?

With a sigh, he put his arm around her shoulders.

She stirred at his touch and rolled over.

"What happened?" She pressed her hand to her head.

"You just had a few too many." He patted her arm, already bored. "I've been watching over you the whole time. Do you know you look like an angel when you sleep?"

Dawn rubbed her eyes, smudging her black mascara. "Did I miss anything? I mean, did we have a good time before I passed out?"

Beau sometimes wondered why he put up with her dim-witted, heavily made-up ass. But through her, he would get closer to what he really wanted.

"We had a great time." He sat up, wiping the sand from his shirt. "One of the best evenings I can remember."

"I'm glad you're pleased." Dawn snuggled against Beau.

Her weight on his shoulder became heavier.

He shrugged. "Dawn?"

She didn't move.

The moonlight on the water brought back the memory of terror shining in Taylor's eyes.

Why was hurting her so much fun?

The rush of power awakened something in him.

Dawn's silky hair tickled his chest. Would she like it rough? She would do anything to please him, and he could try different things to see what he liked.

The chill in the air slipped under his shirt. Beau grew restless. He needed to get back to his party. "Baby, get up." He nudged her. "I have to get you home before curfew."

Dawn sat up, a little unsteady. "Mom doesn't mind if you bring me home late."

He stood and pulled her to her feet. "No, but your dad minds. I don't want him to think bad of me."

Dawn tossed her arms around his neck. "I'm the luckiest girl in the world."

Beau loosened her suffocating grip. He guided her off the beach and through the thick brush back to the path.

A hard rock tune was pounding when they returned to the party. Couples danced in the water, some with clothes, some in their underwear. There was little alcohol left, which didn't surprise him.

Beau led Dawn through the crowds gathered around the bonfires.

He helped her up the slim path. She slipped on the pine needles, but he caught her before she hit the ground. Beau picked her up and carried her the rest of the way. She nestled her head against his chest, and he gazed down at her raccoon eyes. There were times he found her appealing. Like a lost puppy in need of love.

He reached the clearing and searched for his BMW. Thank goodness he didn't end up blocked in by other cars.

He set Dawn in her seat. Her head wobbled, and she leaned back, closing her eyes.

"I feel sick."

Beau cursed under his breath. "Don't puke in my car. I'll leave the door open while I'm gone."

She grabbed the sleeve of his shirt. "Where are you going?"

He pried her fingers off, hating when she got clingy. It reminded him of his mother when she drank too much.

"I've got to find Josh and Mitch and tell them I'm taking you home. They can catch a ride with someone else."

Dawn wiped her face. "I should tell Taylor I'm leaving with you. She gave Zoe and me a ride here."

He patted her shoulder and stood. With no intention of finding Taylor, he said, "I'll let her know."

Her head rolled to the side, and he could tell she'd fallen back asleep.

That was good. The last thing he needed was Dawn talking to Taylor tonight. Although he knew intimidation would keep Taylor quiet. It worked on everyone else in town.

Beau headed back to the beach. He wished he could stay, but he made a point never to give Dawn's father any reason to doubt his integrity. The last thing he needed was John Moore speaking to his dad.

He set out for the bonfires, checking the faces lit by the flames. He found several members of his football team, but there was no sign of Mitch or Josh. He searched the revelers gathered around the picnic tables. Some were sober, most were trashed. A few lay passed out in the sand.

No discipline.

He found Mitch. A redheaded cheerleader from Dawn's squad was all over him. His friend's glassy eyes and clumsy movements bothered Beau.

"Hey, there." Mitch slapped his shoulder. "Where you been?"

Beau dragged him away from the girl. "Have you seen Taylor?"

Mitch nodded. "Wise choice, my friend."

Beau scanned the picnic tables. "No, I was wondering if she's still here. Dawn came with her, but I'm taking her home. Just wanted to let Taylor know."

Josh stumbled up and swung his arm around Mitch. "Dudes. Great party, huh?" He fell to his knees and puked.

Mitch giggled like a girl as he pointed at Josh. "You're wasted."

Beau grabbed Josh by the shoulders to keep him from tumbling forward. "Have you seen Taylor?"

Josh's face sobered a little. "Yeah. I saw her headin' to her car a while back. She was upset about her shirt. She got tangled on a branch or somethin'."

Beau contained his grin. He loved being right about people. "Can you guys get home without me? I need to drop Dawn off at her house."

Mitch waved and almost fell backward. "We'll be fine."

Idiots. Why do I waste my time?

He knew why. They were part of the Beau Devereaux package. He'd spent years cultivating his outward persona—the good student, considerate son, best friend, football star, and respectful hometown boy. But the self-restraint he fought to maintain slipped tonight, and an addictive outlet for his ever-present rage had presented itself. From now on, parties at the river would never give him the same thrill.

Beau headed to the parking lot, grinning.

I've found a much better game to play.

CHAPTER TWELVE

Thud!

Leslie sat up in bed, scanning her darkened bedroom. She remained perfectly still.

What the hell was that?

She tossed aside her comforter and shivered. She stood, staring at the bedroom door.

A faint groan came from the hallway.

She hurried to the door and flung it open. Dawn fell into the room. The reek of alcohol was everywhere. "What are you doing?"

Dawn went to rub her face, but missed. "I'm so wasted. Beau gave me vodka at the river."

"I thought your boyfriend didn't drink."

"He doesn't. He wanted me to drink so I was relaxed before we did it, but I don't think we did it."

"Gross. That's way too much information." Leslie shut the door and switched on the lamp.

Dawn remained on the floor, looking up at her. "I fell asleep, but Beau stayed with me. Isn't that sweet?"

"Yeah, he's a regular Casanova. I hope Mom and Dad didn't hear you. They'll ground your ass if they see you like this."

Dawn struggled to stay upright. "No, they won't. They love Beau.

Everyone thinks Beau's a great guy. Even the pope loves him."

"You're more messed up than I thought." Leslie hoisted her off the floor.

"No, it's the truth. Everywhere we go, people wanna talk to him. It's kinda like dating a celebrity."

Leslie sat her down on a brass day bed, disgusted that no one saw what she did—the monster lurking inside Beau Devereaux.

Leslie grabbed a bottle of water from her nightstand, opened it, and handed it to Dawn. "Drink."

Dawn took a sip.

"I have to practically sneak around with Derek, and you get a parade every time you go out with—"

"It's not always fun with Beau," Dawn interrupted.

Leslie sat back, not sure if she'd heard her right. Dawn gushed about Beau twenty-four seven. "What did you say?"

Dawn flopped back on the bed. "There are times I'm with him that I'm glad when it's time to go home."

Beau's unwanted attention had turned Leslie's life upside down. To finally hear her sister give even the slightest hint that all was not right with her "perfect" boyfriend was huge. "I thought you were madly in love."

Dawn sighed. "I am, but aren't there days Derek gets on your nerves?"

"No." Leslie smiled. "I could spend every day with him for the rest of my life and never regret a minute."

Dawn pushed up, resting on her elbows. "You really love him, don't you? But how? He doesn't have a dime to his name. His mother's a waitress. He drives a beat-up truck. And the best he can ever hope to be is—"

"You're only looking at him from the outside. I know who Derek is on the inside. Can you say the same about Beau?" Leslie took her hand, knowing any meaningful conversation was pointless in her condition. "Come on. I'm putting you to bed."

"Can I sleep in here with you? Like we did when we were little?" Dawn settled back against the bed. "We used to talk about the kind of wedding we would have and—"

"You were the only one who talked about weddings." Leslie peered down at her. "You've always wanted to live like a princess and find Prince Charming to whisk you away to his castle. Beau isn't him. He's no good."

Dawn's dreamy expression changed, and with a slight wobble, she stood from the brass bed. "You're wrong. One day, I'll be Mrs. Beau Devereaux. We'll live in his big plantation home, and I'll be by his side as he runs his father's company. Everything'll be perfect." With a toss of her hair, Dawn strolled, rather haphazardly, into the bathroom.

Prior to Beau's influence, Leslie would have run after her sister and begged her to see reason. But then she remembered something her father once said.

"People are like windows, Leelee. They have to crack and shatter before they change their view."

"I can't drink like that again," Dawn said into the phone. "I mean it, Beau." She kept a pillow over her eyes. She'd spent all day nursing the mother of all hangovers. Just the idea of drinking again made her nauseous.

"Just meet me there, baby. I want to spend time with you tonight."

She liked the insistence in his voice.

"My girl can't stay home and leave me all alone. What would everyone think?"

Ugh! He was right. They couldn't let people think anything was wrong. Her standing as cheerleading captain would be in serious jeopardy if she missed any river party. Sometimes high school could be so hard.

After hanging up with Beau, she wondered why Leslie never seemed stressed about her reputation at school. Her sister didn't care what anyone thought about her, which seemed weird. How could she not want to be popular? If they didn't look so much alike, Dawn would swear someone switched her at birth.

What really bugged her was the gossip about Leslie's choice of boyfriend. It hurt to listen to them talk about Derek's mother and their rundown house. Dawn understood her sister's jealousy over Beau—he was the catch of the century—but she didn't get why she hated him. Leslie had never been a spiteful person. Growing up, she had been Dawn's rock, but lately, she'd changed. She wondered if Leslie's issue with Beau was because of Derek's influence. It would explain a lot.

Dawn downed more ibuprofen and put the finishing touches on her makeup.

Leslie walked into her bathroom. "You going out?"

Her condescending tone almost made Dawn stab the mascara wand in her eye. "Beau and his friends are partying at the river. I'm picking up Zoe and heading over there."

Leslie sat on the edge of the bathtub. "Are you going to spend your entire senior year at the river?"

Not another holier than thou lecture! Dawn's hands shook. "What's wrong with the river? No, wait. Let me guess." She pointed the mascara wand at Leslie. "'It's nothing but a bunch of mindless assholes screwing around.' Isn't that what you said?"

Leslie appeared calm—too calm. "I'm surprised you remembered."

"How could I forget? I'd just started dating Beau, and you were all pissy about it."

Leslie stood and cautiously approached her. "He's not good enough for you. When are you going to see that?"

Dawn swallowed the hurtful things she wanted to say about Derek. She wouldn't stoop to Leslie's level. For months, her sister had taken cheap shots at Beau, even hitting on him to steal him away. Dawn knew why. It was to prove a point—she wasn't good enough for Beau. Leslie always had to be the twin everyone admired. "Go away, Leelee. Don't make me say something we'll both regret."

Leslie left the bathroom without flinging another insult, which was odd. Dawn had grown used to her jabs and one-liners, getting in her point no matter what. Leslie walking away was unusual.

Maybe she finally agrees with me, for once.

A gentle breeze from the river tousled Dawn's hair as she stepped from the car and heard a faint thump of music drifting from the shore. She adjusted her cashmere sweater to show off her boobs and glanced around the lot. There weren't nearly as many cars as the previous night. Fewer people meant fewer girls to hit on Beau. It seemed all she did lately was see who was checking out her boyfriend.

"Sounds like the party's already started." Zoe nodded to the path leading to the river. "Let's go."

Dawn followed her, catching glimpses of the ghostly trees surrounding them. The shadows beneath their boughs came alive in the faint light from the rising moon. They swayed in the wind that circled her. She got a creepy vibe from the darkness at the edge of the parking lot.

Zoe grabbed her hand. "Would you come on?"

Dawn hurried to keep up as they came to the edge of the lot and maneuvered the steep path. She glanced back at the shadows. Nothing.

Familiar faces lit by the glow of the bonfires settled Dawn's unease. The football team, her cheer squad, and other popular kids from school were back. A peppy dance tune stirred her headache.

Dawn spotted Mitch by a bonfire, surrounded by a slew of girls she didn't recognize. Mitch turned to Josh Breeland—the other guy Beau couldn't seem to live without. Josh sheepishly grinned when one of the girls pecked his cheek.

"I'm gonna find Beau," Dawn shouted to Zoe over the music.

"Sure thing. I'm getting something to drink." Zoe took off toward the tubs filled with ice and beer.

Dawn trudged across the sand, eager to spot Beau's sun-streaked hair. He usually met her first thing when she arrived at the river. So where was he?

A tingle in her belly ignited concern. Was he with another girl? That was always a fear—she was never enough for him. Sometimes she couldn't believe the most popular guy in school wanted her. What she hadn't realized was how stressful keeping him would be.

The music grew faint as she made it to an obscure corner of the beach. Then a familiar chuckle drifted by.

Beau?

A breeze shifted the branches, allowing light to shine on an isolated picnic table. Beau sat there, holding a bottle of water, wearing a long-sleeve T-shirt that hugged his broad chest. Next to him was a girl in a pair of black leather pants. Platinum blonde and big-boobed, she had her arm wrapped around Beau's shoulder, gazing into his eyes.

Dawn's outrage escalated like a volcano about to blow.

Seemingly captivated, Beau raised his hand to brush hair from the girl's face—a gesture he'd done a thousand times before.

Dawn stormed across the sand. When she could see the girl more clearly, jealousy quickened her pace. It was Sara Bissell—the smart-mouthed bimbo who told everyone she loved bondage, but no one actually believed her.

"Beau, what are you doing? Get away from her. She's trash."

Sara sat back, a broad, sassy smirk on her crimson lips. "Who you callin' trash, bitch?"

Beau stood, his mouth a thin, angry line. "Dawn, enough!"

His stern voice sent a chill through her. Beau frightened her when he got mad.

"Why are you hiding back here? What are you up to with my boyfriend, Sara?"

"I'm not up to nothin'!" Sara got up, appearing ready to claw Dawn's eyes out. "Your *boyfriend* asked to talk to me. Seems he's looking for pointers."

Beau took Sara's arm and walked her past Dawn. "Why don't you go back to the party."

Sara gave Beau one last smile. "You know where to find me."

Dawn wanted to tear Sara's dyed hair out by the roots. How could he talk to her out in the open where all their friends could see? What would everyone think?

She could hear her sister's voice in her head. "*I told you so.*"

"What the heck, Beau?" She stepped toward him, seething. "You wanna tell me why you were with Bondage Bissell?"

Beau remained aloof as he stood with one hand in the pocket of his jeans. His expression was a mixture of amusement and discontent. The calculating way his gaze glided up and down her made Dawn feel like a rabbit caught in the sights of a wolf.

"You need to lower your voice."

"I will not lower my voice. What were you doing with her?"

Beau dragged Dawn back to the picnic table, his fingers digging into her skin. He pushed her onto the bench and put his water down. Resting his hands on either side of her, he pinned her in.

"We were only talking."

Beau displayed the boyish frown she'd never been able to resist—until now.

He straightened and searched her eyes. "I had questions about her lifestyle."

The disclosure hit Dawn with the force of a tsunami. "What? You don't buy into that whips and chains crap, do ya? It's an act."

He lowered his head until his lips came to a halt right above Dawn's. "This isn't about her. It's about us. I've been thinking about trying some new things."

She didn't recognize the way he spoke or the strange distance in his voice. This wasn't her Beau. "But why not talk to me? Why Sara?"

He kissed the tip of her nose. "I wanted it to be a surprise."

She cocked an eyebrow. "You were hitting on her. Admit it."

He chuckled softly, filling her with doubt. "Baby, why would I want her when I have you? Sara's a nobody. She isn't the head of the cheerleading squad or beautiful, smart, or funny. All the things you are."

He'd described everything she fought to be every second of the day. But Dawn still didn't feel good enough.

"Yeah, but Sara's like a double-D with platinum blonde hair, and all the guys think she's hot because she talks about bondage all the time. How do you think she earned her nickname?"

Beau grinned, looking too cute for her to resist.

"I'm an ass guy, and there isn't a finer one in the entire school." He stroked her hair. "As far as the bondage stuff, well, we could try it. Experiment with some things. What do you say?"

Dawn searched his face, hoping to find the truth. Instead, she became more confused. Was love supposed to be this hard? Was giving in all the time the norm in a relationship? And bondage—she'd just gotten the hang of sex. How was she supposed to feel about something that made her uncomfortable?

Zoe waltzed up, wrinkling her nose at Beau. "Are you, drunk, Devereaux? That Sara Bissell bitch is telling everyone you two are back here fighting because of her."

"This is all I need." Beau ran a hand through his hair. "We're not fighting." He waved Zoe away. "Go on. I'm still talking to Dawn."

Zoe planted her feet. "What am I, your social director? Don't be thinking you can shoo me away, boy. I'm here to protect my friend from your cheatin' ass."

"I'm not cheating, damn it." A touch of outrage tainted his smoky voice.

What's going on with him?

The nervous tickle in Dawn's belly grew stronger. She went to Zoe's side, ready to put some space between her and Beau.

"Let's go back to the party."

Beau slapped his chest, indignation burning bright in his eyes. "You're leaving? We're not done yet."

"Can you blame her?" Zoe stood protectively between Dawn and Beau. "You're a piece of shit, Devereaux."

"Shut the hell up, Zoe." He shifted his focus to Dawn, the tension smoothing in his face. "You need to chill, baby. I've done nothing wrong."

"Yet." Zoe smirked.

"Damn it, Zoe." He raised his hand, looking as though he might strike her, then lowered it. "Don't you dare make Dawn doubt me."

His reaction sent a gut-wrenching jolt through Dawn. Beau had never laid a hand on her, but she'd never seen him teetering so close to the edge. With his clenched jaw and balled fist, he looked downright dangerous.

"Leave Zoe out of this." Dawn stepped forward. "This is between you and me."

His deadly stare cut through her. Where were the kind eyes of the guy she loved?

"How can I compete with people who keep trashing me? I'm your boyfriend. You need to believe me and not your so-called friends."

Dawn's heart wanted to believe him, but her head urged caution. He was different, and she couldn't put her finger on what had sparked the change.

"I'm beginning to believe Leslie was right about you."

"You're going to listen to that twisted bitch? After all the times I've reached out to her, only to have her throw it in my face?" Beau's voice ticked higher. He held up his hands and backed away from her. "That's it. I'm done. Believe who you want, Dawn."

Panic swept through her. She couldn't lose him. "Are you serious?"

"I've never been more serious in my life. I can't hack your drama anymore," he said with a cruel sneer.

The nightmare scenario she'd dreaded was here. Her fear morphed into a crushing weight, sucking the air from her lungs.

Desperate to save their relationship, she got angry. "Beau Devereaux, if you walk away, I will never speak to you again."

He turned his back and strolled toward the party. "Fine by me."

The air thinned, and despite taking deep breaths, she swore she was suffocating. Dawn bent over and grabbed her knees.

"It's all right." Zoe patted her back. "He didn't mean it."

Her cheeks burned. Dawn needed to get away. She took off for the party.

"Wait up!" Zoe shouted.

She reached the partygoers as they swayed to the soft sounds of a ballad. Faces blurred as Dawn rushed past, her gaze focused only on the pine-needle-strewn path returning her to her car.

She was halfway up the embankment when Zoe caught up to her. Dawn stepped onto the shelled lot, her only thought to climb into bed so she could cry without anyone seeing. But the heaviness in her heart got to be too much. As soon as she got to her car, tears streamed down her cheeks.

"You'd better let me drive." Zoe took the keys from her hand.

Sniffling, Dawn opened the passenger door. "I can't go home. Not like this."

"We'll go to my house," Zoe said. "You can stay over. Everything will be better tomorrow."

"Will it?" Dawn didn't think her life could get any worse.

The fire danced around the pine logs in the pit, the crackling of wood carrying across the beach. Beau pictured the red and orange embers running through his bloodstream, flecks of rage surging in his muscles, deepening his desire to cause pain.

Dawn had ignited his fury. No one questioned him. No one.

"I think you blew it with Dawn." Mitch walked up, holding a can of beer. "She looked pissed."

Beau grinned at his friend. "We just had a misunderstanding."

Mitch popped open his beer. "Chicks are hard to figure out."

"Some are harder than others. Like Dawn's sister. Now there's a real tough nut."

Mitch's dark eyes flickered in the firelight. "She's not so bad. She helped me get through English lit. Would have failed without her."

Beau's fingers twitched. "You never told me that." What other information had his friend kept from him?

"You've always been down on her, so I never wanted to say anything." Mitch sipped his beer.

Beau arched an eyebrow. "So, you like her."

Sweat beaded Mitch's brow. "No, man. It was a long time ago. Before she got salty."

"I wouldn't blame you if you liked her, but I'd stay away. You might end up cut out from everything. Like Derek Foster. Know what I mean?" Beau tilted his head, a veiled threat in his voice.

"Yeah, I hear ya." Mitch peered down at the can in his hand. "Whatcha gonna do the rest of the night without Dawn?"

Beau surveyed the crowd. "I'm just gonna hang out with my friends."

Mitch wiped his forehead and toasted him. "You're the king."

Josh came up to them and offered Beau a beer. "I saw Dawn bustin' outta here. You need a drink."

Tempting, but his father's mantra came back to him. "Nah, I'm the designated driver." He slapped Mitch and Josh on their backs.

Josh popped the beer he'd brought for Beau. "Next weekend, I'll drive."

The idea of Josh driving him anywhere almost made him break out in hives. He could trust his defensive lineman on the field, but not on the road. "We'll see. I'm gonna change the tunes. We need some rock." He left the glow of the bonfire and passed through a mass of giggling girls from school. Then someone patted Beau on the back.

"You and Dawn okay?" Sara stepped in front of him.

Beau reined in his irritation. "She's a little pissed, but she'll get over it."

Sara rubbed along his chest. "Anything I can do to help?"

Beau grabbed her hand, turned off by her audacity and crimson lips. "Don't you think you've done enough?" He pressed into the soft spot of her hand, the space between her thumb and index finger. "I heard you were telling everyone me and Dawn were fighting." He squeezed harder. "Is that true?"

She recoiled from his grip. "You're hurting me."

He enjoyed the way she squirmed. "I thought you said you were into pain. That's what you told me before."

"Not like this." She flinched.

It was what he'd figured. Another girl who talked big, but when confronted by genuine pain, turned tail and ran.

He squeezed her hand harder. "What did you say about Dawn and me?"

Then he saw it. That twinkle of fear in her eyes. Much less than the horror Taylor had fed him, but enough to awaken his thirst for more.

"I might have told a few people you were fighting." She twisted her arm, trying to get away from him.

The confession was what he wanted. He let her go. "Do yourself a favor, Sara. Don't spread lies about me." He wondered how loud she would scream if he took her to the cells. He leaned in. "Be careful what you say about me to anyone. It might come back to haunt you."

He thought he saw her lower lip quiver, but then it vanished. The light from the bonfire flashed in her eyes.

He held out his hand, eager to see if she was worth pursuing. "Now, why don't you let me get you a beer and we can talk some more."

"About what?" she asked, sounding leery.

He smiled. "Anything you like."

CHAPTER THIRTEEN

Beau folded his arms, studying the morning fog hovering above the blacktop of the school parking lot, irritation gnawing at him.

Where the hell was Dawn? She always rode with Leslie, but this morning they were late. Had something happened? It would explain why she hadn't returned any of his calls or texts. Sometimes she annoyed the shit out of him.

Mitch strolled up to Beau. "Any sign of her?"

Beau leaned against the hood of his car. "She'll be here soon enough."

"You know, sooner or later, she's gonna wise up about the other girls. She's not stupid."

Beau smirked. "What other girls?"

"I'm just sayin', they always find out." Mitch flicked a leaf off the hood of Beau's car. "My old man tried to keep his cheatin' hidden from my mom for years, but she found out. It's the reason I ended up in this town after the divorce. Workin' at the brewery was the only job my mom could find."

Beau edged closer to him. "Yeah, well, Dawn better not get wind of the other girls from you or anyone else."

"I hear ya." Mitch backed away. "I'd better get to first period before the bell. Mr. Santos is a ball-buster when you're late."

Beau sighed, disappointed. He'd always believed Mitch to be a friend, but what if his favorite wide receiver was just another ass-kisser?

A familiar car entered the parking lot. When it came to a stop, Dawn emerged from the passenger side. Beau uncrossed his arms and stood. He counted to ten before jogging across the lot. *This damn woman better appreciate my efforts.* "Hey, baby."

Dawn ignored him and made a beeline for the school entrance.

Leslie got out of the car. The hate in her eyes bore into him. He studied her, picturing her naked body covered with bruises.

"Damn, you look good today."

"Get away from me."

She walked past Beau, and he fumed. He so wanted to teach her a lesson. "It won't always be like this between us."

Leslie stopped in mid-stride and turned around. "Do you have a problem?"

He moved in closer, analyzing the way her blue eyes never wavered. "My problem is you." Beau lowered his voice to a guttural rasp. "You haunt me. I dream of doing things to you." He brushed the hair from her eyes. "And I plan on making my dreams come true very soon."

She slapped his hand away. "Touch me, and I'll cut your dick off and shove it up your ass."

Beau licked his lips. "I love it when you talk dirty. If you could teach some of that to your sister, I would appreciate it."

"You disgust me." Leslie slapped him.

The sting brought a slow, smoldering smile to his face. Beau stepped toward her, anticipating the day when Leslie was at his mercy. "So, you like it rough. I'll remember that."

With the flush of her cheeks and the rapid rise and fall of her chest, he knew he was right about her. *Foster wouldn't know what to do with her fire*

The magic of the moment siphoned away when Derek stepped between them. "Hey, what's going on here?"

The stupid geek took a defensive stance in front of Beau. He yearned to rip Derek's head from his skinny neck and squeeze it until his brains squirted on the blacktop—food for the crows. But the parking lot teemed with students and teachers, all watching them.

Beau had spent too many years cultivating his image to destroy it for the sake of one nerd. He needed to stay focused. "I was just talking to Leslie about her sister," he said in an easygoing manner.

Derek put his arm around Leslie. "Are you okay?"

"She's fine, Foster." Derek's pseudo-manly gesture of ownership annoyed him.

Derek got in Beau's face, squaring off like a contender in the ring. His tough guy act amused Beau.

"Never touch her. You hear me?"

The tension between them became brittle. Then Derek's caustic gaze withered. Beau knew the little peckerhead would always back down.

Leslie gripped Derek's arm. "Forget about it. Let's just go to class."

Students gathered around, intrigued by their confrontation. Beau needed to use the gossips to kill Derek's rep. He'd employed such tactics to shut down challengers to his river parties and dispense with a few old girlfriends. But this time he had to make sure what he said ended up all over the school.

"I think you should talk with your girl, Foster. I tried to have a conversation about her sister, and she flew off the handle." He smirked at Leslie. "That's not normal. People are talking about how strange she's been acting lately. You should get her checked out. Maybe she's pregnant. You guys aren't riding bareback, I hope."

Snickers from the crowd confirmed Beau's arrow had hit the bullseye. By afternoon, the 'Leslie's pregnant' rumor would be everywhere.

"You asshole!" Leslie charged at Beau.

Derek stepped in and boxed her arms, holding her against him.

Beau turned away and faced the students behind him. He loved how they whispered amongst themselves. With her rep in free fall, she would eventually need rescuing, and he would be there.

A girl wearing a thick black sweater and a cap over her long brown hair cut in front of him. It took him a moment to realize who it was. The change in Taylor's appearance startled Beau.

Her droopy shoulders, lack of makeup, and layers of thick clothes were a far cry from the flirty girl he'd met on the beach. The only thing he recognized was the hate stewing in her eyes. The look she gave him was the same one she'd given him in the cells.

"Hey, Taylor, what's up? Love the outfit. I hear bag lady is in this year."

He heard chuckles from those in earshot.

Taylor never uttered a word. She stood, glowering, and he didn't like it one bit. If she kept this up, people might ask questions.

Leslie put a friendly hand on her shoulder. "Are you okay, Taylor?"

Beau glanced at the crowd chuckling around him. "Maybe you shouldn't party so hard on the weekends, Taylor. You never know where it may lead."

Deciding not to push his luck, he brushed past her, heading toward the school entrance. Sweat beaded his upper lip. *Chill, dude, chill. She won't talk. She wouldn't dare.*

Students rushed past Dawn as she rummaged through her locker with jittery hands, searching for her chemistry book. Beau's actions in the parking lot played over in her head, making her forget what book she needed.

Why do I feel like I'm in the wrong? He's the jerk.

Dawn expected a lot of stares and whispers as she entered school that morning, but the gossip hounds were already deboning their next victim. Just as she found her book, she spotted Beau talking to a girl. Dawn couldn't make out her face, but from the protective way she hugged her book bag, she appeared uneasy.

Beau, on the other hand, seemed aggravated. A stiff posture and lips set in a grim line is how he looked right before he yelled at her for doing something stupid.

The girl darted around Beau, and Dawn gasped. It was Taylor Haskins. "What the hell?" she whispered. Did he have something going on with Taylor? By the looks of their encounter, she thought not. But why was he so annoyed?

Dawn's imagination got the better of her as she remembered the two of them at the river.

She must be why Beau was so odd the other night.

Beau adjusted his book bag over his shoulder and strutted down the hall. The cocky grin on his face was the one he got when he felt powerful and in charge, like at the river or after throwing a touchdown.

Zoe jumped into her line of sight. "Hey, you ready for the chemistry test?"

Dawn peeked over her shoulder, looking for Beau.

"Hello?" Zoe moved her head, blocking her view. "Are you listening to me?" She glanced behind her and then back to Dawn. "Oh, for the love of God. You're not mooning over him, are you?"

Dawn shut the locker. "No."

"After the night you spent at my house crying your eyes out, I hope not. Beau showed his true colors. Why can't you see that?"

Dawn tucked her chemistry book into her bag. "He's a two-timing louse, but I saw ..."

"Saw what?" Zoe inched closer, her voice almost a whisper.

"Nothing." Dawn put on a smile. "Ready for chemistry?"

"Am I ready to fail another one of Mr. Elbert's tests? Yep."

Dawn's mouth went dry. "We have a test?"

Zoe shook her head. "Girl, sometimes your mind even amazes me."

Leslie tensed as she snuck in from the garage. The house was quiet, but she held her breath, waiting for her mother to jump out from a shadowy corner and interrogate her about where she went after school. When she reached the stairs, she relaxed.

How had her life come to this? Between Beau, her sister, and fighting with her mother about Derek, Leslie didn't stand a chance. The stress was getting to her, and some teachers had asked if she was okay. But what could she tell them?

Upstairs, she hurried across the hall to her bedroom, eager to hide from her mother. Yellow light spilled onto the cream-colored carpet from Dawn's open bedroom door. Leslie peered inside, not expecting her sister to be home so soon from cheerleading practice. But she was there, sitting on her pink princess bed, her brow wrinkled, holding her cell phone.

"Hey." She leaned against the open door, studying her pink-themed wall collage of inspirational quotes and puppies. "Where's Mom?"

Dawn never raised her head. "Out."

Okay. Let me ask another question. "What are you doing home so early?"

Her attention remained glued to her phone. "I called off practice and had Zoe drop me off."

Leslie couldn't remember a day when her sister had missed practice. Cheerleading was her life. Well, cheerleading and Beau.

"You still upset about Beau?"

Dawn raised her head and revealed her bloodshot eyes. "What do you think?"

She never liked to see Dawn upset. She wanted to hug her sister, but her support would be unwelcome. The great divide Beau created between them had taught her to keep her distance.

"Are you gonna get back with him?"

Dawn slammed her phone on the bed. "Why do you care?"

Leslie came into the room and shut the door. "For months, I've kept quiet, but there's something you should know. Beau says things to me, awful things. He talks about taking me to The Abbey. It's been going on for a while."

Dawn's eyes narrowed into blue slits. "Are you joking? I heard about your argument at school. Everyone did. You're the one who threatened Beau. How am I supposed to believe anything you say? Is this part of your plan to keep us apart?"

Leslie recoiled in disgust. "I shouldn't have said anything. You're right."

Dawn jumped from the bed. "You're just saying that because you want Beau for yourself. You know Mom can't stand Derek, but she loves Beau."

Leslie's jaw dropped. "Are you out of your mind? I could care less what Mom thinks of me or who I date. I don't need her approval, and neither do you." She held up her hands. "You know what? I'm done. I don't care what you do when it comes to Beau Devereaux."

Dawn jutted out her chin. "Fine. I'll marry him and be the richest girl in town."

Leslie hurried from the room, convinced Dawn was never going to change.

The slam of Dawn's bedroom door knocked a picture of Beau off the dresser. She rushed to pick up the silver frame and gazed at Beau flashing his mesmerizing smile. She studied his chiseled features, sun-kissed hair, sexy gray eyes, and bulging biceps before putting the portrait back in its place. How could Leslie stoop so low as to say Beau had hit on her?

She didn't understand what he meant to her. Years of living in her perfect sister's shadow disappeared the first time Beau kissed her. He was special, and he made her special by loving her. With Beau, she was an individual and not Leslie Moore's twin. All her life, she'd been second best. Now she was somebody, and her sister couldn't stand her newfound sense of self.

Dawn ached to call Beau. She was a better person with him. Maybe she'd overreacted. Leslie had gotten into her head. Listening to her was a mistake.

With a shaky hand, she reached for the phone. She counted the number of rings, and it was about to go to voicemail when he answered.

"It's about time you called me back."

"I was mad." She cradled the phone against her cheek, wishing she was in his arms. "When I saw you with Sara, and then the way you acted ..."

"Nothing happened." He sounded sincere. "But you wouldn't believe me. Dawn, you know you're my baby."

Her heart melted, but then Leslie's words came back to haunt her. "What did you say to my sister today? I thought you were going to stay away from her."

An unexpected silence arose, which struck her as odd.

"I asked her to talk to you for me, but you know Leslie," he said in a matter-of-fact way. "She hates me. She got weird, and then her boyfriend showed up. I'm sure you heard the rest."

"I can't understand what her deal is." Dawn considered how distant they'd become in recent months. "I don't even know her anymore."

"Forget about your sister. Let's talk about us." Beau's voice took on a gruff edge.

She reclined on the bed, feeling happy. "Just tell me you didn't have anything to do with Sara after I left the river."

"Nothing at all. I hung out with the guys. Ask them, if you don't believe me. Don't you know by now you're my number one girl?"

"I'm more concerned about being your only girl."

"You are, and always will be."

Dawn's grip on her phone tightened. "Promise me I'm the only one, Beau."

"I more than promise, I guarantee, now and always."

Leslie's words faded as Beau's declaration won her over. "I've missed you," she whispered. "Not being with you today was horrible."

"When can I see you?" His voice sounded strained, desperate.

"Tomorrow, after school." Dawn couldn't wait to be alone with him.

His sigh felt like a caress against her cheek. "Sounds great. It seems like we've been apart forever."

Dawn giggled. "Well, what are you doing tonight? You could come over."

"Ah, I can't, baby. I've got a major English lit paper to tackle. I've gotta ace it or I'll blow my GPA. I suck at Shakespeare."

"Well, don't stay up too late. I wanna see you first thing in the morning. We can walk into school and show everyone we're back together. I'll bet everyone was talking about us today."

"I don't care what people think," Beau said. "I only care what you think."

"I'll be waiting at the entrance for you." She hesitated, then added, "I love you, Beau."

"Gotta go, baby." Beau sounded rushed. "See you tomorrow." He hung up.

Dawn stared at the phone, euphoric at first, and then she reconsidered the conversation. *Why am I always the one saying I love you.* She tried to push back the thought, but it was too late.

He does love me. Right?

CHAPTER FOURTEEN

The streetlamps nestled between stately oaks guided Beau to his driveway. A crisp fall breeze ruffled his hair as the tall, arched gates of black wrought iron with intricate scrolls loomed ahead. He hated those gates. To the outside world, they marked the entrance to the Devereaux Plantation, but to him, they represented prison. He punched his security code into the keypad.

The lights of Benedict Brewery shone in the distance. There wasn't a day when the brewery hadn't crept into his life. He'd worked every shift, in every building, attended every benefit and holiday party, and sometimes traveled with his father to promote the brand. He hated the brewery almost as much as his home.

After the gates slowly swung open, Beau continued up the drive. The trees crowding the road cast long, eerie shadows. Then his headlights settled on something slithering across the concrete. A black snake raised its diamond-shaped head. Its red tongue flicked as if challenging his car.

The damn creature should have been hiding beneath a pile of leaves, but here it was. He remembered the hours he'd spent scouring the woods for a snake to put in the hole with Jenson. Maybe this was a cousin. Beau pressed the accelerator, wanting to show the serpent who was boss.

His car didn't even register the bump as he plowed over the reptile. One less snake hanging around the estate was fine by him.

A streak of white billowing material caught in his headlights and then disappeared into the trees.

Beau slammed on his brakes, his heart hammering against his chest.

What the hell was that?

He peered into the darkness on either side of the road. Nothing. He debated getting out of his car, but the bitterness lingering in his mouth made him rethink his plan. Getting trapped by whoever or whatever crossed his path terrified him.

Beau let up on the brake, waiting to see if the strange white figure returned.

He clenched the steering wheel. "Get a grip. It was nothin'."

Beau's nerves settled when he spotted his three-story home through the trees.

Built in the 1800s before the Civil War, the house had the customary sweeping galleries and temple-fronted façade attributed to the Greek Revival movement. The home had four white Corinthian columns, balconies trimmed in the same wrought iron design as the gates, and a porch decorated with rocking chairs. His mother insisted the chairs gave the house a homey feel.

Homey, my ass.

The light from the french windows and double front doors reached into the darkness around his car, creating sinewy shadows in the Spanish moss-covered oaks. When he was little, Beau believed ghosts haunted the trees. Now he wondered if the same optical illusion caused by the illumination from the house had startled him on the road.

There were even lights in the round cupola located atop the red-slated roof. His father insisted on the brilliant display for security and made sure it burned until dawn. Beau believed the whole thing a waste of electricity and swore he would stop the silly tradition when he inherited the place.

Hate the house as he did, it had been in his family for ten generations, and he couldn't fathom giving it up completely. Ever since the Frellson family had acquired the land, a male heir had lived under its roof. Their acreage started as a cotton farm, but they turned to other crops when electricity became available. By then, their name had changed to Devereaux—for reasons still unclear to Beau—and the family fortune had expanded to gold, railroads, and banking. The brewery had been his great-grandfather's hobby and had eventually grown into a lucrative source of income. But it was his grandfather, an infamous state senator, who had given the family their political clout in the state. Beau hoped to follow in Edward Devereaux's footsteps, but only after his career in the NFL.

He drove past the house to the five-car garage at the rear.

Once inside the mudroom door, he passed through a set of glass french doors, etched with peacocks. Along the walls, framed magazine covers featured his family home. None captured the disturbing essence of the house.

No amount of rocking chairs would change that.

In the kitchen, the green digital lights from the appliances cluttering the countertop cast an eerie glow. There were an array of cookers and coffeemakers his father had given his mother with the hope she'd take an interest in something other than drinking and shopping.

He yanked open the door of the built-in refrigerator and retrieved a bottle of juice. He perused the containers of freshly prepared meals arranged neatly on the shelves by Leah—the only person in the house who seemed to care what he ate. Turned off by the selection, he closed the door.

He repositioned his book bag over his shoulder and took the shortcut to the staircase through the cypress-paneled dining room, wanting to avoid his father's study door.

The dining room had painted portraits of former Devereaux men. Arranged according to the years they'd lived in the home, the portraits started at the entrance off the main hall with the builder of the plantation, Gerard Frellson. His father's painting hung toward the back. The likeness to Gage Devereaux was uncanny—cold, ruthless, and lifeless. An empty spot on the wall waited for his portrait.

Yeah, that's another tradition I'm getting rid of.

Beau walked across the room and swore the eyes of each family member followed, criticizing him. For years, he'd refused to go to the kitchen at night by himself, frightened the pictures would come to life. Now they meant nothing, but he was thankful for the discipline his fear had taught him.

Self-control is everything.

He passed through the peach-painted parlor, turning up his nose. Heavy curtains pooled on the hardwood floor, a nod to the "Southern tradition" of excess material representing wealth and not taste. His mother preferred the parlor, but tonight she wasn't in her favorite wingback chair with her whiskey. Beau figured she'd moved her drinking to her bedroom—the one she slept in down the hall from his father.

Discovering that other parents shared a bedroom had been a shock. He thought all parents slept apart and rarely spoke. Sleepovers with friends had shown him his family wasn't the norm, they were the exception.

He was about to step into the central hallway when a shadowy movement came from his father's study. Beau tiptoed across the floorboards, keeping to the red and gold runner down the center. When he reached the marble french side table, the damn floor gave him away. The groan echoed through the hall and he cringed, sure his father had heard it.

"Beau, come in here."

Convinced he was in trouble for something—usually not living up to Gage Devereaux's excessive standards—he stiffened and prepared to get it over with.

He took a deep breath and pushed open the heavy cypress door. The room was distinctively male, with burgundy leather furniture, ash paneling, and a red rug covering the original hardwood. Even down to the wide walnut desk his father sat behind, the space reeked of authority.

"Where have you been?" Gage frowned as his son approached.

Here comes another lecture.

With Gage, it was always about talking, never about being heard.

"I had to stay late for a student council meeting after practice."

Gage pushed a small pile of papers off to the side. "What about schoolwork?"

"I got it covered."

The scowl on his father's face summed up a lifetime of memories. Never a smile, never a kind word, only *work harder, do more.*

"You only think you do. That's your problem. You don't study hard enough."

Beau's stomach tightened.

"You need to do more if you want to get into Tulane. Your ACT scores weren't exactly impressive. Neither are your grades."

Beau took a step forward, feeling brave. "I've got other skills the admission committee will look at."

"Are we talking football?" Gage sat back, clasping his hands. "That's not enough."

Beau gave an upbeat grin. "But it will help. Colleges look at athletes before regular students."

"Being good at football will not help you run the family business. A degree will. You're also going to have to set more of an example in this town. I've been hearing some talk about you, your friends, and the river." Gage stood and went around to the leather chairs in front of his desk. "Is there anything I should worry about?"

"No. Nothing." Beau nervously shuffled his feet.

Gage sat on the edge of his desk, eyeing his son. "What this community thinks of you now will influence how you do business in the future. I've had to fight to uphold our family name. It's why I've pushed you so hard not to make my mistakes and earn the respect you will need to be successful."

"People *do* respect me." Beau's voice notched upward, reflecting his frustration. "I work my ass off. I attend all the events put on by the brewery. I'm captain of the football team, president of the student council, and volunteer at the local family clinic. What more do you want from me?"

"What about your anger? Your mother told me what you did with the computer. Are we going to have issues again?"

His father's hard tone directed his gaze to the rug. "No. I have it under control, sir."

"I don't think you do. There are those in this town who'll be watching your every move because they know I'll be passing the reins of everything to you. Remember that. The image you project, and your deeds, are what you're known for. Don't let them see who you really are."

Beau raised his head, giving him a confident smile. "You've got nothing to worry about."

Gage wrinkled his brow and then glanced back at the pile of papers on his desk. "Go do your homework."

Beau hurried to the door, impatient to get out from under his father's scrutiny.

Gage's voice rambled around in his mind, giving him a headache. He couldn't understand why his old man was so mistrusting. Beau never screwed up, and if he did, he covered his tracks.

At the top of the stairs, he peered down the long hall. Light shone beneath his mother's door. Gingerly, he started to cross the floor, praying he could get to the safety of his bedroom without encountering Elizabeth. He hated dealing with her late in the evening.

A lock clicked open, and light from her room spilled out as she cracked the door.

"Beau, is that you?"

Beau cursed under his breath. "Yes, it's me."

Elizabeth stepped into the hallway, wearing her yellow robe. She examined the juice bottle in his hand. "Is everything okay?"

"Fine. I was just going to get started on homework." He made a move toward his room.

"What is it? You don't want to give your mother a minute of your time?"

He halted, suppressing his desire to say what he was thinking. Approaching her open door, he noted its shiny new lock.

"You changed the lock again." He smirked. "Was that before or after I threw the computer across the kitchen?"

She went to touch him, and he backed away. "The last time you got that angry with me, I ended up with twenty-two stitches. I don't want to go through that again."

He shook his head, wondering how the cold bitch could even think of calling herself a mother. "I was a kid when that happened. I didn't mean to hurt you. It was an accident."

"It wasn't an accident." She rolled up the right sleeve of her robe. "You attacked me."

The shiny thin scar on her forearm brought back the memory of the rage he tried day after day to control. It had been there all his life, like boiling water beneath the surface of a still lake. His muscles twitched as he pictured taking the butcher knife out of the block in the kitchen and going in search of his mother. She'd taken away his favorite toy because he'd bitten a boy at school. He was going to show her.

Beau had climbed the stairs and crept down the hall to her bedroom door. He turned the handle, being very quiet, like in his favorite ninja movies. She sat on the bed, her back to him, talking on the phone. The first blow had glanced off her arm, but the second ripped through her flesh. He loved the metallic smell of the blood mixed with her floral perfume.

"I'm not a kid anymore."

Elizabeth rolled down her sleeve. "I just don't want to—"

"I said I'm fine!" His shout echoed through the hall. He hoped his father hadn't heard. His mother on his ass was enough.

She took a step back. "Go do your homework and get to bed early. You know how you are when you don't get enough sleep."

He peered in the open door. She had turned down the comforter on her mahogany four-poster bed, but on the nightstand was an empty glass and bottle of whiskey. The sound of the television filled an uncomfortable silence. "How many have you had tonight?"

Elizabeth tugged at the lapels of her robe. "It's just a nightcap, so I can sleep."

Beau faced his mother, not hiding his tight grimace. He hated the saccharine voice she used after a couple of drinks. "Is that your excuse for the past ten years?"

The caring glint in Elizabeth's gray eyes faded. "I don't like your tone."

"And I don't like you drunk." He let his anger seep into his voice. "Are you ever going to do something about that?"

"Don't lecture me." She shook her head, leaning against the doorframe. "I get enough of that from your father."

He motioned to the bottle on her nightstand. "Is that his fault or mine?"

"You already know the answer to that."

He stepped closer. "You bitch."

She backed into her room, the color draining from her cheeks.

I can smell your fear.

Elizabeth slammed the door in his face. The *click* of the lock put an end to their conversation.

Satisfied, Beau strutted down the hall. Nothing like terrorizing his mother to make him feel better. He clenched the brass handle of his door as he thought of her pouring yet another drink, knowing she would retreat to the bottle to dull her pain. Ever since that night, she'd found refuge in whiskey.

The knot in his chest coiling tighter, Beau shoved his door open. Only a few more months, and he would be free.

CHAPTER FIFTEEN

The warm Louisiana sun crested the towering trees alongside the high school, chasing away the dewdrops on the blacktop. Beau parked in his usual shady spot next to the big oak and searched for Leslie's car.

Good. He'd beaten Dawn to school.

He'd dressed in khakis and a freshly starched shirt, wanting to look his best for her. It was time to put any rumors about their relationship to rest. He couldn't let a girl walk away from him. Beau would end it when the time was right, and Leslie was his.

Across the parking lot, Sara appeared, wearing a flowery and fitted dress, showing off her boobs. She was with Dawn's irritating friend, Zoe. The two girls had their heads together as if deep in conversation.

What are they up to?

He strolled toward the girls. "Hey, there."

Zoe scowled while Sara flashed a radiant smile.

Beau ignored Zoe. "So, Sara, did you finish that last assignment in physics? I could use your help."

Zoe sniffed and shook her head. "I'll see you at lunch, Sara."

Beau waited until Zoe was out of earshot. "I just wanted to say, I had a great time at the river the other night. You're a good listener. I'm sorry if I bored you."

Sara flipped her long hair around her shoulder. "Not at all. I like talking to you. We should do it again sometime."

The last thing he needed was Dawn finding out about his time with Sara.

"I'd love that." *Then I can shut you down for good.* "We could meet up at the river this weekend. I know a special place where we could talk in private."

A faint blush warmed her cheeks. "Sure. I'll be there."

He nodded after Zoe. "What were you two talking about? Didn't know you were that tight."

"We're not. She was just asking me if I wanted to try out for the cheerleading squad. Taylor Haskins quit."

Taylor. His adrenaline spiked. He had to make sure she didn't become a problem. "Well, I gotta go." Sara's tedious smile wore on his nerves.

"What's your hurry?" she demanded in a surly tone.

He scrutinized the odd twist of her lips. "You know how people talk. Best to play it safe."

She left without saying another word. Seconds later, Leslie's car pulled into the lot.

Perfect timing.

Beau set off across the lawn at a brisk pace. Not wanting to appear too anxious, he slowed and put on the amiable smile he knew would win Dawn over.

Dawn stepped out of the car, her hair hanging down her back, her blue eyes clogged with mascara, and her lips stained with thick cherry-red lipstick. His heart sank. She looked like a whore.

Ignoring his revulsion, he went up to her, determined to make a public display. "I've missed you, baby." He kissed her cheek.

Over Dawn's shoulder, he saw Taylor on the school steps, glowering. Her ill-fitting clothes and pale skin made him wonder what the hell he'd ever found attractive about her.

Dawn slinked into his arms. "What was that for?"

"I wanted to start the day off right between us."

Leslie peered over the top of the car. "So, you're back. You're like the bubonic plague, Beau Devereaux. You can never be eradicated."

I know what I'm gonna put in that smart mouth of yours.

"Ignore her." Dawn handed him her book bag. "Walk me to class?"

His fists clenched the straps. "Sure, baby."

Dawn clung to his arm, smiling like a beauty queen wearing her newly won crown, eager to make sure everyone got a good look at them. He tuned out Dawn's chatter, nodding only when necessary.

Beau focused on Taylor. She remained hidden in the shadows alongside the stone steps, the tormented look of a wounded animal in her eyes. Her shirt buttoned to her throat, she reminded him of a nun. Gone was the nymphet wanting to "play hard."

Taylor backed to the side of the steps as he approached, cowering.

He imagined his Leslie acting just as compliant, just as afraid.

I can't wait.

The bell rang, and students crammed the halls. Beau made a beeline for Taylor's locker and put down his book bag. Her behavior bothered him— the change in clothes, attitude, and quitting the cheer squad would raise questions. She needed a quick pep talk to keep her compliant. After the next bell, the frenzied screech of tennis shoes skidding on the tiled floor faded. The hall became still.

He waited, knowing she had an hour free between classes.

The door to the girls' bathroom creaked open. A head poked out, and Taylor scanned the hallway.

Beau hid around the corner from her locker. A slight squeak of shoes made him peek into the hall.

Taylor was at her locker, working the combination. He snuck up behind her, careful not to make a sound. Beau placed his hands on the lockers surrounding hers, trapping her.

"Taylor, where've you been?" His voice turned velvety as memories of their night flooded his mind.

She arched away. "Leave me alone."

Beau put his lips to her ear. "What did I say last time we chatted? Stop staring at me like a stalker. You've kept your mouth shut, right?"

Her breath came in choppy waves. "I said I wouldn't say anything, and I haven't."

Beau ran his fingertip down her neck, loving the way she stiffened. "Good. Let's keep it that way. I'd hate for something to happen to your daddy's job."

Taylor flinched as his breath brushed across her ear.

"You better not go back on your word. Or the next time we're together, you won't walk away."

He pushed off from the lockers and strutted down the hall. If she ever breathed a word, Taylor Haskins would end up as just another victim of the Bogue Falaya River.

Late for class, Leslie hurried down the hall but stopped short when she spotted Beau towering over Taylor. She hid behind a row of lockers, curious about their encounter.

Beau stormed off as Taylor hung her head, visibly shaken. When he rounded the corner, Taylor slammed her locker door. The *bang* resonated throughout the corridor.

Keeping a wary eye out for Beau, Leslie approached her. "Hey, you okay?"

Taylor gave her a weak smile. "Just a lot goin' on."

The way she laced her fingers to hide the slight tremor struck Leslie as odd. "I saw you and Beau. Are you two …?"

Taylor's eyes widened. "No, no. We're nothing. Please, please don't mention you saw us talking to anyone. Especially Dawn." She clung to Leslie's arm.

"It's all right." Leslie spoke as she would to a terrified child. "I won't say anything to anyone."

Taylor nodded and let her go. "Thank you. I don't want any problems with him. I prefer to stay as far away from Beau as possible."

Something had happened to Taylor, and Leslie was confident Beau was behind it.

"Glad to hear I'm not the only one who hates running into him. That's something we have in common."

Taylor cocked her head and frowned. "Why don't you like him?"

"Probably for the same reasons you don't." Leslie inched closer. "He's got everyone in this town believing he's some kind of saint, but he's far from it."

Taylor's shoulders relaxed, her trembling subsided, and she exhaled. "So, why can't Dawn see him for what he is?"

Leslie didn't bother to go into the lengthy list of why her sister stayed with Beau. Instead, she asked, "What did Beau say to you, anyway?"

Taylor's eyes darted around the hall. "I should go. I'm late for class." She raced away.

Derek rounded a corner as Taylor rushed past him. He glanced at her and then walked up to Leslie. "Hey, what are you doing out here? I thought you had calculus."

Leslie's gaze followed Taylor as she disappeared around a corner. "I do, but I ran into Taylor Haskins."

"You run into Taylor all the time." Derek brushed a fallen lock of hair from her cheek. "What's special about today?"

She shifted her attention back to him. "She was with Beau Devereaux."

"Is he going to start bothering her and leave you alone?"

The question jarred Leslie. Could Taylor be suffering the same abuse she had? It would explain her odd behavior.

Derek nudged her shoulder. "What do you think?"

Leslie realized she hadn't heard a word Derek just said. "Think about what?"

"Camping out by the river this weekend?" He grinned, appearing excited. "We could fish and lay out under the stars. We haven't done that in a while, and it'll be too cold soon."

Leslie winced at the prospect of disappointing him. "I've got to go to the lake house with my family this weekend. I've tried to get out of it, but Dad's not letting me or Dawn slide."

He put his arms around her. "Then you need to be with your family."

"How 'bout next weekend?"

Derek touched his forehead to hers. "It's a date. Now get to class. You're not doing that great in calculus."

CHAPTER SIXTEEN

His muscles aching from practice and his hair still wet from the shower, Beau pushed open the gym door and stepped out into the afternoon sun. The nippy air clung to him like cobwebs and tickled his skin. He strutted from the door, lugging his heavy book bag over his shoulder as his stomach rumbled for food.

At the gate to the field, the shadows from the metal bleachers blocked the sun, sending a shiver through him. He halted. The sensation was more than passing from light to dark—it was as if he had changed from one world to another.

Something told him to look up, and when he did, he saw Taylor seated at the bottom of the stands, watching the cheerleaders gathered below her. Their eyes met, and the chill returned with a vengeance.

Taylor got up and went to the steps leading to the oval track next to the field, where Dawn and the other cheerleaders stood huddled.

He hurried to the track, his tennis shoes crunching on the gravel while a bitter taste rose along the back of his throat.

Taylor pulled Dawn away from the squad and whispered in her ear. Since Dawn's head was down, Beau couldn't gauge her reaction, and the knot in his stomach tightened.

"Dawn, you ready to go?" he called to her.

She raised her head, and her smile radiated nothing but love and warmth. Beau relaxed, then shifted his attention to Taylor, picturing her naked, bruised, and bleeding before him.

"Hey, honey." Dawn picked up her bag. "You remember Taylor Haskins, right?"

Beau ignored Taylor and took Dawn's hand. "Let's get out of here."

"What's up with you?" Dawn shirked off his grasp.

"Nothing." His arm went around her. "We don't get to spend much time together. I don't wanna waste it talking to some stuck-up girl."

"You think Taylor's stuck-up?"

Beau's jaw clenched as he opened her car door. "Let's not talk about her anymore." He pecked her cheek. "Now, tell me what you'd like to eat."

She squealed. "Pizza!"

Once Dawn was in the front seat, Beau shut her door and went around to his side. He reached for the door handle and glanced at the field.

Taylor met his threatening gaze, but instead of backing down, she stared as if to say, "I dare you."

He imagined taking her back to his cell and making her pay for her disrespect.

Just you wait.

The sun dipped behind the buildings along Main Street, stretching long shadows over the road in front of Beau's car. The businesses in the shops crowding the sidewalks had a steady stream of customers.

"So that will mean I have to find a new girl," Dawn said, coming to the end of her rambling.

"A new girl for what?" He peered ahead to the neon sign with wavy blue lights resembling the river that cut through town. Framed in bold green letters, it read *The Bogue Falaya Café*—also known as The Bogue.

She swatted his arm. "Weren't you listening to me? Taylor quit the squad." Dawn huffed in her seat. "How could she not want to be a cheerleader anymore?"

"I told you that girl is screwy." He pulled into the parking lot of a brick and glass building. "You need to stay away from her."

Dawn scrunched her face. "Why don't you like her? She's nice."

He selected a spot away from the side entrance of the eatery. "Some of the guys had a run-in with her and said she's a bitch. I don't want her influencing you."

"What guys?" Dawn's heart-shaped mouth twisted into a quirky pout. "She never mentioned that to me."

"I've heard stuff in gym class." Beau opened his door, wanting to drop the subject. "Come on. I'm starving."

Through the windows, Beau saw classmates and members of the football team filling the booths and tables. He opened the door to a whoosh of pepperoni-scented air-conditioning. A bluesy tune blasted from the red, yellow, and green neon jukebox in the corner of the dining room.

He squared his shoulders and plastered on a fake smile. Years of listening to his father's lectures on how to present himself in public had become ingrained.

He nestled his hand into the curve of Dawn's back, guiding her down the center aisle and around the clog of tables set up between the steel-topped counter and orange vinyl booths. The aroma of cooking cheese and meat wafted by while the flurry of conversations and music unraveled his concentration.

"Beau, my man." Carl greeted him from behind the counter. "You going to lead the team to victory against Forest Glen this Friday?"

Beau gave the stocky man a confident nod. "You know it, Carl."

Carl set his flour-covered hands on the counter. "What can I get you guys?"

"Large pizza, the works. Hold the anchovies." Beau held up two fingers. "Two iced teas."

"Comin' right up." He motioned toward the tables. "Take a seat, and I'll send someone over with your drinks."

Beau ushered Dawn along the center aisle to the back of the dining room. He passed a collection of faded pictures of food selections served in the restaurant. Ceiling fans spun while images of Coke floats and ice cream sundaes hung from the fluorescent light fixtures.

Dawn selected an empty booth in the middle of the dining area, much to Beau's dismay. He preferred to keep a low profile in public, not wanting anything to get back to his father.

She scooted across the bench. "Carl must be happy this place will be all his one day. Like you'll have the brewery."

Beau slid in beside her, aggravated by the reminder of his father's plans. He hated thinking of a life stuck at the brewery. In five years, he envisioned himself no better off than Carl Bucelli—trapped in a dead-end job and under his old man's thumb.

As the streetlamps flipped on, the front glass doors opened. Sara Bissell walked in, wearing a tight white T-shirt, high-cut skirt, and tall black boots.

He longed to wipe off her thick makeup and blacken her eyes for real.

Around Sara was a group of girls dressed in revealing clothes, wearing just as much makeup. Beau's appetite waned when Sara spotted him. The smile she flashed did nothing to arouse his passion, only his fury.

"That skank is here," Dawn muttered.

He patted her thigh. "Settle down. Don't start something."

Sara sashayed by their booth, keeping her focus on Beau.

"I'm gonna kill her." Dawn shimmied toward him, attempting to get out of the booth.

Things were tense enough at home without adding this to his pile of bullshit. He refused to move. "Baby, you need to calm down. I told you there's nothin' going on."

Dawn gave him a big push. "I don't believe you. Get me out of here."

He wanted to talk her into staying, so everyone would see they were tight. But he recognized the angry glint in her eyes and held up his hands. "All right. We'll go." Beau stood and headed for the door.

Behind them, a syrupy voice called, "Leaving so soon, Beau?"

He turned around, and Sara winked at him. He hoped Dawn didn't see it, but out of the corner of his eye, he glimpsed her open-mouthed shock.

Dawn was about to step toward Sara's table when Beau tossed her over his shoulder and carried her out of the restaurant.

"Put me down!"

He ignored her and didn't stop until he reached his car, hidden in the shadows at the edge of the lot. He deposited her by the passenger door. "Are you insane?"

Dawn attempted to get around him and head back inside. "Did you see her winking at you?"

"So what?" He held out his arms, blocking her way. "That's no reason to act crazy. There's a lotta people in there. How long do you think it would take before the whole town knew about your little run-in? How would I explain that to my dad? He's always up my ass about how I present myself in public." He gripped her right arm, digging his fingers into her soft flesh. "Damn it, Dawn, do you have no self-control?"

She tried to back away, but he only squeezed harder.

"You're hurting me."

Her pale face became Leslie's. She smirked at him, egging him on. His fingers cinched tighter, tingling with excitement.

"Beau!" a voice called across the lot.

He let Dawn go, and she pressed up against the car. Fear pinked her cheeks and her blue eyes watered.

Carl came running up to them. "Is there a problem?"

Beau's anger cooled when his gaze settled on the man's flour-covered jeans and red apron.

"No, no." Beau shook his head. "I'm sorry we can't stay. I've got to get Dawn home."

"You want me to get your order to go?" Carl asked.

Beau wasn't about to wait around and give Dawn another chance to confront Sara. He'd had enough of both girls for one night. He removed his wallet from his back pocket and handed Carl a fifty-dollar bill. "Give our order to someone else."

Carl slipped the money into his apron pocket. "I'll take care of you, Beau."

After Carl returned to the restaurant, Dawn opened her mouth to speak, but Beau held up his hand. "Don't say another word." He put her in the car and slammed the door.

Once he peeled out of the parking lot, his fury shifted from Dawn to Sara.

"We could have at least waited for our order."

Dawn's high-pitched voice intruded on a daydream of tying Sara to the pipe in the wall of his cell.

"What did you say?"

"You paid for our food. Why not wait for it? Running out like that seems silly."

Beau hit the gas, needing to get her home and out of his hair. "You better be thankful I got you outta there before you did something stupid. I can't have Sara calling the cops on your ass."

"For what? Calling her a whore? Threatening to rip her hair out? That's what I wanted to do."

"That's assault." He gripped the wheel. "For being the daughter of an attorney, you're not too bright."

She got that deer-in-headlights look he hated. It meant a fight was coming.

"If you hadn't been hanging around that slut Saturday night, this wouldn't have happened."

Beau punched the steering wheel. "I didn't do anything with Sara!"

She flinched and shrank into her seat.

A taut expression of fear distorted Dawn's face. She clenched her hands, her knuckles showing white against his sienna leather seats. She hugged the door as if she would jump out at any moment.

Beau had gone too far. He'd let his anger show. His hand throbbed. With the pain came regret.

Keep it together.

"I'm sorry." He kept his eyes on the road. "I lost my temper back there."

Dawn rubbed the red mark on her upper arm. "I should have ignored her."

"Forget about Sara." Beau grinned, wanting to assure her all was well. "Do you really believe I'd wanna go out with that skank?"

"No." A slight smile returned to her lips, but her eyes remained apprehensive. "I'm sorry I was a witch at the restaurant. I promise to do better."

In the beginning, Dawn's sweet disposition and promises to do whatever he wanted—be the girl he needed and follow his rules—pleased him. Now, she grated on his nerves. Maybe it was time to shake things up.

"You can make it up to me at the river this weekend."

Her smile faltered. "Uh, I have to go to the lake house. My dad is being a real pain in the butt about having a family weekend."

Her news didn't bother him at all. There were others he could have fun with. "Well, I'll miss you."

She leaned across the console. "Promise to keep out of trouble and away from Sara Bissell while I'm gone."

He made his grin appear genuine. "I won't have anything to do with her."

The lie pleased her, but he questioned how anyone could be so trusting. Leslie would have never believed him.

Beau's sour mood lifted. With Dawn out of his hair, his weekend looked bright. Beau punched the accelerator. He would invite Sara to join him at the river and bring her to the cells. There, he would exact his punishment for the shitstorm she'd caused. With Sara, he could try something new—and dangerous.

The *vroom* of Beau's engine carried up Dawn's sidewalk as he pulled away from the curb. The stars in the sky and lights from other houses on her street cast a protective glow, chasing away the encroaching darkness.

But the tranquility of the night did little to offset her unease. Stunned by Beau's treatment at the café, Dawn didn't understand what had happened to the guy she knew. She walked along the path to her front door, her upper arm still stinging. Dawn checked the spot again. His red fingerprints remained.

She'd seen another side of Beau tonight. She knew he had a temper, but this was different. He scared her.

I bet Leslie doesn't have to deal with this from Derek.

She abruptly halted on the porch, comparing her relationship with Beau to Leslie and Derek's. They never seemed to fight, have issues with other girls, or even argue about their future. Derek didn't push Leslie to have sex, and he never wanted to party with his friends.

Weak at the thought of a life without Beau, she plopped down on the steps. She had dreaded the coming weekend at the lake house, but part of her wanted an opportunity to think. A little time away from Beau could help her get some perspective. Playing by his rules wasn't as fun as it used to be. It was time to make some rules of her own.

CHAPTER SEVENTEEN

The rustle of people, the clatter of metal bleachers, and shouts of excited teenagers filled the football field of St. Benedict High as fans packed to head home.

In his football uniform, fresh from a winning game, Beau escorted Dawn to the parking lot as her parents waited by the gate.

"Promise to call me every night, even when you're at the river."

He noted the desperation in her voice. "I'll call." He searched the field, hoping to see Sara. "You know I can't go a day without you, baby."

Dawn pulled away. "Remember, I love you, Beau."

His eyes instantly went back to her. *Love?* Did she even know what the word meant? To him, love meant possession, rage, power—not some fuzzy, warm fairy tale.

"I have to go. Coach always wants to do a recap after the game. He'll probably bring up my two touchdowns to Mitch." He kissed her cheek. "Can't miss that."

Beau took off running for the locker room, glad to have gotten away before she pushed for his feelings about their relationship. He didn't have any.

When he made it to the metal doors of the gym entrance, Sara was waiting. His anger for her still smoldered, but he would take care of it. "You and me at the river tonight?"

She gave an ambivalent half-nod. "What about Dawn? I saw you together at the gate."

His gaze drifted down her red top and snug blue jeans. "She'll be gone all weekend. I told her we needed a break, so she's going away with her parents."

"I like the sound of that." Sara's eyes lit up as she moved away from the door. "See you there."

This day just gets better and better.

Mitch slapped the dash as Beau turned into the local grocery for a liquor run. "When you hit me with that twenty-yard pass, I was like *boom*. We crushed it."

A fiery beat blasted from the stereo speakers, cool fall air sifted through the cracked windows, and the high from the game radiated through Beau.

"It was sweet." Beau headed around the back of the store.

"Now we're gonna have ourselves a wild time at the river." Josh leaned forward from the back, his broad shoulders barely fitting between the bucket seats. "So glad Dawn cut you loose for the weekend. I hate to say this, dude, but she's a downer."

Beau turned toward the loading dock. "Lately, she's been different. I'm not sure what the problem is."

"Just train her right and she'll heel like a dog." Josh scanned the inky darkness around their car. "Chicks dig an alpha male."

"My sister reads them alpha male books like they're goin' out of style. All chicks do." Mitch thumped his chest. "Be the beast."

Beau wanted to laugh. *They have no idea.*

"You guys aren't in relationships." Beau parked next to the rear entrance. "It's not so easy just telling women what to do. You have to get them into thinking what you want is what they want."

Josh crinkled his brow. "How'd you do that?"

Beau dialed down the music. "It's a question of power. You've got to assert yourself. You ask a girl what she wants, pretending to be considerate and all, but before she has time to think, you put suggestions in her head. Where to go, what to wear, who her friends are." He thought back on how easy it was to conquer Dawn. "Pretty soon, your wants are her wants. When you've got the little things down, you can manipulate them on bigger things like sex."

Mitch turned to him, eyes wide with amazement. "Dude? You're creepin' me out. You really do that shit?"

"Don't interrupt him." Josh edged closer. "Go back to how you get girls to have sex with you."

Beau wasn't dealing with the savviest bunch, but that was why he hung around them. How he manipulated girls also worked on his friends. "You weren't listening. You sweet talk. You tell them what they need to hear, and once they're addicted, you change the rules."

Mitch burst out in a coarse laugh. "Sounds like the same crap you've done to win over the entire town. The no drugs, no drinkin', no smokin', volunteerin' do-gooder." He hooked a thumb at Josh. "But we know better. You're a badass."

Beau shook his head. *You don't have a clue.*

Josh frowned. "What happens if you do all that stuff, and you still can't get laid?"

Beau just smiled.

The back door to the grocery opened, and fluorescent light bathed the car. Freddie emerged, carrying a box loaded with bottles.

Beau met him at the back of the car.

"Here ya go." Freddie held out the box. "Wish I was going with you guys. I remember the river used to be a blast."

Beau put the alcohol in his trunk. "Yeah, still is. Thanks for the supplies, Freddie." Beau reached into his pocket and handed him some cash.

"Let me know whenever you guys need more." Freddie checked the one-hundred-dollar bills before tucking them in his pocket. "Your liquor runs sure help pay the baby bills."

Beau shut the trunk. The ass-kissing store clerk annoyed him. One of many who saw his family as a meal ticket. *Losers.*

"We stocked up?" Josh sounded exuberant.

"Yeah, we're good." Beau started the car. "Let's make this a night to remember."

CHAPTER EIGHTEEN

D awn and her family arrived at their cabin on the shores of Lake Pontchartrain. The setting sun threw red and orange ribbons across the lake's modest waves. A log home designed with picture windows along the front sat nestled amid a circle of thick pines. A wooden deck jutted out over the edge of the lake with two jet skis secured to the dock.

The log décor added an earthy texture to the walls and beamed ceilings inside the home. The simple furniture with forest green and burnt sienna upholstery complemented the pine hardwood floor. A massive stone fireplace rose from the combination living room and den.

Once in the bedroom she shared with Leslie, Dawn unpacked her duffel bag while the last dregs of sunlight filtered through the window and reached across the white plush rug. She turned to her sister, wanting to broach the subject of her confusing feelings for Beau.

"Did you say goodbye to Derek?" She placed some shirts in her dresser.

"Yep." Leslie took a blow dryer from her bag. "What did Beau say after the game?"

"Not much, but that's Beau." Hand on her hip, Dawn debated how to ask the question on her mind. "When you say, 'I love you' to Derek, does he say it back?"

ALEXANDREA WEIS AND LUCAS ASTOR

Leslie put the blow dryer on her night table. "Yes."

Dawn pressed her lips together. "With you being gone for the weekend, do you trust him?"

Leslie's laugh circled her like the bothersome caw of a crow.

"Of course, I trust him."

Dawn went to Leslie's bed and flopped down. "Why don't I feel like I can trust Beau?"

Leslie sat next to her. "Maybe that's your heart telling you he isn't the right guy."

The wall of hostility Dawn put up whenever she dealt with her sister came tumbling down. She believed she was impervious to Leelee's comments about Beau, but every single one had stuck in her head for months. Dawn kept her eyes on her bag, afraid to look at Leslie. "I've been thinking about the things you said. Things Beau told you." A lump formed in her throat. "When did it start?"

Leslie's sigh cut through Dawn like a razor blade. Her intuition bristled—Leslie had been telling the truth.

"After the first night you two hooked up at the river. He corners me at school, saying ..." Leslie shook her head. "Disgusting things."

Dawn's heart broke into a thousand pieces. She knew why he'd harassed her. It was the same reason she'd refused to acknowledge. "He wanted you that night at the river, not me. He's been making you suffer for turning him down ever since. Beau doesn't like being told no."

Leslie touched her hand. "I was trying to protect you. You seemed so happy with him, so I sorta let it go. Was I wrong?"

Dawn squeezed Leslie's hand. "You can't always protect me, Leelee. I had to see for myself who Beau really is. I believe you." Her lower lip quivered. "I'm going to talk to him and tell him to stop bothering you."

Leslie frowned. "Be careful. There's something very wrong with him."

"Wrong with who?" Shelley came into the bedroom. "What are you girls gossiping about? Or do you still call it gossip? Haven't seen you with your heads together in a long time."

Leslie got up from the bed. "We were talking about Derek and Beau."

Shelley set the bag by the door. "Do I want to hear this?"

Dawn stood alongside her sister. "Leslie was helping me make up my mind about something."

Shelley's eyebrows arched. "Can I ask what?"

"Why isn't anyone downstairs ready to roast marshmallows?" John Moore peered into the bedroom. "What's going on in here?"

Shelley nodded at the twins. "Dawn was just about to tell me she's made a decision about Beau Devereaux."

John folded his arms. "What decision?"

Dawn sat back down on the bed. The pressure of her parents' curiosity suffocated her. She hadn't decided anything yet. "It's no big deal."

"Are you two having problems again?" Shelley took a step closer to Dawn. "Because if you want to talk about—"

Her father held up his hands, demanding quiet. "New rule. For the duration of the weekend, there will be no more talk of boyfriends. No mention of Beau or Derek until we're back home. Agreed?"

Dawn reluctantly nodded, but Leslie never moved a muscle.

John waved at his daughters. "See? Problem solved." He left the room with a grimacing Shelley following close behind.

Dawn sagged into the bed. It was going to be a long weekend.

Moonlight glistened on the beach along the Bogue Falaya River. Vibrations from the pounding speakers sent ripples across the black water. Beau felt the throb of music through his tennis shoes as he watched the dance of light on the shallow waves. The canopy of trees arched over the river seemed to sway with the beat.

He turned, nursing his water bottle, already bored with the festivities. People on the beach danced, with most paired off in couples. Those gathered around the bonfires talked or checked their phones. Guys from the football team had set up a table and were playing beer pong.

How had he found such simple things fun? Before Taylor, the kids at the river had intrigued him. Now, they bored him to death.

Josh and Mitch sat on picnic tables, chatting with two scantily clad girls from Covington High who had heard about the party on social media. Beau loved the notoriety, but not the bigger crowds. He preferred the beach filled with locals who knew who he was and that he ruled the river.

He checked the time on his phone, pissed about Sara. He'd searched for her, wanting to get her to the cells, and if she didn't show soon, he would find another girl.

Mitch stumbled across the sand. "Did you see those two hot babes from Covington High? Beverly and Lana." He slapped Beau's back. "Do those girls rock or what?"

Beau looked around. "You might wanna keep your voice down."

"What do I say to keep them interested?" Mitch's face lit up with a smile. "Help me out."

"I'd offer them some wine, but don't let them drink too much. Girls love it when a guy acts concerned about their welfare. Insist you want to get to know them sober, and I promise they will go out with you."

Mitch gave him a fist bump. "You the man, Beau."

Mitch hurried away, and a leggy redhead caught Beau's attention. Slim hips, an upturned nose, and full coral lips had him wondering how she'd look naked.

"Hey, sexy," a voice whispered in his ear.

Sara eased in front of him. She had on the crimson lipstick he hated. Beau threw his arms around her and lifted her into the air, itching to get her alone.

"Where've you been?"

"I had to sneak out." She kissed him. "Mom doesn't want me here."

"Why not?" Beau put her down.

"Parents at the high school are talking about the drinking and stuff going on here. She said I couldn't come anymore." She slipped her arms around his neck. "Like she can stop me from bein' with you."

His stomach churned. So that's how his old man found out. "I didn't realize. Might be time to tone things down."

"Are you kidding? Every student in town wants to come to your river parties." She smiled. "And after tonight, everyone in town will know about us, too."

"Whoa. What are you talking about?" Beau's desire to take her to the cells fizzled.

Sara gaped at him. "You're dumpin' Dawn, right? I'm takin' her place. Anyone who sees us here tonight will know."

He unwound her snakelike arms from his neck. This possessive streak meant she would be trouble. He thought he'd screened her well enough. Aggressive, outspoken—she had traits he admired in Leslie, but lacked her fire, intelligence, and class.

Beau took a step back, his cool demeanor snuffing out the hint of aggravation in his voice. "I haven't called anything off with Dawn."

"What am I supposed to do?" Her raised tone attracted a few stares. "Wait in the shadows until you're ready for a relationship with me?"

Beau folded his arms, an arrogant smirk on his lips. "Who says I want a relationship with you?"

Sara studied him with an icy glare. "You want me to tell your little girlfriend you asked me here tonight?"

His first instinct was to punch her, but he couldn't do that in front of others. He lowered his voice to a menacing growl. "Careful. You don't know what I'm capable of."

She cocked her arm back to slap him.

Beau caught her hand before she could land a blow. "I could make you pay for that."

"You can't touch me, Beau Devereaux. I don't care how much money you have."

He let her go. "I don't need money to hurt you. All I need is what I already own—the ear of everyone in this town."

She gave him her best "bad girl" stare. "Oh yeah? Who's gonna believe what you say about me?"

Keenly aware of the attention they attracted, Beau stopped and reset. He moved closer, so only she could hear. "The entire football team will after I tell them the things you did to me tonight and are *more* than willing to do to them. What do you think a gang of horny drunks will do with that? Hell, I'll even give them a place to do it. A place no one will hear you scream."

"You bastard." She came at him with her claws out.

Beau cuffed her hands and held her against him. "Don't you dare think you can outsmart me."

Sara wiggled out of his embrace, her cheeks a brilliant shade of red. "You're a sick shit."

He nodded. "Quite possibly. You better never speak to Dawn or even look at her. Break that rule, and my boys will mess you up so bad, you'll never be any good to a guy again."

The color drained from Sara's face as she backed away and took off toward the tree line. She disappeared into the shadows, chased by the whispers and stares of the party.

Beau's edginess returned. He'd planned to teach her a lesson in the cells but had to settle for threats and intimidation. Not what he wanted, and certainly not what he craved, but it would have to do for now.

He'd dreamed of hurting Sara, and like a coiled spring, he was sure to explode if he didn't find another girl to give him that rush. Like an addict jonesing for another fix, he needed the high again.

"You sure know how to throw a party. Beau Devereaux, right?"

The alluring redhead was back. He fixated on her coral lipstick. "How do you know my name?"

Her low-cut blouse offered a tantalizing glimpse of cleavage. "Everyone knows who you are."

Beau sized up her potential. Dressed to tease and raring to go.

"Who are you?" he asked in his husky voice.

She smiled, adding a luster to her dreamy hazel eyes. "Kelly Norton."

"From Covington High?"

Kelly tossed her long red hair. "We've met before. My mom manages an apartment building your dad built in Covington."

The news pleased him. Daughter of an employee—she would be less willing to talk for fear of hurting the family income. He could do what he wanted to her without worrying about repercussions.

"My father owns several properties in the area, but I think I know the building you're talking about." On the hunt to reel her in, he set the trap. "Your mother is Beth Norton, right?"

Her smile widened, adding a dimple to her chin. "Wow. That's right."

Beau put his hands in his pockets and, with a sheepish grin, moved in, wanting to gain her trust. "I work summers at the brewery, and part of my job is helping my father with the books. I've seen your mom's name a lot lately."

"You don't remember me?"

He detected a glimmer of hope in the undercurrent of her voice. "No, I remember." He stepped around, circling her like a predator. "You helped serve the punch at the opening last year." He impressed himself with that one. She was the mousy girl in the pink dress who had been too afraid to talk to anyone—including him.

An uncomfortable silence lingered. Well, not uncomfortable for Beau. Kelly shifted her feet in the sand, tugged at her top, and played with her hair. She was nervous—nervous meant insecure and easy to manipulate.

Beau glanced back at the two girls with Mitch and Josh. "Are you here with them?"

"Yeah." She stepped closer. "That girl you were with before, is she your girlfriend?"

Definitely interested.

"No. She's angry because she isn't my girlfriend." He shook his head. "She's too possessive for my tastes."

Kelly twirled a lock of fiery hair around her finger. "What type of woman do you like?"

He ached to touch her. "Smart. Funny. Interested in the long term. One-night stands aren't my style."

Kelly tilted her head and raised the corner of her mouth in the slightest smile. "You expect me to buy that bullshit?"

A tingle shot through Beau's groin. The comment was just what he would expect from his Leslie. "Would I lie to you?" He grinned. "What do you do when you're not in school?"

She tucked a lock of hair behind her ear. "I work at a vet's office. I love animals."

"Animals, huh?" *I like the wild kind.*

She inched closer, her lips parted. "What do you like to do when not playing quarterback?"

Beau wasn't in the mood to toy with her anymore. He wanted to taste her fear. "Have you ever seen the inside of The Abbey, Kelly Norton?"

Kelly's bewitching smile spread, highlighting the alluring curve of her lips. "No. Wanna show it to me?"

After a quick check to see who was around, Beau clasped her hand. "Come with me. I'm going to give you the night of your life."

CHAPTER NINETEEN

C rickets chirped as Beau eased out of the crack in the wall from the cells. The chill in the air teased his sweaty skin, but the surge of power in his blood was like liquid fire. The rush consumed him.

What if you get caught?

The family name would protect him. In addition to money, his father had hefty political clout in Baton Rouge, thanks to his notorious grandfather.

He headed across the grassy field, already thinking about his next girl. Before he reached the iron gate, movement in the corner of his eye grabbed his attention.

Amid the trees crowding the edge of the property, something darted in and out. Beau could just make out a long, white hooded cloak, fluttering and billowing at the edge of the woods. Then it disappeared.

His heart rocketed to his throat. All the stories of the lady in white at The Abbey came rushing back.

Then he calmed. Someone had to be messing with him. It wasn't Kelly. She'd taken off a bawling mess several minutes before, and he'd heard the slam of the iron gate. He was alone—unless the guys were messing with him.

But they don't know about your room in the cells.

Beau cut across the grass, racing to the gate. He reached the path and glanced back at the trees where he'd seen the ghostly presence. Nothing.

My mind's playing tricks on me. Just like at the house.

Relieved, he made it to the beach, but the spooky incident had killed his high.

The crowd had thinned and those left were packing to go. Most had midnight curfews, including Beau.

He set out across the sand, avoiding bottles and piles of trash in his path. His heels angrily dug in as he walked. He searched the weary faces around him until he spotted the black curls and broad shoulders of his friend.

Mitch sat on a picnic bench chugging a beer. Two girls slept curled up next to him.

"Dude, what's this?" He slapped Mitch's shoulder and motioned at the girls.

Mitch shrugged. "They passed out a while ago."

Beau got a closer look at their faces. "Who are they?"

"Beverly." Mitch stood and wobbled, pointing to the slim brunette sleeping next to him. "And Lana. The Covington girls, remember?"

Josh barreled out of the bushes, tugging his zipper up.

"I was just about to look for you. It's getting late." Beau ran his hand through his hair, his anger creeping upward. "Let's get out of here." He lowered his voice, mindful of the others around them. "I've got to make curfew. My old man will pitch a fit if I'm late."

Mitch tossed his empty bottle toward a trash barrel and missed. "Haven't seen you 'round for a while."

Beau picked up the bottle. "How could you see anything after all these?" Beau motioned to the unconscious girls. "What did you give them? They're out cold."

"Wine." Josh wiped a bit of sand from his shirt, grinning. "Thanks for the tip."

"I said tipsy, not dead drunk." Beau tossed the bottle to the garbage can several feet away, making it in on the first try.

Mitch glanced behind him at the river. "Where's Kelly? I saw y'all headin' off together. You make it with her?"

Beau's heart sped up, remembering her whimpers. "She's not my type. I left her by one of the bonfires."

"You should've given Kelly some wine." Josh snickered and tripped, almost falling to the ground before Mitch caught him.

Lana sat up, weaving as she held her head. "Wait? Kelly left us?" She looked around the beach. "How are we supposed to get home? She was our ride."

Josh helped her from the bench. "Beau will take you home."

Beau's cheeks burned. He was ready to kill. "I've got to make curfew."

Lana wobbled up to Beau, going for sexy but coming across as pathetic. Still very drunk, she rubbed up against him. "I'll do anything you want if you give me a ride home."

Beau pushed her away. "Thanks, but I'll pass."

His phone rang, and he checked the caller ID. Dawn. Beau frowned and sent her to voicemail. He put the phone back in his pocket. He would deal with her later.

Josh put his hand on Beau's shoulder. "What do we do with the girls? We can't just leave 'em."

Lana wrapped her arms around Josh's thick neck. "Take me home with you."

There were times his friends were more trouble than they were worth, but if he left the girls behind, people might hear about it. Best to keep up appearances—just like his old man wanted.

"Get the girls." Beau moved back toward the path leading to the parking lot. "I'll drive them home."

"But they live in Covington." Mitch followed him. "It will take you another hour, at least."

"Josh is right. We can't leave them." Beau checked the clock on his phone. "It wouldn't be gentlemanly."

"My hero." Lana left Josh and went to Beau, slipping her arms around his neck.

Her foul breath and slutty behavior sickened him. He wanted to kick her senseless to teach her a lesson. Instead, he peeled her off and pushed her back at Josh. "It's time to go."

Once everyone settled into his car, Beau left the parking lot and turned onto the dimly lit road. The trees whipped by as he picked up speed, creating undulating shadows reminiscent of the odd presence he had seen by The Abbey. Had someone meant to frighten him? But who? The drunk ramblings of Josh and Mitch interrupted his thoughts—their hyena-like laughter grated on his nerves.

The evening exemplified the difference between boys and men. Boys like Josh and Mitch chased girls who drank too much and gave in too easily. But Beau was a man. He no longer had an interest in women who surrendered. He wanted them to struggle, cry, beg, resist, and scream—just like Kelly.

Beau quietly shut the glass doors to the mudroom and stepped into the rear hall. The exterior security lights filtered through windows as he crept past the kitchen—the clock on the microwave read almost two.

In the main hall, the lights were out. Even Gage's study was dark. Beau tiptoed, holding his black tennis shoes, not trusting them on the hardwood floor. Years of sneaking around at night taught him how to walk and not make a sound. Once he made it up the curved oak staircase, he peered into the darkness, searching for lights. Fortunately, everyone appeared to be asleep. Beau slipped into his bedroom and shut the door.

He flipped on the light and scanned the ornate mahogany trundle bed, flat-screen TV, and the display cabinet housing his collection of toy supercars. The décor didn't gel with who he'd become. He needed to make some changes.

Beau tossed his sand-encrusted tennis shoes aside and set his cell phone on the night table. A light knocking surprised him.

"What is it?"

The door creaked open, and his mother stepped inside. "You're home past your curfew."

After a ragged sigh, Beau raked his hand through his hair. "Yeah, I was making sure some drunk girls got home."

Elizabeth walked into the room. "Is that the truth?"

Beau cringed. "Would you back off? I wasn't doing anything wrong."

"Ever since this school year began, you've been acting like you used to—the rages, the tantrums. Now you're coming in late and shouting at me." Elizabeth gripped the edge of his bed.

He took in her bloodshot eyes. "I'm amazed you noticed."

She tugged at the lapels of her yellow robe. "Don't push me. I went along with your father last time. He buried the incident. But do it again, and I won't remain silent."

"You're never gonna to let me forget, are you?" Beau didn't hide his bitterness. "Every day, you remind me with a look or a gesture." A muscle quivered in his jaw. "You spend your days at the bottom of a whiskey bottle so you don't have to deal with your son."

"Don't you dare speak to me that way."

"What? Have I offended your sense of decency? That's a laugh." He moved toward her. "People are talking about you—the neglected wife of Gage Devereaux. You know how he feels about his precious family name. I guarantee he'll get rid of you long before he ever pushes me out the door."

"God, you're just like your father." She backed away. "You even sound like him when you attack me."

"Maybe you need to take a page out of Dad's playbook and start fucking around." He returned to his bed, wanting to end the conversation. "Might get your mind off me."

Elizabeth balled her fists. "Does Dawn know about you? Has she seen the real Beau Devereaux? I'd hoped that poor girl was getting through to you, but she isn't, is she? Should I warn her to keep the family dog out of your reach? I can tell her what you did to mine."

Beau charged her, wanting to break her skinny little neck, but he refrained. The fear in her eyes gave him a rush.

"If you ever say anything to Dawn, I'll kill you."

Elizabeth wasn't like a high school girl. Her fear faded and a steadfast resolve replaced it.

"I believe you would." She raised her head, becoming the society maven she always liked to portray. "I won't tell your father you were out past curfew. He has enough on his mind."

Beau tempered his anger, not wanting to give his mother the upper hand. "I doubt he'd care. All he needs is an heir for his empire, not a son."

Elizabeth gave him a stern rebuke with her frosty glare and then slipped out the door.

His head pounded. For as long as Beau could remember, he'd hated his mother. She always enraged him to the point of madness.

Beau undressed and climbed into bed, but her comments lingered, and restless energy chased away his fatigue. Unable to close his eyes, he snatched up his cell phone and decided to call Dawn.

"Beau?" She sounded groggy. "Why are you calling so late?"

What would she like to hear? "I missed you tonight."

"I missed you, too. Are you just getting home?"

Dawn's voice melted like butter over a flame.

"Yeah, Josh and Mitch met some girls at the river from Covington High. They were too drunk to drive home, so I took them. Made me miss my curfew."

"What did your folks say?"

"It's all good," Beau added with a boastful lilt. "They like it when I set an example for others."

Dawn sighed. "You're a good guy, Beau Devereaux. Did you have fun at the river? Please tell me Sara Bissell wasn't there."

"She was." He paused, thinking ahead, finding the right words to set his plan into motion. "I put that bitch in her place when she hit on me. She won't be messing with you or me again."

"What did you do?"

He grinned at her curiosity. "I let everyone know what a slut she is. First, she flirts with me, knowing I have a girlfriend. Then she went off with a couple of guys at the river."

"Wow." Dawn giggled. "Wish I could have been there to see that. Her rep will be dirt come Monday."

Done with the subject of Sara, he searched for something to keep her talking. "Are you having a good time at the lake?"

"I'm enjoying myself. Leslie and I are getting along, if you can believe it. My parents are happy about that."

The mention of her sister set off alarm bells in Beau's head. He sat up, his restlessness returning. "What have you and Leslie been talking about?"

"Nothing much. It's been nice spending time with her."

Leslie in her ear was a bad thing. He didn't want Leslie's opinions rubbing off on Dawn. "When are you coming home?"

"Sometime tomorrow night. We're going out on the boat in the morning."

"That sounds like fun." It didn't, but he figured that was what she wanted to hear. "Wish I was there."

"I wish you were, too. If you go back to the river, don't get into any trouble."

"Don't worry." Beau drummed his fingers on the bed, anticipating another night of fun. "After tonight, I don't think the boys will be ready to party too much. They hit it pretty hard."

Dawn yawned. "I'd better get back to sleep. I love you, Beau."

He hesitated, not sure what to say. He didn't love Dawn, but he needed her for a little while longer. "I'll call you tomorrow night."

Beau hung up with images of Leslie dancing in his head. Soon, she would be on her knees, begging for him to hurt her, wanting to feel his hands around her throat.

That's real love. And she's gonna know it very soon.

CHAPTER TWENTY

A foggy tunnel loomed before him. Shadows played along the curved wall, and he heard women screaming. The alluring sound urged him deeper into the darkness until a voice rang out.

"Beau, wake up."

The tunnel evaporated and light pierced the darkness. He opened his eyes and his vision cleared.

Gage Devereaux arched over the bed, his thick brown hair damp, his face freshly shaven, and his dark, harsh eyes glowering. Gage's woodsy fragrance filled his nose.

"What is it, Dad?"

Gage sat down on the edge of the bed, oozing the sense of mastery he commanded wherever he went.

"I got a call from Kent Davis at the sheriff's department this morning. A girl leaving from your river party was pulled over for driving erratically. Evidently, she was upset, looked roughed up, and they had to call her mother to come get her. Her name is Kelly Norton. Do you know her?"

Beau wiped the sleep from his eyes as his heart thudded. "Never heard of her. Does she go to St. Benedict?"

"No, Covington High." Gage checked the time on his gold Rolex. "I'm concerned because Kent's been getting complaints about parties at the river. The noise, trash, and unattended fires are angering people who work and live in that area. You spend a lot of time there, and I want you to be careful."

"We just go there and hang out."

Gage stood. "And drink. I'm not stupid."

Beau kicked his comforter away. "I don't drink. We just have fun, listen to music, and talk."

Gage scowled, not looking convinced. "You aren't like the other kids. Your future is already planned, and you have the family's reputation to uphold. You will be a leader of this community. That position requires a certain sense of responsibility."

Beau suppressed a groan. "I know the drill, Dad, but can we have this talk another time?"

Gage grabbed his shirt and yanked him out of bed. "I want to make myself perfectly clear. When I tell you to mind yourself and stay out of trouble, you will obey me. I will not have you screw up everything our family has built."

Beau stiffened with fear as he stared into his father's dark eyes. "Yes, sir."

Gage let him go and strutted to the bedroom door. "Get dressed. We're leaving in twenty minutes."

Beau wanted to hit something. "You're serious?"

His father opened the door and glanced back. "You broke curfew. You didn't think I'd let you off for that, did you?"

He left the room, and Beau punched the air. "Dammit!"

Gage Devereaux pulled his black BMW up to the front gate of Benedict Brewery. Beau sat next to him, his gaze fixed on the ten-foot-high wire fence surrounding the facility. A private security guard, one of three on duty, waved from the guardhouse next to the gate. Beau glimpsed the multiple TV screens inside, where dozens of cameras monitored everyone coming and going from the site. His father had increased security when he moved all of his business operations to the brewery property.

"New guy?" Beau asked as his father drove through the gate.

"We rotate new guards through the facility every year, except for George Cason, the head of security."

The single black smokestack rose out of the red-bricked processing plant. "Seems excessive for a brewery."

"You know our family owns more than the brewery." Gage navigated a narrow road with landscaped gardens on either side. "We have other business interests to protect. In a few years, when you take over more of the day-to-day management, you will understand."

Beau had just returned from a short stint at Children's Hospital in New Orleans when Gage started working full time from the brewery. He believed the change would give him more time with his father. He'd been wrong.

While the car passed two big metal buildings used for equipment storage, Beau's hopes floundered behind his father's plans. His name predetermined his future.

Beau knew every building scattered across the fifty-acre facility. He'd worked in packaging, shipping, and on the loading docks with the fleet of green Benedict Beer delivery trucks. He'd hung over the giant copper vats where the fermentation process took place and assisted in the sleek glass and steel research and development building where his father's team of "beer fanatics" came up with new brews.

Gage waved to a delivery truck as it pulled onto the road. "We've started sending out Fall Fest Beer for the Oktoberfests happening around the area."

Beau tuned his father out as the sleek car eased into the reserved spot outside the gray clapboard, two-story office building.

"Come November, you'll be spending your after school hours in this building with me." Gage opened the door. "I've let you slide on your duties since football practice began, but once the season is over, you need to get serious about the business."

Beau bit his tongue as his father got out of the car. *This is such bullshit.*

To the side of the building was a straight wooden staircase that climbed to a dark glass door on the second floor—his father's private entrance to his office.

Beau followed Gage up the steps and, once inside, peered down a hallway decorated with framed posters of beer bottles. Strawberry Ale, Bogue Falaya Rock, Crescent Dark Ale, and the Devereaux Special Blend were just a few names Beau had memorized.

Gage unlocked his office door. Beau noted Connie's empty desk down the hall. Beau couldn't remember a day when Gage's longtime secretary hadn't been at her post.

"Where's Connie?" He stepped into his father's corner office.

"It's the weekend. She's off."

Lucky her.

"I want to talk to you about college." Gage took a seat behind his impressive mahogany desk. His office was a replica of his study at home. He even had the same rug on the floor.

Beau sank into a cold leather chair, eyeing the certificates of merit, awards, and commendations earned by the brewery over the years, desperately avoiding his father's eyes.

Gage folded his hands on the desk. "I know you're setting your sights on playing football at Tulane, but I think you need to reconsider."

Beau's irritation festered. "What? You don't believe I have the chops to make a college team?"

"I won't beat around the bush. No." He stared Beau directly in the eye. "You've got talent, like I did at your age, but it's not enough. You need to face that now and commit to your future."

Beau feared his father and the repercussions if he refused to accept his fate. "What if I don't want this future?"

Gage slapped the desk. "I could give a shit what you want."

Beau flinched and sank deeper into his chair.

"You're expected to take over the family business just like I did, and my father did, and his father before him. This is the price you pay for being a Devereaux."

"You can't make me. I'm gonna be eighteen soon. Then I can do whatever I want."

Gage drummed his fingers on the green blotter. He was quiet for what seemed like an eternity. Gage's silence was more insufferable than his lectures.

Beau looked out the window, avoiding his father's disturbing gaze.

Gage leaned back in his chair. "I'll make a deal with you. You can have one shot at football. I'm sure you'll fail, but if you prove me wrong, I'll allow you to play college ball."

Beau perked up, not sure if he believed him. "You're kidding?"

"If you blow this chance, you will devote yourself to your education and working summers here with me." Gage pointed a threatening finger at him. "And you will take your place as head of the company when I say. No more talk about what you want. Your ass is mine."

Beau's rebellious streak resurfaced. "I'll prove you wrong."

Gage gave his son a cursory once-over. "I've got a friend in the athletic department at Tulane. I'll ask him to send a scout to the next game."

Beau couldn't believe it. He jumped up, almost toppling his chair. "Are you serious?"

Gage showed no emotion, not even a raised eyebrow. "They will determine if you're good enough to play. If they pass on you, you will give up this dream of playing football. Either way, you can get your business degree from Tulane and maybe go on for your MBA."

Beau went around the desk and held out his hand to his father. "Yes, sir. You have a deal."

Gage Devereaux studied his son, doubt swimming in his eyes. But he didn't shake his hand. "I think you're in for a rude awakening, Beau. When it happens, you need to promise me something else. No more outbursts." His father stood, rising to his full height of six-foot-four, two inches above Beau. "You will control your anger, and if you can't, I will take action." He then shook Beau's hand.

Beau didn't give a damn what his father said. He was going to impress the scout from Tulane and make the team. Then the brewery could kiss his ass goodbye.

Nobody's gonna tell me what to do.

"Can you believe my old man has a scout coming to the game?" Too excited to sit still, Beau paced in front of his bedroom window.

"Fan-fucking-tastic news." Mitch's voice grew louder with every word.

"I talked to Josh. He's up for celebrating tonight at the river. You in?"

Beau called each one of his teammates to let them know about the scout, hoping to motivate them to be in top form. If they played well, he played well.

"You know me, I'm always game for a blowout at the river." Mitch lowered his voice. "Hey, you heard about Kelly?"

Beau's enthusiasm sputtered. "What about her?"

"Cops picked her up. Word is she got knocked around a bit at the river." Mitch hesitated. "My parents heard about it and asked me all kinds of crap."

Beau tapped his finger on the phone. "My dad asked me about it, too. We'll just have to be more selective about who we tell about our parties."

"Sounds like a plan." Mitch's deep laugh came through the phone speaker. "What time we headin' out?"

"After dinner. I'll pick you up."

"Sweet. I'll be here."

Beau hung up and continued to pace. Everything he wanted was within reach. He wondered who else he could brag to and thought of Dawn. He debated texting, but wanted to hear the reaction in her voice.

She answered on the first ring. "Hi, Beau."

"Baby, I have some news."

"What's going on?" Her voice ticked upward. "Is everything okay?"

"It's fantastic. I just found out Tulane is sending a scout to the game Friday night to see me play. Can you believe it?"

He waited for her to shatter his eardrum with a jubilant scream, but she didn't.

"That's great, Beau."

Her flat, emotionless tone disappointed him. "What? Why aren't you happy for me?" His mouth went dry with disbelief. "This is a big deal. It could mean I—"

"I'm happy for you," she cut in. Her apathy oozed from the speaker. "But I wanted you to go to LSU with me. We talked about this."

Beau almost pitched his phone across the room. Here he was with the opportunity of a lifetime, and all she could do was think of herself. His grip tightened on the phone as he tried to remain calm. "I know, but at Tulane, I've got a chance to make the team. I'll be a big fish in a small pond. Dad and I made a deal. I get to play football as long as I get my business degree."

"But I'll be at LSU. Doesn't that mean anything to you?"

Her whiny tone was like nails on a chalkboard. He let the seconds pass without giving her an answer. His fingers twitched to release his pent-up rage. "I thought you would understand."

"I do, and I'm thrilled you'll get to play. I just wish we could go to college together. That's all."

Dawn had always been someone he could count on to tell him what he needed to hear and never to question him. The shift indicated she'd outgrown her usefulness. It was time to go after the woman he really wanted.

"I gotta go." Beau hung up before Dawn could say goodbye.

Dropping the phone on his bed, he muttered, "Time to find me a new cheerleader."

Dawn sat on her bed staring at the black screen of her phone, debating if she should call Beau back. Maybe she should have been more enthusiastic about his news, but why did he have to go to Tulane?

Leslie walked into their bedroom at the lake house. "Who died?"

Dawn slapped her phone on the blue bedspread. "He hung up on me. He's cut me off before, but he's never hung up on me. I thought he was a gentleman."

"Who? The asshole? What did he do? Dent his BMW?"

Dawn listened to her sister's cocky attitude and shook her head. Why couldn't she be that way with Beau? Might be good for her to hang up on him once in a while. "He called to tell me a scout is coming to the game Friday night to check him out. A scout from Tulane."

Leslie sat on her bed, a crease across her forehead. "I thought you planned on going to LSU together."

Dawn got teary-eyed at the thought of them attending different colleges. She sniffled and wiped her nose with the back of her hand. "Beau thinks he has a better chance to play football at Tulane. I got the impression Gage wants him to go there, too."

Leslie tilted her head. "Sounds like Beau is putting everything else before you."

Dawn's heart sank. Leslie was right. She'd never wanted to see it before, but the truth stared her right in the face. Beau put football, his friends, and the river before her.

This can't be love.

"Is it too much to ask that he think a little more about me?" Her lower lip trembled. "Am I being selfish, Leelee?"

"No." Leslie put her arm around her shoulders, tucking Dawn's head into her neck. "He will always put himself before you."

Leslie's embrace eased her heartache but did little to silence her regret. Beau's mood swings, anger, disregard for others, and the way he hid it all behind a seductive smile left her raw and miserable. How much longer could she put up with him? Would a life without his constant rules and expectations be so bad?

"Come on." Leslie coaxed her from the bed. "Let's go tell Mom and Dad about Beau's news. I'm sure Mom will be elated."

Sparkling pinpoints of sunlight skimmed the surface of Lake Pontchartrain, and a mild breeze stroked the water's surface. Leslie studied her father as he stretched out on a wicker chaise lounge, reading messages on his phone. Shelley sat next to him, her nose in a book.

"Hey!" Leslie called, walking onto the deck, dragging her sister by the hand. "Dawn has good news."

John lowered his phone and raised his eyebrows. "What is it?"

Dawn cleared her throat. "Beau said a college scout from Tulane is coming to the game this Friday to see him play."

"It would seem Beau Devereaux is going to be a green wave and not a tiger." Leslie pumped her fist in the air. "I, for one, am very thankful."

Shelley put her book aside, her face impossible to read. "Dawn, as always, we'll be there watching you and Beau on Friday night." She glanced at John. "Won't we, dear?"

"Of course." John nodded. "Wouldn't miss it."

"It would be nice if you were there as well, Leslie." Shelley patted her husband's leg. "Don't you agree, John?"

Her poor father. How could he answer and keep all three women in his house happy?

"Yes, that would be nice." Dawn stepped in, saving him from a fate worse than hell. "But it probably won't happen."

Leslie folded her arms and smirked. "If Derek could sit with us, I would come."

Shelley's face turned a deep shade of crimson. It was John's turn to pat her knee. "Sounds like a fine idea to me, hon."

Slowly, the hard line across Shelley's lips smoothed. "If that's what it will take for Leslie to come and watch her sister cheer, then he's welcome."

John beamed. "We can make it a family event."

"Does that mean you'll come?" Dawn elbowed her sister.

Leslie grinned, glad to see her father happy. "I'll see what Derek says."

John stood. "Well, this will be a first. The entire Moore family at a St. Benedict football game." He dramatically placed a hand over his heart. "I might die of shock."

Shelley returned to her book. "That makes two of us."

Leslie chuckled. *That makes three of us.*

CHAPTER TWENTY-ONE

Beau's muscles throbbed with excitement for the coming evening as he gripped the steering wheel. With his friends by his side, a favorite song blasting from the speakers, and his dream about to come true, life had never felt so good.

People turned to stare as he drove down Main Street. Word must have gotten out about the scout. It was his time to shine. Not as the senator's grandson, or Gage Devereaux's boy, but as himself—a talented high school quarterback with a chance to go pro.

He pictured the sweet satisfaction he would get after the game when the scout praised his performance. The invitation to play ball at Tulane would shut down his old man.

"You let Freddie know we're comin'?" Mitch asked.

Beau held up his cell phone. "Just sent him a text, but he'll have it ready. Freddie never lets me down."

Josh pointed out the window as they drove past the bright neon sign outside The Bogue. "Hey, isn't that Bondage Bissell?"

Beau slowed down. Sara and a few girls in tight jeans were at the edge of the parking lot. Sara was in a short black skirt, showing off her trim legs.

"Let's see what's up." Beau turned into the lot.

Josh leaned forward from the back seat, wide-mouthed. "Dude, after the way you blew her off, she might scratch your eyes out."

Beau liked the sound of the challenge. "She'll forgive me. I'll even bet she comes to the river tonight."

Mitch held out his hand. "Fifty bucks she turns you down."

With the gods of fortune smiling on him, how could he lose? Beau shook his hand. "You got a bet."

Beau parked next to the SUV Sara perched against. He could see the hate roasting in her eyes, but that didn't bother Beau. He climbed out and went up to her, confident she would do what he asked.

She tossed her platinum hair over her shoulder and sneered. "Look who it is, Mr. Pencil Dick."

Mitch and Josh laughed.

Beau didn't find the comment funny. He longed to teach her a lesson, one she would remember. He gave her a cocky grin. "You're not still mad, are you?"

"Is threatening me your definition of foreplay? Boy, you've gotta lot to learn about women."

If he'd been any other guy at St. Benedict, her interest in bondage would have been intimidating. But Beau understood the game of pain, considered himself an ardent student, and was certain Sara had not practiced what she professed to know.

"Then teach me." His voice dipped into a smooth whisper. "Come to the river tonight."

Sara put her hand on her hip. "No thanks, asshole."

Mitch and Josh hung out the car window. Mitch taunted him with an arched eyebrow, as if insisting he concede.

Beau turned on the charm.

"We're celebrating tonight. A scout from Tulane is coming to watch me play Friday. I'm on my way to going pro."

"I'm not big on football." She took a step back, looking ready to walk away. "You can't bait me with your bullshit."

It was time to move in for the kill. He put his lips to her ear so no one else would hear. "Do you want to find out how far you can go before begging a guy to stop? I can make you a member of the pain is pleasure club."

When he backed away, Sara's mouth opened in an expression of stunned surprise. "How do you know about ...?"

Beau grinned. He'd been right about her—a wannabe who owned a pair of handcuffs but had never used them. "You're not the only one in school who wants to try kinky things. Maybe we could try them together."

Sara said nothing but lowered her eyes. Her relaxed posture told him she debated his proposition. The outward hostility slid from her face, softening her features.

"Dawn won't be at the river tonight, if you're wondering. We called it quits today. I never expected her to turn into such a bitch."

Sara tucked a ringlet of hair behind her ear. "I did."

The high he'd been riding gained momentum. "Say you'll come to the river."

Sara glanced at her friends, hiding her smile. "I'll think about it."

"We'll have fun," he whispered to her. "I promise."

When Beau climbed into the car, Mitch patted his shoulder. "I gotta hand it to you. You had her eatin' out of your hand."

Beau's engine roared to life. "You're about to owe me fifty bucks."

Once he arrived at the local grocery, Beau drove around to the loading dock. He got out and popped the trunk, expecting to see Freddie at any moment.

The minutes slipped by, and Freddie didn't show.

"Hey, man." Josh looked out the window. "Where is he?"

Beau grabbed his phone to text Freddie. The back door opened, and bright light illuminated Beau's car. Freddie hurried toward him. Instead of the usual box, he carried two bottles.

Beau glanced at the meager offering. "What the hell, dude?"

Freddie shoved the bottles at Beau. "The cops came by today, asking about underage kids drinking at the river. You guys left the bottles behind. They tracked them here." He glanced back at the open door. "My manager is all over the clerks about checking inventory and IDs on anyone buying alcohol."

Beau's soaring spirits suddenly took a nosedive. "I need more than this."

"I can't get any more. Take the bottles of vodka on me. When things calm down, we can go back to business as usual. All right?"

Beau carefully appraised the store clerk and weighed his options. "I'll let it slide. But next time, I need a heads-up to make other arrangements. If you can't fill my orders, another guy's waiting to take your place."

"No, Beau." Freddie wrung his hands, appearing desperate. "I can get what you want, but let the heat die down. I need that money."

Beau shut the trunk, intent on getting back at the store clerk. "It would be a real shame if you have to leave St. Benedict after your kid's born."

Freddie stared at him. "What are you talking about? This is my home."

Beau handed the bottles to Mitch, his zeal for the evening returning. "Yeah, but imagine how hard it will be to raise a kid here without a job and a misdemeanor offense for selling liquor to minors on your record." Beau drove his point home with a smile.

Freddie shook his head. "You wouldn't do that. You bought the liquor and would be in trouble, too."

Beau kept up his grin as he got in the car. "But I bought it from *you*, Freddie. That's something the parish DA will be real interested to hear if my next run isn't just what I ordered."

Beau rolled up his window as Freddie came up to the car.

"What's his problem?" Mitch asked.

"Freddie? He's just having a bad day."

Mitch held up the bottles. "How we gonna party with two lousy bottles of vodka?"

"That's all you're going to get." Beau eased out onto Main Street. "Freddie said the cops have been asking questions."

Josh leaned in. "So, what do we do?"

Beau came to a stop sign and looked both ways, his mind racing ahead. "Try to keep the parties to just people we know. No more out-of-town guests."

Mitch tucked the bottles under his front seat. "Good plan, but what do we do in the meantime for supplies?"

Beau was sick of Mitch's whining. "Get creative. Maybe it's time you start scoring the booze."

Mitch adjusted his seatbelt, lowering his gaze. "I ain't you, Beau."

With an insolent grin, Beau hit the gas. "You got that right."

CHAPTER TWENTY-TWO

T he gray light of dusk blanketed the town of St. Benedict. The curved wrought iron streetlights came on as Derek drove his mother's blue truck along Main Street to Mo's Diner. He rubbed his thumb along a torn spot on the leather-clad steering wheel, hunting for a way to say what was on his mind.

"You look worried." Carol, wearing her beige uniform, reached over and ruffled his wavy brown hair. "You thinking about school?"

"Actually, I'm worried about you." Derek exhaled, glad he'd finally found the nerve to say something.

"Me?" Carol chuckled. "I'm fine, sweetie. You've got nothing to worry about."

He examined the bags under her eyes and cheap uniform. There had to be more for her than a life of filling coffee cups and serving po-boys. "Mom, you work too hard. You put in too many hours."

She rested her head against the seat, giving him an indulgent smile. "We gotta eat, Derek. And the diner ain't so bad. I get to pick my shifts, and the tips are good at night, and we've got everything we need, right?" She patted his hand.

Derek's biggest fear was, once he left for college, she would work even more to avoid the empty house. "Maybe you should consider doing something else. A different job or take up a hobby. Do something for you."

"A hobby?" She ran her hand across her brow. "It's been a long while since I've done anything for me. You've been my sole concern for so long. I'm not sure where to begin."

"Mom, you need more than me. What did you like to do in high school? You never talk much about when you were growing up."

"Probably because growing up in St. Benedict was about the same then as it is now." She glanced out the passenger window. "Everyone went to the river, had parties, and hung out at The Bogue Falaya Café. Not a whole lot has changed."

Derek glanced at his mother. "And the Devereaux family? Are they any different?"

Carol kept her face turned away, but he detected a change in her mood.

"Their influence is the same."

"What about Gage Devereaux?" he asked. "What was he like as a teenager?"

Carol shrugged. "He was the quarterback of the football team, like his son, and very popular."

Derek noticed a slight tremor in her hands. "What happened between you and Gage?"

Carol sighed. "We were pretty serious, but his father never approved of me. I wasn't the right fit to be a senator's wife, or so Edward Devereux believed. Gage's mother, Amelia, was a snooty Uptowner from New Orleans. She came from a blue blood family, and she wanted Gage to marry into high society. They sent him off to college in Boston for a year. He said he wanted to marry me after he returned. So, I went to LSU and waited."

Her quivering voice tore at Derek's heart. It was the saddest sound he'd ever heard.

She cleared her throat. "When he came back, Gage refused to speak to me. I called and went to his house, but I never found out why he cut me off. I fell apart and quit LSU, then got my job at the diner. It used to be his favorite coffee spot. I hoped one day he would stop by, order a coffee, and explain what happened. He never did. A year later, I met your dad."

"But you never forgot about Gage." Derek placed his hand over hers.

"Some pain haunts you. It digs in deep and awakens at those moments when you think you're over it. Gage was like that for me for the longest time. Then I had you."

Derek spotted the white neon sign to *Mo's Diner*. His second home. The diner and the people working there had been the closest thing to a family he'd known. Despite his happy childhood, Derek yearned for something more.

He pulled the truck into a parking spot in front of the railcar-style diner. Through the windows, he could easily see every customer inside. They sat in blue booths or on stools at the glass-covered counter, drinking coffee, eating sandwiches, and enjoying Mo's famous strawberry cheesecake.

Derek pictured his mother and Gage Devereaux inside as happy teenagers. "Do you think he forgot about you?"

Carol wiped her eyes. "I honestly don't know, and at this point in my life, I don't care. The boy I loved in high school isn't the Gage Devereaux everyone sees now. He's different—darker, angrier, and more like his father, the senator." She positioned the rearview mirror so she could check her makeup. "When I heard he married Elizabeth, I figured he'd forgotten about me. We've both moved on."

She adjusted the clasp that held back her hair and ran a finger under her lower lip to wipe away a smear of lipstick. When she put the rearview mirror back in place, she smiled, the pain of the past erased. "You want to come in and get some cheesecake before you head home?"

"Naw, I've got homework to get to."

"Then go straight home. I don't want you going to the river. The cops have been circling the area since they pulled over that girl."

"What girl?"

Carol gathered her purse with an umbrella sticking through the top. "Sheriff Davis came in for coffee and told me his deputies stopped a Covington girl coming from a river party this weekend. She'd been roughed up but refused to say who did it. She wouldn't even allow them to take her to the hospital to get checked out."

"Leslie had a bad experience there with some football players. She doesn't like going there, and I'm not part of Beau's crowd, so I wouldn't be welcome."

Carol kissed his cheek before getting out of the truck. "Glad to hear it. Not being part of Beau Devereaux's crowd is a good thing. Pick me up at seven in the morning, and we'll have breakfast."

"Will do, Mom."

Carol walked toward the double glass door entrance to the diner, then turned to wave at him.

Derek was uncomfortable with the idea of his mother working another twelve-hour shift. But what could he do? After hearing her story about Gage Devereaux and why she'd taken the job at the diner to begin with, he understood how she'd gotten trapped there. But, after all these years, it was time to start a new life. He just wished he knew how to help her do that.

The sky grew dark, and he was about to leave when a girl in an oversized black sweater and gray sweatpants walked in front of his truck. Her brown ponytail was askew, and tufts of hair poked out at odd angles.

He sat back in his seat, riddled with astonishment. It was Taylor Haskins.

Her unkempt look didn't bother him as much as why she was at the diner alone. Mo's wasn't the preferred hangout. Everyone gathered at The Bogue. So why was she here?

He opened the door, grabbed his keys, and called after her. "Taylor?"

She stopped. Her back to him, he could almost sense her cringing. She slowly turned to face him, pulling her sweater closer. When their eyes met, Derek became concerned.

Her stony expression didn't belong to the vibrant girl he remembered passing in the school halls.

"You're Leslie Moore's boyfriend."

He moved closer. "Derek Foster."

She folded her arms and slouched her shoulders, appearing uneasy. "Ah, yeah." She eyed the diner. "What are you doing here?"

"My mom works here. I drop her off when she's on the night shift."

Taylor nodded. "That's sweet."

"Why are you here and not the river? I hear there's a party there tonight."

Taylor paled, turning a sickly shade of gray. "I don't like it there. Those parties are ... some crazy shit happens there."

Taylor seemed terrified of something. She took a step back, her fingers nervously twirling her ponytail.

Her behavior bothered him. She was nothing like the cheerleader he'd seen leading pep rallies in the school quad during lunch.

"Are you okay?" He put a hand on her arm, and she leaped back as if he had the plague.

"I'm sorry." Her eyes darted around the street. "It's getting late, and I gotta head home."

"Let me drive you." Derek motioned to his truck. "You shouldn't be out here alone at night."

Her gaze went from him to the blue truck, then back to him. The vein along the side of her neck pulsed. She hugged herself tighter and bit her trembling lower lip.

What happened to her?

"Take me straight home. Okay?"

Where else would he take her? "Sure." He went to the passenger door and opened it. "Get in and tell me where you live."

She stepped toward the truck like a wild animal sizing up a trap—cautious, yet hungry for the bait.

Once inside, she seemed to calm. After he shut the door, Derek went around to the other side and climbed in, his mind racing. He started the engine and waited as she fastened her seatbelt. It took her shaking fingers a while to get the belt locked in place.

"1125 Huntsman Road." She scooted closer to the passenger door.

He nodded and put the truck in reverse. "I know where that is. In the new subdivision near the Devereaux Plantation."

She grasped the edge of her seat with her left hand. "Yeah, I've gotta drive past their black gates every single day."

"You're not a Beau Devereaux fan, are you?"

Taylor turned to her window. "What makes you say that?"

He dug his thumb into the tear in the steering wheel, grasping for a way to get her to open up. "I get it if you don't like him. There's no love lost between Beau and me. I know everyone in this town thinks the sun shines out of his ass, but I know better. Leslie knows better, too."

Taylor settled back in her seat and relaxed her shoulders. "He thinks he's invincible."

"Invincible?" Derek chuckled as he remembered something he'd once read. "'The mighty have a longer way to fall than the helpless. That is why the impact of their demise resonates like a dying star throughout the heavens. But beware their wrath. Such a fate can fashion the monsters men come to fear.'"

The smile on her lips was slight, but he figured it was a start.

"Did you just make that up?"

Derek eyed the last of the buildings as Main Street ended. "It's from a book, *The Dust of Giants*. I forget the author."

At the line of wide oak trees, he turned left, wondering how to keep her talking.

She leaned a little closer. "What's the book about?"

"It's about the Titans—the giant gods who ruled before the Greek gods of Zeus and Hera. They thought they were invincible, but eventually their invincibility destroyed them and turned them into vengeful monsters."

"It sure does apply to the whole Devereaux family."

"Yep, that it does." Derek kept picking at the ripped leather. "Let's hope it's not too long before Beau Devereaux's invincibility eats him alive."

Taylor turned to him, her smile taking on a devilish curve. "Wouldn't it be wonderful? To have that smug son of a bitch suffer, just like those he's tortured. Makes you believe in karma, huh?"

The chilly tone in her voice gave Derek pause. "Why do you say he's tortured people? What do you know?"

"Nothing." Taylor looked away. "I just have a feeling."

The brisk air, the stars shining bright, and the pounding music—it was all for him. The river was Beau's playground, and soon he would leave it behind. For his teammates seated on the picnic benches along the Bogue Falaya shoreline, football at St. Benedict would be as good as it got for them. He would be famous, but these guys would spend their days looking back and not ahead.

Pretty young things crowded the tables—from short to tall, blonde to black-haired, mahogany to lily-white. He could have his pick, but he ached for someone with a little more adventure in their soul like Sara, but she never showed.

Beau started talking to a curvaceous sophomore, but her innocence, and the way she constantly batted her eyelashes, quickly bored him.

He wandered the beach, checking out the girls and aching to take another to his cell. He debated between a perky cheerleader who reminded him of Dawn and a serious-looking brunette with a perfectly round ass— until he spotted a new face. She had a maturity about her, whetting his appetite. She had to be in her twenties.

What's she doing here?

She came across as seductive and sensual, with dark hair and wide-set eyes. He admired how she swayed in time with the music, rocking her hips like a wave rolling over the ocean. Fluid, smooth, mesmerizing—the more he studied her, the more he wanted her.

He followed her around the beach until she ended up in the fading light of the furthermost bonfire.

"I haven't seen you 'round here before. How did you find the place?"

She spun around, and her full lips parted in a tempting smile. "I was at a campground down the river with some friends. I heard the music and came to check it out. But this isn't my scene." She turned to go.

"What's your scene?"

She halted and glanced at him over her shoulder. "Something less noisy."

Beau took a step toward her, his heart pounding. Her condescending tone aroused him. "What's your name?"

She looked him up and down. "Andrea. What's yours?"

"Beau Devereaux."

She didn't bat an eyelash. Either she didn't know who he was, or she didn't care. Nonetheless, she intrigued him. He debated how to get her to the cells. She could be just what he needed to cap off his night.

Andrea folded her arms. "What would a lady have to do to get a drink around here, Beau Devereaux?"

He closed the gap between them. "Well, that depends on the lady."

She got a little closer. "You're cute. How old are you?"

Tantalized by the ivory color of her skin, his gaze drifted down her skintight jeans. "Old enough to know how to please a woman."

Her eyebrows shot up. "I doubt that. Men have a hard enough time figuring out what women want. What makes you think you know, little boy?"

Now he was excited. The challenge in her voice, the way she teased, roused his hunger. "I've got more experience than most men, and I have very selective tastes."

She stood back, reappraising him. Beau sensed her interest as well as her reservations.

She chuckled. "You're cocky, aren't you?"

Beau moved close enough to kiss her. He wanted her to know he wasn't playing games. "For good reason."

Curiosity glistened in her eyes.

He had her.

She scanned the tree line surrounding the beach. "Is there a place we can go to get to know each other better?"

Beau turned to the far side of the beach, where a path led away from the sand. "You ever been inside The Abbey?"

She sank her hands into the back pockets of her jeans, jutting her breasts forward. "I've heard about the old abbey, but I've never seen it."

Beau held out his hand, his every nerve on fire. "Let me show you." He guided her through the crowd on the beach until they came to the path. The spires rose in the starry sky ahead of them.

"The Abbey dates back to the 1800s. The land was given to the Benedictine monks to build their seminary. There are rumors that the land is cursed, but no one believes it."

She nestled closer to him, curling into his arm. "Scary stuff."

He put his arm around her. "Don't worry. I'll protect you."

Andrea didn't resist as they made their way through the high grass toward the cells.

At the forgotten angel fountain, he turned to a thicket of brush. "What I want to show you is in here."

Sensing he was close to his release, to capturing the power inflicting pain gave him, made his fingers twitch.

She's gonna be so sweet.

When he parted the brush covering the crack in the wall, she hesitated.

"It's in there? You're sure about this?"

A twinge of apprehension. He liked that. It meant she was sober, somewhat cautious, and would put up a fight. "Yeah, it's okay. I come here all the time."

Andrea gave him a wary glance as she slipped through the crack.

He followed her in, and on the other side of the wall, took her hand. Beau guided her down the dark corridor to his cell. The air was heavy with moisture. The odor of mold hung around them. She didn't flinch as the pinpoint of light coming through the cracks landed on the skeleton of a rat. Brave, too. Even better.

Once in the cramped room, he lit the candles.

She waited at the doorway, enshrouded in a yellow halo. He admired the play of candlelight and took her hand. Her inviting smile enticed him. Unable to stop himself, he kissed her. A long, passionate kiss. She responded, and her fervor added to his excitement.

Beau scooped her up into his arms and carried her to the cot. He carefully set her on the blanket.

Andrea pressed her hand to his chest, pushing him back. "I'm not like other girls. I don't want you to be gentle and romantic. I'm not looking for anything like that tonight."

Shades of Taylor flashed in his head. "Tell me what you want."

Her fingernails scratched down his chest to the waistband of his jeans. "You ever hit a girl?"

A wary thread snaked through him. Either she was a twisted soul like him, or this was a setup. He didn't trust anyone. "What are you saying?"

Andrea deftly worked the button fly on his jeans. "Some girls like to be spanked. Some like to be tied up or handcuffed." She slipped her hand inside his briefs. "I like rough, hard sex, with all the hitting and biting."

A trickle of disappointment curbed his enthusiasm. The terror he instilled in Taylor and Kelly aroused him more than this half-assed BDSM shit.

She reclined on the cot, her plump lips parted, eager for him, and though he wanted to button up his pants and walk away, he also wanted to show her *his* idea of rough. Beau pushed her hands above her head. "I'm going to give you the night of your life." He ripped her shirt open.

Andrea released a wild cackle. "Don't hold back, Mr. Devereaux."

Beau combed his fingers through her long hair, gripped it in his fist, and then yanked her head back. "I aim to please." He bit into the soft flesh at the base of her neck.

"There you go." She held to him. "Show no mercy."

Swept up in the moment, Beau slapped her face as he stripped her naked. He bit her shoulders, breasts, and inner thighs, waiting for her to beg him to stop, but she didn't. Andrea took everything he gave her. The rougher he got, the more she seemed to enjoy it.

He bound her hands with her bra and secured them to the pipe in the wall. Her lower lip trickled blood, but she smiled through it.

He didn't care for this game. It wasn't fun. He missed the wide-eyed terror, the cries, the pleas, the whimpering. Her grin left him empty.

To offset the numbness her silence created, Beau took his violence to a whole new level. He put his hands around her throat right at that climactic moment. He hoped to frighten her, shape her face in the mask of horror he'd grown to love, but it did nothing. Her smile continued as he choked off her air.

When her eyes bulged and her lips turned a dusky blue, he let her go. Gasping and coughing, she never turned away.

"Don't stop. I deserve it."

Beau hadn't satiated his fury. Determined to have his release, Beau flipped her over, slapped her ass, and started all over again.

This time, he didn't let up on his chokehold. She bucked beneath him as her fair skin turned red and then pale. Andrea kicked violently and jerked, fighting for air. For a split second, he pictured Leslie, and only then did he get off, reaping his satisfaction from the panic in her face. When he let her go, she lay motionless until air entered her lungs in one loud, ragged gasp.

Beau rolled off her. When he freed her hands from the pipe, he noticed the red dots in the whites of her eyes. Proof he'd pushed her to the edge of death. What if he'd gone further? What kind of rush would he have had? The idea floated around his head.

She unwound the bra from her wrists. "Wow. That was insane."

Her hoarse but perky voice rattled him. He preferred a woman's whimpering to her praise.

"That was the biggest rush ever. I thought I was going to die."

That she wasn't frightened of teetering on the edge of death frustrated him. His only enjoyment during the evening ripped away, he got mad. She'd been the one in power all along.

"If you wanted it like that, you should have told me from the start." He sat up on the side of the cot.

She curled into his back. "Don't I get a round two?"

Beau stood and worked his jeans up over a rock-hard body. "We'll save round two for another time."

"I like your style, Mr. Devereaux."

"Don't call me that. Mr. Devereaux is my old man."

Andrea cocked an eyebrow but didn't comment.

Beau studied the cut on her lip, the red handprints on her throat, and the assorted bite marks on her creamy skin. There was something intensely erotic about surveying the damage he'd inflicted. She was like a work of art, and he yearned to paint another.

"When can I see you again?"

Andrea avoided his gaze as she quickly dressed. Then she pecked his cheek before heading to the doorway. "I'll be in touch." She disappeared into the darkened corridor.

Beau straightened up and blew out the candles, then made his way to the crack in the wall. He pushed the vines aside and stopped, reflecting on the bittersweet encounter. He wanted the rush of being with her again, but not the letdown. How much better would the experience have been with Leslie?

Tons better.

Images of Leslie's porcelain skin and blonde hair had meshed with Andrea's during the height of his arousal but dwindled afterward.

How much longer could he go on without Leslie?

Every night he spent with another woman prepared him for the day he would be with her. No matter the depth of pain or type of torment he inflicted, his greatest rush would come with Leslie. He rested his shoulder against the jagged line of broken stone and stared up at the angel on the fountain. The world was his, and with his life getting better every day, it was the perfect time to bring Leslie into it.

An eerie scraping floated down the corridor. His muscles tensed. He turned, peering into the darkness. No one should be there.

Determined to defend his territory, Beau returned to his cell and grabbed the flashlight under his cot. He swept the beam from side to side in the corridor, lighting the narrow passageway. He checked the other rooms and kicked some debris, but discovered no one. Probably a rat or a raccoon.

Time to get back to the party.

Beau left the flashlight in his cell and made sure everything was in place before he slipped into the night.

CHAPTER TWENTY-THREE

Under a cloudless sky, Beau strutted across the St. Benedict High parking lot, ready to begin the week he was sure would change his life. Students sat on car hoods, stood in small groups, or stretched out on the quad, whispering amongst themselves.

They've heard about my scout.

He waited for well-wishers to praise his good fortune, but no one seemed to notice him. Perplexed by the snub, he listened in as two girls with their heads together walked by.

"They said she was beaten pretty bad," one girl muttered.

"I heard she was high on a new drug mixed in someone's bathtub," her friend added.

Guys from his Spanish class sat on the hood of a truck, deep in conversation. He stopped next to them, pretending to adjust his book bag.

"She was from Covington High," a guy said.

"Why was a babe from Covington High at the river?" another student asked.

Kelly.

Everyone should have been talking about him. Then, a surge of pride replaced his consternation. Without him, no one would have anything to talk about. He enjoyed the snippets he picked up here and there. Kelly hadn't told anyone about their little encounter. She had done as she was told.

Leslie's car pulled in the lot. With Dawn back, his future set, and his secret safe, Beau was certain the day would be a good one.

Before the engine had shut off, Beau opened Dawn's door. The girl staring back at him was not the exuberant one he'd dated for the past several months. Her tense features reminded him of the snarling dragon on her cheerleading uniform.

"Hi, Beau."

Her flat tone upended him.

"What's wrong?" He took her hand. "Didn't you miss me? I missed you."

Dawn pecked his cheek, appearing unenthused. "Yeah, I missed you. We just got in late last night."

He didn't believe her. She was different.

Beau gazed across the car at Leslie, wishing he could smell her sweet skin. "Did you have a nice time at the lake, Leslie?"

Her smirk reeked of insolence. God, how he wanted to break her right there.

"Why? Disappointed I didn't drown?"

"Nah. I wasn't there to watch."

"Enough, both of you." Dawn took his hand and pulled him away. "Why do you tease her like that?"

Beau removed her bag from her shoulder, displeased with her line of questioning. It was what he expected from Leslie, not Dawn. "You used to love it when I teased her."

Dawn brushed the hair from her face. "It was cute in the beginning, but it got old."

"I don't understand. You hate your sister."

"I never hated her. We just never talked. But this weekend, we had a good time. I don't want to go back to how things were."

Damn! He needed that wedge between them to keep a handle on Dawn. This sisterly love crap wasn't part of the plan.

"Do you want me to kiss her ass? Is that what you're saying?"

She shook her head. "I want you to be nice to her and Derek. Can you do that for me?"

Beau never said a word. He didn't argue when he got angry—he got even. When he glanced back at the car, Leslie stared at him with a menacing scowl. "If that's what you want, baby, I'll be as nice as pie to your sister."

"Great." Dawn's bubbly demeanor returned as she walked ahead, a bounce in her step. "I told her you would be reasonable. She didn't believe me."

"Your sister just doesn't know the real me." Beau pictured his hands around Leslie's neck. "I'll have to show her who I really am."

Banging lockers and loud voices filled the halls as Beau made his way to the cafeteria. He scoured the students rushing by, carrying lunch bags. None of them were Dawn.

They'd agreed to meet for lunch, and she was never late. Annoyed, he stuck his hands in the pockets of his khakis. With nothing to do, his mind drifted back to Andrea. Beau relived their night, especially when he'd brought her to the brink of death. Images of strangling her excited him more than roughing her up.

"How's it hangin', Beau."

Sara Bissell stood in front of him, wearing a fitted black dress that accentuated her boobs and a silver chain of handcuffs nestled in her cleavage. He wanted to pull the chain tight around her throat and see what she looked like when the life left her eyes.

Beau leaned against the wall and checked out her long legs. "I missed you Saturday night."

"Yeah, I can guess just how much you missed me. Fifty dollars' worth?"

"What are you talking about?"

Sara sneered. "Don't play games with me. Mitch is bragging about your bet all over school."

Her raised voice attracted curious glances from the students heading into the cafeteria. The last thing he needed was Sara's tantrum to get back to Dawn.

Beau stood straight and pivoted to put Sara between him and the wall. "Yeah, I bet Mitch I could get you to the river, but you never showed. I'm glad you didn't come." He lifted her necklace and let it fall against her skin. "You know nothing about bondage. It's all an act. I've tasted the real thing. Would you like me to tell everyone in school what a fake you are?"

"You're an asshole."

Beau towered over Sara, aching to hurt her. "Maybe. But to everyone else, I'm St. Benedict's golden boy. If you jeopardize that, I'll tie you to a bed and beat you within an inch of your life."

Sara tweaked his nose. "Keep talking, big boy."

A torrent of disgust rode through Beau, obliterating whatever attraction he'd felt. "You're a crazy bitch."

She licked her lips. "Takes one to know one. I can see what you've been hiding behind that little Mr. Perfect image. You like the rough game, and if you ask me, you've played it before with someone. Could it be that poor girl from Covington High they found on the road?"

Beau searched her face for any hint of what she knew. He suspected it was nothing, but her accusation flustered him. "Don't start shit you can't finish. I'll make you regret it."

Sara's head turned. "We have company."

Dawn stood a few feet away, gripping her lunch bag. She frowned and then marched through the cafeteria archway, almost running him over.

Sara snickered, sounding like a snake flicking its tongue.

Beau's apprehension grew. He didn't need Dawn going off. When anyone got dumped, it was going to be her—and on his timeline. "This isn't over," Beau muttered to Sara before racing after Dawn.

"Where have you been?" He caught up to her, slipping his arm around her shoulders. "I've been looking everywhere for you."

Dawn wiggled out from under him and kept walking. "Well, you weren't going to find me while you were talking to Sara."

"What? That was a little recon for Mitch. He's got the hots for her." Beau gripped her elbow, urging her to stop. "Baby, talk to me."

With a loud snort, Dawn turned to him. "Beau Devereaux, you expect me to buy that? Everyone says I'm a fool for trusting you."

The comment stirred his desire to throttle a certain someone. "By everyone, do you mean your wonderful sister?"

"Actually, my sister is pretty damn wonderful." Dawn pried his hand off her elbow. "She hasn't lied to me, cheated on me, or made me feel stupid, like some people."

A vein pulsed in Beau's neck. "Let's talk after school. We have some things to get straight about our relationship."

"You hate having conversations about our relationship." Dawn put her hand on her hip and scowled. "Whenever I wanna talk, you say, 'Don't worry about us, we're fine.'"

She tried to imitate his deep voice, which irritated Beau even more. "Well, now I'm ready to talk."

"I can't." Her sassy attitude evaporated. "I've got cheerleading practice, and my mother expects me home for dinner. Shouldn't you be focused on the scout coming Friday?"

The reminder quickened his pulse. He couldn't wait to put high school and girls like Dawn behind him. "I'm not worried about the scout. I'm worried about us. You're everything to me, baby."

She didn't melt, or smile, or even flutter her lashes like before.

"I have to go." Dawn backed away. "I've decided to eat lunch with my sister today."

He didn't want to hear that. "You tell Leslie to stop talkin' shit about me." He tried to temper his coarse tone with a pleasant smile. "She doesn't know me like you do."

"She isn't putting anything in my head. You're the one making me second guess us, not her."

Dawn stomped away, leaving Beau dumbfounded. What happened to the girl he had under his thumb? His grip on Dawn wasn't what it used to be, and it was all Leslie's fault.

Why were all his problems boiling down to one rebel with the same face as Dawn?

Dawn gripped her brown paper bag, a jumbled mess after the encounter with Beau. She crossed the quad, heading to the picnic benches set beneath old oaks trees. A wash of jealousy, betrayal, and sadness coursed through her. What had happened to them? He used to make her heart swell.

She spotted Derek and Leslie on a bench, cuddled together, smiling and laughing. Derek caressed her sister's cheek, touched her hand, and gazed into her eyes. It was genuine—honest to goodness love, and nothing like she had with Beau. Dawn almost felt like an intruder, but she needed the company and her sister's ear.

"Can I join you guys?"

Derek motioned for her to join them. "Absolutely."

Dawn angrily tossed her bag on the table.

Leslie's brow furrowed. "You okay?"

She plopped down on the bench. "Not really. Do you guys ever argue?"

Leslie opened a bottle of water. "Sometimes. No relationship is perfect."

"But when you make up, is the argument over, or does it keep coming back?" Dawn removed a container of celery and carrot sticks from her bag.

Derek rested his arms on the table, frowning. "I don't understand."

"Me and Beau keep fighting about the same things. It's always his problems with me, never my problems with him."

Leslie unwrapped her turkey sandwich. "Then walk away. If the other person in a relationship isn't listening to you, they don't care about your feelings. That's my advice."

Derek bumped Leslie's shoulder. "I listen to you as well as take your advice."

Leslie chuckled. "*Sometimes,* you take my advice."

Derek opened a bag of potato chips. "Well, sometimes you don't give the best advice."

Leslie stole a chip from Derek's bag and threw it at him. "I'll get you later, Foster."

He snapped up the chip and stuffed it in his mouth. "I'm counting on it."

If Dawn had told Beau he gave bad advice, he would've blown a gasket. Then again, he expected her to take his advice and never question it. What to wear, what to say, how much to drink, and how he didn't like her makeup. He even commented when she gained a few pounds, making her terrified to put on weight.

Celery and carrots were what Beau wanted her to eat, not what she wanted. She pushed the container away, her appetite waning.

"Guess what?" Leslie tapped the table to get her attention. "Derek's going to the game with me so we can watch you cheer."

Her sister's excitement softened her heartache. She'd missed Leslie. How had she let Beau come between them?

"Hey, did you hear about that girl at the river?" Derek asked.

Dawn perked up, always interested in gossip. "What girl?"

"Kelly, from Covington High." Derek leaned into the table. "When I gave my mom a ride to Mo's for her night shift, she said Sheriff Davis had been by. Evidently, his deputies pulled over a girl coming from the river.

He said she was pretty roughed up."

Dawn shivered. *What the hell?* "That can't be true. I'm at the river all the time. I've never seen anything bad happen to anyone."

Derek sipped his water. "Taylor Haskins said a lot of crazy stuff goes on at the river. She swore she was never going back."

"Taylor said that?" Dawn couldn't understand. Taylor was her friend—or had been. Since she'd quit the squad, Dawn had seen little of her. "She never mentioned anything to me." Dawn sat back, stunned. Was she that blind? "Why have I never heard this before?"

"Maybe Beau didn't want you to know," Leslie said.

A cloud passed overhead, and Dawn stood, fighting a bout of panic. "I gotta go." She grabbed her lunch bag and left the table.

Every movement became labored, every breath an effort. Dawn swore all eyes were on her as she crossed the quad.

Something else he's lied to me about.

CHAPTER TWENTY-FOUR

With the confining walls of St. Benedict High behind her, Leslie relaxed in her car, breathing in the humid honeysuckle-tinged air coming in the window. She couldn't wait until high school was a distant memory. The only bright spot in her life—the wonderful guy in the seat next to her.

He'd been quiet during the ride, only speaking when she asked about classes or homework.

"What is it?" she asked after a long silence. "You haven't said much."

Derek kept his eyes on the road. "I've been trying to come up with ways to get my mother out of the diner. She works too hard. I'd like to see her in a better job before I go to college. But I just don't know how to help her."

"I could talk to my dad. He might know someone who could help." Leslie turned toward Derek's house.

The crease in his brow eased. "You would do that for me?"

The question knocked her for a loop. Of course, she would. Didn't he know how much she cared?

"Why wouldn't I? Your mother is my family, too. I want to help her any way I can." She pulled to the curb in front of his driveway and parked.

Derek cupped her face. "You're amazing. I love you."

All her worries melted away when he spoke those words. She could conquer the world with him by her side.

"I love you, too. I couldn't picture my life without you."

He touched his forehead to hers. "Every day it gets harder and harder to wait for you. I want you so much."

She took his hands and squeezed them. She longed to share every part of herself, but Leslie didn't want their love consummated in the back seat of her car or on his mother's living room sofa. "I want you, too, but we agreed to wait. Until then, we have high school to keep us busy."

His rumbling chuckle sent a shiver through her as his lips brushed her forehead. "Yes, the trials of sex-obsessed, electronically preoccupied, confused, and sometimes confounding temperamental teenagers will no doubt keep us occupied until June."

She loved how his mind worked. "After that, we'll have college."

"You're going to kill me." He pulled away. "Thanks for helping me with my mom."

"Let's hope my dad can figure something out."

Leslie drove away, and as his house grew smaller in her rearview mirror, she fought the urge to turn around. With every passing day, her determination to wait until marriage weakened. She was in love, in a committed relationship, and trusted him more than anyone. Maybe it was time to find a private place for their special night together. But where would they go? There weren't a lot of choices for two broke teenagers in St. Benedict other than the river.

And I'd rather die a virgin than go there.

With jittery excitement, Leslie shut the door to her father's study. She traced the swirls of grain on the darkly stained wood, going over their conversation about Derek's mom. Her father had encouraged her to help others, and even though she didn't see much hope for Carol Foster's job hunt—especially in the small town of St. Benedict—her father's enthusiasm to join in the search encouraged her.

With a spring in her step, she couldn't wait to get upstairs and text Derek. To offer him some hope and lighten his worries made her happy.

Leslie reached the second-floor landing and noticed Dawn's door ajar. Pitiful sobbing came from within. The sound made all her good vibes vanish.

Leslie tapped on the door. "Dawn? Are you okay? It's me." She peeked inside and saw Dawn in a heap on her bed.

Her sister looked up, and Leslie was struck by the sadness in her eyes. Dawn sniffled. "You must think I'm an idiot."

Leslie walked toward the bed. "You're not an idiot. He's the bad guy here."

Dawn wiped her nose on her shirtsleeve. "You knew what he was and tried to warn me, but I wouldn't listen." She scooted back on her princess bed and hugged her knees. "I should have seen Beau like you did." She snapped up a tissue from the box sitting on her pink comforter. "Some twin I am."

"What are you going to do?"

"I don't know." She blew her nose. "Part of me wants to break it off, but another part doesn't want to be without a boyfriend. Especially with the big Halloween bash at the river coming up. Sounds stupid, huh?"

Leslie sat next to her, determined to make Dawn smile. "It's not stupid. If you want to go to the party so much, go with me and Derek. You don't need Beau."

Leslie shuddered at the thought of The Abbey, but Dawn's happiness was more important than her apprehension. She needed to go to this one river party for Dawn's sake. Maybe it would be a good thing. If Dawn could envision life without Beau, then perhaps she could put him behind her.

Dawn crumpled the tissue. "But you hate the river."

Leslie felt closer to her twin than she had in almost a year. "I can tolerate it for one night. With Derek there, it will be different than before. Who knows, it might even be fun."

Dawn wrinkled her nose. "Beau is gonna kill me if he sees me there and I'm not with him."

Leslie bumped her shoulder. "He'll have to go through me first. And I'm not going to let him touch you. Remember what we always said as kids—together, we're stronger than apart."

Dawn wrapped her arms around Leslie, and all the fighting and snapping over the past few months melted away. "What would I do without you?"

Leslie held her close. "You'll never have to find out. We'll be together forever."

CHAPTER TWENTY-FIVE

Beau counted the seconds until the blare of the last bell rang and hauled ass out of English lit. He fist-bumped guys wearing red dragon jerseys in the hall and shared an enthusiastic *whoop*. The biggest game of his life was hours away.

The only downer was Dawn's continued brush-off. He didn't want to let her go just yet. The squeaky-clean daughter of John Moore helped him sustain his good-boy image. Corrupting her had been a satisfying *fuck you* to his parents, who had deemed her worthy to date. But the week without her at his side had sent the gossip fanatics into overtime. He had to win her back, if only to dump her in a very public fight so he could walk away clean.

Mitch and Josh waited for him by his locker, greeting him with high fives. "Are you guys ready for the big game against Covington?"

"I'm more than ready." Josh shifted his gaze to Mitch. "You call Lana to meet up after the game?"

Mitch nodded. "Yeah, she's comin' with Beverly. They're gonna join us at the river."

"Who's Lana?" Beau asked.

"Lana, the girl from Covington." Josh punched his arm. "You gave her and Beverly a ride home, remember?"

He waved off the conversation. "Who cares? We got a big game ahead of us. Focus!"

"Beau?" Mrs. Evers, the stout, middle-aged head of the English department approached his locker.

Beau turned to her, putting on his standard teacher smile—the one he used whenever he spoke to faculty. "Yes, Mrs. Evers. How can I help you?"

"I wanted to thank you for all the extra time you put in on the school paper last week. We just finalized the issue, and it's wonderful."

Damn right it is. Busted my ass on it.

"I'm glad you're pleased. I wanted to do my best."

"Keep up the good work." She winked. "And good luck tonight. The faculty is rooting for you to make a great show for the scout."

He tilted his head in an *aww shucks* pose. "That means so much, Mrs. Evers. Thank you, and thank the other faculty members as well. Go, Dragons."

The most boring teacher he ever had pumped her fist in the air, looking comical.

"Go, Dragons!"

After she walked away, Mitch chuckled. "Dude, you've got 'em snowed."

"You keep asking how I win people over." Beau shoved a book in his locker. "That's how. I kiss ass around here and do a ton of work I don't need to do, but it pays off. Mrs. Evers is tight with my dad. I keep her happy, he stays off my back."

Josh rubbed his chin. "And here I thought it was just your personality. Dayum."

Mitch leaned against a locker. "What's goin' on with you and Dawn? Haven't seen you two hangin' all week. Word is she's blowin' you off."

Beau stiffened. "That's bullshit. We're still together. Since when has anyone around here ever gotten anything right? They don't know me or my life."

This was all he needed. He had more important things on his mind, but he also didn't want people thinking Dawn had ended it. He would have to fix that ASAP.

Beau slammed his locker door. "Guys, I gotta keep my mind on football, not girls."

Mitch slapped his back. "Dude, chill."

What he craved was a sweet rush of power. Every day, his need to inflict pain competed with his ability to keep up his well-practiced mask. He'd never known such desire for anything in his life, even football. How could something be so addicting and so devastating at the same time? He was like a heroin junkie struggling to show the world how normal he was.

"I have to focus." He touched his head to the cool metal locker, hoping for some relief.

Mitch yanked him away and ushered him down the hall. "What you need is to do some serious damage to someone, and there's only one place to do it—on the football field."

The corners of Beau's mouth lifted into an evil grin.

If only they knew.

Slumped against the hood of her car, Dawn surveyed the students walking on the grassy quad and passing her in the parking lot. She wanted to crawl into a hole and die.

This sucks.

Funny looks, curious glances, and whispers had followed her all week. She knew what they were gossiping about. Since the day she'd caught Beau talking to Sara at the cafeteria entrance, she'd avoided him. She even skipped cheerleading practice so she didn't have to see him. Staying away from him was popularity suicide, but she didn't care about what people thought anymore.

Gawd! When did I turn into Leslie?

A shadow stretched across the blacktop and stopped in front of her. She glanced up and discovered her sister standing a few feet away, her book bag slung over her shoulder.

Dawn peeked behind Leslie. "Where's Derek?"

Leslie retrieved her keys from her bag. "He drove his mom's truck today. I thought you were staying for cheerleading practice before the game?"

"Nope." Dawn cringed at the mention of the game. "I told the squad to be back before it starts. We don't need any more practice."

Leslie went up to her, a skeptical sparkle in her eyes. "Where did that come from? You're always so anal about your squad being perfect."

"Lately, I don't feel much like cheerleading. I wish I didn't have to do it tonight."

Leslie folded her arms and glared, making Dawn uncomfortable.

"You've been out of sorts all week, and I'm not the only one who's noticed. Everyone is talking about you and Beau breaking up. On top of that, you aren't wearing your cheerleading uniform on a game day—you used to love wearing it. I'm worried about you."

Dawn scanned the students around her, who were laughing and enjoying the late afternoon sun. She wished she were one of them.

"I don't want to be around people and listen to all their questions about me and Beau. I don't have the answers. All I know is I don't want to talk to him. I can't trust him anymore."

Leslie tapped the key fob and opened the car doors. "Not wanting to speak to Beau, I understand, but your friends and cheerleading? You love cheerleading."

Dawn hugged her book bag like a shield of armor. "I loved the attention. Particularly Beau's attention. That's why I joined the squad. I was so desperate for him to notice me, I slept with him that first night at the river. I always wanted Beau, and I thought life would be perfect with him. But it wasn't."

Confessing didn't make Dawn feel any better. Wasn't it supposed to be good for the soul or something? What a crock.

Dawn yanked open the passenger door, angry at how stupid she'd been. "I just realized the whole time I was with Beau, I was the same desperate girl on the inside. I'm not strong like you, Leelee." Her lower lip trembled, but she tried to hide her pain by stuffing her books into the back seat. "People around here think Beau is some kinda golden boy, but I'm seeing who he really is. When I look at you and Derek, I realize how meaningless my relationship was."

Leslie walked around to her side of the car. "It's all a part of growing up. Happens to all of us. Maybe take some time before you get involved with someone new. And keep cheering. You're good at it."

The riptide of all her past choices threatened to pull Dawn under. "I just don't want to be here anymore. But I'm also scared to death not to be. I don't even wanna think about graduation."

Leslie rested her arm on the open passenger door. "I've been thinking about college. If we both go to LSU, we could room together. Might help us adjust to all the changes coming our way if we have each other."

Leslie was right. The future wouldn't be so scary if they faced it together. Six months ago, she would've never dreamed of rooming with her sister at LSU. Now she wanted nothing more.

"You're on." Dawn swiped the keys from Leslie. "I'll drive."

"You hate to drive."

"No, I just let you drive because you think you're better." She went to the driver's side door, her mood brightening. "I need to start doing things for myself."

Leslie settled into the front passenger seat. "Just don't get us killed."

Dawn started the engine and adjusted the rearview mirror. She noticed someone in a red football jersey with a dragon logo rushing to the car. "Oh, *no*."

Beau stood with his hands on the trunk so she couldn't back up. "We need to talk, Dawn."

She didn't want to talk. If she listened to him, she might get sucked back into his lies. Beau Devereaux was a drug, one she had to avoid at all costs.

While the car was still in park, Dawn revved the engine.

Leslie grabbed her seatbelt. "You can't run him over."

Dawn nodded to the rearview mirror, a wave of satisfaction egging her on. "No, but I can scare him a little."

Beau headed for the driver's side, his neck muscles tensed.

Leslie quickly locked the doors. "Just go."

Dawn put the car in reverse and backed up. The mirror narrowly missed hitting Beau. He slammed his hand on the hood as she took off. She hit the gas, a sense of freedom coming alive as a red-faced Beau remained behind.

Leslie opened her window and shouted, "Better luck at the game, asshole!"

His figure grew smaller in the rearview mirror, but the predatory expression on his face was unmistakable. A shiver ran through Dawn. She'd pushed Beau too far. Dawn knew his well-hidden bad side, and she feared what he would do. Beau looked like a guy about to lose control.

CHAPTER TWENTY-SIX

The St. Benedict football field was lit in preparation for the night game. A good crowd had already formed in the stands thirty minutes before kickoff. Beau wanted to see if the scout had arrived, but Coach Brewer was a stickler about getting to the locker room on time before a game. He hurried across the grass to the gym, his heart pumping in time with a rock song blasting from nearby speakers. He noticed someone staring at him from the edge of the field.

Taylor.

Her baggy clothes seemed to hang off her. She'd lost weight. He could tell by her protruding cheekbones. The hate burning in her eyes was still there. It was the only attractive quality she had left.

"Well, don't you look like shit," he shouted.

She never said a word but continued glaring.

If she can't handle the rough stuff, she shouldn't have asked for it.

"Where's your cheerleading outfit?" He chuckled.

He was almost to the gym doors when she called, "Ready for the night of your life, Beau?"

He stopped and glanced around to see if anyone had heard her. He walked up to her. "What's your problem?"

Taylor backed away, stepping into the shadows of the stands, her face lost in the darkness.

He licked his lips, longing for another night with her. "Keep your mouth shut." He turned back to the gym doors.

"Do you feel like a man, Mr. Hotshot Quarterback?"

She'd stepped into the light, hugging one of the metal supports below the bleachers.

She was nothing like the brazen whore he'd taken to the cells. "You're one psycho bitch, Taylor."

She inched closer, giving him a deadpan stare. "Did you enjoy yourself in the cells the other night? You might want to be careful next time. You never know who's watching."

Before he could ask what she meant, she broke into a run, heading toward Dawn and the rest of the cheerleading squad gathered in front of the stands.

He thought he heard someone that night with Andrea. She must have been spying on him. Had she seen them? Andrea had wanted it, so he could never be accused of anything.

But what if she'd seen him with Kelly?

He ran his hand through his hair. Beads of sweat gathered on his upper lip. He didn't need this right now. Not with the scout coming. He talked himself down, picturing how he would strangle the crap out of Taylor once he got her alone. After he'd secured Tulane, he would beat what she knew out of her.

His fingers going numb as he gripped his duffel bag, he hurried to the gym entrance.

Before he stepped inside, a shadow crossed before the door. He turned, expecting another member of the team, and sharply inhaled when he saw Kelly Norton.

In a granny dress buttoned up to her throat, she was no longer the seductive girl at the river. Her red hair smoothed back in a simple clasp, she wore no makeup and appeared deathly pale.

"What are you doing here?"

"I came to cheer on my team. Heard you got a scout comin' to the game." Her stormy gaze ripped into him. "Gonna be the night of your life, eh, Beau?"

His pulse raced. She was in league with Taylor. The two bitches had talked.

Shit!

A trickle of sweat rolled down his back.

She stuck out her bottom lip. "What's wrong, Devereaux?"

He got in her face. "Don't fuck with me." He was anxious to see the fear in her eyes, but there wasn't any. Instead, she twisted her mouth into a wry grin and walked away. Beau staggered into the locker room, almost hyperventilating. He gripped the wall inside the door, struggling to calm down.

They were out to ruin his big night. He imagined their blood dripping off his hands. He would show them.

Beau squared his shoulders and went to his locker, greeting a few members of the team with high fives. He dropped his duffel bag on the bench, but his hand trembled when he reached for the zipper.

Pull it together. Self-control in all things.

Cleats tapped the floor, and excited chatter floated in the stale air of the locker room. The clatter of safety equipment and the occasional bang of a locker all came together to unravel Beau's nerves.

He couldn't concentrate. His shoulder pads weighed a ton, his jersey itched, even the laces in his shoes were too tight. He was off, and he knew why.

"Are you ready to roll over Covington High?" Coach Brewer shouted.

Beau ignored the thunderous war cry rolling through the locker room. Taylor and Kelly consumed his thoughts. Had they talked to anyone else? Dawn? Leslie?

I'm gonna kill them if they opened their mouths.

Maybe they wanted money. To blackmail him, or worse, blackmail his old man.

"Hey?" Mitch waved his hand in front of Beau's face. "This is the day you've been waitin' for, so snap out of it. Are you with me?"

Beau slapped Mitch's helmet. "Hell, yeah."

Coach Brewer walked past Beau and opened the doors to the field. "Let's go get 'em, boys!"

A sea of red jerseys rushed past. The coil of knots in Beau's stomach stayed with him while he dashed out into the night air. He took deep breaths to steady himself. It didn't work.

The lights on the field blinded him. Every game was the same, the glaring lights and the aroma of grass.

The last thing to register was the crowd. Their roar was almost like a jet engine. He couldn't distinguish specific voices in the rush of sound, but they were all calling his name.

Coach Brewer pulled Beau to the rear of the pack, kicking up some of the chalk marking the outline of the field. "Don't be a hero, Beau. Don't do anything you think will impress that scout. Just stick to the plan and play like this is any other game." Coach Brewer slapped his shoulder pad. "These guys don't want show-offs, they want players."

Beau jogged in place. "Yes, sir. I got it." He checked the sky, wishing away any rain, and then ran out onto the field, his legs two heavy anvils, sluggish and slow. With a strange ringing in his ears, his heart thudded. He tried to push everything else from his mind, forcing images of touchdowns, perfect spiral throws, and the cheers of his teammates into his head.

He glanced at the home team's bleachers. Taylor and Kelly stood with their heads together near Dawn's line of cheerleaders. Too close for comfort.

They won't run their mouths. They have too much to lose.

A whistle screeched. St. Benedict won the coin toss and opted to receive the ball. After the kickoff, Beau fought to focus, but couldn't shake the images of Taylor and Kelly.

Set up on the twenty-two-yard line, Beau counted off the snap. He pulled back, saw Mitch down the field, and threw the ball. The perfect spiral sailed over Mitch's head, and the referee blew the whistle on an incomplete pass.

"What the hell, dude?" Mitch complained when they were back in the huddle.

Beau's indignation flared. How dare he question him?

"You need to show a little more hustle to get the ball," Beau griped.

On the second play, Beau called for the snap and pulled back from the line, his mind scattered. He made a sloppy handoff to his running back, David Acker, who fumbled the ball.

Beau cringed, knowing he'd screwed up. Luckily, David fell on the ball and recovered it.

Back in the scrimmage, he had to cover his mistake. No point in letting his guys know how frazzled he felt.

"Nice move, David." Beau punched the guy's shoulder pads, venting his frustration. "Get it together, will ya?"

"You get it together, Devereaux." David poked him hard in the chest. "You blew that."

White-hot anger sizzled through his limbs, clenching his muscles. He would show them who was the king on this field.

On the third play of the first drive, Beau shouted for the snap. He stepped out of the pocket and scanned his men scattered across the field. Mitch waved his arms, jumping in place to show he was open deep in the end zone. *Perfect!* His confidence surged. Beau cocked his arm back, lining up his throw, and then everything turned to shit.

A hard shove came from his left, and the ground rushed up to meet him. Beau slammed into the grass, grunting as the air left his lungs on impact. His vision blurred momentarily. He rolled over, got his bearings, then noticed a defensive lineman from the opposing team sharing high fives.

I've been sacked. Nobody does that to me.

Exploding with rage, he scrambled to his feet and went after the lineman who had missed the block—Brett Massey.

Beau grabbed Brett's facemask. "You blew my touchdown!"

Brett shoved him to the side. "Get off me, Devereaux."

The referees ran in and separated them. The punter for St. Benedict came on the field, sending Beau to the sidelines.

"Devereaux!" Coach Brewer shouted when he reached the bench. "What the hell is wrong with you?"

Beau removed his helmet, his cheeks burning. "Massey blew it and got me sacked."

Coach Brewer launched into one of his speeches about playing as a team, but Beau didn't pay attention. He searched the stands.

Where are you two? What are you planning?

Coach Brewer grabbed his chin and snapped his head around to face him. "Stop worrying about the scout and play ball. If you don't, you'll blow it. You understand?"

Beau wanted to laugh. He'd listened to all he could of Brewer's bullshit. He pushed the coach's hand away from his chin. "Careful. You don't want to make me angry."

The coach scrunched his weathered brow, seeming unsure of how to react. He pointed at the bench. "Sit down and get your shit together before you go back out."

Beau sat on the bench, intent on finding Kelly and Taylor. Dawn huddled with her squad on the sidelines, her trademark red ribbon securing her long ponytail. She avoided looking his way. Then, to the right of Dawn, he saw the object of his desire. Leslie, along with that idiot Foster, had come to his game. The negativity choking him since arriving at the field disintegrated. If she watched him play, his luck would turn around.

Right behind her, another face appeared, and his hope sank.

Taylor.

Her glower reignited his rage.

This game is becoming my worst nightmare.

Leslie rubbed her bare arms in the chilly night air, wishing she'd brought a jacket. With the home team's sluggish performance so far, the dull game hadn't captured her attention. Beau wasn't living up to his hype, which didn't surprise her.

Derek took her hand, sending a wave of heat to her fingers. She was glad he was there. It would have been agony without him.

"Beau sucks," he whispered in her ear.

She nodded. "He does, doesn't he?"

John leaned over to them. "He's usually better than this."

"He'll get better." Shelley clapped. "Come on, Beau!"

Derek nudged Leslie's shoulder. "Your mother even cheers for Beau when he's not on the field. No wonder she wants to feed me to the wild dogs at the river."

"She's coming 'round. She called you by name on the way here. That's a big step."

"I know how you feel, Derek." John lowered his voice. "Sometimes I think my wife's going to chop me up for dog food, too."

Leslie squeezed his hand. "See? You're not the only one."

Derek cleared his throat. "Mr. Moore, I want to thank you for helping my mom. She was so nervous about her job interview today, she couldn't stop shaking."

"Glad I could help." John patted his shoulder. "She would be a great fit at the law firm. I'm sure they'll love her."

"I know they will," Derek told him.

Her boyfriend's optimism lifted Leslie's heart. Knowing she had a part in making him happy meant the world to her.

"Interesting game, huh?"

Leslie looked around to the next row up from hers. "Taylor?"

Bundled in an oversized jacket, Taylor was barely recognizable. Her pale skin and blank stare disturbed Leslie. "You okay? Are you here with someone?"

Taylor hunched her shoulders. "I came with a friend from Covington High. She's sitting with her team."

Her soft voice sounded as fragile as she appeared. Something was off, but Leslie couldn't put her finger on it. "Who's your friend?"

"Her name is Kelly. We have a lot in common." Taylor grinned, showing the first spark of life. "You two have to meet."

CHAPTER TWENTY-SEVEN

Clouds gathered, and the breeze turned colder as the second quarter got underway. A restless rumble rose from the St. Benedict stands and drifted across the field to Beau. On the fifty-yard line he had the ball, getting ready to count off the snap. He yearned for some action to show his fans and the scout.

The ball snapped and he pulled out of the pocket, his feet dragging. He spotted an open man close to the end zone, and the sluggishness plaguing him lifted.

You got this!

He threw the perfect spiral pass. It hung in the air, coming right down on his player. But when his receiver stepped forward to catch the ball, Beau got slammed to the ground. He caught his breath and sat up. Beau strained to see down the field, trying to focus. A player from Covington High had the ball and sprinted to the visiting team's end zone.

What the fuck?

He couldn't believe it when the guy kept running without a single whistle blowing the play dead. Beau staggered to his feet, ready to rip into the ref calling the play.

He marched to the official closest to him. "That was a late hit."

The referee shook his head. "Not from what I saw, Beau."

Beau pushed the man. "What are you, blind?"

A whistle blew. Players gathered around Beau, blocking his access to the official.

"Dude, no," Mitch said, urging him away.

The head referee ran into the melee of players, shoving them out of the way. He held up his index finger to Beau. "You've got your first warning, Devereaux. One more stunt like that, and you're out."

The storm inside him raged. His reason, his desire, his hope for the future had gone up in smoke.

"What did I do?" His growl triggered a few shocked looks. "This is such—"

"Devereaux," Coach Brewer hollered from the sidelines. "Get over here."

Beau walked off the field, his cleats kicking up the grass. *What kind of fuckers are refereeing this game?*

"You'd better wise up, boy." The coach yanked off his helmet. "You push a ref like that again, and I'll bench you for the season."

Beau bit his tongue. "Yes, sir."

Coach Brewer poked him hard in the chest. "Park your ass on the bench and get your head in the game."

Every muscle in his body quivered. Every nerve was on fire. Beau wanted to hit someone, hurt someone. Everything melted into one blur of blind rage. Though wound tight and craving for release, he held it all in. He suppressed a scream, letting it burn in the back of his throat.

Beau took a seat on the bench, then scanned the bleachers, hoping the sight of Leslie would soothe him. She chatted with someone behind her.

Fucking Taylor.

Her gaze locked with his, and her grin had *I've got you* written all over it.

Josh took a seat next to him. "What's up with you?"

Beau didn't look at him but kept his eyes on the stands. "Nothin'."

"You've gotta get your head out of your ass. You're costing us the game."

Something clicked inside him. Without giving it a second thought, Beau tackled Josh, knocking him to the ground.

Beau's teammates pulled him off Josh.

Coach Brewer charged up to Beau. "Devereaux, have you gone mad?" The stout little man hiked up his shorts. "What in the hell are you doing, going after one of my players like that?"

"Sorry, Coach. Just a disagreement about a girl."

A dark shade of red tinted the coach's cheeks. "You better simmer down, son." Coach Brewer waved to the gangly second-string quarterback at the end of the bench. "Marty Evans, you're in for Devereaux."

Marty got to his feet, nervously looked at Beau, and grabbed his helmet.

Beau gaped at Marty's back as he jogged onto the field. The hush from the St. Benedict stands echoed his disbelief.

What just happened? He didn't know if it was shock or disgust at his coach's choice to replace him, but he laughed as he approached Brewer. "Are you serious? I'm the best you've got, and if you put Marty in there, we'll lose this game."

Silence descended over the St. Benedict players lined up on the side of the field.

Coach Brewer leaned closer, his prominent belly almost touching Beau. "Devereaux, do yourself a favor and stay out of my face until this game's over."

Beau headed back to the bench and noticed his father chatting with a middle-aged man with gray hair and glasses.

Is that the scout?

Gage Devereaux faced the field, his gaze ripping into Beau. He could hear the lecture he would get, but he didn't care. He'd catered to his father's rules for too long. But when Gage took Elizabeth's elbow and escorted his chicly dressed wife down the steps, his determination faltered. His parents had given up on him.

Beau would expect nothing less from his father. Fail to live up to his ideal, and Gage Devereaux wrote you off like a bad check. He did it to his mother, and after his behavior on the field, Beau suspected he would do the same to him.

The astonished reaction from the crowd sickened him. *Bastards are always hungry for a show.*

His parents, the school, and even the town had held him back. If he'd gone to a big school in New Orleans, he wouldn't have to beg for a scout to come see him. They would have heard of him already.

The emotional blow of his parents leaving was nothing compared to the hurricane of hatred inside him. He wanted to destroy someone. And if his coach didn't let him back on the field soon, Beau Devereaux would give the people of St. Benedict something to talk about for years to come.

The whistle blew, starting the second half. Beau paced the sidelines, kicking up the dirt and holding in his resentment. Thunder accompanied the clouds blanketing the sky, and the air was heavy with the promise of rain.

With Covington High's fourteen-point lead, he was convinced he would be called in to do what he did best—win. He stayed off the bench, keeping his body warmed up and ready to go. Minutes ticked by on the scoreboard, and he agonized over every one of them. With three minutes to go until the last quarter, he'd decided it was time to get back in the game.

"Coach." Beau put on his best ass-kissing grin. "I want to apologize for my behavior. I don't know what happened to me. I got hit hard twice and wasn't myself, but I'm good now."

Coach Brewer turned from the game and gave him a skeptical side-eye.

"I'll be happy to clean up the locker room after the game. Anything you want me to do," Beau added. "I was wrong."

"Don't disappoint me, Devereaux." Brewer nodded to the field. "Get in the game and send Marty out."

That was music to Beau's ears.

Mitch slapped his chest. "You got this. Let's turn this thing around."

Beau's seething bitterness didn't ebb while he put on his helmet—it skyrocketed. He had to sit by while the other team scored, and now he needed to pull a miracle out of his ass to win and impress the scout. But he just smiled at everyone—like his father wanted—and acted like the Beau they all thought they knew.

On the field, he stayed focused, shutting out all other thoughts and suppressing his anger. He threw short passes, connected with his open men, and his confidence returned as his team moved up the field.

His wrath retreated to the black hole inside him. Beau was his old self again. He settled into a rhythm. He backed out of the pocket on third down and found an open receiver. It was one of his best passes ever.

Touchdown!

A tide of jubilation washed away all his discontent. St. Benedict was within seven points of catching Covington High.

Beau remained quarterback in the fourth quarter. The boost was just what he needed.

I'll show that scout, my father, even Coach Brewer. I've got the talent to go all the way.

On the first down, he passed the ball to Mitch for a thirty-five-yard play. The bad beginning to the night forgotten, a rush of exhilaration hit him.

"You're back." Mitch butted his helmet when he returned to the huddle. "Let's win this."

Beau hoped to do just that, but on the next play, the referee called offsides before he handed off the ball. He kept his cool and refocused. He returned to the huddle and glanced at the visitor's sideline. Kelly was there, chatting with one of the off-duty officers working security detail.

Beau almost doubled over.

"Hey." Mitch slapped his back. "Shake it off."

Beau joined the huddle, but kept a wary eye on Kelly and the cop as he called the next play. After the snap, he couldn't find an open receiver, so he ditched the ball to avoid another sack. The blare of a whistle made him look to the right. The line referee called him for intentional grounding.

In the stands packed with cheering St. Benedict fans, he spotted Leslie. She looked right at him, wearing a strange smile.

Taylor stood up behind her and caught his stare. She aimed her finger like a gun and fired.

Beau snapped. "Damn it, Kramer!" He charged the lanky referee. "That's a bullshit call."

Kramer blew his whistle at Beau. "Keep it up, Devereaux, and you're out of the game!"

The line official signaled for play to resume.

His fingers twitched, signaling he was about to lose control. He tried to lock it down, and before he went into the huddle, he glanced one more time at the stands. Taylor had vanished, but Leslie remained with Foster by her side. His nerves settled, then movement to the left distracted him.

The older man he'd seen shaking hands with his father stood, folded a notebook, and made his way down the steps.

The scout. He'd blown his shot.

Fuck!

"Beau!" Mitch summoned him to the huddle.

The flimsy lock on his anger broke. A myriad of dark emotions pumped through him, urging him to run. He barely got out the call for the play. On the line, he counted off the snap, ready to pound into the first person who touched him.

Kramer stood nearby, waiting for the play. His call had cost Beau his future and destroyed his ticket to the pros.

He took the snap, a plan hatching. But he had to be smart.

Don't let them see who you really are.

Beau backed out of the pocket and kept an eye on his open men. To the right, he saw Kramer heading downfield. He cocked his arm back, pretending to aim long for the end zone, even though no one was there.

His temper driving him, he zeroed in on Kramer and let the ball fly. It sailed through the air, a perfect spiral, gaining momentum. The ball came down, and without a single player to catch it, it connected with the back of Kramer's head.

Beau hid his grin as the man went face-first into the grass and didn't move.

Silence. The entire field was in shock.

There's your intentional grounding, asshole.

He relished the moment. He'd gotten him in front of everyone, and no one could say for sure if it was on purpose.

Coaching staff and players from both teams rushed to Kramer's aid. Mindful of those watching him, Beau ran across the field to join the others, ready to convince everyone it had been an accident.

"Dude." Mitch jogged at his side. "You nailed him."

Beau slowed as they arrived at the small group tending to Kramer. "I didn't mean to hit him."

"Devereaux!" Coach Brewer got in Beau's face and ripped off his helmet. "What in the ever-loving hell were you thinking?"

Beau glanced over his shoulder to see Kramer sitting up. He pressed his lips together, hiding his smile. "The ball slipped, Coach. I must have gotten hit when I threw it."

The years he'd spent perfecting his golden-boy persona would pay off in that one moment. Who would believe Beau Devereaux would intentionally hurt someone?

"Bullshit!" Coach Brewer grabbed his collar. "I've watched you throw balls for four stinking years. That was intentional. Get to the locker room."

Beau noticed all the players and coaches watching his every move. He backed away and walked off the field, keeping his head down. He heard the whispers from the St. Benedict crowd as he neared the stands. Then, like a church bell on Sunday morning, someone's throaty laugh cut through the quiet. He glanced up and saw Leslie.

Beau hurried the last few steps to the gym doors. Once inside the locker room, he let go of his rage and flung his helmet, taking out the clock on the wall. He plopped down on the bench in front of his locker and put his head in his hands.

Faces from the game whipped through his mind—Taylor, Kelly, but most of all Leslie. Her insolence needed to be tamed, and he was the only one who could do it.

The locker room door swung open, and Coach Brewer waddled inside. He approached the bench, his face the color of Beau's red jersey. "Devereaux, what in God's name has gotten into you?"

Beau didn't look up, keeping his eyes on the coach's dirty shoes.

"That referee you hit is okay, but probably has a concussion." Coach Brewer waited for him to say something, then went on. "Do you understand what you've done?"

Pushed far enough, Beau stood. "It was an accident. I never meant to hit him. I let go of the ball too soon, got tapped. I don't know, but it wasn't my fault."

"I'm not buying that." Coach Brewer scowled and pointed at the locker room door. "Everyone out there may buy your bullshit, but I know what you can do. This entire game you've acted like you've lost your damn mind." He shook his head. "You're through, Devereaux. Leave your uniform and go. You're off the team." Coach Brewer stomped out of the locker room.

Beau wobbled and sank to the bench. They had four more games, big ones, and they needed him. Not that loser Marty. He raised his head to the harsh fluorescent lights. The walls closed in. The air got thin.

He had to think. He had to get out of that damned locker room and formulate a plan. But how did he win back what was rightfully his?

Beau changed out of his uniform. When he went to return his jersey, he hesitated. He wanted to keep it. He'd worked so long to earn it, but he decided it would look better to leave it behind.

He walked to his car and heard the announcer calling the game. It finally hit him—he'd lost his stardom. The tightrope of control he'd fought so long to keep in check had broken.

Peeling out of the parking lot and speeding away from the school, Beau debated going home. The last thing he wanted was a Gage Devereaux lecture. No, he needed to go where he could recharge his batteries and release his frustration. To the one place on Earth where he was king—the river.

The first raindrops hit Dawn while she stared at the football field. The injured referee sat on the sidelines, a bag of ice pressed to his head, while the St. Benedict team waited for their coach to return from the locker room.

"Can you believe they kicked him out of the game for that?" Zoe tapped her red and white pompoms together. "That was a million to one shot. No one could do it on purpose."

Beau could.

She didn't bother to enlighten Zoe. She didn't know Beau. Dawn had a lot of experience with his chameleon-like personality. She'd never put it all together until she saw the football hit its mark. He had been good at portraying the model son, overachiever, and squeaky clean teenager with a heart of gold. Then, like the Incredible Hulk, his anger would turn him into a monster.

"You think they'll let him come back—"

Zoe's question was cut off as whistles sounded across the field and players scrambled.

Dawn focused on the game, but her lingering apprehension about Beau remained.

The rain fell a little harder as the minutes ticked down until the end of the fourth quarter. She cheered as St. Benedict closed in for a touchdown. Then their drive got blocked, and they had to settle for a field goal.

Anxious and exhausted from the roller coaster evening, she screamed with gusto when her team got the ball back with thirty seconds left on the clock. The rain stopped, and the crowd got to their feet and shouted along with her squad for the home team to score.

With ten seconds left, Marty Evans let go a Hail Mary pass to connect to an open receiver in the end zone.

Touchdown!

Ecstatic, she tossed her pompoms in the air, jumped, yelled, and hugged her fellow squad members. The roar of the home crowd blotted out all other noise.

The players left the field, hurrying back to the locker room. St. Benedict fans lingered in the stands, reveling in the excitement of the win.

Dawn wiped her face with a towel, listening to the gossip circulating through the stands about what had happened to their favorite hometown hero.

"He had an off night," one woman said.

"He was totally stressed over the scout," a freshman girl confided to her friends.

"Too much partying on the river," a faint female voice said next to her on the steps.

Dawn glanced up to find Taylor at the railing, fidgeting and gazing out at the empty field. Her loose-fitting clothes, agitated movements, and faraway look confused Dawn. The Taylor she'd spent hours with at cheer practice was no longer there.

"What do you think will happen to Beau?"

Taylor eased down the steps to Dawn's side. "Nothing more than he deserves."

The venom in her voice surprised Dawn. "I wonder where he went."

"Aren't you meeting him at the river?" Taylor asked.

"No. I'm going home." Dawn collected her pompoms. Why was it so hard to forget him? He hadn't looked her way once during the game, and for some reason it hurt. "I'm not sure I want to go out with Beau anymore. After tonight ... I've never seen him like that in public. He's always so careful to show people what he wants them to see. I'm afraid what will happen next."

Taylor studied the crowds emptying the stands. "He's kept a lot from you."

Dawn's stomach churned. How did Taylor know anything about Beau? "Are you talking about what goes on at the river?"

Taylor's cheeks drained of color. "You don't know how he is when you're not around. He's not what you think."

Dawn hugged her pompoms, feeling sick. "You mean the other girls, huh? I've suspected there were others for a while now. That's why I want to end it. But is there something else?"

"Stay away from him." Taylor gripped Dawn's arm. "He's dangerous."

The terror etched in her face shocked Dawn. Why would Taylor be so worried about her being with Beau? What did she know? What could be worse than his cheating on her?

She needed to find out what was going on. Until she knew for sure, she doubted she would ever be completely free of Beau Devereaux.

CHAPTER TWENTY-EIGHT

Trees draped with Spanish moss cast ghostly shadows along the sides of the road as Beau drove to the river. The rain had cleared, and stars peered out from behind drifting clouds. The only sounds were the hum of the engine and thumping of his heart. Anger flowed through his veins, burning away every ounce of restraint.

The faces of the girls who had cost him the game drifted into his head. He couldn't let them get away with it.

At the river, he parked his car near the entrance and made his way across the shell-covered lot. The crunching of his shoes was the only sound. He was about to head down the path to the beach when a lone howl pierced the air. Beau came to a grinding halt and listened. He didn't want to end up eaten by one of those damn wild dogs. That would be a shitty way to go.

He stepped on the sand, disappointed to see no early birds had arrived. He kicked at the water hugging the shore, thinking about what might have been. Could he still play college ball?

Images of working at the brewery or sitting behind his father's desk left him weak in the knees. He didn't want that life and wouldn't settle for it.

The sound of rushing water reminded him of the roar of the crowd at the game. Beau wanted no reminders of his lost dreams. Craving quiet, he headed across the beach to the path that led to The Abbey.

He stomped through the rickety iron gate, needing something to destroy. Or someone. He set out across the high grass, running his fingers along the tips of the shoots. The tickling sensation added to his throbbing need to pulverize flesh and bone.

Beau turned at the broken fountain, smirking at the praying angel. "Nobody's listening, buddy."

He debated what to do with his life. With his days free from the hassle of football practice, he could pursue other extracurricular activities.

Beau stiffened as he stepped inside the cells. Flickering candlelight danced on the walls. Someone was in his room. He hugged the wall, ready to tear into whoever dared invade his space. He froze in the doorway as he peeked into the room, trying to get an idea of what he was up against.

The flare of a lit cigarette glowed in the shadows.

"Told you I would be in touch." Andrea stretched out on the cot, a coat wrapped around her, staving off the chill in the room. Her dark hair intermingled with a red scarf draped around her neck. A slender sliver of a smile welcomed him inside.

Beau rubbed his hands together, imagining things he would like to do with that scarf. "I needed to see a friendly face tonight."

"I figured your friends would be at the beach by now, and I didn't want to be seen." She put out her cigarette on the wall. "So, I snuck in here."

Beau approached the cot, his desire to hurt her charging to life. "Everyone's probably still at the football game."

She sat up and edged closer. "Why aren't you at the game?"

He arched over the cot, apprehensive about saying too much. "That's a long story."

She traced her finger along the blue vein running up his left forearm. "You've got all night to tell me about it."

He drank in her long legs wrapped in tight jeans. "I'm not in the mood for talking." He took a tendril of her silky hair and sifted it between his fingers. "What I need right now is to forget."

She stood, curling her arms around his neck. "I can help with that."

He pulled her into his arms. "What about your friends? Won't they miss you?"

She ran her hand across his chest. "They're partying in New Orleans. So I'm all alone." She bit her lower lip and then let it go. "And all yours."

Unable to wait any longer, Beau held Andrea by the back of the neck and kissed her. It was a long, slow, deep kiss. The kind he never liked to give, but with her, it just felt right.

A howl came from the direction of The Abbey.

Andrea leaned away from him, listening. "What's that?"

Beau nuzzled her neck. "Wild dogs. They live on The Abbey grounds. There's a couple of legends about them."

"What legends?" She stepped out of his embrace.

He watched her hips beneath her coat, getting turned on by the painful things he would do to her. "They say the dogs stay around The Abbey waiting for the lady in white. She was a gamekeeper for the seminary school and a lover of one of the monks. She died on the grounds, betrayed by the man she loved. Her dogs were kept to manage the varmint population. The wild dogs are said to be their offspring."

Beau slipped the coat from her shoulders, eager to see more of her. "The gamekeeper was found hanging from a tree in a white hooded cloak. It was all kept very hush-hush at the time. After the woman's death, the dogs roamed the grounds and lived off the land. They're said to only appear when death is near."

Beau looked at Andrea to see if she was sufficiently unnerved, and then unzipped her jeans.

"That's just creepy." She glanced at his hands as he tugged her jeans over her hips. "But a guy who brings girls to these abandoned cells is into creepy."

He liked the image the cells portrayed. It was his laboratory, like he'd read about in *Frankenstein*, where he could experiment and create his own monsters.

She cupped his face and brought his mouth to hers. "It's fine for us, but if you find a nice girl, don't bring her here."

He chuckled as he traced the outline of her jaw. "There's no such thing as a nice girl." Every girl who pretended to be nice hid a darker side.

Andrea took the red scarf and lassoed it around his neck. She worked her jeans the rest of the way and stepped out of them. Like an exotic dancer teasing a client, she hooked her fingers along the lacy edges of her black panties and slid them down her legs with an alluring grin.

Her underwear hit the floor, and his mouth watered. Spinning Andrea around, he crushed her against him and kissed her neck. Her light floral scent was intoxicating, adding to his desire to possess her.

He eased her onto the cot, took the scarf from around his neck, and dangled it in front of her.

She held out her wrists. "Now you're talking."

He tied the scarf around her wrists and crushed his lips against hers. Her tongue teased him, driving him mad. He broke away briefly to undress, tossing his jeans and sweatshirt aside.

"I've been a bad, bad girl," she whispered. "Show me no mercy."

That was all he needed to hear. His pulse thundered in his ears as he got a rubber from his jeans and slipped it on. He ran his hands over every inch of her soft, pale skin. But as his hunger grew, his need to inflict pain did, too. He hooked the scarf over the exposed pipe in the wall and flipped her over. Beau caressed the curve of her ass and slapped it.

Andrea moaned.

He didn't like the sound. To teach her a lesson, he spanked her harder. Her body curled inward with every strike, and she trembled.

"This is what you wanted," he murmured against her cheek. "Night of your life, right?"

Beau positioned her hips and thrust deep. Closing his hands around her throat, he rode her, feeding his desire for power. The command he had over her every breath made him squeeze tighter. She fought him, struggling under his weight, and his grip tightened. He thought of the game, the referee, Coach Brewer, and all the people he would love to strangle at that moment.

Andrea's features morphed and shifted, turning into Leslie. His hands around her neck, his power absolute.

Spurred on by his fantasy, his thumbs squeezed into the back of her neck. Her thrashing about on the cot heightened his pleasure. He could see Leslie's tears, feel her nails gouging at his skin, desperate for him to stop.

But he didn't.

He squeezed harder and kept on until she was his. Then a dull *snap* resonated in the room.

Andrea went limp.

Her weight settled in his hands, bringing him back to reality. He moved and waited for her to suck in a breath, but she didn't. "Hey, wake up." He shook her, but she still didn't move. "Stop fooling around."

Beau rolled her onto her back. Her head lolled to the side, resting at an awkward angle. Andrea wasn't breathing. Her dull eyes frightened him.

She wasn't pretending.

He jumped from the bed and broke out in a cold sweat. "Shit! Shit! Shit!" He ran his hands through his hair, feeling like he would puke. "Think, dammit."

He stared at Andrea, her hair fanned out on the cot, but all he could see was Leslie.

"This is your fucking fault! You drove me to this." He paced at the cell entrance, his chest on fire. "If you'd hooked up with me that first night, I wouldn't be here right now. I never would've touched Andrea or those other girls. You cost me my football career. You've destroyed my life!"

Leslie's smile, the smell of her skin, the throaty allure of her voice—she was the reason for his suffering. She would pay for what she'd done.

Before he could deal with Leslie, he had to do something about Andrea.

He gathered up his clothes. "I need to get her out of here before anyone finds out."

Who the hell cares.

The adrenaline pumping through him slowed. No one knew Andrea had been there. All he had to do was get rid of her body and walk away.

You got this.

Beau dressed and grabbed Andrea's clothes, securing them into a ball. He untied the scarf, his fingers caressing the silky material. He raised it to his nose and breathed in her scent. Without a second thought, he put the scarf under his cot. He would keep that to remember this night.

Andrea's eyes remained open, staring up at him. He closed them, but they didn't stay shut. Unable to take her empty gaze, he turned her on her side. Her neck made a funny crunching sound. Yeah, that was weird.

He went outside to listen for any trace of the party beginning at the beach, but it was still quiet. No music, no laughing, no noise at all. Perfect.

In the cells, he thought he saw what looked like a white cloak heading down the corridor toward The Abbey. He was about to run after it when the apparition disappeared.

A cold breeze brushed past him, raising the hair on his arms.

Beau sensed someone watching him from the shadows. It had to be one of the girls from the game. They had tracked him down.

Ready to rip whoever it was apart with his bare hands, he took off down the corridor, going from room to room, convinced someone was there.

He reached the entrance to The Abbey but saw no one. He tried the wooden door, but it wouldn't budge—the damp must have sealed it shut. Beau peered down the corridor. Where had they gone?

Never mind. Get the body out of here.

But where could he hide her?

The river.

He had no shovel, no means of digging a grave. But graves could be unearthed, especially by hungry dogs. The river was the only place he could dump the body and have all the evidence wash away.

Beau picked up her clothes, then hoisted Andrea's body over his shoulder. Maneuvering through the dimly lit hallway wasn't a problem, but when he came to the gap in the wall, he had a dilemma. Beau would have to pull her through the narrow opening.

He set her on the ground and breached the crack. Then he grabbed her feet and tugged her through.

Outside, he thought he heard something. Beau paused, his heart racing, but it was only the wind.

He hurried through the grassy field, straining under her weight, while Andrea's head bobbed against his back. At the path, he heard voices coming from the beach. Sweat beaded his brow.

Gaps in the trees to his left offered glimpses of the rushing Bogue Falaya. Beau lumbered down the embankment, carrying Andrea's body to the shoreline. A narrow strip of beach opened before him.

At the water's edge, he callously dropped her on the sand, the bundle of clothes landing beside her. He found a Louisiana driver's license, forty dollars, and a couple of rubbers in her coat. He threw the license into the river and pocketed the cash and rubbers.

The only other item she had was keys in the pocket of her jeans. Since he hadn't touched or even seen her car, there was no evidence to worry about. He tossed her keys in the river and picked up her clothes. He had to make it look like an accident or an animal attack.

Rip them up.

The shirt was easy—the jeans, not so much. The coat took a lot of effort and had him drenched by the time he'd finished.

Once the items had time to reach the bend in the river, he went back for her. Beau lifted Andrea from the sand and froze. Something watched from the brush along the shore.

An enormous dog stepped from the thick covering. Black, with patches of fur missing, it had a long snout and skinny body. It stood at the edge of the beach, studying him.

They only appear when death is near.

Beau was afraid to move. Andrea's body got heavier, and he didn't know how much longer he could hold her. He clutched the body against his chest and a creepy hiss emanated from her lips.

The hair on the back of his neck prickled.

His thighs burned and Beau gulped in air as the edges of his vision blurred.

The dog growled, then cocked its head and leaped into the brush.

A shrill laugh came from the direction of the party, breaking the eerie spell. Beau relaxed, and Andrea's body almost slipped from his arms.

With the moonlight shimmering on her ashen skin, he pushed Andrea's body into the river, mindful not to get his shoes wet. Her pretty hair spread over the water's surface, undulating behind her. The current took her, and soon she vanished around the bend.

All traces of her belonged to the river.

He rinsed his hands in the water as if he were washing away his sins. He envisioned Andrea being swallowed up by the Bogue Falaya and never seen again. His crime was perfect. She'd come with no one and left with no one.

Erasing his footprints from the sand as he backed away, he reached the end of the slender beach.

The brush to his right moved. It wasn't the wind. The night was still.

Beau cautiously advanced toward the leafy twigs and brushed the vines aside, determined to find out who or what was there. He couldn't see anything through the trees as he climbed the embankment.

The underbrush disappeared, and he arrived on the path from The Abbey. Music pounded in his ears. Or was that his heart? He jogged, searching the surrounding foliage, but all he found was shadows. A spiral of panic rose in his belly.

There couldn't be a witness. He'd committed the perfect crime.

Beau heard something behind him and glanced over his shoulder, but kept moving forward.

Then he ran smack into something and almost toppled to the ground.

"Beau?" Mitch grabbed onto him. "Dude, you okay? I've been looking for you. I saw your car in the lot."

Grateful to see a familiar face, Beau patted Mitch's thick arm. He took in his damp hair and the beer in his hand, then glanced back down the path. "I was just walking around the old grounds and thought I saw something."

Mitch's eyes narrowed. "Something? You mean, the ghost?"

Beau shook his head. "No, this was a person." His voice became strained. "And I'm going to find them."

CHAPTER TWENTY-NINE

Leslie scooped the last of the ice cream from her bowl as the sweetness of chocolate filled her mouth. The clink of the ice maker in the fridge was her only companion in the darkened kitchen. She relished the time alone after the commotion of the game. With her parents in bed and her sister still not back, enjoying her favorite snack in peace was the perfect ending to a rather satisfying evening.

Her mother had been cordial to Derek at the game, Beau was on his way to a well-deserved suspension, and Halloween was almost here—her and Dawn's favorite holiday.

The bang of the door shutting, and the murmur of soft voices, drifted into the kitchen. She put her spoon down when she saw a pale face poking out from under a gray hoodie.

"Taylor?" Leslie took in her disheveled appearance. "What are you doing here?"

"I asked her to spend the night." Dawn set her bag on the breakfast bar. "We got to talking after the game, and she told me some things about Beau."

Leslie picked up her sister's bag and handed it back to her with a scowl. "Half the girls at St. Benedict High could tell you things about Beau."

Taylor twisted her fingers, her eyes darting about the kitchen. "People don't understand how dangerous he is. He's sick and disturbed. Dawn needs to stay away from him."

Leslie recognized the fear in her voice. "What did he do to you?" Silence permeated the room. "It's okay. You don't have to say anything. But when you're ready."

Taylor sucked in a deep breath. "Thank you."

The *plonk* of Dawn's bag hitting the floor made Leslie jump.

"I'll leave you with Leslie while I take a shower." She unzipped the bag and pulled out her pompoms. "I'm soaked from the rain, and I've got to dry these before they wilt." Dawn shook the pompoms, and a few droplets of water settled on the stone floor.

For once, Leslie was grateful for Dawn's cluelessness. She didn't want her to hear something distressing. She'd been through enough.

Before Dawn headed for the stairs, she glanced back at Taylor. "You can tell my sister about Beau." She hurried out of the kitchen.

Running out of a room when conversations got heated or too emotional had been Dawn's coping mechanism for years. In the past, Leslie was the one who handled the tough stuff. Then she would give Dawn a watered-down version of the news to spare her the emotional upheaval. It was something she'd always done for her sister—another way to protect her.

Leslie pointed at her ice cream bowl. "Want some?"

Taylor sat on a stool. "Yeah. Thanks."

Leslie took the carton of chocolate ice cream out of the freezer and grabbed a bowl. While scooping a large serving, she glanced at Taylor and smiled. "You goin' for the grunge look?"

Taylor fidgeted with her hoodie. "I like to be comfortable."

Leslie pushed the bowl of ice cream across the breakfast bar. "Not too long ago, you were like Dawn, wearing your cheerleading uniform to class whenever you could, not hiding beneath a hoodie." She put the ice cream back in the freezer. "What happened?"

Taylor picked up her spoon, keeping her gaze on the bowl. "I'm okay."

"You can trust me." Leslie rested her elbows on the breakfast bar. "Beau's been harassing me for months. Ever since the night at the river when I turned him down. He's never let me forget it." Leslie sniffled, biting back her anger. "He says he's going to take me to The Abbey and make up for the night I should have been his. The worst part is no one believes me. I think Dawn's coming around, but there's still a part of her not willing to let go of Beau." She clasped her hands together, squeezing hard.

Taylor traced designs in her bowl with her spoon. "He's not what he pretends to be."

The voice didn't sound like her. It was colder, deeper, and sinister.

"Beau has taken a lot of girls to The Abbey. And he's hurt some of them."

A numbing cold rose inside Leslie. "Hurt? What do you mean?"

Taylor continued to clink her spoon against the bowl, and the eerie sound carried through the kitchen. "I mean raped."

Leslie gripped the edge of the counter, digging her nails into the granite. "Do you have any evidence?"

Her eyes were dead. There was no sadness, no terror, no fear in Taylor's face, just overwhelming hatred.

"I was at the river. Beau noticed me. I thought he was interested, but then he took me to his 'special place.' A room in those cells behind The Abbey. There was nothing special about it."

The cells. The room she'd discovered with Derek belonged to Beau.

Taylor's flat expression never changed. "He beat me, raped me, and when he was done, he said he would have my father fired from his job at the brewery if I told anyone."

The subdued, unemotional way she spoke scared the hell out of Leslie. She covered her mouth, horrified. "Oh, God, Taylor."

Why hadn't she recognized the changes? The clothes, the withdrawal from friends and school. It was the signs of sexual abuse she'd read about, but hadn't recognized in someone she knew.

I'm an idiot!

"The whole time he was hurting me, I kept thinking, what did I do to deserve this? Was it something I said, something I did, the way I looked? I kept asking myself why." Taylor dipped her spoon into the ice cream and tasted it. The emptiness in her face lifted, and she smiled. "This is good."

A tear trickled down Leslie's cheek as she watched the broken girl eat her ice cream. The barbarity of what she'd endured, coupled with a childhood pleasure, tore her apart.

"He needs to pay for what he did to you." Leslie reached for her hand. "We need to get you help."

Taylor pulled away. "I don't need help. What I want is revenge."

Dawn gripped the railing at the top of the stairs and suppressed a scream. *His special place.* It had to be the cells. The same place he'd taken her countless times. Tears streaked her cheeks as Taylor's humiliation and anger blended with Dawn's. She'd believed in Beau. What kind of person was she for loving such a monster?

Taylor's soft voice and the matter-of-fact way she told her story sucked the strength out of Dawn. She sank to the plush carpet, crying in silence, not wanting to let Taylor know she'd eavesdropped.

Leslie's voice floated up from the kitchen. "Do you know any other girls he's done this to?"

Dawn held her breath, waiting for Taylor's answer.

"Yes. There are more."

The unvarnished delivery of the news sent Dawn curling into a ball. Then, as the strength returned to her limbs, so did her resolve to get even with the psychotic bastard. She could almost hear Leslie scolding her to leave Beau to the authorities. But Dawn couldn't do that. She felt responsible for what had happened to Taylor and his other victims. Leslie couldn't protect her anymore. She wanted to make Beau Devereaux pay for what he'd done.

CHAPTER THIRTY

The breeze coming off the river teased Beau's sweaty skin as he fumed about his Andrea situation. The loud music wasn't helping. And students from St. Benedict and Covington High mingling around his bench made him sick.

His search through the brush to find whoever had been watching him as Andrea drifted away haunted every second. He also couldn't stand listening to the constant retellings of Marty Evans's Hail Mary pass. A few mentioned Beau's nailing of Kramer, but everyone considered Marty the hero of the day.

If that little prick gets my place on the roster at Tulane, I'll kill him.

How had everything turned to shit so quickly?

He knew why.

He pictured Leslie swallowed whole by the river in place of Andrea and smiled. Killing Andrea had given him a rush. Even disposing of her body had been a thrill. What if he could recapture those moments with Leslie? But he would have to be careful. He'd gotten lucky with Andrea. He'd have to plan every detail of his dream night with Leslie.

The party, the game, and losing his future didn't seem so important anymore. Andrea's death had given him an odd sense of purpose. If he could kill her, what else could he do?

"You okay, dude?" Josh kept his distance.

Beau never realized the tool was such a pansy ass. "I'm fine." He sipped his bottle of water.

Josh took a brave step forward. "You scared the hell out of everyone on the field tonight."

"Not to mention that referee." Mitch rubbed his chin, hiding a grin. "You clobbered him."

"It was an accident. I never meant to hit the guy."

Josh had a seat next to Beau, cradling his beer. "Coach Brewer doesn't buy it. What do you think the school will do?"

How could he bother with something as mundane as school? How would science and math help him carry out all the wicked things popping into his head?

A group of laughing girls arrived, dressed in tight jeans with fitted tops. Beau licked his lips, but the surge of sexual attraction he'd experienced before wasn't there. He was more interested in their necks. He pictured his hands around their throats, recreating the high he'd gotten from Andrea. It was like a drug.

Self-control in all things.

First, he had to get Leslie out of his system. Then the world was his.

Beau recapped his water, already bored with the party. "Sounds like Marty pulled out a great end to the game."

"Yeah, the boy has skills." Mitch eased his arm back, imitating the quarterback's Hail Mary pass. "You should have seen it."

Beau squeezed the bottle. "I should congratulate him."

"Are you serious?" Josh didn't sound convinced. "We figured you'd be big-time mad."

He gave them his well-practiced smile. He'd grown so far beyond their simple minds. "Hey, I'm a team player. I just want the best for everyone."

The roar of a bonfire and the crackle of wood filled the air. A cheer went up from the crowd. The party had hit its stride. Three girls dressed in jeans and Covington High shirts had a seat on the other end of the bench.

Mitch tipped his beer at them. "You know those girls?"

Beau found one of them somewhat tempting. With slim hips, blonde hair, and pouty lips, she reminded him a little of Leslie.

The ringing of his phone distracted him. He stood and retrieved his cell. *Dad* showed on the screen. Beau didn't bother to answer. Whatever he wanted, he wasn't interested.

Just when he was about to slip the phone back into his pocket, he received a text message.

Dad: Get your ass home right now. No excuses.

"Something wrong?" Mitch asked.

Beau put the phone in his pocket. "I'm gonna have to take off. It's my old man."

Mitch winced. "Yikes. That ain't good."

Josh patted Beau's shoulder while checking out the girls. "Maybe he didn't hear about you nailing Kramer yet."

Mitch chuckled. "Gage Devereaux? Are you kidding? He knows everything that goes on in this town."

Not everything.

Beau nodded to his friends. "I'll see you guys later." He slipped away and hustled back to the parking lot. His old man never texted, never checked on him. It meant Gage was furious. Beau may not give a damn about his father, but he still needed his money. He opened the car door as his phone pinged again.

Dad: If you are not here in ten minutes, I'm coming to get you.

Beau started the car, cursing his father under his breath. His night was about to take a turn for the worse.

Beau slowly navigated the driveway to his house. Shadows teased him as he headed to the garage. He swore he saw Andrea's face in the gloom, serene and lifeless, as it had been when the river took her away.

When he entered the back door, Gage was there, his thick arms— carved by years of weightlifting—folded across his broad chest.

"Where were you?"

Beau dropped his duffel bag on the ground, knowing he couldn't con his father. "At the river. I wanted to apologize to my teammates."

Gage's cold-blooded expression never altered. "After that stunt you pulled on the field, you should have come straight home."

"You heard, huh?"

His father grabbed him, wrenching his arm. "What have I told you time and again? People are watching us, they're watching you. That lapse of judgment is all some will need to question your integrity and state of mind. How hard have we worked to keep you focused, to keep people from seeing who you really are? And you blow it on a stupid football game."

Beau yanked his arm away. "It wasn't a stupid football game. And it was an accident. I never meant to hit the guy. I lost my grip on the ball. How many times can I apologize for a mistake?"

"You expect me to buy that bullshit?" Gage threw his hands in the air, his voice deep with anger. "I've watched you, studied you. I know what you're capable of, and everyone in this damn town is going to find out. Do you know what that will do to our business? To our reputation? You can't walk around reacting to everything and everyone without thinking your actions through."

Beau shoved his fists into his jacket pockets. "Is that all that matters to you? You don't care I've lost my shot at Tulane, do you?"

"You never had a shot at Tulane." Gage slammed his hand against the wall, inches away from Beau's face. "That scout was only there as a favor to me. He'd looked at your numbers, watched some films on you, and wasn't impressed. You don't have what it takes to make it in college ball, but I tried to give you a chance. A chance you fucked up."

Gage's words cut through Beau. He knew his father was a scheming, ruthless businessman, but he'd never dreamed he would use the same tactics on him.

"Perhaps now you can focus on your studies and put football behind you." Gage headed toward the kitchen.

"But I don't want to give up football," Beau said, following behind.

Gage shook his head, appearing more frustrated than angry. "You're off the team. Brewer won't take you back. He called me after the game. That's how I knew about Kramer. He suspects you threw that ball on purpose. I know you did. So, there will be no more football for you. We'll find other ways for you to handle that problem of yours without playing sports."

Beau's insides boiled. For years, he'd listened to his parents whisper about *his problem*. But he never saw his anger as an issue. It made him stronger and better than the losers at school. And as he pictured Andrea floating away in the river, he knew his bouts of madness had given him another gift—purpose.

He rubbed his hands together to hide their twitching. "What about baseball in the spring? I always play shortstop."

Gage ran his fingers through his hair, his heavy sigh permeating the tension in the room. "Right now, you'll be lucky if the school doesn't expel your ass for that stunt. Ms. Greenbriar called me, too, after the game. I had to do a lot of apologizing to keep her appeased. She plans on having you do community service."

A flurry of expletives was on the tip of Beau's tongue, but he held back. He had a part to play. "I understand." He picked up his duffel bag. "I'll do whatever they want."

"No more trips to the river." Gage snatched the keys out of his hand. "You're grounded. You'll work at the brewery after school and on weekends. Until you prove to me you have a handle on your behavior, you will live according to my rules."

Beau responded with a somber nod and headed toward the stairs.

"Aren't you going to ask about Kramer?"

He'd never even considered the referee. He didn't give a damn about the man. "How is he?"

Gage gripped Beau's keys. "He's got a concussion. I picked up the tab on his ER visit, which you will work off at the brewery. I'm going to put you in the shipping department under Kramer. You can apologize all you want to him when you're there."

Beau gritted his teeth. *So be it.* If he had to kiss every ass in St. Benedict, he'd climb back to the top. And once there, Beau would make sure those who had brought about his misery paid an agonizing price.

CHAPTER THIRTY-ONE

The bright blue sky did nothing to ease the pain in Leslie's heart. Taylor's revelation still tormented her. She'd barely slept, hardly touched her breakfast, and though she and Dawn were on their way to pick up Derek to go shopping, she was miserable. Beau had to be stopped. But who could she turn to for help? She needed evidence to bring to the authorities.

Dawn stopped the car at a red light and glanced at her. "You're awfully quiet."

"Are you sure you want to go to the Halloween party at the river? Beau will be there."

"No, I want to go," Dawn insisted. "Besides, I'll be in costume. He won't know it's me."

Dawn's resolve saturated her voice. Leslie wished she wasn't so damned stubborn.

"I will not run with my tail between my legs whenever I see Beau. We're going to go and have a good time." Dawn hesitated as she turned off Main Street. "What is it? I thought you wanted to go."

Leslie's heart sank as she remembered Taylor's emotionless face. "I just want to make sure you wanna go. We'll have to hustle to get our costumes ready."

Dawn chuckled, sounding upbeat. "It'll be fine. You'll see."

When Dawn pulled into the driveway, her smile wavered a little. "You're sure Derek wants to join us?"

Leslie unbuckled her seatbelt, hiding the apprehension in her voice. "Of course. He wants the three of us to hang out, and what better way than shopping?"

Dawn glanced at the yellow house through the windshield. "You never doubt him, do you? You're always optimistic about your future together." Dawn slapped the steering wheel. "I couldn't even get Beau to talk about going to the same college together, let alone anything after that. But you two seem to have it all worked out."

Leslie wished she could erase all of Dawn's disappointment, but she knew it could have been worse. Dawn could have ended up like Taylor. "He wasn't right for you. Let him go. You'll find the right guy one day."

Tears gathered in Dawn's eyes. "I'm not like you. You've always known what you wanted. Ever since we were little, you had everything figured out while I was still struggling. You were the smart one, the interesting one, and I ... well, I was just trying to keep up."

Leslie raised Dawn's chin, determined to get through to her. "I want you to listen to me. You're just as smart, funny, and definitely as pretty as me. You never have to prove anything to me or anyone else. We're twins, and nothing you do will ever make me love you less. I want you to be happy. That's all I ever wanted. I knew you weren't happy with Beau."

A teardrop trickled down Dawn's cheek. "I'm sorry, Leelee. I was a bitch to you when I was with him. I shouldn't have been. You're my best friend, and I—"

"Hey," Leslie cut her off. "You don't need to apologize."

A knock on the window made both girls jump. Dawn wiped her face when she saw Derek.

"What are y'all doin' in there? Everything okay?"

Leslie opened the door and got out. She longed to chase away her blues. "We're great. Let's go shoppin'."

Derek wrapped her in his arms and kissed her nose. "Shopping? You said we were going to hang out."

Leslie took an extra second to escape inside the warmth of his embrace. The world seemed a beautiful place when he held her. The ugliness, the hate, and the anger didn't touch her in his arms.

"Hey." Derek held her back, examining her face. "What is it?"

She yearned to say something, but it wasn't her secret to tell. "I'm just glad to see you."

"I've got news. Mom got that job at the law firm. She'll be working in Covington. No more diner."

Leslie's troubles lessened. "That's great."

"Yep. She's so excited. I can't remember when I've seen her so happy." He kissed her. "Thank you."

"Hey, you two," Dawn called from the car. "We've got Halloween costume shopping to do."

Before she climbed in, Leslie peered up at the blue sky and thanked the heavens for helping Derek and his mom.

"Are you guys sure you want me to go with you?" Derek fastened his seatbelt. "You could just pick out costumes without me."

Dawn put the car in reverse. "Leslie and I've already decided we're going to have matching costumes." She glanced at Derek. "If you're not with us, we might choose pink tutus and ballerina shoes."

He furrowed his brow. "Yeah, that's not a good look for me."

Leslie relaxed, chuckling at his remark.

Once on the road, she saw the tips of the white spires of The Abbey peeking out over the treetops. The dread lingering in the back of her mind resurfaced, ruining her cheerful mood. There was something off about the place. She didn't know what it was, but Leslie was sure of one thing—it wasn't good.

CHAPTER THIRTY-TWO

Beau tossed the last of his toy supercars from the display cabinet into a box on the floor. The clink of metal settling next to the football trophies and athletic medals he'd discarded sent a ripple of satisfaction through him.

Out with the old me.

He went to the black duffel bag on the bed—his "Leslie bag." It would remain in his cell, ready for his night with her at the river. He checked the nylon rope, handcuffs, duct tape, rags, hunting knife, and lighter fluid. He zipped up the bag, proud of the collection—his new beginning.

He needed to check his cell at The Abbey to ensure everything was ready for the big night. His father had harped for years that preparation was the key to success.

And you didn't think I listened during your lectures.

Though still grounded, he planned to sneak out after dark and head to the river. He'd done it dozens of times before. Beau couldn't join his friends and party—his father might find out—but he could watch from the sidelines. It was a way to weed out who was loyal to him and who was taking advantage of his absence.

He even had an outfit to make sure he remained invisible. A solid black ski mask, black jeans, and a black jacket sat on the bed next to his duffel bag.

A knock on Beau's door startled him.

He shoved the clothes and bag under his bed. "Yeah?"

Elizabeth strolled inside and frowned. "What are you doing?"

"Making some changes."

She'd traded her yellow robe for slacks and a floral blouse. She didn't have her usual drink in her hand and had even done her hair and makeup. Too much makeup, as far as he was concerned.

"Why are you dressed like that?"

Elizabeth skimmed her hand over her pants. "What's wrong with my outfit?"

Beau wondered what his hands would feel like around her neck. "Nothing's wrong." How the bitch dressed wasn't his problem. "I'm just used to seeing you in your robe."

Elizabeth held her head up, reminding him of the ice queen he'd known all his life. The woman had as much emotion as a glacier.

She folded her hands and leveled her gray eyes on her son. "The robe is gone. I'm trying to get better. I want you to do the same. Maybe this is something we can do together."

Ah, he got it now. His asshole father had spoken to her about the game, and this was her solution. What was next? Family counseling and weekends at Disney World? He could just see Gage Devereaux in Mickey Mouse ears.

"Since when do we do anything together?"

Elizabeth scowled. "Since your father decided he wants to make things better for you. I know our strained relationship hasn't helped your problem, so we're going to be around more. I want to try before we end up back in therapy. I don't want that for you."

His mother had attempted to dry out dozens of times. His father had made just as many promises to spend more time with the family. They were both liars.

Beau folded his arms. "It's a little too late for family time, Mother."

Elizabeth's features softened. "I blame myself for last night. If I'd been around for you more, there wouldn't be so much hostility."

"Hostility?" Beau wished he had a knife in his hand to send the woman screaming from his room. "Is that what you think my problem is?"

"Oh, I know exactly what your problem is."

Her harpy voice rang in his ears.

She took a step forward. "But I'm not going to give up on you. I'm not afraid anymore."

He closed the space between them, a sly smile on his lips. "You should be." One sudden move and she would run for the door like a scared rabbit.

"It's not too late for this family. But you have to be willing to work with us." She raised her folded hands, begging. "Will you do that? Will you agree to at least listen? If not, your father will take action."

Dammit!

If he didn't agree, then his father would insist on therapy or, worse, drugs. He'd been down that road before and swore he would never go down it again. Meds created a fog that stifled his mind. It seemed Gage's concern for his family's safety had finally outweighed his need to protect the Devereaux name. He had to play along so he could hold on to whatever freedom he had left.

"All right." He deepened his voice to sound convincing. "I'll work with you and Dad. I'm sorry about the game. I'm still not sure what happened, but I'm willing to take responsibility for my actions."

Her slight smile was becoming. He couldn't remember the last time he saw Elizabeth smile.

She folded her arms. "I'm surprised to hear you speaking this way. It isn't you."

Beau took a step back, trying to get away from her heavy floral perfume. "Me? You don't know me."

"I know you, Beau. I know every thought going on in your head. Don't think you can fool me." Elizabeth turned and marched out of his room.

The confidence in her step was a charade. Elizabeth had spent years at Devereaux Plantation terrified of two things—her husband and her son. One night of sobriety wasn't about to change that.

Beau shut his door and paced the floor, feeling the walls closing in. His parents would restrict his activity like before, but he wasn't a kid anymore.

He needed to know where Leslie was. Being with Dawn had given him a sense of access to her he no longer had.

Beau picked up the phone from his night table, toying with calling Dawn. What should he say? Should he try and win her back to stay close to Leslie?

He dialed her number. On the third ring, she answered.

"What do you want, Beau?"

It didn't sound like Dawn. She was edgier and colder. "Leslie?"

"Surprise!"

Her throaty laugh mocked him, and he tightened his grip on the phone. He imagined the sound echoing through the cells. He would make her laugh like that right before he strangled the life out of her.

"Put Dawn on," he demanded.

"Hell, no. You're the last person she wants to talk to."

Her defiance made him ache to punch something. "I promise you will suffer one day."

"Like you've made others suffer? Stay away from me and my sister, Devereaux." Her voice became a menacing whisper. "Or I swear to God, I'll kill you."

Her threat rang in his ears as the line disconnected. Her smile, her smell, and her laughter circled his head, squeezing out every single thought. It was as if shards of glass worked their way out of his stomach. He could not let her win.

After dropping the phone on the night table, he put his hands together and squeezed, imagining all the power and pleasure he would gain from her end.

When his fury passed, he smiled.

When I'm done, I'll burn her and leave the rest for the wild dogs. No one will ever find any trace of Leslie Moore.

The sky outside Beau's bedroom window was black. Not even the stars poked through the veil of ominous clouds. He lay on his bed with his lights out to let his parents think he was asleep. He listened for the closing of bedroom doors. First his mother's, and then, a short time later, his father's.

It was almost midnight. Everyone at the river would be drunk. It was time to make his move.

In his black jeans and jacket, he felt like the special ops guys he'd read about online. Beau learned a lot from the articles he studied, especially how to sneak around in the dark and not be seen.

He tossed a pair of black combat boots and a ski mask into his duffel bag. The clothes added to his sense of power.

Gently closing his door, he hiked the bag over his shoulder and eased along the hallway, careful to avoid the spots where the floor groaned. Once he was safely down the staircase to the main hall, he picked up his pace. Beau wiped the beads of sweat from his brow as he neared the mudroom. He was almost home free.

The blinking red light on the alarm pad brought him to a grinding halt. Gage had set it—something he never did.

Son of a bitch!

Beau had to get out of the house. He couldn't put his plan for Leslie in place unless he went to the river.

What's the fucking code?

He settled down and then remembered the five-digit code his father had given him—a combination of Gage and Elizabeth's birthdays. Holding his breath, he punched in the code and waited for the blare of the alarm, wondering what he would say if he got caught.

The alarm light switched from red to green. With a sigh of relief, Beau exited the house and slipped into the garage. He stopped to put on his combat boots next to the red McLaren that Gage had bought but never driven. What a waste.

The one vehicle not there was the black 4X4 Jeep used for hunting. Parked around back, no one would notice it missing.

After stepping outside, he glanced at the second-floor windows. Beau then searched the Jeep, patting underneath the tire wells and checking the rack on top. When his hand glided over the spare tire, he found the keys tucked into a small metal shelf.

You can't outsmart me.

The parking lot above the beach had cars crammed into every available spot. The crowd surprised Beau—considering he wasn't supposed to be there. He parked his Jeep at the entrance next to a patch of trees and grabbed his black bag. Putting on his ski mask, he ducked into the woods.

He positioned himself behind a thick oak and spied Mitch on a picnic bench. He was holding a beer and talking to a couple of girls. Beau was about to head to the cells when he noticed a lone girl walking along the path to The Abbey. He kept to the tree line and followed her.

She wore a long black coat and carried a bottle.

"Ellen." Josh stumbled toward her. "Where've you been?"

"You said let's take a walk to The Abbey."

"I wanted you to wait for me." Josh clasped her hand and led her through the old iron gate.

Intrigued, Beau followed them, staying far back. Instead of heading for The Abbey, Josh crossed the grassy field to the cells.

That little prick.

The cells belonged to him. The Abbey was everyone else's make-out spot. But here was his best friend, breaking the rules.

At the angel fountain, Josh glanced over his shoulder and then ushered the girl to the break in the wall.

Beau seethed as they disappeared through the opening. He hurried the last few yards to the entrance and listened before slipping inside.

The flare of a match came from his cell.

"My buddy has quite the setup. He doesn't know I know about it, so shh." Josh's slurred words echoed through the corridor.

Shuffling and moaning followed. The harsh creak of the cot moving on the stone floor came next.

Beau debated what to do. Should he rush in, knock the girl to the side, and let into Josh with his fists? This was his place.

Self-control in all things. Yeah, to hell with that.

His so-called friend had violated *his* territory.

Beau adjusted his ski mask, making sure his face remained hidden. The distinct sound of panting carried down the narrow passageway.

From the doorway, the yellow light of candles flickered. Josh was on his cot with a girl's long legs spread underneath him.

Beau put his duffel bag down and quietly snuck into the room. He waited, poised over the cot, observing the sickening display. When the girl's eyes opened, she parted her lips to scream, but he was too fast. He grabbed Josh by the collar and threw him against the wall.

The girl shrieked as Beau grabbed Josh by the throat. He held him against the cracked wall as Josh's jeans gathered around his ankles. Beau relished the terror in his eyes.

Josh clawed at the ski mask, fighting to breathe.

Not as good as Andrea, but a close second.

The girl ran out of the room.

Beau let Josh drop to the floor, deciding he'd had enough.

"What the hell, man?" Josh coughed, fighting to get to his feet. "Beau? Is that you?"

Beau jabbed his finger in Josh's chest, not bothering to disguise his voice. "If I catch you in here again, you're dead." He slammed his fist into the wall.

Pieces of plaster broke off, tumbling to the ground.

"You're crazy!" Josh scrambled out of the room, pulling up his pants.

The anger in Beau's veins swelled. *That fucker defiled my special place.*

He kicked the cot, smashed the vodka bottle they left behind, and shoved a candle to the floor. He ripped the blanket to shreds and pulled apart the pillow, filling the room with chunks of cheap foam stuffing.

Worn out and breathing hard, Beau slumped to the floor. The world he'd thought was coming together for him was instead falling apart. There was only one thing that could make up for all he'd endured—Leslie Moore.

Something red peeked out from under the chunks of stuffing. He reached under the cot and grasped Andrea's scarf. He lifted the silky material to his nose and inhaled her lingering scent. He'd forgotten he left it there.

You're lucky Josh never found it.

Beau dug his nails into his palms, punishing himself for his slip-up. Maybe he wasn't ready to take her yet. He had to get better organized. He'd have to come back, clean up, and replace what Josh had tainted.

He needed to get back home. He tucked Andrea's scarf in his jacket and blew out the rest of the candles. In the corridor, he groped in the dark and found his bag.

Under the light of the burgeoning moon, Beau ran across the field, creeped out as he peered into the pitch-black trees. The incident with the ghostly figure had never left him.

When he ducked into the brush, he used the light from the bonfires as a guide around the beach, frequently checking behind him.

He got back to the Jeep without issue. All he had to do was sneak into the house and crawl into bed.

Piece of cake.

CHAPTER THIRTY-THREE

Students hung out in the quad, lounging on the grass and soaking up the sun. Everyone seemed to be in a good mood, considering it was Monday. Beau didn't share their sentiments.

The first few stares he got walking through the school parking lot didn't bother him. He expected to get crap for what had happened at the game. But as he approached the quad, several students scurried out of his way.

"Dude, ignore them." Mitch gave him a fist bump. "They're just freaking out about the news."

Beau swung his book bag over his shoulder. "What news?"

"You haven't heard? The cops found the body of a naked woman on the riverbank this morning."

A sting of apprehension rippled through Beau. *How did they find Andrea so fast?* "Where was she?"

"Not more than two miles from where we party. Everyone's scared about going to the river for Halloween. What if there's a killer on the loose?"

"There's no killer. You know how people party on the river. She was probably just drunk." Wanting to change the subject, Beau looked around. "Where's Josh?" He couldn't wait to put the backstabbing asshole's nose to the fire.

Mitch eyed two girls in short skirts walking by. "He's at home sick. He hasn't been right since Saturday night. After he hooked up with some girl, he came back to the bonfire all pale and sweaty. Just hope I don't get it."

"I'm sure he'll be fine by the game Friday." Beau wondered how much Mitch knew. "Y'all have fun at the river Saturday?"

"Wasn't the same without you, but a lot of girls from Covington showed up."

Beau shifted his book bag, trying not to show his irritation. "You hook up with anyone? Go to The Abbey?"

"Nah, man." Mitch scanned the quad. "You know that place creeps me out."

Beau's heart raced when Leslie's car entered the lot. *She's here.*

"Aw, dude, you're not still hung up on Dawn, are you?" Mitch slapped his shoulder. "I thought you two called it quits?"

That Mitch didn't understand the reason for his excitement didn't bother him, but why would he assume he'd split with Dawn? "What makes you say that?"

Mitch's jaw slackened. "It's all over school. Everyone's saying she dumped you."

The air left his lungs. "Are you kidding me?"

Mitch held up his hands. "Don't shoot the messenger. I'm just telling you what's out there."

The black cloud inside him surged into a raging storm. He scrambled across the parking lot to Dawn's car.

"Did your sister tell you I called?" he shouted before Dawn could get out.

She leaned back in the passenger seat, seeming annoyed. "Yes, Beau, she did."

The sarcasm was new. Probably Leslie's influence. He held out his hand to her. "Then why didn't you call me back, baby?"

Dawn climbed out of the car, ignoring his hand. "Because we're through, *baby*. You can party at the river without worrying about me." She folded her arms, smirking. "I know about the other girls. How long did you think it would take before it got back to me?"

He wanted to tear her limb from limb. "What're you talking about?" Students gathered nearby, taking in the show. "You're going to believe the gossip of jealous losers over me?"

"They're not losers, Beau." Leslie placed herself between him and Dawn. "Losers are the ones who hurt people and destroy lives. You're a monster."

His fingers twitched. He needed to walk away before she shredded the tenuous grip he had on his self-control. Her strange power over him had to come to an end.

"You don't want to push me, Leslie." Beau's voice became menacing. "You won't like what I become."

Dawn shoved him out of the way. "That's enough! Leave Leslie out of this."

Beau edged closer. *No one breaks up with me.* "You might want to reconsider pissing me off. I'll make it so no other guy will ever touch you again."

Dawn didn't flinch. She grabbed her bag from the back seat, unflustered. Nothing like the girl he once knew.

"Breaking up with you is the best decision I've ever made. Stay away from me, or I'll tell everyone what I know about you."

Panic shattered his confidence. What did she know? Had Taylor run her mouth? Or Kelly? He couldn't afford loose ends.

He gripped her arm. "What do you think you know?"

Leslie rushed to Dawn's side and slapped Beau hard across the face. "Let her go."

He didn't acknowledge the hit. "What do you know, Dawn? Tell me!"

"Is there a problem, Mr. Devereaux?" In a gray wool suit and high black heels, Ms. Greenbriar stood on the curb in front of Leslie's car, hands on her hips.

Beau let Dawn go and flashed the principal one of his winning smiles. "No, ma'am. Just having a friendly conversation."

Madbriar tapped her shoe on the asphalt. "My office, now, Mr. Devereaux."

Beau backed away from Dawn as a ball of anger burned in his stomach. "Yes, ma'am."

Leslie's throaty laugh followed him from the parking lot. The rhythmic clip of Madbriar's shoes on the asphalt acted like a metronome. He imagined every click as a blow to Leslie's body as he made her pay for her sins.

"Good. You're here," Gage said as Beau walked into the kitchen.

The fact his father was home early, obviously waiting, intimidated the crap out of him. Any deviation from his tight schedule meant Gage was mad—very mad.

He held a mug of coffee, the rich aroma filling the room.

"No need to stay after school anymore, is there?" Beau set his book bag on the floor, bracing for another lecture.

Gage sipped his coffee, eyeing the bag. "Ms. Greenbriar called after your meeting. I guess she bought your 'it was an accident' bullshit and decided not to suspend you. Your one-month probation at school will coincide with being grounded. Since you're no longer on the football team and have been banned from all extracurricular activities, your time belongs to me."

Beau gulped, dreading what was coming next.

"You will be at my office immediately after school every day without fail," his father said in a contemptuous tone.

Gage stepped closer, his unbending gaze devoid of any compassion. "When your probation is over, we can discuss terms for your return to extracurricular activities."

Beau gripped the edge of the copper breakfast bar. "What about the Halloween party next weekend? I can't miss it. Everyone will be—"

"I already said no more river."

Gage's deep voice reminded him of a foghorn at night—cold and impassive.

"They found a dead girl near there. I can't have you around anything that brings even a hint of negative attention to this family. I have business associates who'd ask a lot of questions if the cops showed up on my doorstep. Make them nervous, and I'll make your life hell."

Beau had always suspected the Devereaux family business had a shady side. He wasn't the only one with secrets.

Gage set his mug on the copper breakfast bar. "I noticed the Jeep had been moved Sunday morning. Care to explain?"

Fuck me. He'd have to mark where he parked the damn thing when he went out again. "I didn't touch it."

His father hovered, exasperation written all over his face. "Every evening, I'm locking the Jeep in the garage with the other cars. I've also changed the alarm code."

Someone shoot me.

"Yes, sir."

Gage slapped the bar. "Let me make this perfectly clear. I've remained quiet about your problem, made sure you stayed off the radar of Child Protective Services, kept you out of institutions, and got you the best shrinks to treat you under the table. But fuck up my business and I'll have you tossed into a psych facility you'll never get out of." He picked up his coffee and stood back. "Now, go to your room and stay out of my sight."

His father's threats proved Beau was just another holding in the long list of Devereaux business interests.

He grabbed his bag and slogged to the curved staircase. Never had his father made him feel so insignificant. How dare he treat him like some deranged lunatic? Gage had no idea what he was capable of.

Beau stomped down the second-floor hallway to his room. Once inside his spartan-looking room, he longed to destroy something. He kicked the leg of his bed, slammed his fists into the comforter, and screamed into his pillow until hoarse.

Despite his father's ultimatum, he wouldn't stay away from the river. After breaking Leslie, Beau would have to find another place to act out his fantasies, but he'd always return to his cell. It would become his shrine—a place to relive his greatest triumph.

He rolled over on the bed, worn out, but accepting his situation. He'd have to continue kissing ass and behaving like a model son. When he was back in the good graces of everyone in St. Benedict, he would hunt again.

CHAPTER THIRTY-FOUR

Beau slammed the locker door, fed up with the whispers of passing students. The gossip ate at him. For the past week, he'd been a model student and followed his father's rules.

The confining schedule ate into his time observing Leslie. He'd analyzed her every smile, frown, or faraway look to read her mood. He'd memorized the clothes she wore and what she ate for lunch. Beau kept close tabs on her at school—following her to classes, staying out of sight, and sitting not too far away at lunch. She ignored him but knew he was there. He could see it in her stony gaze.

Unfortunately, Gage kept him very busy after school. So, he turned to another outlet to relieve his tension—the internet. He spent hours searching for ways to hurt women. Sites on rape, torture, and how to get rid of a body became a late-night addiction.

Mitch rested his shoulder against Beau's locker. "Any word if you're gettin' back on the team?"

"No, not yet. Where's Josh?" He didn't see the ass-kissing interloper scurrying behind Mitch like he always did. "I haven't seen him for the past week."

Mitch shook his head. "Don't know what's up with him. He's missin' practice, skippin' classes. He sounds real nervous lately. Like he's scared or somethin'. He says he's got the flu, but I'm not buyin' it."

Beau remembered the sensation of choking his ex-friend. "Must be some flu."

Mitch slapped his back and guided him down the hall to the school entrance. "If I were you, I wouldn't worry about football. The team didn't do half as well without you Friday." Mitch ambled along in his slow style as students went around them.

"And the river?" Beau kept a nonchalant quality in his voice. "How was that?"

"Nobody went to the river over the weekend. After they found that dead girl there, people have been stayin' away. Plus, the cops have been patrollin' like crazy."

"I'm sure it'll cool down by this weekend." Beau scanned the hall for Leslie. He usually saw her about this time. "Won't be a proper Halloween unless we're at the river."

Mitch stopped. "I thought you were grounded. You're gonna be there?"

Beau still had to convince Gage to let him out for one night. But he would devise a way to get to the river. He had to. "I'm working on it."

Taylor trudged down the hall in a lumpy black sweater, hugging her book bag.

Beau gave her a long, icy stare. *You're next on my list, darlin'.* After her antics at the football game, he'd been keeping an eye on her, too.

Before she turned into the bathroom, she shot him the finger.

Mitch chuckled. "What was that about?"

"What's it always about." Beau cracked a grin, ready to start spreading a little gossip of his own. "She's in a snit because I turned her down. She came sniffing 'round not long ago. I don't want anything to do with that twisted bitch."

While descending the steps to the quad, Sara rushed past and purposefully knocked him with her shoulder. Her eyes seared into his.

She was next. When he cleaned house, he would do it in a big way. *Girls will be filling the river.*

"What's her problem?" Mitch ogled Sara's short leather skirt and long legs.

"Man, didn't you hear?" Beau sneered at her back, formulating his smear campaign. "She got caught with some guys in the gym, having their own little bondage party. Ropes, handcuffs, you name it. There're pictures on the internet."

"No way!" Mitch gave Sara a second look. "I got to check that out."

Beau chuckled, knowing anything he told Mitch would get around school faster than the truth. He needed to get some serious revenge on the bitch. "Be careful with Sara. She charges. Works for one of those porn sites."

Mitch's eyes widened. "Are you shittin' me? How do you know that?"

"She told me at the river." He headed across the grassy quad, ready to drive the stake through Sara's black heart. "She does it to help pay the bills. Her old man's a drunk. My father's getting ready to fire him, but nobody knows yet, so keep it quiet."

Beau grinned as the sun hit his face. He would have her transferring to another school by Thanksgiving.

"Oh boy." Mitch directed his gaze to the parking lot.

The sun dipped behind a cloud, covering Beau in shadows. "What?"

Mitch patted his shoulder. "Try and keep your tongue in your mouth this time when you see her."

Derek, Leslie, and Dawn were walking toward their car. Derek held Leslie's hand. He hated that. She belonged to him.

Dawn leaned over and whispered in Leslie's ear, then giggled. The sound turned his stomach.

"When was the last time you two talked?" Mitch's deep voice intruded.

"Last week. You were there." He kept his eye on them as they got into the car. "The time apart did me some good. I needed to get that bitch's hooks outta me."

Mitch snapped his fingers in front of Beau's face. "Then why you keep starin' at her? You got to move on, dude."

Mitch was right, except it wasn't Dawn he kept obsessing over. It was Leslie. He needed to stop following Leslie around, especially if someone as dense as Mitch had noticed. One thing he'd learned from football, if a defensive line keeps stopping your every attempt to pass, then they're reading your plays. You have to shake things up and do the unexpected.

"I gotta go." Beau yanked keys from his pocket. "Gotta get to the brewery. My old man's waiting." He took off across the quad at a slow jog, antsy to get to his car.

It was time to finish with his obsession. Once Leslie was dog food, and the others on his list joined Andrea in the river, he could move on with his life. By then, he would have to expand his sights beyond St. Benedict.

Good thing New Orleans is close by.

There was still enough sunlight branching across the sky for Beau to keep an eye on Leslie's car as it headed down the busier part of Main Street. He stayed back, not wanting anyone to notice. A passerby who recognized his car waved, and he returned the welcoming gesture. The windows down, a mellow tune coming from his speakers, he appeared the same casual Beau everyone knew.

She took a right at the neon sign hanging over The Bogue parking lot.

Perfect!

He parked nearby and grabbed his phone, pretending to send a text as he waited for them to walk inside.

Through the large windows facing Main Street, he watched as they took a seat at a booth—Leslie and Derek on one side, Dawn on the other.

From his vantage point, he couldn't see Leslie's face but could discern a few of her hand gestures. She didn't use her hands as much as Dawn, which he preferred. It didn't take long for his reconnaissance to frustrate him. He yearned to hear her voice, her laughter. To remember it when he made her scream.

Would she be high-pitched like Taylor, or more muffled shrieks like Kelly? Shame he'd never gotten Andrea to scream. Might give him something to compare to Leslie when the time came.

Beau clenched his steering wheel, picturing Andrea on his cot, her neck in his hands, and then the snap. It was a wonderful sound.

He yearned to leave Leslie a present. Something to let her know how he felt.

Beau grabbed his book bag from the seat next to him and rummaged for a pen and piece of paper. The note he scribbled was short and to the point. Soon his fantasy would become a reality. How delicious would life be then?

Time to make my little Leslie sweat.

CHAPTER THIRTY-FIVE

The aroma of pepperoni and cheese, an eighties ballad playing on the flashy neon jukebox, and the murmur of conversation surrounded Dawn. She sat in the booth, her stomach rumbling, trying to ignore Beau's silver car in the parking lot.

Leslie picked up her iced tea. "So, we have our black pants, boots, and billowy-sleeved shirts. All we have left to get are the Cavalier hats, capes, and black masks."

Derek gripped her sister's hand. "We don't have to be exactly the same, do we?"

"We're the Three Musketeers. Our outfits have to match." Leslie sipped her iced tea.

Dawn turned her attention to the window. Beau was still there, sitting in his car and making no attempt to leave. She studied his chiseled profile. It was hard to believe such a good-looking package housed such a demented mind.

His rules and preoccupation with his image had never set off alarm bells, but after hearing Taylor's story, it made sense. The one thing haunting her was his anger. It had been there since the first night, simmering under the surface. The flared nostrils, white knuckles, and tightly pressed lips—warning signs not to push him. But she'd thought it was a guy thing, not a psycho thing.

Dawn didn't bother to tell Leslie and Derek he'd followed them to the restaurant. She couldn't handle another heated confrontation.

"Did you know about this?" Derek's deep voice drew her attention back to the conversation.

"Know about what?"

"Leslie says you're riding to the river together, and I'm to meet you there."

Dawn shot a cool glance at her sister, having no idea what he meant. "I, ah ..."

"I'm trying to talk Taylor into going," Leslie interrupted. "I figured it would be better if the three of us went together and Derek meets us there."

Leslie's easygoing manner was fake. Dawn knew her better than anybody. She was up to something.

"Taylor has been having a tough time lately." Leslie turned to Derek. "I'm hoping some girl time will cheer her up."

Dawn wouldn't argue with Leslie in front of Derek, but she'd ask her about it later.

"I don't like it." Derek rubbed his face and scowled. "I'd feel a lot better sticking close to you. Especially after they found that dead woman near there."

Dawn wanted to warn him from trying to tell Leslie what to do, but it was too late.

"What? You don't think we can take care of ourselves?" Leslie shook off his hand. "Why? Because we're girls?"

Dawn grinned at him. "Choose your next words carefully."

Derek groaned. "I'm just worried about y'all. I want to protect you, not limit your personal freedom because of your gender. Okay?"

The line between Leslie's brows softened. "I appreciate that. But we'll be fine. I can ride home with you after the party. Nothing will happen. I promise."

Derek shifted his attention to Dawn. "What do you think?"

She sat back, folding her arms. "I stopped trying to tell Leelee what to do when we were six. I suggest you do the same. You'll live longer."

Dawn turned back to the window to check on Beau. His car had vanished. She eyed Main Street, but he was gone.

Foreboding clouds passed by as the wind kicked up. Something flapped on the windshield of their car. She squinted. It looked like a note.

A funny feeling swirled in her stomach.

Dawn decided not to mention anything to Leslie and Derek. She wanted to get to the note before they did.

"Hey, guys." She slid to the end of the bench. "I'm going to the bathroom."

With a glance over her shoulder, she snuck out the side door leading to the parking lot. A strong gust tossed her hair in her face. Humidity clung to her skin, and the scent of the coming rain hung heavy in the air.

Dawn ducked as she hurried across the parking lot to their car, trying not to be seen by her sister. She quickly snapped up the note and dashed to the side of the building to get a closer look.

While the acrid taste of dread climbed the back of her throat, she fought to keep the wind from blowing the note away as she read it.

> I'm going to give you the night of your life.
> Derek will never be able to fuck you again.

There was no signature, no scrawl of letters at the bottom—nothing.

A rumble of thunder rolled across the sky.

Dawn leaned against the building and closed her eyes, her pulse racing. What should she do? Beau had left the note for her sister. The excessive teasing, the strange questions, the weird comments about Leslie all made sense. Gut-punched, Dawn's fear mounted. Leslie had been the one he wanted that first night at the river. The one he still wanted.

A heady aroma of magnolias and honeysuckle from that night came back to her. She had gone to the party with one goal—Beau Devereaux. In a short black dress that showed off her cleavage, she'd flirted with him, laughed at his jokes, and done all the things boys liked. But his interest was in her sister until she'd offered something he couldn't refuse.

"Leslie's a prude. She's saving herself for someone special."

Beau had grinned at her. *"And who are you saving yourself for? Or have you already found someone special?"*

She recalled the tingle in her belly as he'd looked at her. He'd been her obsession since ninth grade. *"I'm saving myself for you."*

Tears clouded her vision. Dawn believed when she gave him her virginity, his attraction to Leslie would end. She'd been wrong.

She'd spent months with a guy who had never cared about her. A guy she'd never known. A hollow emptiness enveloped her. She'd been an absolute fool.

Beau was a sick, psychotic bastard, and he'd set his sights on her sister.

Through her tears, she reread the note, and this time the bitterness rising in her throat didn't recede. She retched, then wiped her eyes and crumpled the paper in her trembling hand.

Taking a deep breath, Dawn suppressed her growing fear. "You've destroyed enough lives, Beau Devereaux."

The headlights stretched ahead as darkness enveloped the Spanish moss-covered trees on either side of the road. While she drove the last few miles home from Derek's house, Dawn gripped the steering wheel tight, her insides a jumble of nerves.

"What's up with you?" Leslie asked as she moved Dawn's long hair behind her shoulder. "You never said a word after you came back from the bathroom at The Bogue."

She relaxed her shoulders, not wanting to give herself away. "Just tired, I guess."

"You?" Leslie chuckled. "I don't buy it. You've always been the Energizer Bunny."

Dawn turned down their quiet street. "What was that BS you told Derek about Taylor back at The Bogue? We never talked about riding with her to the river. I didn't think she even wanted to go."

Leslie sighed and faced her. "She doesn't. I made that up because I've got a surprise planned for Derek Saturday night. I need to get to the river ahead of him, so I can be ready."

Dawn tensed. The porch lights to their home were just ahead. "What surprise?"

"I plan on showing him how much he means to me."

Dawn's waning patience cracked. "Are you going to have sex with him there?" Her insides turned to ice. "There's nowhere at the river to be alone. Everyone's all over the beach unless you plan on doing it in the woods, and even then, there's those damn dogs to worry about."

"I'm not having sex at the river. Gross." Leslie grimaced. "I'm going to meet him at the cells with a bottle of champagne. We found this room there. I want to tell him about my surprise without anyone around. Then, after the party, we'll go to a boutique hotel in Covington. I saved up some money and—"

"When did you decide this?" Dawn hit the brakes hard after she pulled into their driveway. She had a weird feeling her sister wasn't being completely honest.

Leslie lurched forward and grabbed the dash. "Dammit, Dawn. What are you doing?"

Desperate, she grabbed her sister's arm. "Meet him at the river, but skip going to the cells. It's a nasty place. You don't want memories of your first time to begin in something that looks and smells like a dungeon." Dawn turned off the engine, avoiding Leslie's eyes. "Beau took me there. I didn't like it."

Leslie leaned closer. "What happened?"

Dawn kept her eyes on the steering wheel. "We just fooled around. That's all."

She wanted to tell Leslie the truth about everything that had gone on in Beau's special place, but was ashamed. Her time with him, and what he'd done to others there, made her feel dirty and ugly. She regretted every second she'd spent with him, but to tell her sister would hurt too much. It would confirm what had always been her worst fear—that Leslie was the better twin.

"Just promise me you'll stay away from the cells. Save the champagne for the hotel." Dawn smiled, putting on a brave face. "That's how Lisa Faucheux lost her virginity."

"Lisa?" Leslie's mouth slipped open. "Really? But she's Pastor Faucheux's daughter. She tells everyone she's saving herself for her husband."

"Yeah, well, Lyle Burgundy beat him to it."

Dawn opened her car door, relieved to distract her sister from the subject of the cells. She hoped she'd done the right thing by not telling Leslie about Beau.

CHAPTER THIRTY-SIX

Beau shouldered his way through the students clogging the halls. He stomped across the tile floor, pissed at Coach Brewer. All around, excited voices chattered about the coming football game against Beddico High Friday night. He wanted to smash all their heads into the lockers.

"Marty'll pull out a win," the team's first-string running back said as he walked past. "He's turning into a good quarterback."

"I heard the team doesn't want Beau back." A girl leaning against a locker blew a big bubble with her gum.

The wildfire in Beau's stomach spread to every muscle. He was the quarterback of St. Benedict High, and he deserved his spot back on the team. But Coach Brewer had been adamant when he met with him in his office.

"Forget it, Devereaux. You have to complete your probation."

"But the season will be over by then," Beau had argued.

"Maybe you should have thought about that before you threw the ball at Kramer."

Beau needed to get away from the noise, the students, and the tight hallways closing in on him. He longed to head to the river for some time to think and prepare his cell for Leslie, but his father would hear about his skipping class. It seemed no matter where he turned, Gage Devereaux's chokehold never let up.

He turned a corner, desperate to get outside, when he came across Leslie. She was a few feet away, but the jutting corner of the lockers kept her from seeing him. She looked beautiful in her sweater and jeans. Her perfect porcelain skin glowed without an ounce of makeup. Her lips were pressed together in a classic Leslie scowl as she searched her locker.

Zoe, Dawn's obnoxious cheerleading friend, was at Leslie's side. The girl had a thing for gossip. What was she doing with Leslie?

"Dawn told me y'all and Derek are going as the Three Musketeers this weekend." Zoe hugged a Spanish book to her chest.

"Yep, we're all set." Leslie shut her locker door. "We've got our Cavalier hats, masks, fancy capes, black pants, and white shirts. It should be fun."

Zoe hesitated, her smile slipping. "Is everything okay with Dawn?"

Leslie's eyebrows knitted together. "Dawn? She's fine. Why?"

Beau's morning was looking up. Any juicy gossip to keep his ex in line was all right with him.

Zoe moved closer to Leslie, casting a wary eye to the students passing in the hall. "She just seems out of sorts. Preoccupied. Dawn said you're planning a romantic evening with Derek, but she looked real upset about it. She also mentioned you want to drive over early to surprise him with champagne in the cells. Ew, really?"

What? It can't be. This was better than he'd hoped. She would come to him. His prize was within his reach.

Leslie's scowl returned. "Dawn had no right to tell you about my plans."

Zoe held up her hand. "Look, I know you two haven't gotten along since she was with Beau, but now that he's history, she's worried you will make the same mistake. I mean, Beau was a total douchebag."

He clenched the grip on his book bag, ready to tear it apart.

Leslie stiffened. "Derek is nothing like Beau. All we want to do is spend some time alone together."

"Doing what? Bird watching?" Zoe chuckled.

Leslie rolled her eyes. "Laugh all you want. Derek loves me and isn't trying to rush me into having sex."

"That boy wouldn't have to rush me." Zoe hugged the book against her chest. "I'd of jumped his bones after the third date. I can't believe you're still a virgin. That boy is hot."

The peckerhead?

Leslie lowered her voice. "I want my first time to be special."

"Special?" Zoe paused and cocked her head. "Girl, you're in for a big surprise."

She sure is.

Beau's head swam, picturing all the things he would do to her. He envisioned the rush thrusting into Leslie would give him. His cock throbbed. It would be better than Taylor, Kelly, and Andrea combined.

Zoe hooked Leslie's arm. "Come on, let's get to class."

Zoe's gaze briefly connected with Beau's. A wave of dread froze him to his spot. Zoe didn't say or do anything as they walked away. Leslie never saw him, thank goodness. He didn't want her changing her plans. He wanted his prey to be calm and happy when she arrived at his special place. It would make her final scream so much sweeter.

Dawn adjusted her pompoms under her arm and then tugged the red ribbon holding her ponytail. A brisk breeze caressed her bare arms, sending a chill through her. She headed across the track in front of the bleachers where her cheer squad waited to start practice.

"Hey girl, you got a sec?" Zoe jogged up to her.

Dawn inwardly groaned. She knew that look. It went along with Zoe's yearning to share some juicy rumor she'd picked up around school. The last thing Dawn needed was more gossip.

"When was the last time you talked to Beau?" Zoe asked.

Dawn hadn't expected that question. "It's been a while. Why?"

"He's been acting funny."

Dawn scrunched her brow. "Well, I've not seen him with Mitch and Josh lately. They usually go everywhere together."

"Word is he and Josh had a fight." Zoe shook out her pompoms. "I tried to talk to Mitch about it, but he shut me down. He's such an ass."

Dawn peered ahead to her waiting squad. The girls stood around talking. Not a good sign. She needed to get them to work. "Zoe, is there a point to this? Because, if you haven't noticed, Beau isn't my problem anymore." She made a move toward the field. "We gotta get to practice."

Zoe rushed in front of her, her brow etched with concern. "Look, I asked Leslie about her Halloween plans at the river with Derek, and—"

"What the hell, Zoe?" Dawn snapped. "I can't believe you blabbed that. I trusted you."

"Sorry." Zoe's shoulders drooped. "But I caught Beau staring at Leslie from behind some lockers. If I didn't know better, I'd swear he was listening."

Dread tightened her throat, making it hard to breathe. "What did he hear? I need you to tell me every word you two said."

"Um, Dawn ... what's going on?"

Dawn dropped her pompoms and grabbed Zoe's arms. "Tell me."

Zoe shook her head. "I don't know. We talked about her plan to make Saturday night special for her first time with Derek. How she wanted to get to the river early to surprise him with champagne in the cells."

"He heard that. The part about the cells?"

"Yeah, I guess." Zoe pried Dawn's fingers off her arms. "The way he stood there was just plain freaky. He had this look in his eyes ..."

Dawn stepped back, her mind a blur. She stared at the open field next to the gym, where the football team ran drills. "Do me a favor, don't mention this to Leslie. I don't want her upset or to ruin her night with Derek."

"Be careful around that boy." Zoe picked up Dawn's pompoms and handed them to her. "Something's not right with him."

CHAPTER THIRTY-SEVEN

T he glow from the security lights filtered into Beau's bedroom window. He admired the blank expression on his Michael Myers mask and tossed it on top of the contents in his black duffel bag. Everything was ready. Under the mask was Andrea's red scarf. He touched the fabric, imagining it around Leslie's neck.

A knock on his door startled him. Beau hurriedly zipped up the bag and shoved it under his bed. "Come in."

Gage pushed the door open and boldly stepped into his bedroom.

Beau noticed his dark pants and white dress shirt, and then he got a whiff of his father's expensive cologne. "You going out?"

"Business meeting in New Orleans." His father tossed something at him. Beau caught the object in mid-air. It was the keys to his car.

"I need you to go to the brewery tonight and get out the Halloween decorations for the employee party this Saturday. They're in the storage building. Have the security guard on duty help you load everything into a truck and take them to the meeting room in the administration building."

He stared at his father, confused. "Why tonight?"

Gage fiddled with the gold Rolex on his wrist. "Because, tomorrow after school, you'll be decorating the meeting room."

Beau frowned. Decorating was a girl thing. "Anything else?" He didn't bother to keep the cockiness from his voice, even though it would anger his father.

Gage stepped closer, his lips in a firm line. "It's not forever. When you've served your time, you can go back to hanging out with your friends."

Served my time? Beau's hand tightened around the keys, squeezing the metal into his flesh. "Even prisoners get time off for good behavior."

His father's sigh hung in the air. "You want something. What is it?"

Beau perked up. "I'd like to go to the Halloween party at the river Saturday night."

"No. You're going to the brewery party Saturday night with your mother. We're going to put on a united front for the staff."

Beau clenched the keys harder. "I just want to go for a couple of hours. Then I'll head to the brewery. If I'm late, you can call the cops on me."

Gage's eyes crinkled at the corners. Something he did when considering a proposal.

"Since a deputy will already be patrolling the river, there'll be no need. Davis wants to assure parents their kids will be safe."

That will kill the party. Good thing I have other plans.

"Then you have nothing to worry about. You can call Sheriff Davis and have me arrested."

The cold indifference emanating from his father didn't surprise Beau. It had been there all his life.

"You better be at the brewery by eight-thirty, or I'll ground you for another month."

Beau's grip loosened on the keys. "Yes, sir."

Gage looked him over. "Leah left a roast for dinner. Make sure you eat. You're getting skinny."

Beau glanced at his flat stomach and baggy pants. He hadn't noticed the weight loss. "Haven't had much of an appetite lately."

Gage nodded. "You'll start hitting the gym with me. Otherwise, people will think you're sick and ask questions."

Beau grinned. "And we can't have that, can we?"

Gage jabbed a finger into Beau's chest. "Let's cut the crap, shall we? You're my son, which doesn't mean shit to you, but it does to me. I've stood by you, put up with your crap, and kept my mouth shut when your behavior has embarrassed this family. I sometimes wonder if you have a shred of responsibility in you, or if you plan on spending your entire life with your head up your ass." Gage threw his hands in the air. "I've done everything I can to keep you under control, but it's not enough. I hope you prove me wrong and become a man people can rely on, but I have a feeling you'll end up their worst nightmare. If that day ever comes, I'll cut all ties with you. You'll be dead to me."

The admission wasn't a shock, but a relief. Beau had been well aware of his father's distaste for him ever since he was a kid. But after the *incident*, things had never been the same. The last tether keeping him grounded to his life as Gage Devereaux's son had finally snapped. He was free to be who he wanted, do what he wanted, his family name be damned. "I'm glad we cleared that up."

Beau relaxed his grip on the keys. His palm was wet and stung like mad.

"Your mother will be waiting up until you get home from the brewery. She's going to call me as soon as you get in, so don't think you can go out and fool around with your friends."

Beau shook his head at his father's stupidity. "It's Thursday. Nobody goes out on a school night."

"Keep up with that smartass attitude, and Saturday's off." He turned for the door and strutted out of the room.

Beau should have been livid, but he remained calm. Fate was on his side, giving him the chance to be with Leslie. It was the only way to explain how everything had fallen into place.

The throaty roar of an engine drew him to the bedroom window. Gage's red McLaren headed down the driveway.

"Business meeting, my ass."

The car, the clothes, the cologne—he had a date. Probably a new woman. *He's so predictable.*

Beau glanced at the keys in his hand. Flecks of blood showed against the silver. He wanted to paint the world in the ruby shade. He would show everyone he was his own man—a man to be feared.

He retrieved the duffel bag from under his bed and hoisted it over his shoulder. He had a stop to make before he went to the brewery.

Beau patted the bag. "My party will be the talk of the town."

The brush of tree limbs against his car was the only sound as he slipped into the shelled lot by the river. His headlights cut through the darkness and didn't land on any other vehicles. Good. He was alone.

Beau parked below some low-hanging branches on the far side of the lot to stay hidden from the deputy patrols. He retrieved a flashlight and flung the duffel bag over his shoulder, ready to head for The Abbey.

Rustling leaves spooked him. Beau stood still, holding his breath. After several seconds, he shook his head and brushed off the noise. He set out across the lot and when he came to the sloping path leading to the river, he ducked into the brush.

Low-lying twigs scratched his hands as he moved through the dense foliage. When he stopped to adjust the heavy bag on his shoulder, the crash of something in the underbrush came from behind. A rush of adrenaline overtook him. Was it the deputy sent to monitor the party?

He spun around, but no one was there.

A patch of green leaves shook.

He shined his flashlight, and the greenery stilled. "Who's there?"

Nothing. Then dark eyes, low to the ground, reflected the beam of his light. A black nose and scarred snout poked out from the brush. A large black dog, its fangs dripping with saliva, drew closer.

He spotted a thick stick on the ground. He kept his eyes on the approaching dog and slowly picked up the small branch. The animal's growl got steadily louder. Determined not to be intimidated by the mangy creature, Beau remained calm. Right before it got too close, he hurled the piece of wood at the dog's head.

A yelp pierced the air, but the mongrel didn't back down. It glared at Beau with intense hatred.

He picked up another smaller stick and threw it, followed quickly by another. "Come on, you fucker."

He waited for the animal to charge. Instead, it turned and raced into the brush.

Smug with his victory, he turned back toward The Abbey. At the iron gate, he raised his head to the night sky. The stars weren't twinkling, and there was no moon. Perfect.

He cut across the field of high grass. Not far from the cells, the lone howl of a dog stopped him in his tracks. Silence. Seconds ticked by, but the only sounds were the chirp of the crickets and the occasional croak of frogs.

When the dogs appear, death is near.

He chuckled. Maybe the dogs knew what he had planned.

Inside the abandoned ruins, he directed his flashlight to the floor. A rat scurried by, startling him. Beau kicked the defenseless creature. It landed a few feet away on a pile of leaves, stunned. He thought of things he could do to it, but there wasn't time. He needed to set up his room and head back to the brewery.

The cell was in the same disarray as after his encounter with Josh. Beau set his flashlight down and dumped his duffel bag on the cot.

He removed several new scented candles from the bag—honeysuckle and rose. Leslie would appreciate their aroma. He tried to find one that smelled like her, but none seemed to have her essence. After lighting candles, he set them around the room, on the floor and ice chest, eager to capture the right ambiance. Once satisfied, he collected the black garbage bag he'd brought, along with a small broom.

Beau took his time, sweeping up the wads of foam, broken glass, and torn fabric from the floor. He found the preparation for Leslie soothing. The way he felt before Christmas morning as a kid, knowing he would get what he wanted. He just had to wait.

With the room freshly swept, he retrieved the new blanket and pillow from his bag and set them on the cot. The last thing he took out was Andrea's red scarf. He gently draped it on a pipe jutting from the wall.

He left the other toys he brought in the duffel bag and placed it under the cot. The flickering light from the candles added to the eerie atmosphere of the room. Beau hoped Leslie would appreciate his attention to detail. Still, something was missing. It needed a homey touch.

Flowers. Yes, of course. He would pick up a bouquet of white roses and set them in a nice vase. Leslie loved white roses. He'd seen Derek bring her some at school.

Breathing in the musty odor of the room, Beau trembled with anticipation. He would act out every depraved fantasy, ending his obsession with Leslie. Then life would be perfect. The annihilation of Leslie Moore would be his greatest work of art, but not his last.

Satisfied, he tied off the garbage bag, blew out the candles, and headed back outside.

A glimpse of white slipping through the break in the wall sent a jolt of panic up his spine. He was not alone.

He took off for the opening. Several precious seconds passed as he pulled the garbage bag through the narrow crack. Once out in the night air, he scanned the grounds.

A strange mist had appeared since he'd entered the cells. It hovered around the grass. The tall blades rose from the dense fog and wiggled like fingers, beckoning him to follow. Beau dashed through the weeds, unsettled by the ghoulish atmosphere.

Ahead, a white cloak floated near the trees. His anger returned. "I'll get you."

He reached the spot where he'd seen the strange apparition and examined the ground with his flashlight. There were no footprints, no disturbance to the grass.

A long, low howl sliced through the air.

His heart pounding, Beau hurried in the direction the gate, sweating under his long-sleeved shirt despite the chill. He headed into the brush, cutting off his flashlight, ready to kill the conniving little bitch playing head games with him.

Beau carefully maneuvered through the brush, not making a sound. But when he emerged in the parking lot, no one else was there. The pale streetlight filtered through the trees and across the shelled surface, revealing no other cars.

He stood by a pine tree, attuned to every noise. He stayed still for several minutes before his fear of being late to the brewery urged him on.

Beau tossed the garbage bag into the trunk and got in the car. Once behind the wheel, aggravation gnawed at his gut. Someone had followed him. He ran through a list of suspects.

What if it's the ghost?

The childish notion made him laugh, and he started the car.

It was a person. It had to be. Any other explanation meant his grip on reality was slowly slipping away.

CHAPTER THIRTY-EIGHT

"I can't wear this, Leslie."

Derek arched over the rickety kitchen table, attempting to stay in front of the camera on his phone. He secured the black mask, debating how to get through the evening wearing it with the Cavalier hat. "These pants only have one pocket. How am I supposed to carry my phone, wallet, and keys?"

"Put them in your hat." Leslie's velvety warm chuckle floated through the speaker as she smiled.

He loved her laugh. He loved everything about her. Her costuming skills, however, remained iffy. "You do realize I will run into everyone. I can barely see." He tried on the hat. "Tell Dawn the hats are too big."

Dawn stuck her face in the screen. "Stop complaining."

Derek grimaced. "Hi, Dawn."

"She's already dressed and rarin' to go," Leslie added. "But you're right, the hats are too big."

"Aw, come on, you guys." Dawn swatted her sister. "They're fun."

"Derek said he doesn't have enough pockets for his stuff," Leslie explained.

"He doesn't need a phone. We'll have ours," Dawn said. "He can't cop out and change his costume so he can carry stuff."

Derek caught her eye roll and laughed. Before Dawn's breakup, he thought she was bitchy, between her obsession with popularity and obliviousness to Beau's cruelty. But, since then, she'd won him over with her humor, resilience, and almost childlike innocence.

"You heard that, right?" Leslie asked.

"Yeah, I've got my orders." If Dawn insisted he wear the same outfit, he would. The costumes represented their friendship, and the evening marked a significant milestone—he'd won the trust of the entire Moore household. Even Shelley had warmed to him.

"You need to get dressed, Leelee. We need to go."

A tingling sensation shot up his spine. "What? I didn't think we were meeting until much later. It's not even six yet."

"We're getting there early." Leslie's tone changed to right above a whisper. "I have a surprise for you."

He tossed his hat on the kitchen table. "What surprise?"

"Just meet me at The Abbey. It's not a surprise if I tell you now."

Derek played with the feather in his hat, disturbed by his growing sense of unease. "I thought The Abbey creeped you out?"

"It's only a place to meet. We won't be hanging around there for long."

The front door opened, and Carol Foster rushed in carrying file folders and a laptop slung over her shoulder.

"Hey, Mom." Derek went to help her. "What've you got there?"

Carol handed him the pile of folders. "Cases from the firm. Mr. Garrison wants me to go through them and type up his notes. He even gave me a laptop. It will probably take me all weekend." Carol kicked the door closed and set her purse and keys down.

"Is that your mom?"

"Hold on," he told Leslie as he carried the files to the kitchen table. He set them down and picked up his phone. "Yeah, Mom just got home from work."

"Is that Leslie?"

He held up the phone to Carol, and Leslie waved.

"Tell your dad thank you again." She went to the coffeemaker and carried the empty pot to the sink. "The job is wonderful. The Garrisons are giving me more responsibility every day."

"I'm so glad everything is working out," Leslie said. "I'll tell Dad after he gets home from the party at the brewery."

Derek watched his mother refill the coffeepot and chat with his girlfriend. To see her doing so well gave him a sense of relief. How had he gotten so lucky? A great mom, a girlfriend he loved, and a new family.

"Leelee," Dawn shouted. "Get off the phone. You have to get dressed now."

Derek heard a strange rustling off-screen. "Everything okay?"

"Leelee will see you at the party, Derek," Dawn said.

"Okay. Leslie, I love—"

Click.

Derek sighed and put the phone down.

Carol flipped on the coffeemaker and checked out his costume. "What are you? A pirate?"

"No." He picked up his Cavalier hat and put it on. "Leslie, Dawn, and I are going as the Three Musketeers."

Carol chuckled. "Lose the hat, keep the mask. You're more convincing as a pirate."

CHAPTER THIRTY-NINE

A bouquet of fresh white roses sat in a green glass vase atop Beau's ice chest. He arranged the stems, wanting them perfect for when she walked into his cell. The burning candles filled the room with the scent of honeysuckle.

Set out on the cot were a roll of duct tape, handcuffs, a hunting knife, lighter fluid, and the finishing touch—his Michael Myers mask. Beau stood close to the entrance of his cell. He wiped a sweaty palm down his black jeans and then cleaned a smudge on his black combat boots. Everything had to be perfect. He glanced at Andrea's red scarf still hanging from the pipe. When the essence of life left Leslie's eyes he would reveal himself, and make sure his face was the last thing she ever saw.

He'd fantasized about this night, but there were times he doubted it would happen.

The sound of shuffling, like someone trying to get through the crack in the wall, came from the corridor.

She's here.

He retrieved the mask from the cot and quickly put it on.

An audible gasp drifted into his room. Beau grinned. She was early.

Energy surged through him. He peeked at her through the doorway, holding his breath, afraid to make a sound and scare her away.

Leslie eased along the corridor, heading toward the candlelight. She wore a Three Musketeers costume with a black mask, Cavalier hat, and carried a bottle of champagne. He waited as she inched closer, aching to get his hands on her.

She stuck her head in the door and glanced around.

Beau kept to the shadows, his back pressed against the stone wall. When she turned her head, he grabbed her and slapped his hand over her mouth. The champagne bottle hit the floor, shattering with a loud *pop*.

She struggled, almost making him laugh. With one hand over her mouth and the other around her neck, Beau dragged her to the cot. He ripped off the hat, disappointed to find her blonde hair secured by bobby pins.

She screamed as he forced her to the floor. He snatched the duct tape and wrapped it around her head and over her mouth.

Her mewling cries filled him with such satisfaction.

Beau peered into her blue eyes. "No one can hear you, my Leslie."

She fought against him even harder. He liked that. Straddling her, he retrieved the handcuffs from the cot. With her hands immobilized, he could now take his time.

Beau removed the pins holding her hair. He ran his fingers through her shoulder-length tresses, reveling in the silkiness.

He picked up the knife, debating which end of her costume to start with—the top or the bottom.

Decisions, decisions.

He wanted to see her breasts. Beau sliced down the center of her white shirt, careful not to graze her skin, and then slashed open her bra. When the cold air hit her breasts, her nipples hardened. He licked his lips as he pinched one of the rosy tips.

The duct tape muffled her shrieks as she bucked against him.

To cut her pants away while she fought took some skill. By the time he ripped off her underwear, his breath stilled—awestruck by the beauty of her naked body. Here was perfection. The woman who haunted his dreams, there for the taking. Beau ran the flat edge of the knife down her chest, picturing blood oozing from her wounds.

Beau hoisted Leslie off the floor and placed her on the cot. "You wanted your first time to be special. I'm going to give you the night of your life."

She didn't fight him as he secured her handcuffs to the pipe. He didn't like that. In his fantasy, he'd imagined her resisting so much more.

He took a moment to marvel at her slender body and long legs in the candlelight. Perfection. He touched his nose to her skin, eager to inhale her scent. Unfortunately, the heady aroma of honeysuckle from the candles obliterated her faint perfume. *Damn!*

Beau needed to feel her against him. He pulled off his boots and fumbled with the button and zipper on his pants, trembling with urgency. After sliding out of them, Beau stood naked before her, wearing his mask and fully aroused.

She kicked when he climbed on top of her. There was his feisty girl. Her resistance excited him. It was what he'd longed for.

Beau slowly peeled off the mask. "That's it, Leslie. Fight me."

She thrashed harder, trying to free her hands from the pipe.

"Keep that up, and you might cut yourself." He laughed. "I don't want you bleeding yet."

He savored the feel of her and raked his nails down her chest. Finally, he had his prize. He wanted to make his enjoyment last.

He tenderly kissed her stomach, attempting to catch her scent. When he licked her nipples, Leslie kneed him in the balls.

Beau winced and hunched over. "You're going to pay for that." He punched her face.

Blood trickled from her nose, dripping down the duct tape over her mouth. He delighted at the sight. He went back to kissing her thighs, but soon his kisses turned to bites. Beau sank his teeth into her flesh, and she struggled to arch away.

The taste of blood turned him on. He moved to her breasts, scraping his teeth over her nipples.

Beau stared into her eyes. "I've had virgins before, but your cherry will be the sweetest." He pried her knees apart, throbbing with anticipation. He'd not brought rubbers with him, wanting to enjoy every inch of her.

Holding his breath, he braced her hips and thrust fast and hard inside her.

Tears streamed down Leslie's face as she screamed into the duct tape.

"How's that feel? Was it worth the wait?" He put his mouth to her ear. "All those times you laughed at me, your comments, your bitchy attitude, I swore this moment would come. I promised I would have you."

He retrieved Andrea's red scarf from the pipes and put it around her neck.

Leslie gasped as tears mingled with the blood streaking her face.

The metallic scent blended with the perfume from the candles as Beau rammed into her, tightening his grip on the scarf. The rush, the wave of power was so much more with her. Not able to hold off any longer, he let out a low, guttural groan as he released into her.

He collapsed on top of Leslie. The night had gone even better than anticipated. He moved to sit on the edge of the cot. She curled into a fetal position, sobbing. He didn't like the sound—he wanted silence, so he punched the side of her head.

After a minute, Beau noticed she wasn't moving. He shook her, but nothing. Not even a moan. He checked her pulse. She was still alive. He slapped her ass. "Too bad I have somewhere else to be."

Beau unhooked the cuffs from her wrists and discarded them. Lifting her battered and bloody body from the cot, he thought it a shame he couldn't keep her somewhere to revisit later.

Once he had positioned her on the floor, he crossed her arms over her chest like a corpse. She would be one soon enough.

He dressed and went into the corridor. After collecting several handfuls of dry leaves and twigs, he scattered them around Leslie. He added her torn clothes to the pile and doused the debris with lighter fluid.

A nice slow burn was what the internet advised to destroy a body. Beau set a few candles on the floor next to the debris.

After gathering up his things and returning them to his duffel bag, he examined the room. Beau would miss the cozy little space. He'd created so many fond memories there.

Leslie had not moved the entire time. He figured she was almost as good as dead. Just about to leave the cell, his bag over his shoulder, he glanced back at her.

"The best and last night of your life."

Once outside, Beau sucked in the crisp night air. He looked at the forgotten angel on top of the fountain, feeling invigorated. Why couldn't it be like this all the time?

He eased forward as his eyes adjusted to the night. His desire for another girl crept into his thoughts. But who would replace Leslie? Who would be his next prize?

Something moved up ahead, and he squinted to get a better view. He wished he hadn't. Three large dogs had gathered. They snarled and hunched their backs.

His euphoria spiraled into fear.

Beau headed toward the gate, determined to get out of there before the dogs came after him.

CHAPTER FORTY

Derek parked next to Leslie's car. The lot appeared full with a collection that ran the gambit from a high-end Mercedes to his beat-up truck. The one vehicle he did not see was Beau's. Perhaps he'd caught a break and could enjoy an evening at the river without running into that idiot.

With his Cavalier hat in his hand, he followed the music to the beach. Hopefully, Leslie's surprise involved something away from the noise of the party. A night of binging movies and popcorn was far more palatable than this.

Navigating the well-trod pine needles, he got down the embankment to the beach. When he stepped onto the sand, he adjusted his black mask and put on the aggravating hat. Anything to make Leslie happy.

He searched the crowd but didn't speak to anyone. He stuck to the line of trees and thick green bushes, avoiding the partygoers, anxious to meet Leslie.

At the gate where The Abbey property began, a handful of revelers with vapid gazes drew his attention. Their heads raised to the sky and their mouths open, they held up phones videotaping something.

He followed their line of sight. A trail of smoke rose in the air. It came from The Abbey. "Oh my God."

He pushed the gawkers out of his way, horrified. Derek tossed his hat and mask to the ground and rushed across the field.

Others joined him along the way. Princess Leia, Han Solo, Captain America, and Wonder Woman tossed their shields, golden lassos, and lightsabers aside as they ran across the high grass.

Beau stuck close to the rim of the beach, then stopped to check behind him. He would come back with his shotgun and make sure he killed every one of those damn dogs.

Shouts erupted from the direction of The Abbey. The thump of music abruptly stopped.

"Fire! The Abbey's on fire!"

His little pyrotechnic show must have spread past the cells. So be it. The old wreck needed to go. Everyone in town would talk about the fire—and the body left behind—for decades to come.

Beau made it to the parking lot and put the duffel bag in his trunk. He checked his phone. Plenty of time to make the party at the brewery. If he didn't, he had a hell of an excuse.

He combed his hands through his hair and straightened his shirt. Time to tell everyone he'd just arrived. Act surprised like everyone else and enjoy the show.

And Leslie?

Beau pictured her charred remains pulled from The Abbey in the aftermath. Or maybe the partygoers would reach her in time to remove whatever was left. He couldn't wait to see the tears in Foster's eyes, or the pain Dawn would experience at losing her twin sister. The thought of their grief made him happy.

"Might make for a very interesting evening."

Sick with fear, Derek ran as fast as he could across the high, clingy grass. A spindle of smoke wafted upward into the black sky from the cells. Flashes of orange light coming from The Abbey lit his way. A fire would spread quickly through the dry, derelict structure. Reaching the entrance, he found it blocked by flames. Remembering a way in through the cells, he took off at a sprint. Past the angel fountain, he found the crack in the wall and slipped inside. His fear for Leslie pushed him through the thick smoke.

With his eyes burning and tears stinging his cheeks, Derek walked blindly through the haze.

Small patches of red and orange flames spread along the corridor, carried by piles of debris. He followed the smoke to a cell. Inside the dilapidated section, in the room he and Leslie had found, the fire raged.

Derek covered his nose and mouth with his cape. On the ground, just outside the cell, was the body of a naked girl. Derek's knees buckled. She was on her stomach as though trying to crawl to safety. Leaves and twigs were tangled in her blood-soaked hair. Duct tape covered her mouth. Wounds, along with red and pink patches—some dotted with blisters—covered her skin.

Leslie! His throat tightened as he scooped her into his arms. "No, no, no. God, please not her." He almost fell to his knees but pushed on. He had to get her out of there.

She remained limp in his arms.

"Leslie? Wake up, love. God, please wake up."

She didn't respond. Panicked, Derek carried her to the gap in the wall. In the seconds he'd been with her, the fire had swelled and filled the corridor, heading toward The Abbey at an alarming speed.

Smoke, vines, and bushes made getting out even more difficult. Once clear, Derek gasped for air, coughing up the smoke he'd inhaled. His vision blurred, he could barely see where he was going, but he ran. Carrying Leslie, he summoned every ounce of strength.

At the edge of the grassy field, people gathered watching the fire. Derek stumbled and fell to his knees. He set Leslie on the grass. She was like ice. He ripped off his cape and covered her, yelling, "Help!"

Several stopped filming the fire and turned the cameras toward them, but only two guys hurried to his side.

He searched his pocket for his phone. He'd left it in the truck.

"Holy shit," one guy said. "What happened?"

"Call 911. Get an ambulance out here. Get the fire department. Get everyone."

While one of the boys dialed 911, Derek gently removed the tape from around her head and mouth. Bile burned the back of his throat as the tape pulled away some of her skin. "Noooo!"

Blood drizzled from her nose. Her lips appeared swollen and split, her cheeks were a bright shade of red, and her jaw was discolored. He could not imagine what she'd endured.

"The paramedics are coming," one of the boys said. "Let's get her to the parking lot. The faster she gets to the paramedics, the better."

Derek carefully lifted Leslie into his arms. He held her close, willing her pain away. The thought of giving her to strangers sent a wave of panic through him. He didn't want to give her up. What if this was the last time he would hold her? What if this was the last memory he would have of her?

The crowd at the gate parted as Derek approached. They gawked at the half-naked girl in his arms.

With the two strangers as his guides, Derek carried Leslie to the parking lot. The whole time, he kept repeating, "She'll be okay." An existence without her was unimaginable. He wouldn't survive it. His heart belonged to her. Everything good in his world came from Leslie.

At the parking lot, he heard the screech of sirens. "Hold on. Help is coming."

Seeing the headlights of the ambulance, they screamed and waved to get the driver's attention. The vehicle pulled alongside, and a man dressed in blue hopped out of the back.

The EMT rushed up to Derek. "What happened?"

"She was, ah ..." Derek fought to keep from sobbing. "In the cells. They're on fire. I found her like this."

The man checked her pulse and quickly took Leslie from his arms.

Derek didn't want to let her go.

The EMT rushed her into the back of the ambulance and placed her on a gurney. Derek followed, needing to see her. If his gaze stayed on her, he wouldn't fall apart.

"Can you tell me anything about her?" the ambulance driver asked coming alongside. "Do you know her name?"

"Leslie, Leslie Moore."

"We need to go now," the driver said. He moved Derek aside to shut the back doors. "We'll take it from here, son."

"Can I go with her?" Derek's voice cracked.

"You can follow us to the hospital." The driver then rushed to the front of the ambulance.

Derek stood shaking, unable to move until they sped away, their harsh yellow lights disturbing the darkness surrounding the road.

A hand slapped his shoulder. "Get in your car and follow her."

Without even glancing at the boys who had helped him, Derek ran to his old blue truck. Panic had his hands shaking so hard, he could barely get his door open.

Just as he left the lot, fire trucks sped past. But he didn't care about the fire. All that mattered to him was Leslie. He hit the accelerator and the old truck chugged, gaining on the bright lights of the ambulance ahead.

"Please, dear God. Save my Leslie. I'll do anything. Just don't let her die."

Reeking of smoke, Derek paced the scuff-marked floor in the waiting room. He vacillated between the scorching pain of guilt, the sour knot of fear, and the sickening grip of grief. Minutes felt like hours.

"Are you the young man who came in with Leslie Moore?"

Derek wheeled around to see a man with troubled hazel eyes. The name stitched on his lab coat pocket read Dr. Jeffers.

"Is she okay?" He shuddered as the words escaped his lips.

The doctor's faint smile did little to reassure him. "How do you know her, son?"

"She's my girlfriend."

"Do you have a number where I can reach her parents?" he demanded. "I need to ask them some questions."

"I called her dad. I got his voicemail and left a message. He was at a party, but I'm sure he's on his way." Derek's lower lip trembled. He was going to be sick.

"What's your name?" Dr. Jeffers asked.

"Derek. Derek Foster."

"Derek, do you know if she has any drug allergies? Any medical conditions she might have told you about?"

"She wasn't allergic to anything. Last year, she got the flu. Other than that, she's healthy."

Dr. Jeffers scanned the faces of the other people in the waiting room. "Is there anyone with you?"

Derek shook uncontrollably. The doctor wouldn't ask that unless it was bad—very bad. "No. I followed the ambulance and ..." His voice dried up. The lump forming in his throat made it impossible to go on. Derek lowered his head.

Dr. Jeffers clasped Derek's shoulder. "I think you should come with me, son."

Derek reached for the wall. "She's gonna be all right, isn't she?"

The doctor put his arm behind Derek's back and urged him through a pair of double doors. "Your girlfriend is in critical condition. Maybe if she heard your voice, it would help her."

A long white corridor stretched before him. Derek's trembling got worse—a lot worse. He could barely stand. The smell of antiseptic blended with bleach and the smoke clinging to Derek's clothes. Conversations of staff, patients, and others in the hallway came and went, but he couldn't make out any words. His world shrank until the only thing he could see was the white tile floor and the reflection of the harsh fluorescent lights.

"She's hooked up to machines," Dr. Jeffers warned as he stopped before a room at the end of the hall. "She's sustained trauma to the brain." He pushed the door open. "Just let her know you're here."

Derek fought back tears. Brain trauma. He may be in high school, but he'd watched enough medical shows to know that was bad. What if Leslie came back and wasn't his Leslie anymore? What would he do?

Digging his nails into his palms to keep from breaking down, he entered the room. Then he froze when he saw Leslie on a bed.

Machines with blinking lights surrounded her, and she had a breathing tube in her mouth. Her pallid hands rested on her stomach. Bright red lines cut into her wrists. Burns blistered her arms, and her bruises had turned a pale shade of blue.

She was so still, so empty of life. This didn't seem real. Derek's throat burned, and his eyes stung with tears. Machines hummed, and the monitor above the bed beeped with her every heartbeat. The noises whirled in his head. The heaviness in his heart sent a wash of numbing cold through him, erasing every thought.

"Is he family?" a nurse at the bedside asked.

"No, but I'll take responsibility," Dr. Jeffers said. "Let him stay with her."

The nurse moved a chair closer to Leslie. "Have a seat."

Derek willed his legs to move, approached the bed, and became transfixed by the pattern of bruises on her face. The red mark around her neck left a patchwork design embedded in her skin. Her lips, her jaw, and her nose appeared distorted and swollen. Her beautiful hair, now partially shaved, lay spread out on her pillow.

This can't be real.

"You can hold her hand," the nurse encouraged.

Derek lifted her fingers, caressing her skin. Still shaking, he slipped his hand into hers, hoping for some sign of life, something to let him know she was in there. She was so cold. He almost asked the nurse to get her another blanket. Leslie's hands had always warmed and strengthened him.

Memories of her laugh, smile, voice, and beautiful eyes inundated him. He curled inward, unable to breathe, unable to speak. "You can't leave me." He didn't recognize his voice.

This can't be happening.

"We have our whole lives ahead of us. There's college and law school. We have to open our law practice together. And we're supposed to get married, remember? Who's going to teach me about feminist literature and watch movies with me on Friday night." Tears poured down his cheeks. He couldn't stop them. "I'll be lost without you, Leslie. I can't go on without you. You're everything to me. You can't leave me."

A loud, harsh buzzer rolled around the small room. Dr. Jeffers and the nurse raced to the bed, shoving Derek out of the way.

"Give her an amp of epi," Dr. Jeffers ordered.

More hospital staff stampeded into the room, moving Derek farther from the bed. He wanted to hold Leslie's hand, to beg her to fight, but he couldn't get to her. "What is it? What's happening?"

The monitor alarm above the bed continued to sound its god-awful screech.

In the back of the room, Derek waited. He was nothing more than an observer, helpless to interfere. He became a shell—absorbing everything but registering nothing.

He flinched with every raised voice. The pounding on Leslie's chest horrified him as someone administered CPR. This was nothing like his basic life support class. Leslie wasn't a doll. They were hurting her.

They added medicine after medicine to her IV while the doctor stood by and waited for the flat line to change on her monitor.

Derek begged God to save her, but the line never wavered. It stayed flat and ugly, bereft of life.

A hush settled over the room, and then Dr. Jeffers turned to Derek.

Their eyes connected, and he saw it. The pity he'd endured as a kid when others spoke about his struggling mother and absent father.

No, God, please.

Dr. Jeffers raised his gaze to the clock on the wall. "Time of death, ten-fifty-three."

"No!" Derek cried out. "You have to save her."

Dr. Jeffers grabbed his shoulders. "She's gone. There's nothing more we can do."

Derek ran out the door and along the corridor. Blinded by tears, he smashed into someone and fell back onto the floor. He glanced up. John Moore stood over him.

Derek covered his head with his hands, wanting to disappear. "She's gone. She's gone." The pain in his chest was like an anvil splitting him in two.

A hand reached down and helped Derek off the floor. Arms went around him and held him close. Through his tears, he saw dirty-blonde hair.

His voice caught in his throat. "What am I going to do? I won't make it without her."

She took his hands, squeezing them. "Derek, what happened?"

Her hands were so warm, like Leslie's used to be.

"I don't know." Derek's deep breath rattled in his chest. "When I arrived at The Abbey, there was smoke everywhere, and when I went inside ..."

"Why would she go there without me? I'm supposed to protect her, but she never gave me the chance. Why didn't she tell me? Why?"

Dawn's voice sounded different, deeper. It frazzled him. Derek wiped his tears. Her beautiful face came into focus, with blue eyes and every feature she shared with Leslie—but then she tilted her head. Her bearing was discerning, questioning, tough.

"Leslie?" Derek whispered.

Her slight nod took away the strength in his legs. He wobbled and then sat on the floor, hyperventilating.

She knelt in front of Derek and hugged him tight. Grabbing onto her, he sobbed into her hair.

"Tell me Dawn's okay," Leslie pleaded.

He glanced back at the room. How was he going to tell her? Derek squeezed her harder than he ever had. "I'm so sorry. I ..." His voice vanished.

Her painful, high-pitched cry broke his heart, but a selfish piece of him rejoiced. He hated himself for feeling that way. "I don't understand. How are you here?"

Leslie shuddered. "Dawn took my phone, the car, and even the bottle of champagne I had for us." She struggled to speak between sobs. "I went to a neighbor's and called you, but you never picked up. My parents had already left."

He sat back and touched a lock of her hair. "I thought she was you. Her hair was shoulder-length like yours."

"She cut it." Leslie's brittle voice sounded so frail. "I found her hair in the sink in her bathroom. Why would she do that?" She collapsed in his arms. "It was supposed to be me. I should have never told her the truth about where I was going."

"I don't understand. Why would she pretend to be you? Why did she go to the cells?"

Leslie grew quiet as she looked into his eyes. A dark shadow swept over her face. Something in her changed.

"I will never forgive myself." Leslie's voice took on a bone-chilling edge.

Dr. Jeffers came into the hall. Cries rose around him as Shelley and John learned of their daughter's passing.

"What happened to her?" Leslie kept asking.

Derek never let her go. "I love you with all my heart."

She would find out the horrible truth soon enough.

CHAPTER FORTY-ONE

S niffling, reverent whispers, and quiet sobs filled the gym at St. Benedict High. Beau sat surrounded by teary-eyed students and faculty gathered around the basketball court. Some carried white roses in memory of Dawn Moore. The podium in the center of the court had a black sash across it. The rain tapping on the roof seemed an appropriate accompaniment for the solemn occasion.

He remained irritated by the news. *Dawn?* How was that even possible? He should have known. But she had shorter hair and the bottle of champagne. The adrenaline rush of his fantasy becoming a reality must have clouded his mind. The high of his kill deflated the moment he learned it wasn't Leslie.

If Beau was going to pursue his new passion, he had to smarten up. Besides, what if he'd discovered it was Dawn? He would've killed her, anyway. She'd been a means to get closer to Leslie, nothing more. Dawn was just a practice run.

Leslie wasn't at school, which really ticked him off. But with his anger came a speck of optimism. He could still take her. No one knew it was him, so he had another chance. There was a silver lining to his disappointment, after all.

"The river is off-limits until further notice," Sheriff Davis announced from behind the podium. "The beach is closed, as well as the ruins of The

Abbey. The area is going to be patrolled day and night until Dawn Moore's killer is apprehended. Two women have been found dead, and we fear a killer is on the loose."

"Is this a serial killer, Sheriff?" one of the female faculty members asked.

Sheriff Davis slapped his Stetson against his thigh, looking uncertain. "Federal authorities are coming in to help with the investigation. That's all I can say."

The rumbling of student conversations echoed throughout the large gym.

"This is bullshit," Beau muttered.

"Yeah," Mitch agreed. "We'll have to get around the cops."

The challenge gave Beau a buzz. It might make parties at the river even more thrilling. Then there was the matter of The Abbey. He longed to visit the scene of his crimes. Find out if he could still use the abandoned location to serve his needs. "We'll make it work."

The idea of returning to the river, and planning for a night with Leslie, made his pulse quicken.

The clatter of students climbing down from the bleachers awakened him from his daydreams. He followed them to the gym doors after the meeting ended.

"Big game against Jesuit High coming up." Mitch butted his shoulder. "You think Coach might let you play?"

"Seriously doubt he'll let me finish the season."

"Go talk to him today during practice. He might feel sorry for you after ..."

But Beau didn't hear the rest. Someone in the crowd grazed by him and whispered "I know" in his ear.

He stopped. A few students gave him dirty looks when they almost ran into him. He looked around, searching for the culprit, his breath trapped in his chest.

"Dude, you okay?" Mitch slapped his back.

Students clogged the doorway. He nervously examined their faces, sweat beading his upper lip. The swing of a brunette ponytail secured with a red ribbon caught his attention. Beau stood on his toes to get a better look. The girl wearing the red ribbon stopped, turned, and her eyes met his.

Taylor Haskins grinned at Beau and then ducked out the gym doors.

He elbowed students out of the way, anxious to catch up with her.

"Hey, watch it, Beau," a girl snapped at him.

He reached the doors, but there was no sign of Taylor.

Sweat dripped down his back, and an unsettling feeling twisted his gut. Had she been the one watching him at The Abbey?

He had to find out what she knew and shut her down.

Leslie's chest ached as she lay on her sister's princess bed and stared at the pink walls. When her gaze landed on a framed picture of Beau, fury ignited in her gut.

She was the reason her sister was dead. She'd made the mistake of telling Dawn her intentions to go to the cells instead of The Abbey to meet Derek on Halloween, and Beau found out. The son of a bitch should have been at home, grounded. She'd hoped to sneak into his room in the cells, find evidence of his crimes, and then slip into The Abbey to meet Derek. But her plan backfired when Dawn went in her place. She must have known Beau would be there, but how?

A gentle rap on the door made her sit up. She wiped her eyes, not wanting her parents to see her grief. She didn't need to add to theirs.

Her father shuffled into the room. His usually bouncy step disappeared that night at the hospital. His bloodshot eyes reminded Leslie that his pain was just as great as hers.

John moved toward the bed and lifted one of Dawn's pink stuffed animals. "Are you okay?"

Leslie sniffled and wiped her nose on her sleeve. "Doubt I will ever be okay again, Dad."

He stared at the bunny in his hands. "We'll get there one day. We have to go on. Dawn would want that."

Her anger resurfaced. "I'm not sure I can. This is all my fault. I killed her."

John dropped the bunny and went to her side. He wrapped Leslie in his arms. "No, honey. This wasn't your fault. Never think that."

She squeezed her eyes closed, willing back the tears. "I was supposed to be there. Not Dawn."

He leaned back. "What are you talking about?"

She wiped her face. How much should she tell her father? Would sharing what she knew about Beau make things worse for him? Gage was his employer and close friend. No matter how ingrained her desire for revenge against Beau, he could never learn the truth.

"I was going there to meet Derek. I told Dawn, and she didn't want me to go. She said bad things happen in those cells. She tried to talk me out of it, but you know how I am." Leslie glanced at her hands, her heart breaking all over again at not telling the truth to the one person she respected most.

She gazed into his eyes, searching for strength. "How do I live with this guilt? How do I make the pain go away?"

Her father tucked her head under his chin. "You let it go. No amount of beating yourself up over what happened will bring Dawn back. And she wouldn't want you to be unhappy. She loved you so."

Leslie's eyes flooded with tears.

He stroked her hair. "Until they catch whoever did this, I don't think any of us will find much peace. It's not until justice is served that the families of those left behind begin to heal. I saw that in my early days with the DA's office. We might think we're a peaceful culture, but revenge is still the best medicine against grief."

Overcast skies dulled the light in the school library, making it difficult for Beau to read the computer screen. He'd tried to change stations, but the bitchy librarian had glared at him for making noise. He was about to look up news articles on Dawn's death when he received an unexpected message through the school's in-house email system.

I know.

That was it. No name, no sender info, nothing. The kick to his stomach knocked him back in his chair. He sat up, avidly searching the other stations around him. Everyone had their heads down. He even checked for Taylor's red ribbon.

He rubbed his face. "Okay, let's play."

Beau opened the messenger system. When a blank screen appeared where his notifications should have been, his breath rattled in his throat. An entire semester of messages had been wiped clean from his account.

"What the fuck?" He retyped his login twice, thinking there must be a glitch. But the same empty screen came back up. Even the newest message didn't show on his board.

Beau slammed his fists on his keyboard, cursing under his breath.

"Is there a problem?"

He expected to see Mrs. Peters arching over him. The hag loved to patrol the computers for students searching for porn.

"Yes, I have an issue with—"

Sara Bissell leaned over his chair, smiling sweetly, a red ribbon tied around her ponytail.

He tried to speak but lost his voice. His eyes remained fixed on the red ribbon.

"What's wrong, Beau? Cat got your tongue?"

He wanted to smack her across the face. Instead, he stood and grabbed his books. "You think you're smart? I'd start sleeping with one eye open if I were you."

The last bell of the school day echoed in the hall. Lockers banged closed while students around Beau still gossiped about the tragedy at the river. The constant mention of Dawn's name and his never-ending performance as the grieving ex ate away at him.

Outside, he stormed across the wet grass on the quad, the cool November air teasing his face. Eager to give Coach Brewer another try, he headed to the gym doors. He missed the game, the glory of being the quarterback, and the physical outlet. There was no better place to let go than on a football field.

He stopped in front of the gym entrance, distracted by a few cheerleaders on the practice field. He couldn't make out their faces, but it wasn't the entire squad of eight girls, only four. Why were they on the field and not in front of the stands?

A practice happening so soon after Dawn's death struck him as odd. Intrigued, he walked closer. The wind picked up as he neared the stands. The breeze circled him, and the hair stood on his arms.

The girls stopped in the middle of their cheer when they spotted Beau and turned their backs. The red ribbons securing each girl's ponytail danced in the passing wind.

He wanted to know who they were, but he wasn't sure if he should waste time confronting them or head to his meeting with the coach. Perhaps the ribbons were their silly way of commemorating Dawn.

When the wind died, the girls lined up, hands on their hips, and chanted in unison. "Hey hey, ho ho, you think it's a secret, but we know. Hey hey, bye bye, a tooth for a tooth, and an eye for an eye."

Stunned, he dropped his book bag.

One girl turned around and stepped forward. It was Leslie, wearing Dawn's old uniform.

He stumbled and almost fell. It could have been Dawn coming back from the dead. But why would she be wearing—

Taylor turned and joined Leslie. In a cheerleading uniform, she looked like the confident girl he'd known before their encounter.

His mouth dry, his stomach turning, he picked up his bag, ready to forget about his meeting with Coach Brewer.

A third girl merged with them. Sara—also dressed as a St. Benedict cheerleader.

Kelly Norton spun around, a St. Benedict red dragon on her chest, and pointed a pompom at him. Her venomous gaze reminded him of a cobra.

The girls linked arms and marched shoulder to shoulder toward him, their faces like stone.

"I know," Kelly said to him.

This was too much.

Before he could sprint away, a hand came down on his shoulder, paralyzing him with fear.

He expected to see Sheriff Davis, ready to arrest him, but it was Mitch.

"What's up with that whacked-out cheer?" Mitch pointed his helmet at the field. "I thought they weren't practicing today because of Dawn."

Beau's skin was on fire, and the air around him thinned. They all knew what he'd done. Even Leslie.

"I've got to go," he muttered, and took off for the parking lot.

"Hey, Devereaux! I thought you wanted to talk?" Coach Brewer shouted.

Beau didn't stop to look back.

The wind picked up in the sparsely filled lot. All the students not involved with after-school activities had taken off. The eerie silence added to his sense of unease.

Someone watched him from the shadows beneath the oaks. He could feel it. He scoured the trees for the girls—nothing.

Keep it together. You're in control, not them.

He scrambled to his car, looking over his shoulder while wrestling his keys from his front pocket. He needed to regroup and come up with a plan. They might be out to get him, but they couldn't beat Beau Devereaux.

"Stupid bitches think they can scare me?" He was almost to his car when the keys slipped from his shaking hand. He bent down to pick them up.

"Where you off to in such a hurry?" Sara stepped out from behind him.

"Get out of my way."

"You seem flustered, Beau." Taylor appeared on his right.

He jumped back and bumped into someone.

"Whoa, dude, watch the uniform."

Beau wheeled around to see Kelly.

"You can't touch me. None of you can. I can say what I want about each of you. It will be your word against mine."

"No, Beau," another voice said on his left. "No one's going to hear your side."

When he faced Leslie, his throat closed. It was Dawn, staring at him from beyond the grave. "Get away from me. I had nothing to do with what happened to your sister."

Leslie's cold, hollow eyes burned into him. She eased closer. "We know better."

Fed up, Beau cocked his arm back to take a swing at her when something pricked his neck.

He clasped the spot below his left ear. "Ow, what the hell was that?"

Kelly held up a syringe. "Any last words?"

"You bitch!" Beau swayed, becoming woozy. "What did you give me?"

She capped a needle. "I swiped it from the vet I work for. I figure if it can knock a horse out, you haven't got a prayer."

Leslie stood in front of him. "Just a teaser of things to come."

"You won't get away with this." He sank to his knees.

Taylor leaned over him. "Oh, yes, we will."

He pitched headfirst into the parking lot just as everything went black.

Beau awoke in blurry darkness, his mouth a desert. He blinked a few times, and when things came into focus, he wished they hadn't.

He was in the charred remains of The Abbey. Burnt pews and fallen beams littered the blackened, debris-covered floor. He could see the clear night sky through the hole in the roof. The acrid smell of smoke burned his nose. He tried to move, but couldn't. Zip ties secured his hands and legs to a wooden chair. Around his feet flickered several candles.

"Seems fitting to bring you here," a female voice said. "Back to the scene of the crime."

He raised his head, woozy with the movement. Shapes formed beyond the golden aura of candlelight.

Kelly, Taylor, Sara, and Leslie, still in their cheerleading uniforms, stood in front of him. The red ribbons in their hair matched their heavy red lipstick, giving each girl a macabre, Joker-like appearance.

Beau, still a little drunk from the drug, laughed. "So, what is this? Some kind of hashtag Me Too revenge club? You've got nothing on me."

"We've got *you*, Beau." Leslie leaned over the candles, her eyes aglow in the fiery light. "You could go to jail for murder one, do you know that?"

Her smoky voice reawakened all the wonderful plans he had for her. "I didn't hurt anyone."

Taylor charged at him. "You lying piece of dogshit. What about me?"

"Or the sick, perverted things you did to me in the cells?" Kelly added.

Sara folded her arms. "Try and talk your way out of that, asshole."

They couldn't touch him, and he knew it. They had more to lose by talking and would never risk it.

"What are you going to do? File charges? With what evidence? Even then, who would believe you? You all got what you wanted."

"What about my sister?" Leslie slapped him hard across the face. "Did *she* get what she wanted? You killed her."

The sting incited his outrage. His fingers twitched while he struggled against the zip ties. "I never touched Dawn. I cared for her."

"Cared? Like you *cared* for the girl who ended up dead in the river?" Taylor held up her phone. "Remember her?"

The video was grainy, but she'd captured Andrea's face, her head tilted toward the camera while Beau trailed kisses down her neck.

"I didn't get a chance to hang around and get more. You almost caught me. Tomorrow morning, this video will be sent in an anonymous email to Sheriff Davis. Then the police will find out you knew her."

Leslie took the phone from Taylor. "What do you think your daddy will do then?"

He looked from one girl to the other, his fear evaporating. "Nothing. I had sex with the girl. She happened to show up dead in the river. I didn't do it."

"No, Beau." Leslie shook her head. "We know you *did* do it. The same way you killed Dawn. You have to pay."

He was done with their games. They were only four stupid girls with nothing on him that would hold up in court. Leslie wasn't the only one with a head for the judiciary process. Ready to take control, he rocked the chair back and forth, attempting to free himself.

He pushed too hard, and the chair toppled over, scattering some of the candles. Beau hit his head on a charred beam and yelped in pain.

With a newfound fury, he fought harder against his restraints. *How dare they think they can treat me like this.*

Kelly patted the top of his head. "You're going to have a long night on the floor like that."

"Let me go!"

Taylor snapped a picture with her phone. "No, you will stay right there, so the police will know where to find you in the morning."

Taylor, Kelly, and Sara backed into the shadows while Leslie moved closer.

Her smirk inflamed his rage. He ached to be free. The acidic burn of panic flooded his mouth. He thrashed, gulped air, and strained until the zip ties cut into his wrists. Then black spots formed in front of his eyes from the exertion.

Leslie knelt beside him. "You're going to spend a long time in prison, having done to you what you did to my sister and these girls. Enjoy hell, Beau." She stepped over him to join the others. "I just hope the dogs don't get you before the sheriff does."

Their figures melded with the darkness. They reached the burnt arch that was once The Abbey doorway, and he lost them completely.

When the only sound he could detect was the cold wind whipping through the charred beams above, Beau's outrage was replaced with fear.

Seconds turned into minutes. Beau continued to struggle, but the zip ties were too tight.

Think. There has to be a way out of this.

He ran through one scenario after another, searched the ground for something to free his hands, then closed his eyes when a brutal headache shut down his capacity to think clearly.

Would they call the police, or was this just a game?

His mind drifted, plotting ways out of his predicament, the blackened ruins around him as silent as a tomb. A howl rang through the night and alarm heightened his senses. He became attuned to every creak and groan inside the structure.

Another howl, this one closer. Beau renewed his attempts to free his hands. When another howl sounded right outside the church, panic quickened his breathing.

Something glimmered at the entrance. White and flowing, it glided toward him. He thought the candlelight was playing a trick on his eyes. Then a figure in a long white cloak materialized.

Beau rested his head against the cold ground, the stench of ash and burnt wood in his nose. "Are you done having your fun, whoever you are?"

The cloak concealed the slender shape of a woman. He couldn't quite make out her features beneath the hood, but he knew she was real.

"I'll hunt you down and take my time before I kill you."

A low growl rose from a shadowy portion of the ruins, followed by another, and another. Out of the gloomy corners of The Abbey, dogs appeared, the whites of their eyes shining against their matted coats. The snarling dogs gathered around the hooded figure.

She drifted closer, coming into the candlelight. "You're the one who will die tonight," she whispered.

A black dog slinked up to her, resting its head under her hand.

Beau didn't like this. The dog had the oddest look in its eyes—an almost human, vengeful glint.

"I don't scare easily, and you would never—"

The dog trotted up to him, its teeth bared in a grotesque snarl.

"Scared now? You were right about the pack living here. But they're not wild, just very hungry." She patted the dog. "And they never forgive ...

like me."

The dog frightened the crap out of him, but not the girl. He recognized her face as she dipped into the light.

"I'm going to give you the night of your life." She backed away, and the pack closed in.

Frantic, Beau wriggled in his chair, desperate to escape. Several of the creatures stood around him, their bared teeth gleaming in the candlelight.

"No!" His muscles quivered with fear. "Get away!"

The black dog drew closer to his face.

He stared into its fiendish eyes, and the cold tentacles of abject terror slithered through his body, paralyzing him.

The dog opened its mouth—the stench of rot and death on its breath.

Beau screamed, the primal sound echoing throughout the crumbling abbey.

Then the candles went out.

CHAPTER FORTY-TWO

A black body bag closed over the pale face of Beau Devereaux. God, he hated the sound of that zipper. Kent Davis removed his Stetson from his head and wiped his brow. Around him, several officers combed the beach for clues as to how the kid had ended up there.

Two men from the St. Tammany Parish Coroner's Office lifted the body bag and carried it across the beach to the parking lot.

"Did you see those bites?" one officer asked Kent. "I've never seen a person chewed up like that."

Kent put his hat back on, disgusted. "The bites didn't kill him, Phil. Something else did."

A heavyset man with black glasses approached. "I'll get to his autopsy as soon as possible."

"Did you note the zip tie burns on his wrists, Bill? Looks like he was tied up somewhere." Kent needed another coffee to get him through this. "See if you can get me any fibers. We have to figure out what happened."

"What *happened*?" Bill removed his glasses. "You get a look at that kid's face? Whatever killed him, he was terrified by it. I've seen a lot of shit as coroner of this parish, but never that."

"Fear isn't a cause of death," Kent insisted.

The coroner returned his glasses to his nose. "No, but it's a clue as to what killed him. Or who killed him." Bill shook his head. "I'll have a preliminary report for you in the morning."

Kent stifled his urge to get the hell away from the creepy crime scene. He hated the nasty ones.

"What are you going to tell his old man?" Phil asked.

He shook his head, sick at the prospect. "I have no idea. This is going to kill Gage. He had big plans for his son."

"Just goes to show no one's invincible," Phil said. "Not even a Devereaux."

Kent studied the rushing waters of the Bogue Falaya River. "I guess someone forgot to tell that to Beau."

"He knew, Sheriff." Phil glanced back across the treetops to the remains of The Abbey's charred steeple. "By the look on that kid's face when he died, I'd say he got the message."

EPILOGUE

The cold November breeze streamed through Leslie's open car window as she eased into a parking spot outside the gray clapboard, two-story office building.

She cut the engine and turned to the duffel bag on the seat next to her. Memories of that night came rushing back. Memories she wanted to forget, but knew she never could.

Bag in hand, she climbed from the car and headed for the straight wooden staircase alongside the building. She opened the dark glass door on the second floor and stepped inside.

She entered a hallway decorated with framed posters of the company's products. She'd never look at a bottle of Benedict Beer again without thinking of the animal who killed her sister.

Leslie checked the secretary's desk, not surprised to find it empty on a Saturday.

She slipped inside the open door to her right. The office had certificates of merit, awards, and commendations touting the excellence of the brewery. She found the décor distinctively masculine and a reflection of the man who sat behind the carved mahogany desk.

Gage Devereaux never looked up, busily writing as she walked across the red rug.

Leslie dropped the black duffel bag on top of his desk. "I'm returning this."

Gage put his pen aside and glanced at it, but never acknowledged her.

He stood and unzipped the bag to inspect the contents.

Leslie watched him, seeing flashes of Beau in his face and his movements.

Gage reached inside and lifted the hem of a white cloak. His face a mask of stone, he leveled his dark eyes at her but said nothing.

She didn't expect him to.

He stuffed the cloak back into the bag and zipped it shut.

"When you came to me for help after Halloween and we made our plan, I promised he would never hurt you again." His voice had a cold, hard edge.

Gage turned to the window behind him.

"And now, he never will."

A NOTE FROM ALEXANDREA WEIS:

Since writing about a psychotic young man and the depraved acts he commits on young women, I'm often asked how I could help pen such a violent and abusive storyline. It's a good question, but in a culture saturated with the #MeToo movement and pro-women agendas, we must realize that no matter how much we think we're progressing, we haven't accomplished a whole hell of a lot where violence against women is concerned.

In the State of Louisiana, where the St. Benedict series is set, 600 to 700 acts of sexual assault in high schools are reported annually (Bale, L. 2018). Many mental health counselors feel the actual amount is three to four times that number. In a small state like Louisiana, that is a huge problem. And archaic laws in the state make it impossible for the CDC to track sexual violence among minors (Bale, L. 2018). So we may never know the true extent of the horror.

Put those numbers on a national or international scale, and the image is horrendous. What does that say about how we regard women, not as a culture or nation, but as a world? Women make up half the planet, but are bullied and suppressed, beaten, and raped every minute across the globe. So why aren't all these women reporting these crimes? For the same reason women have kept quiet for centuries—threats, intimidation, shame, and no one to listen to them.

The victims of Beau Devereaux's debauchery keep quiet for the same reasons many young women in high school do today—fear of reprisals, humiliation, peer pressure, and lack of trust in "the system." When high school counselors and teachers don't listen or believe a young woman's reports, she will more than likely never seek help. These girls will withdraw, change their appearance, live in dread of being discovered, and feel shame over what occurred. Before strides can be made to stop the abuse against women, we must embrace a perspective of not assigning guilt to any victim, and stop blaming women for being women. Their sex, personality, behavior, or clothes did not lead to the attack—the disturbed individual and their twisted disregard is the culprit. Sexual assault was the choice he made, not her.

What saddens me is how little things have changed since I was in high school. In the eighties, there was less education, no counseling, and only whispers shared in the halls about sexual assault. Despite the millions of dollars schools pour into programs today, the numbers and experiences have not turned around. I remember watching firsthand a schoolmate suffer the aftermath of her sexual assault, but no one knew what was happening at the time. No one spoke about such atrocities.

Popular, beautiful, a cheerleader, and a kind person, Lady L was admired by the girls in my class and got noticed by all the boys. When she scored a hot date with a popular, wealthy boy from another school, rumors swirled in the halls. Especially about this guy's penchant for date-rape. But no one told Lady L about it. Weeks after her date, everyone noticed the change in her. A young woman who had once dressed well and took pride in her burgeoning social calendar was seen in baggy clothes and withdrew from all activities. I remember noticing and having others mention it to me, but I never put the signs together because no one had taught us what it meant.

Thirty-five years later, this high school classmate finally told her family, husband, children, and friends what happened to her. She lost her virginity to a man who had drugged and raped her. He never paid for his crime. His wife and children do not know what he did. But I remember, after reading her post on social media, how sad I was that I didn't recognize the signs and reach out to help her. If I had, I often wonder what I would have done.

Part of me wanted to write this novel for her, my Lady L. To open the eyes of young people about what can happen, even in the smallest of small towns. Books and movies can reach a large audience and educate individuals faster than word of mouth, social media, or the news. Perhaps more attention needs to be paid to this taboo subject by literary and motion picture companies. A truthful depiction can open the door for discussions, let victims know they are not alone, and spread the word that nothing justifies sexual assault—NOTHING! And like the girls victimized by Beau Devereaux, women can band together, fight back, and get justice. We have a voice.

Find your voice. Speak up and speak out against any form of sexual harassment, assault, or violence. If it happens to you, please seek help. Talk to officials, friends, family, and never keep quiet. If you know someone who has been a victim, stand beside them, support them, and believe what they tell you. Having someone listen is the first step to getting help. Talk to everyone you can, and be an advocate for change. Get loud, get angry, and fight back against antiquated judicial systems and state and federal laws that protect the guilty and hurt the innocent. Individually, we may be regarded as just women, but together, we make up half the planet and are a force that no man can ignore.

So, to answer the question of why I helped write such a dark and sinister tale about sexual assault, let me say this; until we confront the ugliness we keep hidden beneath the surface, the suffering of women in our society will continue to be the impetus for novels like this. Change isn't easy, but it is possible, even if we have to tackle it one book at a time.

Bale, L. (2018, 18 September). *High school sexual assault a common problem across America*. Retrieved from https://www.wwltv.com.

ABOUT THE AUTHORS

Alexandrea Weis, RN-CS, PhD, is a multi-award-winning author, screenwriter, advanced practice registered nurse, and historian who was born and raised in the French Quarter of New Orleans. She has taught at major universities and worked in nursing for thirty years, dealing with victims of sexual assault, abuse, and mental illness in a clinical setting at many New Orleans area hospitals.

Having grown up in the motion picture industry as the daughter of a director, she learned to tell stories from a different perspective. Infusing the rich tapestry of her hometown into her novels, she believes that creating vivid characters makes a story moving and memorable.

A permitted/certified wildlife rehabber with the Louisiana Wildlife and Fisheries, Weis rescues orphaned and injured animals. She lives with her husband and pets outside of New Orleans.

Weis is a member of the International Thriller Writers Organization and the Horror Writers Association.

www.AlexandreaWeis.com

Lucas Astor is from New York, has resided in Central America and the Middle East, and traveled throughout Europe. He lives a very private, virtually reclusive lifestyle, preferring to spend time with a close-knit group of friends over being in the spotlight.

He is an author and poet with a penchant for telling stories that delve into the dark side of the human psyche. He likes to explore the evil that exists not just in the world, but right next door, behind a smiling face. Astor currently lives outside of Nashville, TN.

www.LucasAstor.com

WELCOME TO ST. BENEDICT...

The Devereaux family fights to keep their grim skeletons hidden after the sins of their heir apparent unravel the idyllic Louisiana town they control. But the arrival of a handsome stranger and the discovery of bones long buried beneath the river threaten to awaken dangerous ghosts in this Southern Gothic Thriller series filled with mystery, a rising body count, and a chilling pact between unlikely friends.

"The dynamic duo of Weis and Astor make magic together. A wholly evocative world propels this small-town mystery to epic heights. Highly recommended." ~*BestThrillers*

THE STORY CONTINUES IN BOOK TWO

Not all secrets can be kept silent.
Some eventually find their way home.

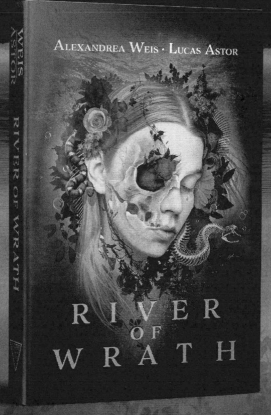

ALEXANDREA WEIS · LUCAS ASTOR

RIVER OF WRATH